MEGHAN QUINN

Prologue

KELLER

"Come in."

I adjust my tie and then push through the ornate, wood-carved door to the king's bedroom. The curtains are drawn despite the time. Just the smallest of cracks in the velvet fabric let the morning rays filter through, lighting up the room so I can see King Theodore resting in his four-poster bed, covered in heavy burgundy fabric.

His attending doctor, Armann, buckles up his bag, adjusts the spectacles on his nose, and then heads toward the door.

"See you tomorrow," King Theodore calls out.

"Yes, tomorrow." Armann glances in my direction, offering an annoyed glare, before he heads out of the bedroom, leaving me alone with the last-remaining royal.

"Keller, my boy—" He turns his mouth into his crooked elbow and heaves a horrendous cough that has plagued him for the last few weeks. After two bouts of pneumonia, Dr. Armann has now placed him on bed rest in order to get him

1

back to his fully functioning self. "Excuse me." He takes a deep breath, but it falls short from the lack of lung capacity. "Thank you for meeting with me."

As the private secretary to the king, I'm his right-hand man, his most trusted advisor. Unfortunately for me, it's been an uphill battle with this job. My predecessor had forty-five years on me before he passed away, and when I was hired, few believed a thirty-two-year-old belonged in this position. The only person who'd trusted me was King Theodore, or Theo, as I call him only when we're alone.

By the side of his bed, there's a burgundy wingback chair that I take a seat in. Pen and notebook in hand, I cross one leg over the other and say, "It sounded urgent when you called me."

"Yes, well, this is an urgent matter," he says right before coughing again. His light blue eyes squeeze shut, and the sparse pieces of hair on the top of his head hitch with every violent hack. He rests his head on his pillow and presses his large, meaty hand to his chest. "I need you to find her."

Confused, I shift in my seat and ask, "Find who?"

He's silent, catching his breath before he opens his eyes and says, "The only heir left."

This is where things get tricky.

Let me give you a quick rundown.

Theo is an only child and the sovereign of our country. He married Katla and had four children.

They more than covered the old verbiage, "we need an heir and a spare." They doubled down.

Pala was born first. The picture-perfect princess who always wore lavender, delighted the people with her flower crowns, and was well-known to try to sneak her cat, Norbit, into every state dinner. When she was at university, she met Prince Clinton of Marsedale, fell madly in love, and married him. But, because Clinton would one day become king of

2

Marsedale, that trumped Pala's throne, and she abdicated to live with him. It's a sore subject.

Second born is Rolant, the troublemaker. Always pressing his luck, never following the rules, and single-handedly created the Fire Task Force—also known as *Rolant fucked up, and now we need to put out the fire*. His demise was inevitable. One drunk night led to him rolling around on one-thousand-year-old sacred moss, and the next day, he was exiled from the country.

Third born, the most promising of the four, despite being the third in line for the throne, is Sveinn. The listener, the do-gooder, the humanitarian. Known as the earth lover, Sveinn was good at everything. He married Kristin. After five years of marriage and no offspring, they were brought into the king's quarters where Kristin admitted to having an affair with her lady's maid. A brilliant lesbian love affair. They ran off together. Sveinn, on the other hand, found the nearest boat, set sail, and is still yet to be found—despite the king's men's best seafaring efforts—six months later.

So that brings us to Margret, the youngest. Fascinated with travel, she was bound and determined to flee from the chilling temperatures of her homeland and explore the humid climate of Miami, where she met the love of her life, Cameron Campbell, a larger-than-life food tour guide. And together, they had one child.

"You want me to find your American granddaughter?" I ask.

Theo slowly nods his head. "You must. Without her, we jeopardize losing our country."

"What do you mean?" I ask, now leaning forward.

"As you are aware, we are a constituent of Arkham, and according to our bylaws, if there is no heir to the throne, then the monarchy dies with me."

Which would be detrimental to the country.

"And with the battles we've fought over the years with

Arkham, there is no doubt they will not only destroy our culture, but they'll take over our people." A cough bubbles up and he sputters a few moments before regaining himself. "I can't have that." With his tired eyes fixated on me, he says, "If it were my choice, you, my son, would take my place, but it must be blood."

"I know," I say, my throat choking up.

I failed to mention the fifth child because the fifth doesn't matter. The fifth grew up in the palace just like the other four, but lost his servant parents at twelve, was orphaned, and then one fateful Christmas Eve was taken in by the king and queen.

He has no right to the crown.

Instead, he . . . or I . . . have dedicated myself to protecting what is mine. This palace, and this man resting on the bed in front of me, practically lifeless with a gray complexion, are mine to protect.

"I need you to find her, Keller, and I need you—" He coughs again. I wait patiently for him to finish before picking up a glass of water from his night table and offering it to him. He nods as a *thank you* and takes a sip. "I need you to train her."

My concerned brow pinches together. "Train her?"

He nods slowly before resting his head on the pillow. "Yes, she will not know of our country, our traditions, or our culture. If she is to take the crown, she must be prepared. The country will not take kindly to an outsider." His tired eyes flash to mine. "And if anyone can prepare the next sovereign, it's you."

Chapter One

LILLY

"Three . . . two . . . one!"

My truck siren goes off.

The crowd erupts in cheers.

I unleash my hose, spraying the men and women wearing white T-shirts in front of me.

"Shimmy for me. That's right," I shout into my headpiece, my voice projected by the speakers attached to my bikini truck. "Let me see your best moves."

Two girls to the right rub their thong-clad butts together.

The man directly in front of me pelvic thrusts at the crowd while sporting a cowboy hat.

And the couple to the left, well . . . they've stopped dancing and are now just making out, drinks clasped in their hands.

"Dry me up," I say to Timmy Tuna, my best friend and co-founder of the Splash Wagon, South Beach Miami's one and only bikini-and-swimsuit store on wheels.

He turns off my hose and then sounds the siren one more time. Timmy Tuna moonlights as a DJ down at the Neon Bar. He's well-known for playing his remixes of popular Afro-Cuban music. He can get a crowd jumping with one beat drop.

"Do we have a winner, folks?" I ask into my microphone. The crowd cheers, boisterously calling out who they think looks best in a wet T-shirt. I walk up to the couple on the left and hold my hand next to them. "Who wants the couple who can't keep their hands off each other to win?" The crowd cheers. I motion to the two girls on the right. "What about these two ladies?" The crowd grows louder. And when I approach the single guy in the front who is still pelvic thrusting the crowd, I ask, "And what about our single gentleman?" The crowd erupts.

It's clear who the champion is.

I knew he was going to win.

It's always the man with the beer belly that wins. Every single time.

I lift his arm and say, "We have a winner!" I hand him a gift card to the Wagon while everyone cheers some more. "Clap it up for the rest of our contestants, who are all receiving a twenty-five-percent off coupon to the Wagon." Timmy Tuna sounds off a blowhorn and then hands out the coupons. "Before we close up for the afternoon, I'll walk around as always for some simple Q and A."

After every wet T-shirt contest, I always work with the crowd to see if I can drive business to any of my local friends. In my lime-green triangular bikini top and yellow sarong, I walk up to a couple who have so much sunscreen on, that their faces have been washed out with white goop.

"Do you have any questions about the area?"

"Yes." The gentleman clears his throat. "Where is the best place to get a Cuban sandwich?"

Smiling, I cup my ear and ask, "Best Cuban, folks?"

Together, the crowd shouts, "Peter Palms!"

I smile at them and say, "Down the road to the right. Tell them Lilly from the Wagon sent you. They'll give you ten percent off."

I move to a group of single ladies.

"Anything I can help you with?"

"We need men," they whine, but in a cute, pouty-face way. "Where can we find the perfect man for a one-night stand?"

I turn toward Timmy and say, "Timmy Tuna, we need some single men."

From his perched spot on the hood of the Wagon, he shouts, "Word on the street is, some of the single players from the Vancouver Agitators are in town and they're staying at Moxy Miami. The bar serves the best rum runners in town. Tell them Timmy Tuna sent you, and get your first drink for free."

The girls squeal and take off. Bet some hockey players get lucky tonight.

I turn to the right and spot a beautiful man—tall, broad-shouldered with blond hair and a menacing scowl. He's dressed in stark black dress pants and a black button-up dress shirt. The sleeves are rolled up to his elbows, displaying ink wrapped around his thick forearms. His presence feels threatening, like someone is about to get into a world of trouble. Thankfully, it's not me.

"Looks like someone didn't get the swimsuit memo," I say as I walk up to him. "Dear sir, do you realize it's summer in Miami?"

His chin juts out as his jaw grows tight, displeasure written all over his face. Maybe someone needs to grab a rum runner with the ladies.

"I need to speak with you," he says in a low tone. The type of tone a father would use when he catches his teenager partying past curfew.

But, hey, I'm here to help, despite the puzzling expression on this man's face.

"Sure," I say into the microphone. "What can I assist you with? Looking for some cigars? Maybe a decent lap dance to help you loosen up? Not saying I'm willing, but I have been known to offer a lap dance with the right drink in me."

His eyes narrow. Nostrils flare.

Man, he might need more than a drink and a lap dance.

"Privately," he says through clenched teeth. "I need to speak with you privately."

Oh, okay, psycho. Yeah, let me just go somewhere private with the angry man. Sounds like a really good idea.

Keeping a smile on my face, I say, "Flattered, but I fly solo."

I turn to talk to someone else when I hear him say, "It's pertaining to your mom. Margret."

My body freezes, my muscles stilling from the mention of my mom's name.

Slowly, I turn back around and remove my headset so my conversation isn't blasted for all of Ocean Drive to hear. "What did you say?"

"I need to speak to you about your mother. I doubt you want to do this with a crowd." He reaches into his pocket and pulls out a black card. Printed in gold is a singular address. When I look back up at him, he says, "Eight tonight, meet me there." His eyes scan my body before saying, "Wear something decent."

"Excuse me?" I say. "How fucking dare you?"

But he's turned around and walking away before I can expand on my tirade.

"What the actual fuck," I say as Timmy walks up to me, the crowd now dispersing.

"Who was that?"

"Some sicko," I say, still clutching the card. "Says he wants to speak to me privately, something to do with my mom."

"Your mom who passed away when you were seventeen? Seems sketch. Need me to call the cops on him? You know Luis would be more than happy to do his blonde goddess a favor." He isn't wrong about it sounding sketch. Mom died when I was seventeen. *It's been a long time since I've heard someone speak her name.*

I watch as the man gets into an unmarked black sedan, my mind reeling. "He knew my mom's name. He said, *Margret.*"

"Wait, really?"

"Yeah." My hand shakes as I look down at the card again. "915 Washington Ave. Is that—is that the Moxy?"

"It is," Timmy says. "Does he work there? Maybe he wants to hire you. Or maybe hire the Wagon for a private event."

"But what would that have to do with my mom?" I ask.

"Not sure, but there's only one way to find out." He flicks the card in my hand.

"Are you saying I meet up with this man?"

"If he knows something about your mom, maybe about your dad? I would if I were you."

I roll my teeth over my bottom lip as I continue to stare at the card.

Who is this man, walking in on my turf, looking like some sort of uptight security detail with his burly, tatted forearms and thick neck? And what could he possibly know about my mom?

Timmy is right, there's only one way to find out.

But if he thinks I'm coming "decent," then he has no clue who the hell he's dealing with.

I FLIP my long blonde ponytail over my shoulder, adjust the deep V of my dress to make sure things are covered, and then, in my four-inch heels, I click-clack across the tiled floor of the Moxy, unsure of where to go from here.

All that was written on the card was the address. A name could have been useful. Possibly more of a meeting destination other than a vague address. But you know how it is with elusive men, they try to gain the upper hand with confusion. Little does he know, I'm not falling for his outdated tricks.

Instead, I stand in the middle of the lobby, people bustling around me, take a compact mirror out of my clutch, as well as my bright pink lipstick, which matches the boisterous flowers on my dress, and I reapply. I'm capping my lipstick when a man in a dark suit and sunglasses approaches me. "Miss Campbell, please follow me."

I don't move, and when he realizes that, he turns back around, a confused look on his face. Well, I assume he's confused. Can't really tell from the sunglasses and inanimate facial expression.

"Do you expect me to just follow you, a man I've never met before?" I shake my head. "Think again. I'm going to need to see your boss, or whoever sent you out here to get me. And I will need his name, as well. And his cell phone number."

Looking far too confused, the man presses his finger to his ear and asks, "Did you hear that?" It's all very secret service-type behavior, and it's all quite comical. This is movie-quality theatrics, not everyday. "He will be right down."

I know what you must be thinking—*Lilly, what the hell are you doing? You don't go off with strangers.* And you're right, I shouldn't, but there's something you have to understand—I lost my parents when I was seventeen to a horrible boating accident. I have no family. No grandparents, no brothers and sisters, no aunts and uncles. My dad was an only child, and his parents passed away when I was five. My mom, well, she never spoke of her side of the family. So, being the strong, confident, and smart twenty-seven-year-old that I am, I'd normally tell this man to fuck off and go on with my day following Miami's trendsetters so I can make sure I have everything in stock in the Wagon. But, the little girl inside of me, the girl who misses her parents, the girl who will cling to any piece of them, she's the one leading the show tonight.

Cut her some slack.

Folding my arms over my chest, I nod toward Mr. Suit and ask, "So, been doing this for long? You know, fetching young women for your boss?"

Stiff, avoiding me at all costs, he doesn't say anything, but I catch his mouth twitch in humor.

"How much do they pay you? Do you have a gun? Or do you consider your hands lethal weapons? From the looks of it, they seem like Grade-A chokers. Have you ever choked anyone? Wait, don't answer that, I don't want to be an accomplice in your murders."

He continues to look around, not saying a word.

"Ah, I see what's going on. They must dock your pay every time you say something, right? You know, I get it. You have mouths to feed, probably. How many kids do you have? Wait, wait, let me guess, that will be more fun. Hmm." I tap my chin. "I'm going to say ten. You look like the kind of man with strong lovemaking genes. Like a workhorse in bed, pounding that semen, one right after the other, having that wife pop them out—"

"Miss Campbell," comes the silky, English voice from earlier.

I turn to see Mr. Mysterious standing behind me, still wearing the black pants and button-up shirt from earlier, but now he has a suit coat draped over his broad shoulders, and he's clouded in a masculine scent that reads more like fresh mountain logger than shadowy assassin. Man, this guy. He's got to be at least six three with a jacket size no smaller than forty-six long. They build them big where he's from.

"Well, hello, there. How lovely of you to show up." I

thumb toward Suit. "Not much of a talker, this one. Do you dock his pay for talking?"

Completely ignoring my question, he says, "I believe you have requested my phone." He reaches into his suit jacket and pulls out his phone. He offers it to me, holding it out in his large hand.

Take a look at those fingers. Hello, *lover.*

"Is that really a phone, or perhaps a bomb acting like a phone? I need you to prove to me that it's a phone."

That anger I saw rear up earlier reappears as he taps the screen, entering a passcode so fast that I only catch two numbers: three and eight. He then turns the screen to me, showing off his black wallpaper with all his apps lined up in folders.

"Who doesn't have a wallpaper on their phone? Seems a bit psychotic, don't you think?"

"Miss Campbell, what I have to talk to you about is of high importance. Please take the phone and follow me."

I take the phone and then say, "First, I need to make a phone call."

I might be following a strange man to God knows where, but I have gained some form of self-preservation over the last few years.

I punch in Timmy's number and then put it on speaker.
"Hello?"

"Timmy, baby, it's me."

"Do they have you captive? Remember our safe word."

"We're in the lobby. The Viking look-alike is about to take me wherever we're going. Is Luis there?"

"Yes, he's tracking the conversation."

I smile to myself. "Good." I glance up at the monstrous man in front of me and say, "You may proceed with wherever you're taking me."

The man adjusts the cuffs of his jacket and starts making his way through the lobby, me following behind him and the suit behind me. Like ducklings in a row, we cross the tiled floor.

We dodge a few of the single ladies looking for a good time from earlier. They already have drinks in hand and are eyeing the hotel bar for any incoming hockey players. We move past a restaurant full of the glitz and glam of vibrant Miami fashion and to a back door that leads to a private rooftop overlooking the pool.

"What's going on?" Timmy asks over the phone. "Have they bound and gagged you?"

"No, they're just taking me to a private rooftop area. It's all very dreamy out here. We really need to hang out at the Moxy more."

Flowers cascade down perfectly placed pergolas draped in string lights, and red couches line the back wall, with round, stone coffee tables placed in front of them. Candles are lit up on every surface, while the aroma of fresh flowers, sunscreen, and this evening's dishes float through the air.

"You know, if I didn't know any better, I'd think you brought me up here to propose." I glance around. "Is this some sort of hidden camera thing? One of those blind marry-me shows?" Calling out to empty space, I say, "Okay, camera crew, I'm onto you, come on out."

The Viking gestures to a red couch and says, "Take a seat."

Okay, he's unamused.

I set my clutch on the coffee table in front of me and then maneuver my body down to the soft surface of the couch, sinking in further than I expected. I adjust my V-neck once again and when I glance up, I catch his eyes on me, studying.

"What?" I ask. "Did I have a nip slip?"

Without a word, he takes a seat next to me on the couch, not so close that I feel like he's going to make a move, but not so far that I have to shout to have a conversation. A respectable distance.

"I thought I told you to wear something decent?"

"Ooo, I missed the memo on when you became the boss of my body."

"Good one," Timmy says on the phone.

"Thank you." I chuckle.

"I'm going to need you to end that phone call," the Viking says. "What I'm about to tell you is highly classified."

"But they're making sure I'm not murdered."

"Trust me when I say it's in my best interest not to murder you. Now hang up," he says in such a forceful tone that I lean in to the speaker of the phone.

"Uh, I think I need to go. You have the phone pinned?"

"Yes," Timmy answers. "Call me after. I want to know what's highly classified."

"Don't worry, I'll tell you later." I hang up the phone and hand it over to its faithful owner.

He sticks it in his coat pocket as he says, "You will not be discussing this conversation outside of the two people involved: you and me."

"Okay, sure." I wink at him.

"Miss Campbell, this is not a joking matter."

I cross one leg over the other and wave dismissively at him. "I'll be the judge of that." I rub my hands together and ask, "Okay, so what's all the secrecy about?"

Chapter Two

KELLER

Go find her.

Bring her home.

Train her.

Seemed simple at the time. A task I didn't want, but something I was more than willing to do because my country means more to me than anything.

After seeing Lilly Campbell, King Theodore's one and only heir, spray water on scantily clad women and a man who found humor in humping the air in public, I realized this is going to be a huge undertaking. *And possibly, an erroneous mistake.*

"Soo . . . I'm waiting," Lilly says, blinking those dangerously light blue eyes at me. Ones I've looked into many times. *Theo's eyes.*

But what I wasn't expecting was how absolutely stunningly beautiful Lilly would be. *Is.* Long, white-blonde hair that falls just over her small yet perky breasts, eyes the color of ice crystals, full lips stained in light pink, and a slender frame still

15

curvy enough in all the right places for a man to grip on to. And those lashes of hers—long and dark—which reveal a depth to her eyes I'm sure she's unaware of.

But it's her attitude, her vibrant sass, that I know will make this task of not only training her to be the next heir—*plus convincing her to drop her life and come with me*—very difficult.

"Miss Campbell—"

"Ugh, call me Lilly. That *Miss Campbell* shit is so stuffy. And you know, it might not hurt you to introduce yourself."

"I was getting to that."

"Takes you long enough."

I clench my teeth. "My name is Keller Fitzwilliam, and I'm the private secretary and advisor to King Theodore."

"Oooo, you sound fancy. Fitzwilliam, so posh." She looks over her shoulder. "Seriously, though, where are the cameras? Are they buried in the flowers?"

"There are no cameras. This is very serious. Please regard it as such."

She folds her arms and stares me up and down. "Where do you get off talking to people like that?" In a snooty tone, she says, "'Please regard it as such.' What acting school did you go to? Your accent could use some work."

Christ.

I push my hand through my hair, irritation now ripping through my veins. "Your mother, Margret—what do you know of her family?"

Lilly straightens up, the straps of her revealing dress pulling on her delicate shoulders. "Why do you want to know?"

"Because what I'm about to tell you pertains to that."

"Do I have family I don't know about?" she asks with a dreamy look in her eyes.

That dreamy look, the intrigue, the hope . . . it's all there, which means, I've found my way to capture her.

"What have you been told?" I ask.

"Uh, well, that my mom fled from somewhere in the Scandinavian area and came to America, where she met my father. She never spoke about her family too much. Why, what do you know?"

She's in for a goddamn culture shock.

"Your mother, Margret, is one of four children."

"Four! You mean I have aunts and uncles?"

Technically, but I don't need to go into details about them just yet.

"Yes. And you have grandparents."

"Grandparents?" she says, her eyes welling up. "Really? Like, actual grandparents? Like two old people who sit in rockers and throw shoes at the street youth for being a nuisance to the neighborhood? Two old people who smile when they fart? Who call you *honey* and wear small blankets over their shoulders because they're always cold? Two old people who talk about sciatica and send you five-dollar bills in a birthday card? That kind of grandparents?"

Not so much.

If Theo or Katla ever smiled while they farted, I wouldn't be sure what to fucking do.

"No," I answer honestly. "They aren't that kind of grandparents."

"Oh." Her shoulders sag. "I always wanted old, cranky grandparents. When I was young, we lived across from this old couple. We weren't friends with them, but I would sit on my porch and watch them from across the street as they yapped and yelled at the kids riding their bikes. I found it endearing. Sometimes I wished that they had been my grandparents. I even asked—"

"They are King Theodore and Queen Katla," I say, unable to deal with her jabbering.

"Excuse me?"

"From Torskethorpe."

"Torske-what-now?"

"Torskethorpe, a small island in the Scandinavian waters, just north of the British Isles."

"Torskethorpe?" she asks, her nose curling up. "That, uh . . . that doesn't really roll off the tongue well, does it?" She pauses and then says, "Wait, you said *King* Theodore and *Queen* Katla."

"Correct."

"Hold on." She blinks a few times. "Are you *really* trying to tell me that these long-lost grandparents I've never heard of in my entire life just happen to be royalty of some far-off country that frankly I don't even believe is on a map? Torksy-to-da, was it? Dude, that was not in my geography books."

"Yes, I am."

The corner of her lip twitches.

Her eyes flit around the empty rooftop.

She smiles.

She chuckles nervously.

And then she stands from the couch. "Okay, Fitzy—"

"My name is Keller."

"Whatever it is, this is some fucked-up reality show." She grabs her clutch from the coffee table and tucks it under her arm. "You must have done some serious research to prey on an innocent girl with a secret yearning to learn more about her family." She scoffs. "Wow, you really are a little, little man. I hope karma comes back and deliberately places a painful zit on the tip of your dick." She spins on her heel, the fabric of her dress floating against the wind, and as she takes her first step away, Brimar blocks her departure with his large body.

"Lilly, I suggest you sit down," I say.

Her eyes widen as she turns toward me. "You can't possibly believe you can detain me. I'll have you know, that I have some serious friends in the Miami Police Department. They will take you out."

Fuck, she's feisty. This is why I prepared.

Hoping it wasn't going to come to this, I take out my

phone, unlock the screen, and go to my pictures. I find one of her mom and point it to her. "Does she look familiar?"

Lilly leans in, taking a closer look, and when recognition crosses her face, she slowly lowers back down to the couch as she takes the phone from me.

"Where did you find this picture?"

"It's one of many Theo and Katla have of Margret. Flip to the right. You'll see more."

Her hands shake as she moves her thumb across the screen, and picture after picture, I see tears well in her eyes until they cascade down her face.

Pictures of Margret in the courtyard with her siblings.

Pictures of Margret embroidering—one of her favorite Torskethorpian traditions.

Pictures of Margret outside the palace walls, talking with the people.

They're all there, and as I watch her flip through, I notice the shake in her hand and the tears that fall to the fabric of her dress. From the side, Brimar tosses me a pack of tissues that I gently hand to her. With a curt nod, she takes one and dabs at her eyes, only to gasp when she gets to the last picture.

"How did you get this?" she asks as she shows me a picture of her mom in a hospital bed, an infant curled in her arms, with her dad's arm wrapped around her mom.

"Your mom sent that to Theo, her father. She would send a pack of pictures every year at Christmas. That is one of many."

"She . . . she did?" she asks, scrolling through the pictures again. "But—I don't understand." She meets my gaze. "Why would she send pictures, but never talk about her family?"

"From what Theo told me, it's because she wanted to explore the world. She wanted a simple life. She wanted to live in a place where she could create a world of her own. To my understanding, she did just that."

Another tear falls down her cheek before she wipes it away

and hands me my phone. On a deep breath, she sets her shoulders and asks, "Do you have any ID?"

"What?" I ask, confused.

"I need to see your ID or passport, something that tells me who you are."

I fish into my pocket, pull out my wallet, and hand it to her. She flips it open and stares at my identification. She doesn't just glance, she studies it. She then asks for Brimar's, and he obliges. She brings them both together and compares them, giving them a thorough read-through. When she's done, she folds up our wallets and hands them back to us. "Okay, I might not be convinced, but I am listening. So why are you here?"

"King Theodore requests your presence."

"Requests it?" she asks. "He wants me to go up to Torky-porty?"

"Torskethorpe."

"You should really reconsider the name. It's quite jumbly in the mouth."

"The island is over one thousand years old. There's no changing it." *Why are you arguing with her? Get to the goddamn point. This has taken longer than I planned.* "Tomorrow morning, we leave."

"Uh, excuse me?" she asks.

"What do you not understand?"

"Well firstly, I don't understand where you get off telling me what to do. And secondly, who's to say I'm going with you?"

Fucking insolent woman.

At this point, she's either in or she's out. If the pictures don't convince her, I don't know what will. So, I stand from the couch and button my suit coat while staring down at her. "We leave at eight." I reach into my pocket and hand her another black business card. "Here's the address. If you're not there by eight, we leave without you."

She stares at the card and then waves it at me. "Did you get these printed for this one-time occasion? That's really freaking weird."

"Good night, Miss Campbell."

"It's Lilly."

Brimar follows me as we head toward the door that leads into the main hotel.

"And don't wait around for me, Fitzy. You don't tell me what to do. Do you hear me? You're not the boss of—"

The door shuts behind us, silencing her.

Brimar places his hand on my shoulder and says, no doubt with an eye roll, "*Americans.*" He shakes his head. "Good luck with that one."

Fuck, I'm going to need it.

Chapter Three

LILLY

"Holy shit. Look, right here it says 'Margret Edwina Ingrid Strom, Princess of Torskethorpe'—woof, the country name is awful to say." *Tell me about it.* "'Is the daughter of King Theodore and Queen Katla.'" Timmy sets his phone down and looks me in the eye. "Girl, you're royalty."

"What? No, I'm not . . ."

His smile stretches from ear to ear, like the Cheshire cat, as he nods. "Yes, you are. If your mom is a princess, that makes you a princess as well." And then, before my eyes, he lowers himself into a curtsy and bows his head. "Your Majesty."

I push at his forehead. "Men don't curtsy, and I'm not royalty." I pick at one of the fried plantains on our shared plate and plop it in my mouth.

"What does it feel like to just sit there in denial?"

"Comfortable," I answer while chewing on my plantain.

Timmy leans on the apartment island, where we're sharing a late-night snack. When I left the Moxy, I told him to meet me at my place ASAP. I know Keller said our conversation was confidential, but let's be honest, it's all such a fictional farse, so how could I possibly keep that confidential? I couldn't. I told Timmy, who of course I swore to secrecy, you know, just in case there is some sort of legal action that could be taken against me.

"Lilly, you know I love you, right?"

"Oh boy, here comes the heart-to-heart," I say.

"You can't deny the facts, and the facts are—your mom hid you away from a world where you have grandparents, an aunt, uncles, and well, a family. And correct me if I'm wrong, but isn't that what you've always wanted? A family?"

"I have a family," I say, reaching out and taking his hand in mine. "You're my family."

"As much as I like claiming you as my own, this is your chance to get answers. This is your opportunity to see where your mom is from, to see the place she grew up. Haven't you always wanted that?"

Yes.

I have. It's been one of my biggest life questions.

That, and why I wasn't blessed with any sort of rumba hip action. No matter how hard I try, my hips just don't sway like everyone else's.

"I have, but, seriously, Timmy, do you really expect me to fly off to some foreign island with a man who looks like Thor's brother?"

"Sounds like a dream to me."

I roll my eyes. "What about the Wagon? With your DJ schedule picking up, you can't cover all the shifts."

"You admitted even yesterday how Shari and Carrie need more shifts. The days they work, our sales are always double. You can't deny the power of a pair of Latina twins in bikinis."

He's right. My boobs have nothing on theirs.

"And they've been looking for more shifts as well. What other excuses do you have?"

"Uh, how about I just signed up for a monthly Pilates membership? That's just careless money management if I don't go at least once a week."

"I know Karen down at the shop. I can get her to put your membership on hold."

"Yeah, well, what about my apartment? You know there's an ant problem. If I'm not here, watching over the invasion, they very well might take over. And then what? I come back to an empty apartment? You know ants can carry up to fifty times their weight? Have you heard about furniture gone missing around here? It's the ants. They're selling people's possessions on the black market, and to hell if I will be subject to such behavior."

Timmy places his finger under my chin and forces me to look him in the eyes. "We just got this place sprayed. No ant will be penetrating these walls. And I promise to stop by to make sure none of your furniture is sold on the ant black market. Face it, Lilly, you have no real excuse to not go."

"How about getting on a plane with a stranger to a weird country I can barely pronounce, let alone heard of, to meet my so-called grandparents? That's not making smart decisions. And, seriously, you really believe this royal thing?"

"Only one way to find out."

"This seems really irresponsible. We don't know these people."

"They know you." He heaves out a heavy sigh and grips my hands. "Listen to me. This is a once-in-a-lifetime opportunity, and if you don't end up going, you know you're going to regret it for the rest of your life. So, let's grab your suitcase, fill it up, and get some rest. You're catching a flight tomorrow morning."

"Will you stay with me tonight? Drive me to the airport tomorrow?"

"You know I will, baby girl." He kisses me on the head,

then takes my hand and walks me to my bedroom. "Time to get packing."

———

"SO . . . HOW LONG IS THIS FLIGHT?" I ask, tapping my fingers on the lavish armrest. There are gold flecks in the wood. Could be real, could be fake, but I'm on a private plane with royal emblems everywhere, so my guess is it's real. Naturally, I took a picture of the gold flecks so I can send it to Timmy when we land.

Straight across from me sits Keller Fitzwilliam—the man with little personality and a whole lot of muscle. I'm not one to gawk, I grew up in Miami for crying out loud—shirtless, muscled men are everywhere—but the three inches of skin revealed above where his buttons stop is doing more for me than the muscle-bound men on the beach. I am slowly gaining an understanding of the appeal of cleavage to a man.

Too bad the brain inside the brawn is a total dud.

Dude hasn't said one word to me since we took off into the sky.

He's buried in a book that has a protective cover on it so I can't see what he's reading. The only people I know who use protective covers are old ladies at the beach, and you don't need to see the cover to tell what they're reading—their cheeks are flush. Grandmas into smut are my favorite kind of grand-mas. Hmm, I wonder if my grandma is into smut?

"Eight hours," Keller says, speaking up before flipping a page in his book.

"What's that?" I ask, forgetting my initial question.

He peers up at me with eyes a shade of blue that I've never seen before. They're dark, like the ocean at night, with a singular ring of gold around the pupil. Intimidating. "You asked how long the flight is. It's eight hours."

"Ah, right." I smile. "So, should we play the get-to-know-you game? The only thing I know about you is that you sort of act like an ass, so things aren't boding well for you at the moment." I hold my arms out. "But, hey, you have eight hours to change my mind."

His eyes flit back to his book. "I'm good."

Brimar—the suit, I learned his name when I stepped onto the plane—coughs, pulling Keller's attention. They exchange a look, and to Keller's chagrin, he shuts his book and says to me in an annoyed tone, of course, "What do you want to talk about?"

"Well, as you seem so overjoyed to have a conversation, where do we even begin?"

Brimar chuckles quietly to himself right before Keller shoots him a withering glance. I think we can all assume who wears the pants in *that* relationship.

"Listen, Miss Campbell—"

"Please, just call me Lilly. This *Miss* shit is really not settling well. I'm only twenty-seven, and I don't think I've earned that sort of respect yet. So, Lilly, please."

He purses his lips together. "Lilly, it is not my duty to get to know you, it is my duty to bring you to Torskethorpe, and from there, we'll see what happens. Until then, I think it might be better if we don't speak."

"Sheesh, what crawled up your behind? Is there some sort of indigenous ass-crawling mouse in Torske—uh, Tors-kethrope I need to worry about?"

"You should worry about your constant swearing."

"What . . . is it not legal there?" I ask. "Because, boy oh boy, will that be a problem. I have quite the potty mouth."

"I've noticed."

I scoff. "As if you've never said *fuck* before."

His eyes lift to mine again. "*Fuck* is my favorite word." Oooo, it sounds like it is. The way he pronounces the *F*, all breathy and erotic, yeah, that was nice on the ears. *Unlike Tors-kethorpe.* "But I am allowed to say it, whereas, you are not."

"Oh, hell no. Is this country some misogynistic place where women are repressed? If so, hand me a parachute now, because I'm out of here."

"It is not." Keller opens his book again.

"Okay, then how come I can't swear?"

"Why don't you just go to sleep? You have bags under your eyes, and you're going to want to look fresh when you get off the plane."

Bags under my eyes? What a dick!

You know what? I take back what I thought about his man-cleavage. I think it's repulsive.

"SERIOUSLY, WHY CAN'T I SWEAR?"

Keller slams his book down and growls. Actually growls.

Okay, maybe I've asked him the same question for the last two hours, but it's starting to drive me nuts.

Thick brows pulled together, the veins in his neck harden as he says in a very controlled voice, "Leave the questions for when we arrive."

"Why?"

"Because I'm not at liberty to discuss anything with you," he snaps.

"Sheesh, you don't have to yell."

"I'm not yelling," he yells. "I'm just——" Through clenched teeth, in an even voice, he says, "I'm trying to tell you that it's not my place to say anything until we arrive. So, sit back, close your eyes, and be quiet."

I cross my arms and study him. I don't think I've ever seen such an angry human. "Have you had enough Vitamin D?" I ask him. "It seems like you're really angry. Maybe a little more sunshine. Nature might do you some good. Do you go outside?"

"Yes," he answers as he turns back to his book.

"What kind of stuff do you do outside? Stand on the grass and just yell at people?"

Brimar chuckles again but quickly covers up his laugh when Keller shoots him another look.

Leaning across the small aisle, I ask, "Is he always like this? Agitated?"

"Don't answer that," Keller says.

"I'm going to take that as a yes," I say. "Hmm, maybe it's the book you're reading. Is it a suspense? Maybe a murder mystery? Are you feeling stabby?"

He rests his head back and pinches the bridge of his nose.

"You realize this frustration is self-induced," I continue. "All you had to do was talk to me, and now we're at this point, where you're about to explode, and I can't stop thinking the worst about you. How about this—how about we just start from the beginning, okay?" I lend out my hand. "Hi, I'm Lilly Campbell. I own a bikini truck with my best friend, Timmy Tuna, and I'm currently on my way to some faraway mythical country called Torske, uh, thrope"—*nailed it*—"where I'm about to meet my estranged grandparents, who, according to a Google confirmation, happen to be royalty. I'm nervous, but excited. Okay, your turn."

Those dangerous eyes stare back at me, unwavering as they peruse my face. My cheeks, my chin, my mouth—he gives me such a thorough exam that I feel the need to suck my cheeks in, give him different angles to ogle at.

Finally, he says, "I'm Keller Fitzwilliam. I've been working for the palace since I can remember. My loyalty and allegiance rest with them. The book I'm reading is a collection of poetry. And when I'm not working, I spend my time hiking, because the country you're about to visit is stunning. It's impossible not to spend your spare time outside." He opens his book again and lifts one brow at me when he says, "Is that good enough for you?"

I wet my lips. "There are a few things in your statement I

would like to explore, but for now, it works." I offer him a smile and then sink into my chair where I close my eyes.

"If you really want to sleep, there's a bed in the back."

"Really?" I ask, my eyes shooting open. "Well, don't mind if I do."

<hr />

"LILLY."

"Mmm, muffins," I mumble, curling into the softest pillow I've ever felt. No doubt, it was made by angels, stuffed with clouds, and sealed with a kiss.

"Miss Campbell, we have arrived."

"Huh?" I lift my head, my hair drooping over my face as I look around. "What do you mean? In Torskethorpe? But, isn't there a landing protocol? Like, fasten your seatbelts?"

"That's commercial, this is private. We make the rules."

I drag my fingers across my face, pushing my hair out of the way, and find Keller standing tall, suit jacket on, waiting impatiently for me at the door.

"Oh, well . . . I should get up, then." I fling the covers off me and roll to the edge of the bed, where I collect myself. I stretch my arms over my head and let out a yawn. "You should bag up these sheets and sell them, because, wow, I zonked out." I slip on my shoes and then stand from the bed. Smiling at the grump, I hold out my arms and ask, "How do I look?"

"Rumpled," he answers.

I glance down at my romper and attempt to straighten it. "Well, we can't all be Instagram ready, now, can we?"

He doesn't say anything, instead, he steps back and moves toward the front of the plane with a simple, beckoning head nod.

A man of few words.

I gather my purse I left by my chair and head toward the plane door but stop short before stepping outside.

"Holy mother of fuck!" I yell as I claw the side of the door.

"What?" Keller asks, startled.

"It's fucking freezing! What the hell, it's summer!"

"Yes, but you're in a subarctic country. Eighty percent of the terrain is glaciers."

I curl around my bag and say, "That would have been nice to know when packing."

There's a waiting car with the door open that I'm assuming is for us. My eyes make contact with where my body needs to be, and before I take another breath, I fly down the stairs, past Keller, and I sprint across the tarmac like I'm tiptoeing across fiery coals, and fling myself into the waiting car, head first.

"Blast the heat," I say as I shiver in the corner.

Keller joins me, takes a seat, and then turns toward me while I feel around the shared bench seat.

"What are you doing?" he asks, irritated.

"My nipples. I think they fell off. Do you see them?"

"Jesus . . . Christ," he mumbles before strapping his seat-belt on.

Jesus Christ is right. We're going to need some help from the Almighty above if this is what summer is like.

⊏⊐

"WAIT, is Torskethorpe like Alaska? Where the sun is up all the time during the summer?"

"Yes," he answers as I plaster myself against the window.

"Can you see the northern lights?"

"Yes."

"Are there volcanoes?"

"Yes."

"Have you seen active lava?"

"Yes."

"Holy shit, active lava and glaciers? Talk about not being able to make up its mind. And it's so green, but then there's black everywhere, and, look, a waterfall. The beach is nice and all, but this is . . . this is unreal. Is the whole country like this?"

"Yes," he answers again.

"Well, I can see what you're talking about, wanting to be outside all the time." I prop my chin on my hand. "It's gorgeous. Are all the houses always like this? Brightly colored?"

"Yes."

"Do you say more than just *yes*?"

"Yes," he answers again.

"You know, I'm not going to let your piss-poor attitude ruin this for me. My nipples might have fallen off, and I can't feel my toes at the moment from how freaking cold it is, but ohhhh no, I refuse to let you bring me down."

"Whatever you wish, Miss Campbell."

"Huh-ha," I say in triumph. "Got you to say something other than *yes*. God, rookie play. And don't call me *Miss Campbell*."

"As you wish . . ."

I eye him suspiciously. "You wanted to say *Miss Campbell* again, didn't you?"

But he doesn't answer me, and that's all I need to know —he did.

31

Chapter Four

KELLER

I know what you must be thinking—*this Keller guy is an asshole.*

Well, you're right, but I'm usually not this irritated.

Let's rewind back to last night. I reported to Theo, letting him know I made contact with Lilly, and told him we would be on a plane the next morning. I wasn't sure she would be on the plane per se, I just counted on it. Thankfully, she showed up. But it was the text I received in the middle of the night that has set me into a tailspin of irritation.

There was a leak in the palace and a gossip magazine has speculated about a long-lost granddaughter coming into town. You can imagine the security breach that is. The plan was simple—find Lilly, get her on a plane, and get her to the palace to meet Theo and Katla.

Those plans have changed.

Here's the thing. We don't know if Lilly is going to want to live the royal life, and until she's made up her mind, we don't want her exposed to the public. Now that rumors are circulating because of the leak, we can't take her to the palace.

Therefore, we're headed to the opposite end of the country, to the abandoned summer castle on the southern peninsula. No one will find us there, since the castle hasn't been inhabited for years, and according to Theo, it's where we'll conduct our training until he believes the time is right for the country to be introduced to Lilly. I've been assured that the necessities are at the castle, but there's no staff to serve us, not that I need serving, so that means it'll just be me and Lilly, with two guards, Brimar, and his girlfriend, Lara.

My irritation is justified.

"Are we headed to the palace?" she asks as she stares out the window, looking perfectly content now that the heat is blasting in the car. I, on the other hand, have had to strip out of my jacket and roll up my sleeves for fear of heat stroke.

"We are not," I answer.

"Oh." Her brow crinkles when she turns toward me. "Why not?"

"There's been a security breach," I answer. "King Theodore will offer more of an explanation when we arrive at our destination."

"And what is our destination?"

"Harrogate, the summer castle on the southern peninsula."

"Oh, sounds dreamy," she says before turning back to the window. "I've never been to a castle before, but I've seen plenty of pictures. Does it sit on a hilltop?"

"No, it's at the edge of the peninsula." I fail to mention it hasn't been visited in years. Or that it's covered in lifeless vines and has the great chance of smelling like dead fish.

"Cool. Is, uh, King Theodore meeting us there?"

"Unfortunately, no," I answer.

"Really?" she asks, her face falling. "Why not?"

"He will explain when we get there."

"Seems like he has a lot of explaining to do," she says before turning back to the window.

Yeah, he sure does.

"YOU'RE KIDDING, RIGHT?" Lilly asks, clutching my suit jacket that she's drowning in over her shoulders. Staring up at the castle, she has a worried look on her face. "We're supposed to live here?" She points to the pile of stones in front of us.

Hell, I remember this place being bigger. Then again, I haven't been here since I was a kid. The castle is on the smaller side—four bedrooms in total with two bathrooms. It was once a painting sanctuary for Theodore's mother during the summers. Not at all ostentatious, or large like Strombly Palace, it settles more on the earthy side, with its natural, unkempt stone with moss growing all over the perimeter. The backdrop is the vast ocean, one of the reasons Queen Miah loved it here, but the wind whips through the plains, creating at times a chilly vortex. The castle resembles more of an old stone cottage with two separate wings, one tower that leads to the roof, and a gravel driveway.

"Yes," I answer her. "This is Harrogate."

"What does that even mean? *Pile of rocks?*" she asks.

"Actually, it translates to *heap of stones.*"

"Well, that is quite accurate." She shivers and bounces in place. "Please tell me there is heat in there. Electricity?"

"Harrogate was modernized in the fifties. It is quite capable of keeping you warm and comfortable."

"Okay." She lets out a deep breath. "I'm sorry. I sound ungrateful, I just . . . I wasn't prepared for how cold it was going to be or for not seeing my grandparents right away. I had a vision of what it would be like when I arrived, and this is not it."

"Trust me, my plans were thrown off too." I pick up her suitcase as well as mine and head toward the front of the castle.

"Where did Brimar go? Is it going to just be you and me?"

I shake my head. "He headed into town. He's picking up his girlfriend, Lara, who's been doing some shopping. She's been instructed to find warmer clothes for you."

"Oh." Lilly pauses on her way to the entrance. "That was nice of you guys. Whose idea was that?"

"Mine," I answer. I reach the castle door and open it.

"You thought of that? Fitzy, does that mean you care about me?"

"Please don't start," I say as I hold the door open for her.

"But you do." She walks up to me and pokes me in the side. "You care about me."

"No, I just don't want to hear your constant jabbering about how cold you are."

"Ahh, smart man. Also, can we talk about how you just walked in here? No key or anything?"

"Once Brimar and Lara arrive, they will be securing the castle appropriately."

"Well, that's reassuring." She pauses in the entryway of the castle. "Wow, it's, uh, it's drafty in here. Isn't it?"

I glance around the stone walls. There's not a thing hanging on them, not a piece of furniture in sight. *Drafty* is one way to put it. "The rooms are more comfortable," I say, hoping that's the case. "We'll be on the second floor."

"*We?*" she asks. "As in, we'll be sharing a room?"

"No," I say sharply. "There are two rooms upstairs, joined by a bathroom. For security purposes, Brimar and Lara are taking the downstairs bedroom while we will occupy the upstairs."

"Oh, I guess that makes sense. But do we have to share a bathroom? I hope you don't hog the sink."

"There are two sinks."

"Perfect." She pats me on the shoulder. "We can become best friends while brushing our teeth together. Show me the way."

Bags in hand, I move up the narrow staircase to the second-floor suite. I open the door, revealing a small sitting area, no bigger than the private plane we were just on. Although partially decorated with wood-carved couches and a matching table, it lacks a sense of comfort . . . and a pillow. Floor-to-ceiling curtains of damask gold drape on either side of the thin windows, a mere sliver compared to the palace. It's a step up from a jail cell.

Perfect.

"Well, this is . . . different." I see her swallow hard and can only imagine what might be going through her head. Regrets. A massive number of regrets. With trepidation in her eyes, she asks, "Which room is mine?"

"On the left," I answer.

She follows me to her door, where she takes a deep breath, places her hand on the doorknob, gives it a twist, and pulls, but the door goes nowhere. She tugs again. And again.

But nothing.

Finally, she turns to me and says, "Perhaps you'd like to give it a try."

I set down our bags and grip the doorknob before giving it a pull, yanking the door wide open with a loud creak that echoes through the stark space.

We both peek into the pitch-black room. She glances at me and then pushes my shoulder forward. "You first. I'll, uh, I'll cover your back."

I've never been in these rooms, so I have no goddamn clue what I'm searching for, but given the way the castle is set up, I'm assuming if I walk straight, I will reach the—

BANG.

"Motherfucker!" I shout as my shin radiates with pain. "Fuck," I repeat.

"What happened?" Lilly asks from the doorway. "Did something hit you? Did you hit something? I have no ability to defend myself other than with this oversized coat."

"Table," I groan out as I hobble closer to the wall, taking it slower now. A few more steps and I'm touching the stone wall, feeling around for something soft, praying it's not a dead animal's tail but rather a curtain. When I connect with velvet fabric, I know I've found what I'm looking for. I tug on it, and a crack of light spreads through the room, illuminating a very bleak and simple space.

The window can't be any larger than two feet wide, and from the look of it, it's the only window. Planted in the center of the room, up against the wall, is a four-poster deep mahogany wood bed with navy-blue bedding. On either side is a night table with an accompanying lamp. Across from the bed is a matching dresser with a mirror. And that's it.

No rug.

No pictures.

Nothing to make the space comfortable.

Fuck.

She's going to run right out of this "heap of stones."

"Maybe the other room is more comfortable," I say as I make my way to the pocket door that leads to the bathroom. It screeches open, a sound so horrifying it makes me believe the trees that sacrificed their lives to make the door are suffering through a slow, agonizing death.

Her lips pull together as the concern on her face grows. I don't blame her.

I flip on the light switch to the bathroom and stop in my tracks . . .

Ah, hell.

The space is completely covered in stone, with another sliver of a window. There is no shower, only a wood-planked circular tub that looks as though it has seen better days. Next to it is the toilet, which has to be only five inches off the ground. Might as well set a bedpan on the floor.

On the opposite side of the bathroom are two exposed-pipe sinks with cloudy mirrors hanging above them on the wall and rickety gold sconces flanking each mirror.

I scratch the back of my neck. I don't care about a lot of things, but this is even a bit low for my standards.

Maybe the room on the right is better.

I move to the other pocket door and use all my might to push it open, revealing another dark room. Being smart this time, I carefully work my way through the space and find the curtain to the window. I pull it open and, to my chagrin, find a replica of the bedroom we were just in. But instead of navy-blue bedding, this one has green.

This does not bode well for convincing her to stay.

When I turn toward her, I can see true regret in her expression. Her frown takes over her face, her lip trembles fast enough for me to notice from a distance, and as she wraps her arms around her waist, I know she's mentally clicking her heels together, wishing she could be sent back home.

"It won't be forever," I tell her. "Just until things calm down."

Her eyes meet mine as a lonesome tear cascades down her cheek. With a quick wipe, she says, "It's . . . it's fine. Just different, is all. At least it's not super cold." She takes off my jacket and hands it to me. "I guess I'll get unpacked."

"Lilly—"

"It's fine, really." She walks through the bathroom and then to her bedroom, where she tries to shut the pocket door and struggles immensely. She uses her shoulder, leaning into her attempt to shut it, and then even yanks on it, but when it doesn't move, she tosses her hands up in the air in defeat and mumbles something under her breath.

I can only imagine what it was. Most likely included a swear word. Or six.

Shoulders slumped, a depiction of giving up, she walks over to the bed, and without bending at the waist, she flops forward on the mattress face-first. And that's where she stays, practically suffocating herself in the velvet of the comforter.

The feeling is mutual.

———

"I REALLY APPRECIATE these clothes you picked up for me, Lara," Lilly says as she cuddles into her light-blue pajama set and matching slippers. "I can't tell you how grateful I am."

"Not a problem at all. I just wish the staff had prepped the cabin more, although, I did hear they had a short time frame, not wanting to give away the location."

Lara and Lilly are sitting in front of the fireplace, a low roar of a fire in front of them, while Brimar is in the kitchen, making some soup. I'm attempting to fix the Internet by turning off the router and turning it back on while cursing under my breath.

It's a windy night, and my guess is we're not going to have any sort of signal until the morning.

"Any luck with the Internet?" Brimar asks as he steps into the main living space, which consists of two couches, one sitting chair, a coffee table, and a dining room table.

"Probably not going to work until tomorrow morning, when the wind dies down," I answer. "Is the soup ready?"

"Yes. It just needed heating."

From the couch, Lilly stands and presses her hand to her stomach. "Would it be okay if I skipped dinner for the night and went to bed? I'm not feeling too great and I think I just want to lie down."

It's obvious she's not feeling herself. Ever since I introduced her to her jail cell, I mean bedroom—my mistake—she's been quiet, withdrawn. She perked up a bit when Lara brought her warm clothes, but that was only temporary. She's spent most of the last half hour staring into the flames of the fire, probably questioning every decision she's made in the last twenty-four hours.

This was not the welcome I'd envisioned. I assumed we'd take her to the palace, let her meet Theo and Katla, and go from there. But having to stay in a distant castle that has seen better days with three strangers that have no family connection to her . . . it can't be easy.

"Are you sure?" Lara asks. "I don't want you to be hungry."

"I honestly don't think I could stomach anything right now, and I don't mean that to sound rude, but I'm just feeling weird and I think I want to lie down."

Lie down, run away . . . probably the same thing.

"Would you like me to walk you up to your room?" I ask.

Her eyes connect with mine. They're weary, tired . . . scared. She shakes her head. "I can handle it. Thank you."

Fuck, this is not going well at all.

Harrogate has totally squashed her personality into smatterings of nothing.

Convince her to stay here and train? Yeah, good luck to me.

When she heads toward the stairs, I say, "I know this isn't what you expected, and I'm sorry we had to switch things up on you, but tomorrow, Lilly. You'll get answers tomorrow."

With a curt nod, she takes off toward her bedroom, leaving the room silent. A deafening silence, and I'm pretty sure we're all thinking the same thing.

She's bolting the first chance she gets.

Brimar brings out some bowls of soup. Lara helps him with drinks, and I grab the bread. Once we're all seated, Brimar whispers, "Think she's regretting her decision?"

"Yes," I answer while I break a piece of bread. "I doubt Harrogate is what she envisioned when she said yes to coming.

An old, broken-down castle doesn't really scream thriving sovereign."

"I wish they made it slightly more inviting in here," Lara says with a shiver. "Even I'm slightly weirded out by the drab interior and lack of warm textiles."

"Well, we weren't supposed to be here and there wasn't enough time to fix the place up before we arrived. It's all spur-of-the-moment, thinking on our feet because there's a damn leak." I let out a frustrated breath. "Fuck, who could it be?"

Lara dips her spoon in her soup—potato and cheese—and says, "We're trying to figure that out as we speak. Ottar is attempting to weed out people by questioning them. He believes it might have been someone close to Theo's doctor."

"He better find out soon, because the last thing we need is the press snooping about. I sent a message to Henrik to see what media control is happening and he's put out an official statement. I haven't been able to read it because of the goddamn reception here."

"I know for a fact the Internet works here, it's just the wind for now," Brimar says. "Patience."

"I don't have any patience," I say as I rub my head, a headache forming from the tense day.

"I noticed. You seem to have forgotten the term ever since you met Lilly."

Speaking quietly, I lean in and ask, "Can you blame me? This whole attempt to convince a woman who has never heard of our country to be a royal is a goddamn joke. You've seen her." I point toward the stairs, keeping my voice low enough that it won't be picked up by the bustling wind. "She's not even close to princess material. She swears, she has zero decorum, and she's a full-fledged American with her offhand colloquialisms. Do you really think our country, *our quaint, small* country with its heavy traditions, is going to welcome an outsider?"

"She's not an outsider," Lara says. "She's been hidden to our people. She is one of us, she just doesn't know it yet."

Still whispering, I ask, "Do you know what I have to train her in? Not just etiquette, which will be a feat on its own. For fuck's sake, she asked me where her nipples were in the car because she thought they'd *fallen off.*"

A loud laugh escapes Lara's lips. "Oh, I might like this girl."

"That's just one of the things she needs to learn. But I have to teach her the history and culture of our country. Meaning . . . she needs to learn to embroider, whittle, and become an inspired kulner. She needs to learn to bake, to paint, to speak to the people of Torskethorpe with care and interest. We're talking about a woman who I found soaking random strangers in wet T-shirts when I arrived in Miami. Do you really think she's going to be able to sit down and cross-stitch until her fingers bleed?"

"You never know," Brimar says. "She had precise accuracy with the hose."

I hate to admit it, but she did.

"It was an embarrassment. Not to mention, what kind of dirt could be dug up on her if she does fall in line with the crown? We're talking about a former bikini-selling American turned queen. Tell me how that's going to go over well. Hell, we exiled our very own prince for rolling around in moss."

Brimar holds up his finger. "One-thousand-year-old sacred moss. He deserved what was coming to him."

"She doesn't even know how to pronounce the country's name without stumbling." I drag my hand over my face. "This is not going to go well. I'm going to spend all this goddamn time training her, and when it comes down to it, she's not going to be good enough. Or worse, she's going to realize she's way out of depth and that Torskethorpe is not for her."

"You don't know that," Lara defends. "You're assuming she'll fail without giving her a chance. You never know, she just might surprise you." Lara leans forward and presses her hand to mine. "I know your first instinct is to think negatively, but that'll do us no good in this situation. As much as you don't want to admit it, she is our last chance at continuing the legacy that Theo has made for all of us. If you're doing this for anyone, you're doing this for him."

I lean back in my chair, feeling defeated.

If anyone else understands the meaning of "doing it for Theo," Lara and Brimar do. We all grew up together. Our parents all worked in the palace. My dad was a pastry chef, my mom was in charge of preserving the art collection, and both Brimar and Lara had parents who were servants within the palace walls. We would spend our summers running up and down the servant halls together. I can remember the day we first met Theo, face to face. We were playing tag, being far too loud, and he came barreling into the hallway through a secret door that led to the throne room.

The pure terror and shock beat through me as King Theo stood there, staring down at three servants' kids. We froze on the spot, our tongues tied, our bodies shaking with nerves. All I could think about was how much trouble we were going to be in when our parents found out.

And just as I felt tears start to well up in my eyes, an onslaught of apologies on the tip of my tongue, Theo leaned down, pressed his hand to my shoulder, and called out, "TAG," before taking off down the hall. It took us a few seconds to react, but once we did, we chased him all around the palace until he led us into the kitchen, where we shared a bowl of cookies and four glasses of milk. I still consider it, to this day, one of the best days of my life.

After that, he was like a grandfather to us, and we were the grandchildren he never had.

"She's right," Brimar says. "You need to not only give her a chance, but you need to make sure she succeeds, if not for the fate of the country, then for Theo."

I roll that around in my head, and the fact of the matter is, he's right. They both are. I love this country more than my own life. I have dedicated my world to protecting the people and the king, so why is this any different?

Why is she any different?

She isn't.

Chapter Five

LILLY

You're okay.

You're okay.

It's just wind.

It's not some scary ghost, lurking in the corner, making scratching noises, preparing to swallow you whole and bring you over to the dark side.

To say this is not what I was expecting when I arrived is an understatement. Maybe I got too caught up in shows like *The Crown*, but . . . I mean, I wasn't expecting an old, creepy stone castle in the middle of nowhere as my place of residence. Can you blame me? I've tried to convince myself all night that my decision wasn't made in haste, that I did the proper fact-checking, and that I'm here for a chance to learn about my mom, but ladies, if you're listening . . . this is what nightmares are made of.

I pull my covers up to my wide-open eyes as I stare at the drafty ceiling. My legs rattle under the sheets, my heartbeat is thrumming in my throat, and my ears are playing tricks on me by sending signals to my brain . . . *did you hear that?*

What about that?

I think someone is in the room.

No! No one is in the room.

I fluctuate between being absolutely freezing thanks to the "summer" weather, to a frantic heat beat every few minutes because of the nerves bouncing around in my body. One moment I'm able to convince myself that everything is going to be okay, and then the next, I believe the Loch Ness Monster is tapping on my window, waiting to take me into its loch forever.

And before you jump on my back, yes, I realize the Loch Ness Monster is a Scotland thing, but that's how insane my brain has been tonight. It's traveling all the way to the land of kilts to scare me.

Tap. Tap. Tap.

I freeze.

See, did you hear that?

It's a ghost, spooking the brave yet stupid American lying in its bed.

My hands shake as I pull the blanket up even higher. Someone is outside that sliver of a window with an axe, mentally fucking with me. Every few seconds, they're tapping the window, letting me know that they own my thoughts and my nightmares.

I lift the sheet past my comforter and wave it in the air, metaphorically waving my white flag.

I give up, okay? Take me as your prisoner, but just do it already and stop fucking with me. I can't do this all night. Take me to the hollows of your phantom hotbed where you feast on souls.

Tap. Tap. Tap.

Ahhh! I didn't mean it!

Don't take me to the hotbed. I'm too young.

Tap. Tap. Thud . . .

I let out a scared squeal as I plug my ears and squeeze my eyes shut.

This is not happening. Nope. There isn't some poltergeist oozing from the stone walls, ready to light up the room with its neon, radioactive spook vomit.

Everything is fine. Dare I say, on the up and up.

Think good thoughts, like . . . flowers. Those are pleasant.

And . . . uh, cat tongues. Love that sandpaper feel.

And I hate to admit it, but Keller's man cleavage, that's . . . that's a nice image.

Tap . . . tap . . . tap.

God, I hate Timmy.

Ohhhhh, go be a royal.

It will be fun, he said.

You will be living out a dream.

Well, guess what, Timmy *Tuna*, this is not a dream, this is death knocking at my door. A slap in the ass by the medieval monsters lurking around for fresh blood. They can smell it from ten miles away. They know I'm weak, they know I'll bow down before them, they know the lightest of taps will turn me into a ball of anxiety, ready to bend over for whatever they have in store for me.

I'm pathetic.

This place is too freaky.

So, just take me.

Take me.

Fucking—

"Are you okay?"

"AHHHHHHHHHHHH!" I scream, jack-knifing straight off my bed, levitating about five feet in the air before falling to the floor. Quick to my feet, I grab the lamp on the night table, and like a bat out of hell, I start swinging it around, blaring my war cry as I jab the midnight air in front of me. "Back, you beast. I have a lamp and I know how to use it. Fa-bam. Fa-bam." I jab.

"Whoa, Lilly, it's Keller."

Keller?

I pause my jabbing and stand tall. I reach under the lamp shade and switch it on, illuminating the dark room. And sure enough, Keller is standing in my room in a pair of sweatpants and a T-shirt. If my heart wasn't about to beat out of my chest, I would actually appreciate his loungewear, but I'm hanging on by a thread at the moment.

"Keller," I breathe out. "What . . . what the hell are you doing?"

"I heard a weird . . . squealing and thought I'd check on you."

"Why would you do that?" I ask, heaving a heavy sigh of relief. "That's being kind, but correct me if I'm wrong, I'm not sure you're a kind man toward me."

"It's not that I'm not kind, it's just that you irritate me."

"You know, if I wasn't so fucking terrified right now, I'd have a witty response, but I'm afraid to say it, this Hagrid place is spooky as shit."

"Harrogate."

"Whatever." I set the lamp back on the night table and sit on the edge of my bed. "My nerves are absolutely fried. What the hell is that tapping sound?"

"What tapping—oh, I was drumming my finger on my night table. Is that what you were hearing?"

My nostrils flare in aggravation. "You've got to be kidding me. What the hell are you doing, tapping your nightstand at night? Sending a morse code to the ghosts to freak me the hell out?"

"There aren't ghosts in here."

"BAH!" I say loudly. "If you truly believe the haunted aren't living in these stone walls, then you are suffering from a severe case of the delusions." I jab my finger into my bed. "This place is crawling in spooks."

"You're playing tricks on yourself."

"Don't you tell me what I'm thinking. I can smell a ghost from a mile away, and they're standing in this room, laughing at us as we speak." I toss my arms up in the air. "Laugh all you want. You don't scare me."

I think we all know that's a giant lie. I'm surprised I didn't piddle the bed.

"Seems like you were scared."

I flash my disdain at Keller. "Is there a reason why you were tapping on your nightstand?"

"My pen was drying up."

"Your pen? What, are you writing in your diary or something?" I laugh but he just nods.

"Yes, I was."

"Wait. You have a diary?"

"More of a journal, but, yes. It's my responsibility to record history, just like every other private secretary before me."

Huh, well, I guess that makes sense.

"So . . . did you happen to mention me in your journal?"

"Yes."

"Can I read it?"

"No."

"But it's about me."

"It's still my private thoughts."

"Uh, it's not private if it's for history." Good one, Lilly. Got him there.

"I record everything, and then it's my choice when I retire if I want to contribute them to the royal archive. It's not a requirement."

"Well, still, I'd like to know your thoughts on me."

"You really don't," he answers.

Tilting my head to the side, I say, "You know, you seem to

have an attitude problem. Are you aware? It's very surly, unpleasant, and—"

"Need I remind you whose jacket you borrowed this afternoon?"

"Eh—well, that was yours—"

"And must I bring it to your attention who had Lara pick up clothes for you so you're comfortable while staying here?"

"Yes, that was in fact you, but—"

"And despite wanting to go to sleep, I came in here to check on you because it seemed like you were scared."

I let out a frustrated breath. "Yes, that was all you, but, you know . . . it wouldn't kill you to be a little nicer in conversation."

"It's not my job to be nice in conversation. It's my job to protect you." He takes a step back toward our slightly ajar pocket doors—shutting them has been a severe, unwanted burden, so we decided to leave them as is. "Get some sleep. You're going to need it tomorrow."

"Why? What's tomorrow?"

"Good night, Lilly."

"Wait, I have questions. Can you just explain to me what the hell is going on?"

But he keeps moving into his bedroom.

"You realize I can still talk to you, even though there's an archaic bathroom between us with pipes that jiggle when you turn on the water. I know you can hear me." I stare into the dark abyss that is his bedroom. "Hello . . ." I pause. "Did a ghost get you? Are you a ghost? Is this some alternate reality I've flown into when I got on the plane? Why does it have to be so cold during summer? Are your nipples hard? Mine are. Hello . . . Keller?"

Urgh.

I flop back on my bed and slide under the bedding.

Get some sleep. Sure, easier said than done.

"MISS CAMPBELL, it's, uh, it's time to wake up," Lara says, patting my bed.

Grumbling under the covers, I push at them and slowly slide out from the foot of the bed where I've been sleeping all night. I pull the covers around my head like a cloak and roll into a warm cocoon while I stare up at the ceiling, blurry-eyed. "Call me Lilly."

"Lilly, did you sleep like that all night?"

I take in my surroundings and then rest my head back down. "Yes, I felt that it would be harder for the ghosts to penetrate my soul if I was fully immersed in my blankets. Seems as though it worked. I'm alive and well this morning. How did you sleep?"

"Great, thank you. Brimar hogged the bed only slightly, but he kept me warm."

"Must be nice working with your boyfriend."

"It has its pluses and minuses. Given our line of work, there are always concerns, but I can assure you about something, Lilly, there are no ghosts in this castle."

"Ha! Okay, Lara, it's nice that you're trying to assure me, but I know the truth." I let out a long yawn. "What time is it?"

"Six in the morning."

"Six?" I say, popping up. "Why the hell are you waking me up at six? The only people I know that wake up at six are overachievers who like to get a workout in before the day starts. And trust me, Lara, I am not one of those people."

"Ah, so . . . that might make this morning's activities a bit of a challenge." She winces. "Brimar and Keller are waiting downstairs with their running shoes on."

Running shoes? She can't possibly be serious.

"Hold on." I swipe my blonde locks out of my face. "Are you trying to tell me that you're in my room at six in the morning, knocking on my sheets because we're going on a run?"

"Yes. It's the protocol that as bodyguards, we go on a run in the morning to keep up with our fitness. Keller joins us, and given the circumstances, you can't be left alone. Therefore, you will need to join us."

She must have lost her mind. Me? Run?

At six in the morning?

"You have got to be kidding me. What circumstances?"

"I'm not at liberty to say."

"Isn't that convenient?" I whisper. "So, what you're telling me is that you'd like me to join you this morning."

"I'm afraid you don't have an option. If we are out of the castle, so are you. You're required to go on the run."

Isn't that just rich?

"Jesus Christ," I say, flinging my covers off me. Of course it's a requirement. Freaking Torskethorpe and their healthy bodyguards and whatever the hell Keller is. Maybe instead of running, they just eat a banana. That's healthy. I hop off my bed in a fit of irritation, only for my leg to get caught in one of the sheets, causing me to tip forward and land flat on the stone surface below me. "Mother . . . fucker," I groan.

"Lilly, are you okay?"

I hold up my hand. "Fine. Fine." I shake my foot free of the sheet and stand. "I'm going to assume you purchased workout clothes and shoes?"

Once again, she winces. "I did." She gestures toward the dresser. "I actually laid them out for you before I woke you up."

"Well, that was kind of you." I move past her, scoop the clothes off the dresser, and then head to the bathroom. "Let me get ready."

"Okay, and, uh, Keller told me to tell you to not take too long. There's a schedule for the day."

There's a schedule for the day—that was said in a very immature, mocking voice.

Deep breaths, Lilly.

She's just the messenger. No need to lash out at her.

"Thank you, Lara." I smile and then slip into the bathroom.

Not take too long . . . where does he get off?

And forcing me to work out? Timmy is going to drop dead when I tell him I went for a run. Running is not my thing. I'm more of a Pilates kind of girl—you know, a little ab work here and there. Nothing too strenuous. Nothing that's going to force me to gasp for air.

But it seems that attitude doesn't work for today's schedule.

Irritated and bitter—a whole lot of bitter—I take care of my business on the tiny toilet, brush my teeth with the freezing cold jiggling-pipe water, and then slip my clothes on and throw my hair up into a ponytail.

I stare at my reflection and say, "This is the best they're going to get."

Lucky for me, the clothes and shoes fit amazingly, and Lara was smart to include a long-sleeved workout shirt for me. Given how cold my room is this morning, I can only imagine what it's going to be like when I step outside.

I head down the stairs to the entryway of the house, where Brimar, Lara, and Keller are all standing, waiting for me.

With a fake smile plastered across my face, I sarcastically say, "Lovely morning for a run, isn't it?"

"Good morning, Miss Campbell," Brimar says.

"Lilly, for the love of God, please, all of you, call me Lilly," I nearly screech and then realize the tone of my voice. When I reach the bottom stair, I grip the banister and take a deep breath. "I apologize for that outburst. I'm not much of a morning person, nor do I tend to run for fun. So, I'm slightly on edge at the moment. But, please, call me Lilly."

Keller steps up and says, "Lara has informed us of your indifference toward working out this morning. But it's required of them, and I like to stay in top, physical form as well."

Yes, well, that's obvious from the man-cleavage I had the privilege of staring at on the airplane.

"I'm well aware of everyone's desires to stay physically fit, but I need to warn you—I am not in tune with my lung capacity when it comes to running. Therefore, there might be a lot of walking in your future."

Brimar and Lara exchange worried glances. "I'll stay back with her," Keller says. "I know you two have a routine."

"Ah, a nuisance *and* a white knight." I pat Keller on the shoulder. "An all-around catch for the ladies." I gesture toward the door. "Shall we get this torture over with?"

Together, we all exit the castle, and Brimar locks up with some special device I've never seen before. Here I was expecting a fresh-from-the-iron skeleton key, but this device is high tech, utilizing a keycode, beeping sound, and laser.

So, we can have a spaceship laser key, but the doors in the bathroom can't shut properly. Yup, makes sense.

Brimar pockets the laser thing, and then, like someone just hit the start button, Brimar and Lara take off in a run.

And so does Keller.

Wait, what about a warmup? Stretching? Maybe a moment to procrastinate?

"You coming?" he asks, looking over his shoulder.

"Yes, but I expected a warmup. These old limbs haven't worked like this in a while." I gesture to my legs.

"You're twenty-seven, there is nothing old about you."

"Tell that to the bunion on my big toe."

Ew, why did I just say that?

From the wretched look on Keller's face, I can tell he's thinking the same thing.

"It was a joke," I say as I catch up to him, my body aching everywhere as I try to pump the gas. Come on, body. Get moving. Wake up. "There's no bunion." He doesn't say anything but continues forward. "I do have calluses, though. Rough and crusty when not treated. Do you have any?"

"No," he answers.

Ha, okay.

"So, I'm to believe that if I took your shoe off, I couldn't use the bottom of your foot to shave my leg?"

"No."

"Do you have secret soft baby feet I'm not aware of?"

"Yes."

"You are such a fucking liar," I huff out, trying to keep pace. But he doesn't say anything after that and with the heavy workload on my lungs, I decide to end the conversation. Best save all the strength I have and not waste it on battling him about his feet.

We all know he's lying. There's no way he has soft baby feet.

I turn my attention to the gravel road in front of us.

From the drive in yesterday, I noticed that, although the terrain's a beautiful shade of green with rolling hills, there is a lack of trees. Not one in sight, and along the rocky edge of the coastline are black rocks with jagged tips. The kind of rock you don't want to be washed up on. But the water, it's such a beautiful blue, and the crash of the waves gives me some peace of mind, reminding me of home.

"You're falling behind," Keller says, pulling my attention back to the current state of misery I'm in.

I pick up my pace and don't say anything, because not only can I barely breathe, but I don't know what to say.

I don't even know what to think. This isn't what I expected. Any of it. I truly thought I was coming here to meet my grandparents and find out more about my mom, but the moment I stepped on that plane, everything has been hush-hush. No one is telling me what's going on and . . . oh . . . my . . . God . . .

I stop dead in my tracks as the last twenty-four hours of events flash through my mind.

The secrecy.

The weird castle.

The whole not leaving me alone thing . . .

"What are you doing?" Keller asks as he annoyingly jogs in place.

"Am I . . . am I a captive?"

"What?" he asks, stopping now and resting his hands on his hips.

"I've been captured, haven't I? That's why I can't be alone in the castle, because you're afraid I'll run away." It's all making sense now. "Well, guess what, buddy, we're in the middle of fucking lava land, my cell phone is conveniently not working, and I have nowhere to go or anyone to call. I'm in my worst nightmare. I've been stolen!"

Keller pinches his brow and mutters, "Jesus Christ." He then looks at me and says, "If you want to leave, tell me the word. I'll get you on a plane quicker than you can change out of that outfit. We are not holding you captive. This isn't a fictional storyline you've created in your head."

"This isn't what I signed up for."

"Me either, but we're fucking here, so make the most of it," he huffs out, and can I just take a moment to admire the way he said *fucking*? It sounds so delicious with his British-sounding accent. And it pains me to admit that, given our disagreeable nature, but it did sound really nice.

"Fine," I say as I walk up to him. "But you need to slow down on your pace unless you feel like giving me a piggyback ride all the way back to the castle."

"Fine," he shoots back at me. "You set the pace . . . a running pace."

I tap the side of my head. "Smart man, adding running in there because I would've walked."

"I figured."

I set out in a comfortable jog. I'm sure it's more of a bounce up and down for Keller, but he can deal, and together, side by side, we say nothing as we exercise.

Timmy wouldn't believe his eyes if he saw me now. Running around in a field with what I can only assume is a Viking next to me, not talking, but sweating enough to look like one of my wet T-shirt contestants.

After what feels like forever, Keller asks, "How are you feeling?"

"Like death," I answer as I slow to a walk and put my hands over my head. "Can you tell . . . by my . . . lack of breath?"

In an untaxed voice, as if he's been out for a leisurely stroll, he says, "Your breathing seems labored."

"It is. How far have we gone?"

"Half a mile."

"What?" I grip his arm, his very stiff, muscular arm. "Half . . . a mile? How is that . . . possible?" I ask, still catching my breath.

Half a mile? No freaking way. Easily two miles by now.

"Would you like to turn around?"

"Yes," I pant out, still gripping his arm. "But walk. Let's walk."

Sighing, Keller turns me around, and we walk back down the path we came from, the castle in the far distance. Huh, maybe it has been only half a mile.

Once I feel like there's sufficient air in my lungs, I ask, "How come there isn't a single tree around here? That seems really odd. I mean, it's green everywhere, but no trees."

"The Vikings stripped the land when they first found Torskethorpe. They used the wood for boats, houses, fuel—they used trees for everything. When they left, a few settlers stayed and developed the country from the rubble left behind. Those settlers found that the soil wasn't rich enough to support tree growth due to the lava fields."

"Seriously?" I ask. "But things can be grown here?"

"Yes. Ash from the volcanoes has actually enriched some of the soil. On the western side, it's rich with moss. Fields and fields of it."

"Huh, interesting. Are there active volcanoes on the island right now?"

He nods. "Yes, Loki is constantly flowing with lava."

"Loki, as in . . . the biological son to the frost giants in the Marvel movies?"

"No. Loki, as in Norse Mythology, a god of fire."

"Well, look at that, you learn something new every day. Here I'm thinking Torskethorpe has been inundated with Marvel fans. So, we could go see this active volcano if we wanted to?"

"Yes, we could."

"That seems fascinating. I've never seen a volcano before, in real life, that is. You always see them bubbling on shows and you wonder how much of it is real—"

"It's real. Very real."

"Fascinating. So, there's an active volcano on the island of Torskethorpe. What else is there? Is it inhabited by animals? Should I be concerned about a bear lurking around the corner?"

"The only native land animal on the island is a Nordic fox."

"Wait." I pause on our walk. "You're telling me there's nothing else on this island besides Nordic foxes?"

"Key word being native," he says, continuing to walk. "There are wild reindeer that you can spot every now and then."

"Wow, so I shouldn't expect a rabid puma to spring from the moss and claw my eyes out?"

"No."

"No alligators waiting to snatch your leg when you're least expecting it?"

"No."

"What about a snake waiting to scare the ever-loving shit out of you when you leave your house?"

"There's not one single snake on the island."

"Now that's something I can get on board with. Florida has trained me to be on the lookout at all times for snappy alligators, sneaky snakes, and jumping lizards. Not to mention the bugs. What about whales, do you see them a lot on the coast?"

"Marine life is a different story. You'll probably see more mammals in the ocean than you're prepared for."

"That seems fun. I like the ocean." I nudge his shoulder with mine. "See, look at us having a conversation without arguing. I'm proud of us."

"I'm sure it won't last long."

"Not with that kind of attitude. Now, tell me, what is the island food here? Anything special I should try?"

I see the smallest of smiles tug on the corner of his lip. "Yes, Torskethorpe is quite known for one thing in particular. It's their pride and joy. The island is actually named after its main ingredient."

"Torskethorpe means something?"

He nods. "Yes. Torske means *cod* and Thorpe means *settlement*."

"This beautiful island is named cod settlement? As in, the fish?"

"Correct. We are surrounded by cod, and with fishing sanctions implemented in our water space, we'll never have a shortage."

"Well, cod is . . . nice. Dare I ask what the delicacy is?"

"Fermented cod cakes."

"Fer-fermented?"

He nods.

"As in, like . . . brined fish?"

"Yup. I'm sure you'll get your fill while you're here."

I highly doubt that'll ever enter my mouth. Brined fish cake doesn't really scream appetizing to me.

"Think you can run again?" he asks.

"I mean, I know I can. The question is—do I want to?"

"The answer is yes," Keller says while getting behind me and pushing.

"Hey, watch it, handsy." I swat at him. "I don't need you touching my sweat."

THERE IS something incredibly humbling about taking a sitting shower in a wooden bathtub. And I use the term *bathtub* pretty loosely—some might call it an oversized bucket, or perhaps the receptacle used for laundry. It's just missing a washboard.

After we returned to the castle, I secretly watched Keller do lots of variations of pushups while I pretended to stretch my legs. Regular pushups, wide pushups, narrow pushups, one-handed . . . pushup jacks. You name it, he did it. He asked if I wanted to join him in his ab routine, and of course, being well versed in an ab workout, I felt confident enough to say yes. That was, until we were seesawing what felt like a boulder back and forth. After five up and downs, I was spent.

Once Brimar and Lara arrived—looking as though they barely even worked up a sweat—I stumbled into the kitchen in need of breakfast and coffee. Brimar made a giant pot of apple oatmeal. Not my first choice, as I was sniffing out more of a Danish option, but I'm going to tell you right now, the moment I took my first bite, I asked for seconds.

Not sure what kind of magic potion Brimar put in his oatmeal, but I had two bowls. After that, I made Keller swear to stay downstairs while I took a bath/shower, because of the doors. He obliged, and I spent a good portion of time learning how to shower without spraying water everywhere. I found if I held the sprayer with my legs while I lathered, that worked best, but at one point, the surprisingly hard water pressure shot straight up the vag and it felt . . . nice.

Anyway, now that I'm dressed for the day, had that "solid" workout, and am fed, I'm ready for what's next.

"Please tell me the Internet is working," I say, wanting desperately to connect with Timmy and tell him about the number of muscles I saw rippling through Keller's arms while he did pushups. Twenty-two, in case you were wondering.

Wearing black-rimmed glasses—hello, hotness—Keller taps away on his computer, pauses, and says, "Yes, we have Internet."

"Oh, sweet Jesus," I cheer as I pull my phone out. "What's the password? I'd love to talk to Timmy."

"Only one device at a time," Keller says.

"Uh . . . are you saying we have dial-up?"

"I'm saying it's close enough to it." He checks the time on his watch and then says, "We have five minutes."

"Five minutes before what?"

"Before the call."

"What call?" I ask. Lara and Brimar are outside tending to some "security" thing while Keller and I sit on a couch together.

"The call with King Theo."

"Wait . . . you mean I'm actually going to meet them? Over a video call?"

"Yes, and before you ask why, they'll explain it all."

"Are you going to stay for the conversation?"

"Yes," he answers. "It's my job to be a part of your business."

"Is that so? Well, then maybe you should know when I took a shower today, the sprayer hit my private parts and it felt good. There you go, how's that for being in my business? Going to write it in your diary?"

His eyes zero in on mine, his brows drawing together,

and for the life of me, I can't stop chanting over and over in my head, "Spank me. Spank me," when he gives me that look.

Before he can say anything, his computer chimes and he says, "They're calling."

"They are?" I quickly sit up and adjust my long-sleeved shirt. "Oh God, how do I look? Do I have anything in my teeth?" I flash Keller my teeth. "How about my hair? I feel like it needs more volume. Do I need more volume?"

Ignoring me, he accepts the call and says, "Your Majesty, it's good to see you."

Your Majesty? Oh God, is that what I should call him?

Maybe Your Grace?

Possibly Kingy . . .

"Keller, my boy, how's everything at Harrogate?" a deep, rich voice asks, causing my mouth to dry up immediately.

That's him. That's my mom's dad. A person I never thought existed.

"Everything is well. The winds have tampered with the Internet out here, but I'm glad we were able to get it running."

"Me, as well. I've been antsy to meet Lilija."

I freeze.

The sound of my name, said just the way my mom used to say it . . . it feels like a spiral of shock hits me all at once, straight in the chest, squeezing my heart until I feel as though I can't breathe.

"Is she there?" he asks.

"Yes," Keller says as he sets the computer down on the coffee table, pulling me into the frame.

When my eyes land on the screen, I can immediately see familiarity in his features. Although more masculine than my mother, they share the same eyes.

"My dear," he says as he folds his hands together. "Lilija, you—" He chokes up. "You look just like Margret."

Nerves bend my words as I try to formulate sentences. "He-hello, Your, uh, Your King Majesty."

He softly smiles at me. "Please, Lilija, call me Theo. I assume it's too early to offer the title of Afi just yet."

I wet my lips as I attempt to get comfortable, not sure it's going to be possible because this is . . . this is mind-blowing.

Throat tight, I say, "Hi, Theo."

"Hi, Lilija. Tell me, how are you liking Torskethorpe so far?"

"Well, it's colder than I expected," I say.

He chuckles and then coughs, a deep, almost scary cough. He holds his fist up to his mouth and says, "Excuse me. Yes, I'm sure it's colder than you were thinking it would be. High fifties is a nice summer day for us, but probably a chilly day for you."

"Just a little," I answer nervously. "I'm sorry, this is all kind of strange to me. I didn't think my mom had family, let alone . . . royal family. It feels all very unbelievable."

"Yes, I can see how that might be hard to believe, but trust me, my dear—" He coughs heavily. "It is quite true."

My head tilted to the side, I ask, "Are you . . . are you sick?"

I can see his eyes flit to someone else in the room before he focuses back on the screen.

"Well, I guess we should be honest with you now, shouldn't we?" He clears his throat. "I trust Keller can explain more once I get off this call, but the reason we brought you out here is that you, Lilija, are next in line for the throne."

What?

I glance at Keller, who nods, and then I look back at the computer, a laugh bubbling out of me. "Oh, is that right?" I cross one leg over the other. "So, what am I? Tenth? Twelfth in line?"

"First," he answers, causing my jaw to hit the ground.

"First?" I blink a few times. "First, as in . . ."

"As in, if I pass away, and your uncle Sveinn doesn't return to Torskethorpe, which we're sure he won't, you are the rightful owner of the crown."

I can't help it, I let out the loudest guffaw ever guffawed. It blows back Keller's blond hair, whipping it over his forehead. It moves a vase of fake flowers, disrupting the well-thought-out, put-together arrangement. The guffaw is so obnoxious that it actually shakes the sheer rubble we're sitting on.

"This is a good one." I clap. "Like, really good, you guys. Who put you up to this? Was it Timmy Tuna? I mean, I know I pranked him last month by tying his shoelaces together while he was napping and then scaring him with a blowhorn, but come on, this . . . this is next-level." I lean closer to the computer. "Is that a green screen behind you? I can't tell. Are you all hired actors? How much was the flight up here? I know Timmy is from a rich family, you know, tuna really does sell, but I didn't think he would do something this crazy. And he even created the Internet searches, too? This is crazy. I mean, kind of cruel to trick me with a family I always wanted, but I have to applaud the commitment."

"Lilija—"

"And that name, so odd that you're calling me by my real name. No one ever called me that besides my mother. I don't think Timmy even knows that . . ."

"This isn't a prank, this is real and I don't have much time to talk, but you are at Harrogate for a reason. Keller can explain the rest." He coughs a few times, his eyes squeezing shut. "But, please, listen to him." Growing incredibly serious, he says, "Keller will be handing you a letter, so please read it, Lilija. You're my only hope."

And before I can say one more thing, he shuts the computer, blacking out the screen.

Uh, what is happening?

You're my only hope? Who is he, Princess Leia?

Keller picks up his computer and sets it on his lap. "We

should start with family history and what's put you into this position," Keller says, getting right down to business.

"Wait, hold on." I hold up my hand as I stand from the couch. "Are you just going to ignore the fact that a huge bomb was dropped on me?"

"No, I was going to go into detail as to how this all happened."

"Like a robot," I shout at him. "Can't you for a second realize that this all might be very weird and very strange for me and that I might need a goddamn second to process it?"

Keller leans back on the couch. "How much time do you need?"

"Uh, I don't know, Keller, a fortnight?"

"Do you even know what amount of time that equates to?"

"No," I yell before fleeing the main living space and storming up the stairs to my bedroom. I attempt to shut the door, but all it does is groan against my push.

There's no use.

I flop on my bed and drape my arm over my eyes.

A royal.

Not just a royal, but the next in line to the throne.

That can't possibly be true.

There's a light knock on my door, and I move my arm to see Keller walk in with an envelope in hand. He holds it out to me and says, "This might help you understand. I'll be down-stairs when you're ready."

I take the envelope from him, and he leaves, giving me some space.

With shaky fingers, I open the envelope and unfold the letter.

Dear Lilija,

My dearest granddaughter. You might not know who I am, but I am quite familiar with you. Ever since you were born until your mother passed, I received pictures of you and letters, telling me what a brilliant and kind girl you are. I was there when you went through your Barbie phase. I was there when you cut your fringe despite your mother's protests. And I was there when you got your very first job helping Mrs. Odom roll balls of yarn. I've been a part of your life from a distance and have always respected your mother's wishes of keeping her two lives separate.

But there has come a time where I need to break that promise, not for selfish reasons, but for reasons greater than the love I have for you and your mother.

The country is at risk of losing its territory, of having its land destroyed, of hurting its people. Without an heir in line to take the throne, our country is lost. I realize this is a lot to ask of you, since you have your own life in Miami, but, Lilija, I beg of you, consider staying here, learning about our country, our culture, where your mother is from. There's so much of her in you, and I would love for you to see that, to reconnect with her roots.

Please, Lilija, give us a chance. Let us train you in our culture, in our heritage. And after two months, if you don't feel this life is for you, we'll hold you close to our heart but part ways. This is your choice, but before you say no, please give us a chance first.

Sending much love to you, my dear.

Theo

(Afi—grandfather)

I have a grandfather. A grandmother too. But where have they been for the last ten years? I get that Theo wanted to respect my mother's wishes, but ten fucking years after her death is a long-ass time to neglect your own granddaughter.

And he wants me to give up my life for Torskethorpe.

For people I don't even know.

My fingers collide with another piece of paper and I bring it forward, only for the tears gathered in my eyes to fall.

It's a picture of me and my mom, standing in front of our house in Miami. She's kissing me on the cheek while I'm giggling. *Oh God, I miss you, Mom. So, so much.* I rub my thumb over my mom's face and quietly ask, "What should I do, Mom?"

Chapter Six

KELLER

"Is she still up in her room?" Brimar asks as he hovers over another pot of soup.

"Yes," I answer. "She hasn't come down since I delivered her the letter."

"Should I go up there and talk to her?" Lara asks.

I shake my head. "No. I think this is a moment when we need her to come to us. We can't press her."

Looking worried, Brimar asks, "What do you think she's going to say?"

I lean on the wood-block counter of the rustic kitchen and fold my arms over my chest. "I don't know. If I were in her position, I'm not sure what I would do."

"Yes, you are," Brimar says. "You'd step up because that's your personality. Not saying there's anything wrong with Lilly, but I fear this might be all too much for her. She has a great life in Miami."

"She does," I say. "The only way she'd stay is if she wants to find a connection to her mother."

Lara steps in closer and says, "What if she doesn't find that connection? What's going to happen to the country?"

"Not something we need to worry about right now," I say as I push off the counter. "When's dinner going to be ready?"

"Ten minutes," Brimar says. I head out of the kitchen but stop in the doorway when I spot Lilly coming down the stairs.

Her eyes are puffy and red, the normally vibrant girl I met only two days ago is completely gone, and a morose woman steps forward. When her eyes connect with mine, her lips tremble as she says, "Keller?"

"Yes?"

"Can I . . . can I speak with you? Privately?"

"Of course," I answer. She walks back up the stairs, and I don't bother looking back toward the kitchen, where I know Brimar and Lara are probably shaking in their slippers.

What's the worst that could happen if Lilly doesn't take the throne?

Arkham takes over—which means, we could lose everything. Everything we've ever known. Our memories, our identity, our connection to what's important to us. Our purpose. We could lose it all, and that is a fact that's far too terrifying to even consider at this moment.

So, I grip the banister tightly and walk up the stairs to Lilly's room, where she's sitting on her bed. When her watery eyes connect with mine, she gestures toward the mattress, so I take a seat and wait for her to speak.

After a few moments of silence, she finally says, "I need you to tell me why."

"Why what?" I ask.

"Why me? Why does this fall on me? I thought I had aunts and uncles."

She's looking for answers, and now that I have the

freedom to explain to her, I can give her exactly what she needs.

"You do. Two uncles, to be exact, and one aunt. How much do you know?"

"Nothing." She swipes at a tear. "I know nothing."

I nod gently. "Pala's the oldest. She married Clinton, who happens to be the Prince of Marsedale, next in line to the throne. Because of his duty to his family, being the only child, she abdicated and is living with him now."

"Okay."

"Rolant is the second born. He wasn't necessarily built to be a royal."

"What does that mean?"

"He caused a lot of trouble. Was never doing the right thing and was more of a liability than a help. He never truly appreciated the culture and spent many nights out partying. He ended up being exiled because he haphazardly rolled around on sacred moss."

"Wait . . . the thousand-year-old moss?"

I nod and watch as the crease in her frown disappears.

"What an idiot."

I chuckle, feeling better, that maybe this might not be too bad, given the ridiculousness of the family's history.

"And then there was Sveinn. He married a woman named Kristin."

"Where is he? Did they have kids?"

I shake my head. "Kristin turned out to be a lesbian and ran away with her lady-in-waiting."

"Wait, seriously?"

"Unfortunately, yes. Sveinn did not handle it well and took off on a boat. We haven't heard, seen, or found him yet. It's been six months."

"Oh God."

"Yeah, which brings us to your mom, Margret. And you."

"Yeah, I guess so." She looks away and leans back on the

headboard of her bed. "This is all kinds of fucked up, you realize that?"

"I do," I answer.

"I had no idea any of this even existed, and then one day, I'm hosing people down and you show up. I thought coming here was just going to be one giant family reunion, you know?"

I nod. "I do. I'm sorry if it was misleading, but you must know, I was not at liberty to tell you anything until you spoke with King Theo."

"I know, but it's just . . . God, I wasn't expecting any of this. It makes me, well . . . it makes me mad."

"Mad?"

She brings her legs to her chest and nods. "I'm mad because my parents should have said something. Why did they hide this from me? And why did it take ten years after my mother passed for my grandfather to reach out to me? Why leave me all alone and then . . . not?"

I stare down at my hands, keeping them posed together as I think . . . *I know why they hid it from you.*

"Wait . . ." Lilly's fingers slip under my chin and force me to look at her. "Do you . . . do you know, Keller?"

Hell.

I swallow hard. "I'm not at liberty to say."

"Don't," she whispers. "Please don't start with that bull-shit. I know we barely know each other and that your loyalty doesn't lie with me, but, please, Keller, if I'm going to consider this, I need to know the truth. Why didn't my mom tell me anything about this part of her life?"

Fuck. She's right, my loyalty rests with King Theo and Queen Katla, but those crystal-blue eyes are pleading with me. I can see the pain in them, the confusion. They're a window to her very soul and it's messing with my head.

She tugs on my arm, her eyes blinking. "Please, Keller."

They're mesmerizing, truly a color that feels like it's

piercing to my very core, sweeping through my veins, and bringing me down to my goddamn knees. From the moment I met her I've found her to be a flighty, independent free spirit. Someone who doesn't have responsibilities and therefore doesn't take much in life seriously. But she's surprised me with how deeply she's allowed this to affect her. And if I'm honest, seeing how vulnerable she is, how despondent, it feels like . . . a fracture is forming.

A fracture in where my loyalty rests. *I want to protect her.*

And despite the trustworthy, honest, steadfast man I've grown to be, I find myself faltering, and I'm unable to stop from speaking the truth.

"There was a fight," I say. "Between your mom and Queen Katla."

"What kind of fight?" She scoots closer to me, her body nearly pressing against mine.

I shouldn't be telling her this, it's not my information to tell. Then again, I already cracked, and if I have any luck in this moment, then maybe what I'm about to say will help her understand why she's here now.

"You must know, Queen Katla has taken her role within the royal family very seriously. Her self-proclaimed duty was to have children, to raise them, and to make sure they contributed to the country in a positive way. When Pala came home with Prince Clinton, the dynamic of the family changed. Queen Katla had been priming her to take the throne, and when they found out her intentions, of leaving Torskethorpe for another country, it felt like a betrayal to the queen, especially because of how hard she worked."

"I can understand that," Lilly says.

"The scandal behind the firstborn leaving was almost too much for Queen Katla to bear. So, that night, there was a proclamation made by the queen, that no one was to betray their family again. That their duty, their service, their lives belonged to Torskethorpe."

"And did my mom not take that well?"

I shake my head. "From what I've been told, your mother loved her country more than anything. She enjoyed the rich culture, the simple traditions carried on from generation to generation, but she also was a free spirit, and before she dedicated the rest of her life to the country she loved, she wanted to explore. Queen Katla was so worried that she'd lose Margret just like she lost Pala that she forbade it."

Lilly winces. "Knowing my mother, she didn't take that well."

"She didn't. And one spring morning, she told King Theo that she was leaving to explore, and he could either support her or lose her forever. He went behind Queen Katla's back and supported her, because even though King Theo knows the fate of the country rests in his hands, he never put it first. He always put his family ahead of everything else."

"That's why Mom sent him pictures and letters."

I nod. "Yes."

"So . . . he let her have the life she wanted, sacrificing himself for the sake of her happiness. This means the country must really be in peril if he's asking me to drop the life I love and take on this complex responsibility."

"Very much in trouble. But you can't base your decision on the consequences." She gets it. Even though it still pains me that I spoke out of turn, I know I did the right thing, because there is clarity in her eyes now. Knowing dinner must be ready, I stand from the bed. "You must base your decision on what's best for you and you alone, Lilly." I walk over to her door and place my hand on the doorframe. "Will you be joining us for dinner?"

She shakes her head as she crawls back onto the bed and slips her legs under the blankets. "No, I'm not very hungry at the moment, and I'm afraid I wouldn't be great company either. Please apologize to Brimar for me." I nod and start to walk away when I hear her call out, "Keller?"

"Yes?" I ask, looking over my shoulder.

"I know that was hard for you, but thank you for telling me. It means a lot."

I offer her a curt nod and continue down the stairs, where I pause at the landing. My hands twist the wood of the banister as an uneasy feeling flips through my chest, an unrelenting grip attempting to squeeze the air out of my lungs. Realization hits me.

That was private information.

Kept secretly in the vault of undisclosed royal history.

And yet, I so freely offered it to Lilly.

I know the reason why I did it, but I barely blinked before offering it up.

That's unlike me. I'm a steel trap of information. Growing up in the palace, you learn quickly that the royal family respects you more if you're able to refuse to disclose valuable information. My parents instilled in me that earning their respect was the highest of honors. So, I became a vault over the years, and it's one of the main reasons I'm the private secretary to the King of Torskethorpe, because I'm trustworthy.

But Lilly, she just . . . fuck, she pulled that information out of me with one bat of her eyelashes, with one pleading stare. If she can easily pull that out of me, what else can she cause me to divulge?

And what kind of hold does this woman I barely know already have on me?

Chapter Seven

LILLY

Stomach growling, I quietly make my way out of my room and to the stairs that I know creak and crack with every step.

After Keller left my room, I lay in my bed and stared up at the ceiling, hoping for any sort of sign. Anything that would help me make this monumental, life-changing decision. I considered texting Timmy, now that my phone is connected to the Internet, but I wasn't sure he was the right person to talk to. Not because he wouldn't give me good advice, but because I'm not sure how classified this information is. Also, I'm not sure he would quite understand. Not sure anyone would understand the position I'm in.

Coming up short, with no answers, I closed my eyes and took a nap. Unfortunately, that nap was at dinner time, and now that I'm awake at one in the morning with a stomach needing food, I'm desperate to make it to the kitchen.

Gripping the banister, I lean over it and lift my feet up, precariously balancing on the wood, and shimmy myself down so I avoid making the steps creak. How I plan on getting back up, I have no idea, but I haven't thought that far ahead yet.

It takes some great effort on my end to not tip over to my death, especially with a fresh batch of sore abs—thank you, boulder Olympics—but when my feet land at the bottom of the stairs, I pat myself on the back. That landing easily would have scored a nine point nine out of a possible ten.

Now, planning ahead for a dark-ass first floor? Not so much on the genius level. Who knew a heap of stones could be so dark at night with the curtains drawn?

Probably everybody. Everybody knows that.

Hands extended, I shuffle through the eerily silent castle, attempting to remember where furniture was placed and hoping there's something in the fridge for me to eat. Something that isn't fermented cod cakes. Yes, I'm judging them before I even try them.

Seriously, Torskethorpe, why fermented?

Continuing my shuffle, one hand high, one hand low, I work my way all the way through the living room and into the kitchen, the promised land, where I smooth my hand along the wall, looking for a light switch.

My fingers rub against stone, along molding, and then . . . wait, what is that? Is that a light switch? It's a knob. Yes, this is what I'm looking for. I turn it, illuminating the space just enough for—

"Ahhhhh!" I scream as a whicker broom hurtles toward my face.

I duck and cower against the wall but the propelled broom crashes into the side of my head, causing me to crash to the ground with a large smack.

"Oh, dear Jesus," I hear Lara yell right before she's at my side, slipping her hand under my head.

The stairs creak with the pounding of a thousand elephants careening down them.

Lights are flicked on.

Swear words are thrown into the formerly still night air, and the moment I open my eyes, not only do I see Lara with a scared look in her eyes, but I also spot Brimar and Keller, both of their chests heaving with what I can only imagine is a healthy dose of adrenaline.

"What the hell happened?" Keller asks, his hair mussed and his jaw coated in a five o'clock shadow.

"I heard a noise," Lara says. "I came to investigate, and when the light turned on, I reacted. I had no idea it was Miss Campbell."

"Let's get her off the floor," Brimar says.

I half expect them to all take a side and lift together, but I'm scooped up into a cradled position against a warm, bare chest.

Slightly dazed, I open my eyes to find Keller carrying me over to the living room, his arms holding me with what seems little effort as he gently lays me on the couch. He takes a seat on the coffee table across from me and leans forward.

A bit dizzy, a bit out of it, it takes me a second to notice the lack of shirt on Keller's chest, but when I do, I can't help myself, my eyes wander over his body shamelessly. Call it the knock on the head, call it pure curiosity, but my oh my what do we have here?

Let me break it down for you: an intricate tattoo spans his thick, muscular chest, connecting to a powerful set of shoulders that ripple with tension in the sexiest of ways. His arms are a work of sculpted art as they reach out to me, one of his large palms falling to my hand, easily eclipsing mine. And his torso is a feat of brawny density, the kind that makes it seem like he rips logs open for a living. Immense, dominant, and striking, he's the model-like man you only see in magazines, very rarely on the streets.

"Lilly," he says, "are you okay?"

I blink, startled, but it doesn't stop my eyes from falling to the stack of abs that are still defined despite his seated, crouched-over position. Yup, he's a beautiful, beautiful man.

"I . . . I think so," I say, as I press my fingers to my hairline.

A warm, wet substance slides across my fingers, and when I bring my fingers into view, I hear Keller say, "She's bleeding. Grab the first aid kit."

Feet shuffle across the room while Keller scoots closer, his masculine scent still strong, even in the middle of the night. It's a woodsy scent. Something only a man with a chest tattoo would wear.

"I'm going to tilt your head to the side," he says, while gently placing his hands on my cheeks. "Tell me if there's any pain." When he makes the first attempt to move me, he asks, "That okay?"

"Yes," I answer as he turns my head so now my eyes are in line with his crotch. His very large, very on-display crotch. Just sitting there, all . . . bulgy. Why is it so bulgy? Wait, is he wearing . . . is that . . . "Are you in your underwear?" I ask him.

Still gently turning my head, he answers, "I didn't have time to dress."

Lucky me, because there's a whole lot of man-thigh in front of me and not a lot of coverage.

Thick, masculine legs carry his heavy torso. His briefs cut all the way up to his hips. Yup . . . his hips. Not sure I've ever seen a man in a pair of black briefs, I've only seen boxers, but there's something about the way the thick waistband wraps around his narrowed hips that is holding my attention, compelling me to wet my lips and wonder what it would be like to slip my fingertips past the black elastic.

"Is it a big cut?" Lara asks, her voice shaky.

"No," Keller says. "Just a butterfly stitch should be fine."

They move around me as I keep my eyes fixed on the bulge between Keller's legs.

It's a great bulge. A large bulge for a large man. I can only imagine what it's like when he stands. Probably hangs heavy. It's the only way I can imagine it.

"I'm so sorry," Lara says, her voice emotional, which of course snaps me out of my bulge-haze.

When I pull my eyes away from the Adonis in front of me and glance up at Lara, I'm gutted to find tears in her eyes.

"Hey, it's fine," I say, attempting to reach out, but quickly put my hand down when I feel a wave of dizziness wash over me. "You were doing your job, and might I add, a job well done. Not sure many people could have such accuracy with a broom."

"I should've waited. I reacted first. I know better."

Brimar puts his arm around her shoulder while Keller opens the first aid kit and gets to work. "I'm glad you were on alert," Keller says while he presses some gauze to my forehead. "For all we know, it could've been an intruder."

"Yes, but still, I should've waited. I know better."

"Lara, it's really fine," I say. "I shouldn't have been walking around at night."

"I didn't hear the stairs. That would've tipped me off that it was one of you."

I smile despite myself. "I slid down the banister on my stomach."

Keller pauses and levels with me. "Why would you do that?"

"I didn't want to wake anyone." I take in the three pairs of eyes all staring down at me. "Then again, looks like I woke up everyone anyway."

Brimar cleans up the first aid kit, while Keller asks, "Are you able to sit up?"

"I believe so," I answer. He takes my hand in his, his warm palm to mine, and then he slips his other hand around my back and slowly helps me up to a seated position.

"How's that?" he asks.

"Good," I answer, just as my stomach growls loudly

enough for the neighbors across the countryside to hear. I smile sheepishly. "Sort of hungry."

"Let me grab you something," Brimar says, but Keller stands and holds his hand out to pause him.

"No, I'll grab her something. Why don't you both go get some sleep? We'll need you alert."

Brimar nods, but Lara takes a seat at the coffee table, where she leans forward and takes my hand in hers. "Are you truly okay? I'm so sorry, Miss Campbell."

I place my hand on hers and say, "Once again, call me Lilly, and, yes, I'm quite all right. I actually feel better knowing there's a badass broom thrower in our midst. Like a javelin, it nailed me dead in the head. I really have to give credit where credit is due."

"She's always had a supreme aim," Brimar says with pride in his voice.

I smile at Lara and say, "I promise. I'm good. I think you actually did me a favor, because"—I dramatically drape my hand across my forehead—"I don't believe I'll be able to work out tomorrow with you guys. I'm much too fragile."

Lara laughs, and then to my surprise, she pulls me into a hug. Shocked, stunned . . . comforted, I loop my arms around her and return the hug.

Quietly, she says, "I know you might leave, but I just—I'm so glad I got to at least meet you." When she pulls away, she gives me a very kind smile and stands. Brimar holds his hand out, and together, they walk back to their room.

When Keller returns, he has a plate in one hand and a glass of water in the other. He sets everything down in front of me on the coffee table and takes a seat.

"You know, I've never been served by a nearly naked man before. All you need is a giant palm leaf to fan in front of me."

He barely cracks a smile as he hands me the plate. It's full of fruits, cubed cheese, and slices of artesian bread that have been buttered. Just what I need.

With concern in his eyes, he asks, "Do you need any pain medication?"

"I don't believe so. I mean, my head hurts but not enough to warrant medication." I take a bite of the bread and moan as I lean into the couch cushions. "Good God, this is delicious. Did you make this?"

He shakes his head. "Brimar loves baking bread in his spare time."

"A man of many talents," I say as I feel Keller's eyes on me, examining me. "You know, I'm really okay. You don't need to worry that much."

"You're my responsibility. If you get hurt, that's on me. Don't tell me not to worry when I'm not doing my job," he says, his voice stern.

"Hey, no need to get angry. It was an accident. Why is everyone walking on eggshells?"

"Because you're important to this country," Keller says, his chest heaving with what seems to be frustration. "If something happens to you, that means we failed at our job. And to us, this job, this country, it means everything. If something happened to your bikini wagon, wouldn't you take it to heart?"

"Well, I guess when you put it that way . . ." I somberly take a bite of my bread. "Yeah, I would be upset."

Keller reaches out and loops his index finger under my chin, lifting my gaze. When our eyes meet, the sheer intensity from his expression causes my pulse to thump harder. There's an underlying sense of ferocity behind his pupils as he says, "You matter most, Lilly. Even if you decide you don't want to be part of the royal life and you go back to Miami, until that time has come . . . you . . . matter . . . most."

I swallow the gooey, mangled-up piece of bread that's just resting in my mouth, because holy . . . shit.

This is the first time that a man has EVER looked at me the way Keller is, with such heavy sincerity but laced with a pinch of possession. Like if I gave him the slightest of nods, he would mark me, claim me, own me. It's distressing, but not in the way that you might think. It's distressing my soul, because oddly, that pinch of possession, it's what I've always wanted in a man. And the fact that this sexy, large, over-bearing god-like man is sitting right in front of me, telling me I matter most, it's messing with my head.

"Do you understand?" he asks.

I wet my lips as my pulse thrums on his every word, straining my veins with an awakening I wasn't expecting.

"I . . . do," I answer.

"Good." Then he stands, his crotch right at eye level, and for the life of me, I can't tear my gaze away, not when the fabric of his briefs clings so desperately to his length, defining the head of his cock. I would say I've seen a few penises in my lifetime, and even through the fabric, I can claim that Keller most likely has the nicest one I've ever seen. "Lilly."

"Huh?" I say, snapping my eyes up to his, but instead of the concern, I'm met with hungry eyes.

He caught me staring.

Does he also notice the way my breathing has picked up?

Or how I can't seem to stop wetting my lips because my mouth feels like the desert?

"Don't," he says, his tone so direct that I feel a shiver creep up my back.

"Don't what?"

"Don't look at me like that."

"Like what?" I ask, trying to play the clueless card, because I know exactly how I'm looking at him. Like he's easily the sexiest, most delicious man I've ever seen, and now that I've had the pleasure of regarding him in nothing but a pair of briefs, I won't be able to think of anything other than his tight, muscular body or his thick, heavy bulge when he's in the same room as me.

In a low, commanding voice, he says, "Like if I gave you

the chance, you would drop to your knees and swallow my come."

Oh.

My.

God.

Fucking hand me a fan because things just got intense.

Intensely wet.

Do you know who says things like that? The dirty ones, that's who.

The ones that pin you against a wall unexpectedly and press their cocks against your leg, showing you know how you tease them.

The ones that whisper in your ear while you're at a dinner party about how they're going to lick your pussy when you get home.

The ones that show up to the bedroom with blindfolds and ropes, and demands prepped and polished on their tongues.

The kind of man that knows of only pleasure with a pinch of pain.

The kind of man that I crave to my very core. The kind of man I've always wanted.

Before I can respond, his hand slips under my chin, tilting it high before he walks toward the stairs. And because I'm in a whirlwind from his words, from his lack of clothes, I don't even bother looking away from his tight rear end as he retreats.

Dear God. Keller isn't just a grump. He's a sexy, dirty grump . . . the best kind.

⸺

"IS THIS REALLY NECESSARY?" I ask as Keller drapes a blanket over my body.

"Yes. You could have suffered a concussion, and unless you

want to share a bed with me upstairs, we'll sleep here and I'll wake you up every hour."

After Keller's panty pageant and the shocking revelation of his filthy mouth, I wouldn't mind an impromptu sleepover, especially if it includes a gentle nuzzle from each of his tatted pecs.

But I know arguing with him won't get me anywhere, so I settle into the plush couch and turn on my side so I'm looking out toward the fireplace. The position helps avoid placing weight on my bandaged head, which doesn't really hurt, other than a dull thudding.

Now in a pair of shorts and a T-shirt—boo—Keller takes a seat in the chair next to my couch and props his legs up on an ottoman.

"You're going to be uncomfortable," I say as he squeezes his broad shoulders into the tight space of the wingback chair.

"I've slept in much worse conditions," he says while pulling a blanket over his lap and propping a small throw pillow against the side of the chair.

"Oh yeah? Like what?"

"Nothing you need to know about," he says. "Now go to sleep." He shuts his eyes but I continue to look at him.

His strong, carved jaw.

The hint of a tattoo that pops up from his neckline.

The singular curl of hair that floats over his forehead.

Seeing him in a different light—ahem, in man panties— and hearing him speak so deliciously with a dirty tongue, has unlocked this feral beast deep inside me and I can't lock her away. She's uncharacteristically ravenous.

He must feel my gaze, because his eyes pop open just in time to catch me perusing his shirt-covered chest. "What?" he asks.

You're hot.

"I can't go to sleep on command," I answer instead. "I

have a full stomach and I'm wide awake. My internal clock is messed up right now. Maybe you can talk to me."

From the disgruntled look on his face, I can tell that's exactly NOT what he wants to do, but to my surprise, he asks, "What do you want to talk about?"

"Tell me about Torskethorpe. What kind of traditions do you have? You said they've been passed down from generations, ones my mom enjoyed."

I'm still trying to process everything Keller told me earlier about my mom and Queen Katla. From an outsider looking in, I can see how the queen might look like the villain in this storyline, but being someone who has lost two of the most important people in my life, I can understand the need, the drive, to keep the ones you love close to your heart. I'm not saying what she did was right, but the intention behind it, I can grasp.

And from my mother's perspective, I also know the feeling of having to escape, to not fall in line with what's expected, because I shared many fights with my parents about not attending college. They wanted me to earn a higher education, but their dreams didn't fall in line with mine. When they passed, I grieved their dreams, and for a semester, I attempted college but quickly found it wasn't for me. And it took courage to push past expectations and do what I believed was right for me.

My mom did the same.

But beneath her urge to flee from Torskethorpe, there was a woman who truly loved her country—according to Keller—and I want to know that woman, even if it's through some of the activities she used to enjoy.

"I never met your mother," he says quietly, "but King Theo has told me so much about her that I almost feel like I do know her."

"Tell me something special about her."

"She was an expert at hardanger embroidery."

"What's that?" I ask.

"It's an intricate form of embroidery using white thread on white linen. It's painstakingly difficult and takes great patience, but when done right, it's beautiful."

"Really?" I ask. "Do you know . . . do you know if any of her pieces are around still?"

Keller nods. "King Theo has quite a few of her pieces in his bed chambers. My guess is he'd be more than willing to part with some if they're in the right hands."

That makes my throat grow tight. After my parents passed, all our belongings went into probate, and one by one, I saw my parents' valuable items get sold off to pay their debts. It was painful to watch, and it left me with barely anything of theirs. So, to have something my mother made would mean the world to me.

"I don't think you know how important that'd be to me. After my parents passed, I didn't have much to remember them by."

He glances away and nods, and I can see that there's something he wants to say, but he doesn't, he keeps it close to him instead.

So, I continue, "You've seen them?"

"Yes, I have. There's one on his nightstand, in particular, that's quite complex but expertly done. King Theo keeps it close on purpose. She was very skilled, Lilly."

The more Keller talks about Theo, the more I'm starting to feel like I know him. He seems to carry the same loving traits as both of my parents, and it feels like home to hear stories about him.

"What else?" I ask him. "Tell me more about Tors-kethorpe."

"Vinatarte."

"Vin-a-what now?"

He gently smiles and, oh my God, is it a gorgeous smile. "Vinatarte. It's a traditional dessert that's usually served during the holidays, but it's also a popular dessert during Torg."

"What's Torg?"

"Torg is an annual summer celebration where the country gets together to celebrate our culture. We trade, we dance, and Kulners call on their herds. There are live wood-carving contests, feasts, and the traditional toast where we drink mead."

"Okay, back up. Is this like a festival of sorts?"

"Yes. It's always at the end of August. It gives our people a chance to show off the skills we've acquired throughout generations. King Theo's favorite part of the year. He always leads the mead toast."

"Now, I don't want to sound rude," I say, "but when you say *mead*, that seems like it could possibly be something like . . . goat's blood. Or fox saliva. Is that correct?"

He chuckles, the sound so deep, so rumbly, that it warms me up under my already warm blanket. "Mead is fermented honey water."

"Fermented?" I gulp. "Why is everything freaking fermented?"

He laughs again. "It's actually really sweet. Delicious. It's used quite a bit as a natural remedy when people are ill. The toast of mead is to indicate a healthy start to the oncoming colder months."

"Do you take part in these traditions?"

"I do."

"What is your favorite thing to do?"

"I enjoy wood carving. I've always found it therapeutic in a way." Why do I find that so enticing? His large hands, maneuvering tools over a piece of wood . . . "My talent isn't as admirable as others, but it does act as an escape for me."

"I'm sure whatever you carve is a thousand times better than what I can do. I don't have many skillful talents like that, or at least that I've tried. I think the best tool in my toolbox is my ability to rally and convince a crowd to let me spray them down with water."

"A talent in itself."

He closes his eyes and leans against his pillow. I can sense he wants to go to sleep, so I take a deep breath, wanting to ask him one more question. "Keller?"

He peeps his eyes open. "Yeah?"

"Do you think I could do it? Do you think I have it in me to take on this role?"

My question is met without an immediate response, which worries me.

And as he gives it some thought, I feel myself shrink deeper and deeper into the couch, my nervous stomach filling with trepidation. I have no idea about my abilities to be a *gulp* queen. My knowledge on the matter feels like a negative ten out of a scale of one hundred and, I don't know, maybe some reassurance could help me decide what to do.

When his eyes finally meet mine, I'm greeted with a gentle expression, a far cry from the dirty man from earlier. He speaks softly, but with a sense of validation in his voice.

"I think your life is in Miami, but your soul rests among the moss and lava rock. You belong here, Lilly." And for the first time since I met Keller, I feel as though he doesn't dislike me. And that's when I realize I want that from him. I want him not to be disappointed in me. I want to make him smile more.

With that, his eyes drift shut, leaving me with a newfound sense of wonderment.

What if he's right?

What if I do belong here?

What if . . . what if I was supposed to be here all along?

What if I'm supposed to be queen?

"HOW ARE YOU FEELING?" Lara asks as she takes a seat next to me on the couch. She offers me a handkerchief of ice that I press gently to my cut. Brimar and Keller went out for a long jog this morning, despite the bags under their eyes or the yawns that wouldn't evade them.

Lara said she would get her workout in later so she could stay and tend to me. Frankly, I think it's ridiculous, it's a minor cut on my head, but no matter what I say, none of them will listen.

"I'm feeling pretty good. Sore, tired. Keller wasn't kidding when he said he would wake me up."

"It's protocol. But I'm glad you're doing okay. I just want to say—"

"Lara, do not apologize again, do you hear me?" I say to the beautiful blonde. Standing at six feet, she's a total babe with her strong, athletic frame, thick thighs, and smooth facial features. Sitting next to her, I know there's no chance anything could happen to me.

"I do." She winces. "But I am."

"I know you are," I say. "But honestly, I think it was really badass what you did last night. If I heard something in the middle of the night, I wouldn't have used a broom like a spear to stun the attacker, I would have crawled under my bed and prayed to the Lord above that I was invisible."

She laughs. "I've always been a bit of a daredevil and faced fear head-on."

"God, you're so cool. And the fact that I have a female bodyguard watching over me . . . can we pause and offer a round of applause to feminism? I love that you're here with us."

"I do too. This is momentous in our country's history, and I'm excited to play a small part in it." She worries her lip. "Not to pressure you, but have you made a decision about what you're going to do?"

"I think maybe I have."

"Really?" she asks in a hopeful tone just as the men walk through the front door of the castle and join us in the living room. Both of their faces are red, chilly from the wind whipping around this morning, but even though I know it's a damp morning with a light sprinkle, there are still sweat stains on their shirts, a deep *V* marking the front of their chests.

"Everything okay?" Keller asks, walking up to us.

"Yes," Lara says. "I was just going to go grab some breakfast for everyone. How's oatmeal?" That hopeful look on her face seconds ago disappears as she goes into work mode.

"That's great," Keller says.

"I'll assist you," Brimar offers, following Lara into the kitchen.

When they're out of earshot, Keller takes a seat on the uneven stone floor and says, "It seems like you were talking about something important."

"Lara asked me if I've made a decision about what I'm going to do."

"Ah," Keller says, his eyes drifting down as he stretches his legs. I know avoidance when I see it—he's worried about what I'll say, so he doesn't look me in the eyes. I'd probably be doing the same thing if I were in his position. But what he doesn't realize is that he's already said some extremely compelling things.

"You matter most, Lilly. Even if you decide you don't want to be part of the royal life and you go back to Miami, until that time has come . . . you . . . matter . . . most."

Admittedly, that rocked me. In a good way. I. Matter. Most. *Wow.* Things were great with my parents, but I'd never felt so championed than in that moment.

And then he told me he had confidence in me with *"I think your life is in Miami, but your soul rests among the moss and lava rock. You belong here, Lilly."* Maybe . . . that's true.

"Don't you want to know what it is?"

"Yes," he says, and I can see the tension in his shoulders rise as the anticipation of my answer hangs in the air.

"I'm not sure what all of this entails, the training, the responsibility, but I feel like if I don't at least try, then I'm going to regret it." His eyes pop up to mine, hope resonating in his pupils. "Being here, hearing about my mom, I already feel like I've found a piece of me I've been missing, and I don't think I'm ready to give that up. So, I'm going to give this a try. I will give the king two months."

He controls his smile, never letting it reach his eyes, nor does he allow his excitement to shine, but in the subtle way his chest puffs, to the faint wrinkles in the corner of his eyes, I know my decision has truly brought him joy.

And even though I'm in this to find my soul, like Keller pointed out, I can't help but feel like bringing Keller joy is something I was meant to do.

Chapter Eight

KELLER

"She agreed," I say quietly into the phone.

Theo coughs on the other end but then follows up with a choked-up, tear-filled response. "Really? Truly she wants to stay?"

"She said she would give you two months." I'm almost whispering, not wanting my voice to carry. I snuck up to the bathroom for a shower but knew I had to relay the information to Theo as quickly as possible.

"That's fair."

"How do you suppose I convince her in two months? I know we said I would train her, but do you actually want me to do that? It'll be grueling. It might not be the best way to convince her."

"No, it's the only way to convince her," Theo says. "The idea of painting a perfect picture of what her life could be is appealing, but it's not the reality of the situation. She needs to understand what she is getting herself into. I might be desperate, but I refuse to deceive my own granddaughter."

And this is exactly why I love Theo. He's a man of his word, a man with a conscience. He won't set out to circumvent you, he'll be truthful and honest.

"You don't want me to take it easy on her?"

"No, because if she becomes queen, she needs to be mentally fortified in order to take the brutal hardships of the responsibility."

"Understood. Shall we remain here, at Harrogate?"

"Given the swirl of media and rumors, I believe it's best."

"And Katla—does she know?"

"She does," Theo responds. "I'd like to say she's happy, but I think she's more worried than anything. I'm not sure she wants to meet Lilija out of fear she'll lose her. I'm attempting to convince her otherwise. She's lost so much, so I understand her apprehension."

"I see. And what should I expect with your involvement in this?"

"Not much." His voice comes out breathy right before he falls into a litany of coughs that only makes my chest feel tighter. I know he's getting better, the doctor has said so, but the cough is still frightening. "We haven't found the leak and I don't want anyone bothering her. I need to keep my interactions small."

"Okay, but I can guarantee you, her reason for attempting to try is based on the connection she feels toward her mom, and toward you."

"I'll do my best. You know I wish this was different. You know I wish I could be there."

"I know," I say softly. "But I think you should at least try to talk to her."

"We'll try to make that happen. I'm just . . . I don't want her to see me sick like this. I don't want that to make her decision for her."

"I understand," I say as I stare at my reflection in the mirror.

"I have faith in you, Keller, my son."

I squeeze my eyes shut as a bout of emotion wreaks havoc on my mind. "Thank you. I'll keep you updated."

We say our goodbyes, then I hang up the phone and set it on the ledge of the sink before gripping the porcelain and leaning forward. The weight of the world rests on my shoulders. The future of the country. Lilly's trust . . . it all rests in the palm of my hand.

And what terrifies me the most . . . is crushing Lilly's trust.

I felt the way she looked at me last night, the way her eyes ate me up. I'd have to have turned a blind eye to not see it, and I'll be damned if it didn't have a damned machismo effect on me.

Fuck, it made me feel like a goddamn man.

The hitch of her breath. The licking of her lips. The inability not to stare. She was unashamed of her perusal, and even though I told her not to look at me like that, I'd be lying if I said I didn't like it.

Because I did.

I liked it way more than I should have.

And I need to lock those feelings up, right now.

DAY ONE OF TRAINING, here we fucking go.

Deep breaths.

She's already been annoying this morning by pestering me about why I brush my hair with my left hand instead of my right, but no big deal.

And at breakfast, she burped louder than a sailor, rattling the table we were sitting at—still, no big deal.

And right before we came into the room to start training, she told me a story about a guy who once painted her breasts in front of a live audience, once again, still not a big deal—just hoping to God Himself that there's no photographic evidence.

"Why does this feel like an interrogation room?" Lilly asks as she shifts on her chair. "And why is there nothing else in this room, but it has the most windows? What the hell is this?"

"It was an art room."

"Ah, that makes sense." She gestures to the windows. "All the bright light. I can see how this would appeal to someone with a paintbrush." She presses her hands to her thighs and looks up at me. "Okay, so this is kind of weird. Are you going to interrogate me? I feel like I'm in trouble. Am I in trouble?"

"No, but this is where we'll be doing your training."

"Ah . . ." She glances around. "Cozy." Her sarcasm hangs heavy in the air. "Wouldn't hurt to have more than a chair."

"I don't want to be distracted."

"I see." She slowly nods. "So, an area rug would distract you?"

I pinch the bridge of my nose. Why did I think the first day would be a breeze? I want to do a good job, I want to teach Lilly everything she needs to know, but she also knows how to grate on my nerves—and quickly—especially when I feel stressed.

And I'm stressed to the max right now.

"An area rug isn't necessary."

"What do you mean *an area rug isn't necessary?* Every interior designer will say an area rug is essential for warming up a space. Look around, Keller, we're surrounded by stone walls. Also, are you just going to stand the whole time? That's kind of weird."

"I'm not someone who sits often."

"Why is that?" she asks, crossing one leg over the other.

"My job requires me to move around."

"I see. What about a table? This is a wooden chair that my

ass is occupying at the moment, a simple wooden chair. Don't you think I'm going to want something to rest my arms on?"

"Are you that unsteady that you need something to prop your body on?"

"You were witness to my attempt at running. Do you really think I'm sturdy?"

Good point.

"And, you know, it's less intimidating, having you sitting with me. Also, when you pictured today, did you really envision me in this uncomfortable chair, sitting ramrod straight all day, not a surface to lean on while you pace the room like a—sorry to say it—psychopath, grinding your feet into an area rug-less surface and expect me not to nauseate over the fact that you're not only rubbing your feet raw, but also that there isn't one single plant in this room to help with the oxygen flow?"

Jesus.

Fucking.

Christ.

Through clenched teeth, I ask, "What do you need in order to be comfortable?"

"Well, you know, perhaps a seat for yourself? Maybe a table? A plant."

It feels like our first meeting all over again when she wouldn't stop jabbering. But if this stuff will get her to be quiet so I can start the training, then she can have whatever she wants.

Without a word, I tear out of the room, flinging the door open and startling both Brimar and Lara, who are sitting on the couch together.

"I need a table, an extra chair, an area rug, and a plant in that room. Now."

Lara snags a plant and a chair. Brimar drags a table, and I walk into the entryway, roll up the rug, and hoist it over my shoulder. Together, we all lay it out in the room while Lilly startles out of her chair, drags it to the corner, and watches us unfold everything.

Once Brimar and Lara leave, shutting the door behind them, I pick up Lilly's chair and move it to the console table so it's across from mine. I leave it partially out and gesture for her to sit down.

"Well, I can't say you're not efficient." She smiles and takes a seat. She places her hands on the table and tests it out, making a show of it. "This can work. It's no talk show set with comfy couches and a mahogany desk with secret compartments, but it will work just fine. Although . . ."

"What?" I ask her.

"Not to be too bothersome, but should I have a notepad?"

"Do you want a notepad?"

"It might be nice to be able to write things down."

Growling under my breath, I stand from my chair and open the door. "Notepad and pen."

Within seconds, Lara is bringing several pens and pads of paper into the room. Brimar follows with water and cookies— an added touch that will hopefully get Lilly to be quiet so we can start our training.

Once they leave, I cross one leg over the other and ask, "Anything else?"

She picks up a cookie and takes a nibble. "No, this is quite nice. Thank you." She smirks and then nudges my leg with her foot. "Lighten up, this will be torture if you don't."

It already is.

"There are five main categories we'll be going over." Her eyes widen, and I hold up one finger, counting them off. "Appearance—"

"What's wrong with my appearance?"

"There's a certain standard that must be upheld when you're in the public eye."

She kicks up a foot on the console table. "Ah, so, no

loungewear, I presume?" I flick her foot off and it plops to the floor.

"No. Then there is etiquette—"

"Ooo, is that when I drink with my pinky out?"

"Can you refrain from commentary while I get through these?"

She leans both arms on the table and props her chin up with her hand. "I can sense irritation, and I'm going to tell you right now, that's not going to work for me. Why don't we try a kind voice? It will make this easier."

"Well, don't irritate me and I will use a kind voice."

"When have you ever used a kind voice?"

"How about when I bandaged your head? Or when I was telling you about your aunt and uncles, or how about—"

"Okay . . . settle down. I can see you're getting yourself worked up. Let's try a different question. How do I irritate you?"

Is she really that obtuse? Can she not see that I can barely get a sentence out without her popping in to interrupt me? I have two fucking months to convince her this is where she should be. That's a lot of pressure on me, and I don't want to let Theo down. The fate of the country might rest in her decision, but her decision is based on what I do. And I can't fucking do my job if she keeps needling me with question after question after question . . . questions that don't pertain to what I'm trying to teach her.

"This," I say, gesturing between us. "This constant jabbering. Just let me get through the five topics, for fuck's sake."

A smile creeps over her lips as she leans back. "Ooo, you swore. I'm going to guess that is a big etiquette no-no." She lifts her glass of water to her lips and takes a sip—her goddamn pinky lifting toward the sky.

"Yeah, but I'm not the future queen, now, am I?"

Sputtering water on the table, she sets her glass down and starts coughing. I give her a few moments.

When she wipes her face with a napkin, she asks, "Can you refrain from putting it like that? My ass just clenched, and I'm not sure it will unclench for hours. Do you understand how uncomfortable that's going to be? Especially on this chair, which I can only assume was too hard for Goldilocks."

I smooth my hand over my face and take a deep breath. "Okay, but can you let me fucking talk?"

"Deal." She crosses her arms over her chest and gestures for me to proceed.

Christ.

Finally.

"The five categories are etiquette——"

"Oo, sorry, one more question."

The grumble that flies out of me shakes the collar of her shirt.

"I know, sorry, but will there be a test after this? I'm horrible at taking tests, one of the reasons I had no desire to go to college. If there is, am I allowed to use a cheat sheet, like a full length of paper? Because, if so, I'll start taking small notes now."

Deep breaths.

In and out.

"There will be no exam. This isn't a university."

"Oh, wonderful." She picks up another cookie. "You may proceed. You were saying, there are five whoosey-whatsits."

With a strained voice, I say, "The five categories we'll be going over are: etiquette, appearance, Torskethorpe history, crisis management, and cultural traditions. If you're in line for the throne"—she winces—"then you'll need to master all five." She raises her hand and I hold back my eye roll. "Yes?"

"Crisis management, is that like . . . customer service? Like how to take care of a disagreement in the village?"

"No. You're not a moderator by any means. This isn't the eighteen hundreds where you decide whose cattle belongs to who. Crisis management would be if you were ever captured or kidnapped, something like that."

Her smile droops into a frown. "Wait, captured? Kidnapped? Is that an actual possibility?"

"Anything is a possibility. That's why we need to prepare you."

"Huh, okay. So, a follow-up question—what kind of kidnapping are we talking about?"

"I'm not sure what you mean."

"Like . . . you know, what would they do to me? Because I've heard some weird things in my time. Like, this one girl who lived in South Beach was once kidnapped by a drug dealer, strapped to a chair in an empty warehouse, and she was tickled with feathers every hour on the hour. Like . . . that's some real freaky shit. Or are we talking about a normal kidnapping?"

I blink a few times.

She's unlike any person I've ever met.

"Do you want us to prepare you for tickle torture?"

"Wouldn't hurt." She taps the table with her finger. "Add it to the list." She lets out a deep breath. "Well, I'm glad I asked that question. Can't be too prepared, right? So, where do we start?"

Sarcasm in my voice, I say, "Given your knack for hard-hitting questions—"

"Thank you." She clasps her hands together and bows, as if she's a celebrity receiving a compliment.

"Let's start with something simple. Appearance."

Can't imagine that will draw up too many fictional scenarios in her mind.

She glances at her sweatshirt and leggings and then back up at me. "I'm guessing I'm missing the girdle?"

Christ.

"When around the palace, when you won't be seen by the

public, you're welcome to wear what you want. Queen Katla has a vast array of comfortable clothes that are still stylish."

"Uh-huh. As in, my grandmother . . . who I haven't even spoken to? That grandmother?" I can understand why she's sounding annoyed by that one. She hasn't heard that her grandparents *want* to meet her, but just *need* to meet her. And nothing at all from her grandmother. *But how do I reply to that one?*

"Well, yes, your grandmother. I'm sure you'll at least speak to her soon, Lilly."

"Right." She looks away for a moment, and I have no idea how to read her. And then she does something incredibly surprising. She composes herself and asks, "And what about when I'm in public? What does a royal of Torskethorpe wear?" *Huh.*

"Depends on the event you'll be attending. You might be required to wear a dress or a pantsuit—"

"A pantsuit." She chuckles. "Man, from bikini to pantsuit, that should be the title of a book." She flips her hair and says in a movie-trailer voice, "She was the hometown hero, wetting every tourist with the spray of a hose. Known to the public as the girl in the lime-green bikini, a true free spirit, now turned into the posh, uptight, pantsuit-wearing killer of Torskethorpe. Murder wasn't always on her mind, but the pantsuits . . . they did her in. Coming this year, in two months."

She smiles brightly.

I remain neutral.

Unfazed. Not amused.

She huffs. "Well, I'd watch that movie. Anyhoo, what about this mop on my head? Am I going to have to do something with that? Or makeup?" She purses her lips at me and then blinks rapidly.

"No, you're quite beautiful." The words slip past me before I can stop them. But it's true, sitting across from her . . .

even with her eyes purposefully bugging out like that, she's quite alluring. Her skin is like velvet—soft, smooth. Not yet distressed with wrinkles and worry lines. And her lips—full, plump, luscious. So enticing that I could see men begging her for attention. And her eyes, crystal as the sky, so blue that they actually feel intimidating at times.

You see, this is why she needs to stop jabbering because she's loosening me up. She's making me say things I shouldn't even be thinking.

That smile of hers returns, and she sits taller. "You think I'm beautiful, Keller?"

Yes. But not just beautiful. Breathtaking. Extraordinary beauty that stops you in your tracks and forces you to stare. A beauty so strong that it can take down even the strongest of men to their knees.

I clear my throat. "Let's move on."

"Oh no, I really want to spend some time on the whole *beautiful* comment." She taps her finger on the table, and my eyes watch the movement with annoying curiosity. Fuck, pull it together. This is the possible future queen. She's not to be played with. She's not one to fantasize about. *She's not for you.*

Controlling myself, I ask, "Do you have any tattoos?"

"Not wanting to spend time on the *beautiful* comment, huh? Okay, fine, but that's logged in my head." She raps her temple. "But just to return the favor, I think you're incredibly hot. The whole briefs thing was a refreshing new fantasy I didn't know was essential to my personal rub club, if you know what I mean." She waggles her eyebrows.

Jesus Christ, not information I needed to be branded into my brain.

And I'd like it to be known that it was not my intention for her to see me in nothing but a pair of briefs, but when I heard the crash downstairs, I sprinted out of bed, neglecting any sort of decency, because my number one thought was to make sure Lilly was okay. And then when I finally realized I was wearing only my briefs, there was nothing I could do other than allow her to stare. And she fucking stared. I hate to admit it, but the more her eyes landed on my crotch, the more I didn't want to dress. The more I wanted her to continue to eat me up with those desperate eyes of hers. They were hungry, ravenous, and even though she had a head injury, it didn't stop her from gawking. And I liked every goddamn second of it.

But that's neither here nor there.

"Lilly," I say, "please refrain from bursting out with personal commentary."

"Made you uncomfortable, didn't I? Are you a shy one, Keller? Strong and mighty, but squishy and soft? Can't take a compliment?" She shrugs. "Sorry to say, but facts are facts—you're a hottie with a body . . . and a weenie that's *not* so teenie."

"Lilly," I snap. "Just . . . stop. Okay?"

She smirks, because she knows what she's doing. She's getting under my skin, and it's obvious that's her intention. *Does she possess a self-controlled bone in her body?* And if so, will she fucking use it?

"Do you have any tattoos?"

Still smiling, she shifts on her chair and answers, "I do."

"Where?" I ask the question for the crown, not my own personal knowledge, but I can feel the increase in my pulse from the thought of her having a tattoo. To me, they've always been a way to express myself. The stories behind them, the placement—they all mean something. And the fact that she has one makes her that much more attractive in my eyes.

She pulls back her sleeve and flashes me the underside of her left forearm. On her wrist, just below her thumb, are three pea-sized hearts.

"I got this when my parents passed away. The three hearts represent us as a family and also our symbol for *I love you.* Every night, before bed, my parents would squeeze my hand three times while saying, *I love you.* One squeeze for each word." She smooths her fingers over it. "I can't get rid of it, if it's going to be a problem."

I take her wrist in my hand and run my thumb over the hearts, feeling her gentle pulse pick up while I stare at the ink embedded in her skin. A marking of family. A marking of love.

It's subtle, yet . . . incredibly sexy. And honorable . . . *as it shows loyalty. That's something I can work with.*

When I look up and our eyes connect, I say, "This won't be a problem."

She wets her lips, her gaze holding mine. A stroke of heat pierces through the thick air forming between us. My hand is still gripping her wrist, and I feel the connection between us, tugging me in her direction. "Ar-are you sure?" she asks, her voice trembling slightly.

I sweep my thumb over her wrist again and nod. "King Theo has a few tattoos. The question wasn't to say you're not allowed to have them, but more so, are there any inappropriate ones. This isn't inappropriate."

Even though I don't want to, I let go of her hand.

"Oh. Okay." Her teeth roll over her bottom lip. What I wouldn't give to know exactly what's going through her mind right now. Because for once, she's quiet, not voicing her thoughts.

"Do you have any others?"

She shakes her head, and then she drags her finger over the wood of the table when she says, "I do have something else that I'm not sure if it matters or not."

"Tell me. I need to know everything."

"Are you sure?"

"Yes, we need to be aware of everything. The worst thing you can do is not divulge information and then we're surprised later."

"Okay, well, my nipples are pierced . . . and so is my clit."

Uh . . . what?

My eyes snap to hers to see if she's serious, and when I see that there's not a hint of humor in her expression, my cock hardens immediately.

Like a goddamn rock.

Her clit?

Her actual clit is pierced?

Fucking hell.

My mouth waters at the thought of it. A tattoo, a feisty spirit, her love for family, and now this . . . she, hell . . . she's everything I'd want in a woman. *But she's not for you, Keller. Not. For. You.* This is for Theo. For Torskethorpe. "Well, um—"

"I'm not sure if the pierced nipples are going to be an issue," she says while I try to keep myself from panting. "I know no one will see my clit, but you know, I've had a few one-night stands back in Miami. Not sure if anyone would care to say what's going on down there, but I figured I should lay it all out there. I've also had sex on a balcony, and on a car in an empty parking lot. On the beach once. The back of a movie theater— don't worry, it was an R-rated movie. Uh, in a bar bathroom, in a restaurant bathroom, in an aquarium bathroom—something about all that water got me randy. I'm also known for a good skinny-dipping. I've streaked twice, and I also always wear thong bikini bottoms." She cringes. "I don't think there are any pictures, but thought I'd give you a heads-up since everyone has a camera in their pocket now. Oh, and I also went to a sex club a couple of times. I never did anything, I just watched."

I dig my fingers into my thighs. Her litany of confessions is like a shot to my libido with every single one. I attempt to control the desire ripping through me, screaming at me to throw this table to the side and pull her onto my lap. I'm a sexual man, someone who thrives off dominance, and from the sounds of it, she would be the quintessential woman for me. There aren't many women here that I'd pursue. Although I'm not high-profile, given my job, I need to ensure I'm discreet and professional. *Not for you, Keller.* Do not forget your place here.

"Is my sexual history going to be a problem? I hope not. But I can assure you, no sex tapes or naked selfies, which I know seems off-brand for me. But I never partook in recording myself despite being intrigued by the whole act of fucking in front of the camera. I've always been very into my sexuality, but I've also been smart about it. Well . . . for the most part. The public sex was risky, and sure, maybe someone could recognize me from the sex club, but I never paid for a membership. I was just dating this one guy, a millionaire in Miami, and his kink was sex clubs. I was into it. But we always had a mutual understanding that what we did together was between us."

I drag my thumb over my jaw. "Was he your Dom?" My mouth waters a second time, waiting for the answer.

Her crystal eyes flash up at me through her thick lashes. "He was," she answers almost breathlessly.

Fuck. My cock strains against the zipper of my black jeans as my mind reels with what she would look like, on her knees, waiting for my command . . .

"Are you involved with anyone at the moment?" I choke out.

She shakes her head. "No. I'm free . . . ripe for the taking."

She wets her lips again, and fuck me, I'm moments from grabbing her by the back of her neck and seeing how serious she really is about being "ripe for the taking."

I want to take her.

I want to grip her jaw, part her mouth open, and claim her.

And from the look of it, she wants the same thing.

How the hell did we go from training to this? Where the air grows heavy between us, the unsaid swirling around, wrapping like a vise around my will, squeezing so tight that my hand itches to reach out . . .

Knock. Knock.

Lilly and I both startle as Brimar walks in, clueless about the tension, and says, "Supplies have been delivered to an undisclosed location. I'm going to go pick them up. Lara will be here."

"Okay," I say before clearing my throat and shifting around, my erection painful as hell. When he shuts the door, I pull on the back of my neck, trying to get myself together. "We, uh, we should move on."

"Yes. We probably should."

But when I meet her gaze again, her smirk tells me everything I need to know. She knows exactly how uncomfortably charged that conversation made me. And knowing her, she's not going to let me get away with it that easily.

Chapter Nine

LILLY

"Brimar is so good at cooking," I say to Lara as we take a walk together along the rocky coastline.

It's been a long day in that tiny, stone-walled room with Keller.

It's been a long day of staring at his handsome face.

Listening to his dreamy voice.

Watching how the muscles in his jaw twitch when I say anything sexual.

And it felt like everything was sexual when we spoke about appearance today. Everything.

And the way his eyes would turn dark when I answered his questions. I started to grow more sensual with my answers simply because I enjoyed the way he would react. Sure, I shouldn't be trying to turn on the guy who is supposed to be training me, but even though I reprimanded myself over and over again, I couldn't stop.

I couldn't stop, because the moment he caressed my tattoo, I was gone.

Every swipe was like he was imprinting himself into my bones.

After our session was done, I had to go up to my room and take a few deep breaths . . . and then shower to cool myself down.

"He's always enjoyed cooking. When we have time off, we like to travel to different food festivals. He loves finding new ingredients and using them in his recipes. At one point, he talked about putting together a recipe book, but of course, his loyalty lies with the crown, so he wouldn't do anything to jeopardize that."

"How would putting together a cookbook jeopardize that?"

"He doesn't like to lose focus. I know when he's in the kitchen, I have to be extra alert because he's truly zeroed in on what he's creating. It's a good, relaxing outlet for him. Being on guard all the time can be tiring."

"I can imagine," I say. "What do you do to relax?"

"I enjoy making doilies. It's one of our country's traditions."

"Oh right, uh . . . hard—uh . . ."

"Hardanger embroidery."

"That's right. Keller told me my mom was very good at it."

"She was. I've seen her work. Exquisite. I could only hope my pieces look half as good as hers."

"I'm sure you do beautiful work as well."

The wind whips past us, kicking my hair over my shoulders and flapping behind me.

"Are you cold?" Lara asks as I pull on my long sleeves.

"Just a bit, but after a day in that stuffy room, I want to spend a little more time out here. Fresh air does the body good."

"That it does. How was training?" We pause at a boulder, and together, we take a seat and watch the ocean roll into the black rocks below us.

"Interesting. Sort of boring at times, and I know I shouldn't say that, but going over etiquette and what dress to wear when is not at the top of my list of things I want to learn. Can't there just be a guide that I reference on all of that? Why do I have to remember it now?"

"I think Keller's trying to give you a glimpse into what life will be like. He's laying it all out on the table so you can make the best decision possible."

"I guess that makes sense." I look behind my shoulder and ask, "Is it true that as queen, we're expected to pose naked for our first portrait?"

"What?" Lara asks, turning to face me. "Did Keller say that?"

A roar of laughter escapes me as I shake my head. "No, but your reaction was priceless."

Lara presses her hand to her chest. "Goodness, I was going to charge back to the castle and ask Keller what the hell he was telling you."

I chuckle some more. "No, he did talk about the process of the first portrait, though. That was an unnecessary interlude. He did mention that I had to button up a bit and not swear. That's going to be *fucking* hard for me."

She chuckles. "Just put on your child filter when out in public. Don't say anything you wouldn't say to a child."

"Huh, that's an easy way to put it rather than Keller listing off the things I'm forbidden to say." I smirk. "I upped my swearing during the training just to press his buttons."

Lara smiles. "You sure are giving him a run for his money. I don't think I've ever seen him as concerned as he was when I nailed you in the head with the broom."

I nudge her shoulder with mine. "I'm glad you can joke about it now."

"Me too. But he was . . . he was distraught. I offered to watch over you that night, but he insisted it be him." She pauses and says, "He's very protective of you."

You matter most.

I still think about what Keller said. I matter most.

I'd like to believe that there's something there, something between us. I saw a glint of arousal in his eyes when I told him about my piercings. And when I unleashed my sexual history, there was no mistaking the way he shifted in his chair or how he clenched his jaw tighter. But I also know if Keller actually felt something for me, he'd never act on it. I haven't known him long, but his loyalty and pride toward his country are too strong. He would never mess anything up that would put Torskethorpe in jeopardy.

"He's protective of his country. I'm part of that," I say.

Lara brings her legs to her chest and says, "I don't know, there's something different about him when you're around. I'm not sure what it is, but it's there. Who knows, maybe you're right, maybe he's being extra cautious, given the circumstances we're in. But he does seem to stick close to you."

He does, but I don't think it's because he finds me attractive or anything like that. I truly believe it's because he's doing a job.

"Well, I'm glad we're able to get some girl time. I don't have anyone to really talk to about all of this. I can't explain this to my friend back in Miami, Timmy Tuna. I don't think I could explain this to anyone. But you get it because you're living it with me."

"I'm here, whenever you need to talk, and not just as your bodyguard, but as your friend."

"That means a lot to me, Lara." I wrap my arm around her and give her a hug as she leans against me. "I can't imagine getting close to the one you're protecting is a smart choice, though."

"We run things differently here in Torskethorpe." She winks.

"I'm starting to realize that." I stare up at the bright sky. "I can't believe it's nine at night and it's still light out. Crazy."

"You'll get used to it, but we should probably start heading back. Keller will start to worry."

"Yeah, you're probably right. Plus, I have to finish my Netflix binge."

We both stand from the rock and head back to the castle together.

"What are you watching?" she asks.

"Binging *Bridgerton*, of course. I have to educate myself. I already watched *The Crown*, so I have that aspect of the royal life covered, but *Bridgerton*, that's a whole other lifestyle."

"You realize that's not what our country is like, right?"

"Yes." I secretly smirk. "But how would I be able to get through these training sessions without driving Keller nuts with *Bridgerton* references?"

"Oh, Lilly, I truly think we'll be great friends."

"I think so too."

"I'VE BEEN THINKING," I say as Keller slows down next to me on our jog back to the castle. This morning workout thing is not my jam, just going to make that known.

There's nothing appealing about dragging my half-dead carcass out of bed, slipping on workout clothes, and jogging about on grassy trails. The only thing that keeps me going, that pulls me from my slumber, is the knowledge that I'll get to see Keller's ass in a pair of running shorts jog in front of me. Or I get to watch his large, muscular pecs bounce up and down while he pedals backward, watching me attempt to catch up to him. The jiggle is nice. The jiggle pulls me forward.

"You've been thinking?" Keller asks. "Why does that feel like a bad thing?"

We pause outside the castle, where Keller picks up our boulder. Great, abs *again*.

I wave my hand at him as I try to catch my breath. "No, do your pushups first." I lean my hand against the stone wall of the castle and take a deep breath.

He sets the rock back down, then reaches behind his head and pulls his sweaty shirt off, dropping it to the side before he gets down on the grass and into the pushup position.

Oh, don't mind if I do.

My eyes fall to his arms that are bulging with muscles, rippling sinew weaving from his shoulders to his hands. His back muscles flex, his robust strength on full display as he goes up and down, up and down, with absolute ease.

Yes, that's right, just like that.

Keep it going.

I wet my lips.

If only I was under him while he was performing his pushups, feeling his large body cover mine only to push back up. In my fantasy, we're both naked and his penis is dipping in and out of me.

I have no shame, and I'm okay with that. Just look at the man, he's easily a fifteen out of ten. His muscles have baby muscles, and those baby muscles have micro muscles. There are so many muscles on the man that my nipples aren't sure if they should be hard, or just dislodge from my body and join his.

"Are you going to tell me what you were thinking?" Keller asks, snapping me back to the present.

"Huh?" I ask.

"You said you've been thinking?"

"Oh yeah. I've been worrying about something."

He pauses and sits up on his knees, resting his hands on his thighs. Ooof, look at that remarkable male specimen. The tattoos, the burly torso of a fit man, his concerned brow. Makes me want to drop to my knees, grip the back of his head, and shove him right into my non-existent cleavage.

"What are you worrying about?" he asks.

"Well, I've been doing some serious research on this whole 'royal' thing, and I'm concerned about the amount of time we're spending together alone."

His brow creases even more, and I just knew watching *Bridgerton* was going to not only entertain me but provide me with the perfect material to test Keller's thinning patience. Got to have a little fun with the grump somehow, am I right, ladies?

"Why are you concerned?"

"Because, we're alone, with no chaperone, and the assumption can be made that you're . . . you're stealing my virtue." I roll my teeth over my bottom lip and say, "We might have to get married."

His face switches from concerned to annoyed in a second. Shaking his head, he goes back to his pushups. "Christ, I thought you were serious about something."

"I am. You know how it is, one assumption can destroy a woman's character."

"Us being alone in a room is not going to destroy your virtue. It's the countless hours you spent conducting wet T-shirt contests that will."

I step toward him and nudge his shoulder with the tip of my foot. "I'm being serious, Keller." I'm really not, but my acting is really on point. "We're going to have to get married."

Growling his frustration—uh-oh—he hops up from the ground and towers over me, his chest looming with irritation, his sweat glistening, reflecting the sunshine. "You want to get married? Fine. Brimar is an ordained minister." He crowds my space. "I'll get married right here, right now. But I'll tell you this—you're not going to enjoy being my wife." He crowds me so much that I'm pushed up against the castle now, hands behind my back so I don't succumb to sweaty skin. "I take what I want, when I want it. And if my wife dares disobey me, there will be consequences."

Ooo, so hot.

Does he realize that's more of a turn-on than a turn off?

Mr. Tattooed Man Meat wants to own me? Where's the marriage license? I'll sign right now.

I wet my lips. "You fail to recognize how much that appeals to me . . ." And just because I feel the dominant in him come out, I add, "*Sir.*"

His eyes narrow on me. His jaw clenches. And boy oh boy does he make the most delicious growly noise I've ever heard. "Don't, Lilly."

"Oh, do you prefer *master?*"

His hand strikes the stone next to me, his palm pressing against the hard surface, startling me, but also turning me on at the same time. "Don't fucking test me."

I swallow hard as I curl into the feel of him so close, his warm, heated body nearly pressing against mine. I love the controlled anger in his voice, but the yearning I see in his eyes? I knew it. I knew he was into the kind of kink I am. I could see it the minute I mentioned the sex club yesterday. This just makes him exponentially more appealing.

"Not testing you," I say. "Just letting you know my concerns."

He leans in even closer, his forehead nearly touching mine as he says, "If you're that concerned, then I'll have Lara sit in on our training."

I love Lara, but I don't want that. I like being alone with him.

Hand to my chest, I bat my eyelashes at him and say, "Are you telling me, by being alone with you, you won't be stealing my virtue?"

He pushes off the stone wall and goes back to his pushups.

After the second one, he says, "Trust me, Lilly. If I were stealing your virtue, you would fucking know I was."

———

"OKAY, so the king is briefed every morning on the current events. Got that. Makes sense." I lean against the console table and ask, "But what about the note?"

Keller, who's now showered, smelling like a freaking dream—there are no fermented cod cakes in his pockets—grips the unruly hair on the top of his head. "What note?" he asks in frustration.

We've spent the last two hours going over regimens, accountability, and political protocol. I started to fall asleep during the political protocol talk only for him to slap the table with his bear-like hand and startle the shit out of me.

"You know, the note."

"Does it look like I know what you're talking about?" he asks, arms wide, his voice oozing with irritation. We've had a day, can you tell?

"Ugh, Keller, the note from Lady Whistledown, where she tells you all the gossip of the inner circles. You know, the good stuff."

His brow creases, and then I watch as he slowly processes what I'm saying. I half expect him to yell at me, to roll his eyes, to slap the table again with that burly man-paw of his, but he doesn't.

There's a shift in his expression, almost . . . an understanding. Like we just fell in cahoots together. "Oh, the note."

Wait . . . what? There *is* a note?

"That comes in the morning, with the other news."

"Wait, seriously?"

He drags his hand over his mouth. "It's called the Informative, though."

Here I was just joking, and this is actually something that

happens? A gossip that calls the shots? Now we're talking.

"What kind of stuff is in it? Did you get it today?"

"That's classified information, and until King Theo gives me the go-ahead, you're not privy yet."

"Can you give me a hint as to what's in it?" I zip my lips and throw away the proverbial key. "My lips are sealed. You can trust me."

"No," he answers.

"But, Keller, I could really be a vital help—"

"I said . . . no."

"Well, you're a freaking wet blanket."

"Glad you see it that way. Now, let's go over the lineage of your ancestors."

I slouch in my chair. "Sounds riveting."

<hr />

"ARE YOU PAYING ATTENTION?" Keller snaps.

My eyes shoot up from where I was staring at a precarious hole in a stone. "Uh, yes," I answer, even though I have no idea what we're talking about. Day four in this hellhole of a training room and I think I'm on the verge of losing it.

"What was I saying?"

How did I know he was going to ask that?

"Well, let's see. You like to hear yourself talk, so it's hard to remember where you were at—"

Smack.

His hand wallops the poor table, which has taken a beating every day with his frustration. He stands from his chair, pushing it out so fast that it tips over and crashes to the ground.

"Jesus, Lilly. That's the third time today."

Fourth, technically, but the second time I was able to pull an answer out of my ass. I even impressed myself with my quick flexibility in lying.

"I'd say I was sorry, but I think I need to be honest with you at this point. You're boring me."

"I'm not here to entertain."

"That's obvious from the number of times I've had to pin my eyes open."

He gestures wide as he says, "This is your history, you need to know it."

"Do I really need to know the type of steel that was used to make the very first needle Queen Regina used?"

"Queen Regana."

"That's what I said."

"You said Regina."

I awkwardly smile. "Pretty sure I said Regana."

"You said . . . Regina."

"Are you sure about that?" I ask, crossing my arms over my chest. "Because they do sound similar, and you look tired, you could have misheard me."

"You fucking said Regina."

"Whoa, whoa, whoa," I say, holding up my hands. "No need to get heated. It's a simple mistake, hearing one word when someone really said the other. Doesn't mean you need to start swearing."

His nostrils flare.

His teeth crunch together.

And I actually spot a vein in his neck that looks like it's at DEFCON 1 levels of exploding.

Oh dear, maybe I pushed him too far.

But for the record, angry Keller is very, very . . . *very* hot. I think that's why I keep pushing his buttons because he becomes all growly and agitated and flexy with his muscles. Positively yummy.

"Lilly, I'm going to fucking lose it on you."

"Because you think I said Regana?"

His eyes snap to mine as his mouth thins out. "You fucking said . . . Regina!" His black boot sails up into his wooden

117

chair, careening it at supersonic speed right into the stone wall and breaking it into two pieces, before he storms out of the room, slamming the door behind him, only for it to flap open.

"Uh . . . does that mean we're done for the day?"

———

"MARBLES. Wait, no, uh, Yeezel. No, no, hold on. It has to be Jeremy. Is it Jeremy? It's Jeremy, isn't it? It's got to be Jeremy."

Keller leans back in his new chair, a replacement for the one broken in yesterday's fiasco, and pinches the bridge of his nose. "If you stopped fucking speaking for one goddamn second, I'd be able to tell you the cat's name was Whiskers."

"Whiskers?" I say in an outburst. "Where's the originality in that?"

"And you think Jeremy is original?"

"Uh . . . yeah," I say, flitting my hand at him. "Everyone knows naming an animal a regular person name holds more humor in it than something like Whiskers."

"Can we get back on topic?"

"We're still on topic. You were talking about the cat who had babies in the ballroom during a state dinner. Frankly, it's the most interesting story you've told since we started this lecture-fest five days ago."

He releases a heavy sigh. "I need a break." He stands from his chair and walks over to the open window. He places his hands on the windowsill, which bunches his shirt around his shoulder blades. There's no mistaking the tension resting in those muscles.

He's been short and clipped the entire day.

"You seem irritated with me," I say.

"What on earth would give you that idea?" he huffs.

"Well, the sarcasm in your voice, for one, and your lack of patience, for another. But there's something you need to know, Keller. I'm irritated with you as well."

He turns around and leans against the sill now, arms crossed. "What could I have possibly done to irritate you?"

Well, he keeps showing up with clothes on. These lectures would be far more riveting if he was naked.

"You find it necessary to tell me every little thing about the history of Torskethorpe. I'll tell you right now, I'll probably remember one percent of it. Stop regaling me with the distinct color of the drapes in some old warden's bedroom. What are you? A Stephen King novel?"

"You need to know everything."

"Oh my God!" I rise from my chair. "Do you really think some Torskethorpian is going to come up to me on the streets, tap me on the shoulder, and say, 'Lilly, do you happen to recall the name of Regina's cat who had babies in the state room?'"

"REGANA!" he shouts. "Her fucking name is REGANA!"

"THAT'S WHAT I SAID!" I shout back before placing my hands under the console table and flipping it right over before storming out of the room.

━━━

"I'D LIKE to say things got a little heated yesterday, and even though I was very frustrated, I want you to know, it wasn't your fault. I was out of line." I rub my hand along the console table. "I'm sorry. Do you forgive me?"

Keller is standing to the right of me, arms folded, a sneer on his brow. "Are you done apologizing to the goddamn table?"

I hold my finger up to him and lean my ear toward the wood. When I feel like I've been forgiven, I give a slow nod and say, "The table has chosen to give me another chance."

"Then let's get started." He flops a journal on the table— my new friend—and points at it. "This is for you."

"A present? Aw, you shouldn't have."

"It's a journal so you can start writing down your thoughts."

"Ah, right, for history." I pick up my pen and flip the journal open to the first page. "'*Dear Jerry*—'"

"Jerry?"

"Is that not a good name for my journal? I think it has a nice ring to it—Jerry Journal."

"Your journal doesn't need a name. You're not writing *to* it. You're just writing your thoughts down."

"Oh, okay." I let out a large sigh and tap my pen to my chin before I start writing again. "*Today Keller did fifty-two pushups. Ten of them weren't proper form*—"

He tears the journal from my grasp, causing me to laugh.

"Lilly, this is serious."

"I know," I groan. "But, Keller, this is slowly killing me. It's been a week of these mindless lectures in this small stone room. I can't sit here anymore. It's boring. It's monotonous. It's slowly taking away my will to live. And, sure, you're nice to look at, and the whole chair kicking and table flipping brought some life to our days, but I can only look at you for so long before I start to lose my mind. And I can't possibly hurt my friend the table again." I whisper while stroking the tabletop, "I made a sacred promise to always protect it moving forward."

"But you need to learn this information, Lilly," he says, more deflated than anything.

"Well, teach me in a more fun way. This jail-like cell you have me captured in is making this experience unbearable. Can we at least walk around? Study in the living room? Make a cake and talk about history? Drive around? Something, please?"

"We're not at liberty to drive around just yet."

"Why not?"

"Because."

"Because why?" I press.

He paces the space, hands behind his back. "Because I said so."

"Ah, I see. So because you said so, I should just be okay with that?" I stand as well and approach him. When I'm about a foot away, I poke him in the chest and say, "Well, I'm not okay with it. I'd like to know why we can't go about visiting the country. Don't you want me to fall in love with it? I mean, this castle is nice and all," I lie, because it's actually dreadful, "but you talked about glaciers and volcanoes. I want to see them."

"You can't."

"Why not?"

"Because you need to stay hidden," he shouts, causing me to step back. He grumbles something and then says, "The royal line of succession has been a joke. Four children born into the monarchy, none of them able to take the throne—granted, your mother is a different story—but still, we're at the precipice of losing everything, and the last thing this country needs is to consider your reign a joke."

"A joke?" My forehead crinkles as I fold my arms. "Why would it be a joke?"

"You're an American. You know nothing about the country. You don't know any of the traditions. And if I were to present you in front of the country right now, they would laugh at you, rather than welcome you. We don't need you being spotted. We don't need the rumors."

"Wow," I say, taking a step back. "Well, maybe if you did something more than drone on about the history of needlepoint—"

"Hardanger."

"Whatever!" I throw my hands up in the air. "If you taught me actual useful things, things of real-life importance, I wouldn't be such a joke."

"What I'm teaching you *is* important. You need to know this. You need to know it all so you can make a decision."

"Well, how's this for a decision—I'm done for the day," I say, moving past him and toward the door, but just as I reach it, Keller places his hand on the wood, preventing me from opening it.

"You're not going anywhere," he says in a menacing tone.

I look up at him, note that his chest is vibrating.

"I suggest you move unless you want me screaming bloody murder."

"We need to work."

"And you need to figure out a better way of teaching me, because I am not sitting in this room with you one more day, droning on about flower crowns and how to properly curtsy." I move his hand from the door, open it up, and storm out.

———

"ARE YOU OKAY?" Lara asks, taking a seat next to me on the couch.

"Sort of," I answer, knowing the boys went out for their second jog of the day. Keller mumbled something about needing to run off some frustration.

I took care of my frustration by dipping my nose in the kitchen and sniffing around for something sweet. Imagine my disappointment when I came up completely short. Freaking health nuts with their morning workouts and their healthy soups. I clung to a loaf of bread and took three large bites before sticking it back in the breadbasket.

"It's only been a week of this training, but it feels like a never-ending form of persecution. And the strange thing is, I know Keller can be more fun, I've seen it. But when we get in that room, it's like he shuts down and becomes a robot."

The front door opens, bringing in a whip of wind that floats through the living room before the door quickly shuts. Keller stands in the entryway, sweat dripping down his brow, heaving heavily, looking as if he just ran a marathon rather than went out for a casual jog. When he looks in our direction, our eyes connect, and something magnetic forces me to keep my eyes on him.

Call it our mirrored frustration.

Call it the crazy pull I feel between us, but his eyes remain on mine as well while he continues to breathe heavily.

Proud chest, sweat dripping down his neck to the collar of his shirt, rosy cheeks from the stark winds . . . he's still so freaking yummy to look at, even though he's absolute torture to be around.

I wet my lips.

His eyes fixate on my mouth.

We stare for a few more beats before Brimar steps into the castle, places his hand on Keller's shoulder, and whispers something. Keller nods and heads up the stairs. Wonder what that could've been about?

Doesn't matter. I turn back to Lara, only to catch her staring at me.

"What?" I ask.

"Oh boy, I can't wait to see how this turns out."

"How what turns out?" I ask her.

"That energy between you two."

"There's no energy," I lie, because, yeah, there's energy. There's attraction, there's annoyance, and there's frustration. Some might say it's a lethal combination.

"Lara," Brimar calls out from their room. "Can you help me with something?"

Lara stands from the couch but grips my shoulder before she leaves. "There's energy, and I'm just waiting for the moment when it's going to explode." Then she takes off.

Explode? *Pfft.* Sure, as I said, a lethal combination, but would it really set me off?

No.

Because here's the thing: we all know there's some attraction there, I've been quite frank about how hot he is, but given the man's stiff upper lip, I doubt anything will happen. I wouldn't be surprised if he's wearing a miniature chastity belt over the head of his cock to prevent him from ever having sex. Not that I'm here to have sex with an infuriating man-beast. My purpose of being here in this castle isn't to seek out an orgasm, but to learn about what my future could be like.

Although, a freaking orgasm might help the tension.

It would help the tension between everyone. And when I say *everyone*, I mean Keller and me. There's no tension between Brimar and Lara, and it's probably because they're giving each other ORGASMS.

Grumbling to myself, I stand from the couch and head up the stairs to my bedroom to check my phone. I texted Timmy earlier, letting him know I'm still alive. I'm hoping he responded.

When I make it to my bedroom, I sit on my bed and pick up my phone from the nightstand. He did text back. I open the text.

Timmy: *Took you long enough! God, woman. I'm over here, selling bikinis, trying to act all casual, like my best friend isn't in some foreign country.*

I chuckle and start to text back when the clearing of a throat interrupts me.

I raise my head to find Keller standing in the doorway of the bathroom, his arms braced in the doorframe, his torso completely bare, and his shorts riding dangerously low on his hips.

Yes . . . sir.

"What happened to privacy?" he asks. Screw privacy, take your shorts off.

"Oh, yeah. I was, uh . . ." God, look at his chest. What I wouldn't give to just drag my fingers over his pecs, dig my nails into his sides, and lick his abs.

"You were what?"

Oh shit, right.

"Texting," I answer, holding up my phone. "And before you jump down my throat about confidentiality, I haven't told Timmy anything."

"I trust you," he says in a light tone.

Wait . . . a light tone? There was no snap in his voice. No crackle of thunder booming from his chest. It was . . . pleasant. Man, that run must've really helped his frustrations. He was even able to run off his scowl.

"Oh, okay. Well, I guess I should give you your privacy."

"Before you go," he calls out, "I spoke with Brimar, who spoke with the head of our security. We all agree that it would be okay for you to receive the Informative."

I prop up even more. "Wait, you mean, the gossip going around town?"

"Yes. We feel it will help you connect better and, since it's about the people of the country and not the inner workings of the state, you don't have to be classified to receive it."

I clap my hands together in excitement. "Oh my God, this is so thrilling. How will I get it?"

"It comes to me through text every morning. I'll copy and paste and send it to you."

"Ahh, this is so much fun. Ooo, I hope there's some juicy scandal in tomorrow's edition. Something to kick things off with. Thank you for asking, Keller. That means a lot to me."

"You're welcome," he says softly and then adds, "Tonight, after dinner, we're going to do some more training."

My excitement falls, like a contestant on that Wipeout show. *Ka-blamo*, splat, right into the water. "Wow, you really wear that killjoy title well, don't you?"

"The training won't take place in the room."

I perk up again. "Really? Where will it be?" What a roller coaster of emotions.

"Just dress warmly." He pushes off the doorframe and backs into the bathroom, where I hear him turn on the shower. He moves toward the sink, and I can't tear my eyes away as he loops his fingers into his shorts and drops them, revealing those briefs again. And the side angle does not disappoint as I take in the bulge between his thick thighs.

Curved, the head of his cock pressing tightly against the fabric, it's so tempting. If it's this big flaccid, how large can it be when erect? Curious minds want to know. Curious hands want to touch. Curious mouths want a solid fuck.

"Lilly?"

"Yeah?" I respond, my gaze snapping up to his.

"Are you going to stay and watch me?"

Can I?

Don't mind if I do.

Let me grab some popcorn first.

"Uh, no. Sorry." I clutch my phone to my chest. "Got my phone. All set. You, uh, you have a nice shower. See you at dinner." I squeeze past my door and down the stairs. I sit at the base of them, my face flushed, my fantasies running wild.

My phone buzzes in my hand.

Timmy: *Have you hooked up with Thor yet?*

If he only knew. I text him back.

Lilly: *No. We've spent the last week hating each other to the point of tossing furniture. Also, the man is a steel trap—even if he does want me, it'll never happen. But I'll tell you this, if he asked to suck my nipple, I wouldn't say no.*

Timmy: *Tossing of furniture? Sounds like a solid dose of sexual tension to me. And girl, he'd be so lucky to have your nipples in his mouth.*

Lilly: *Given how sexually frustrated I am at the moment, I think we'd both be lucky.*

Timmy: *Urgh, I love sexual tension. Have you seen him with his shirt off? Is he the god I believe him to be?*

Lilly: *I've seen him all the way down to his briefs, not boxers . . . just briefs, and let's just say, it looks like he has two large bananas shoved down there. TWO, Timmy.*

Timmy: *I'm sweating. Lawrd help me, I'M SWEATING!*

Lilly: *You and me both.*

Chapter Ten

KELLER

There are a few things you need to know.

My intent in training Lilly was not to bore her but to help her make an informed decision.

But after the disastrous week we've had, clearly, she needs to be trained in a different manner.

There's also no such thing as the Informative. Yup, I made it up. I saw right through her goddamn jokes and I've decided to twist it back around on her and dish her some fake gossip. Serves her right with all the shit she's been giving me.

I'm not going to be able to hold back if she keeps looking at me the way she is, like she could drop to her knees and devour me in a second. And fuck, when she called me sir, I felt my entire body inflate with life. What I wouldn't give to hear her call me that while my cock runs over her lips.

It was also unbelievably hot seeing her flip the table. The combination of her taking charge, her flushed cheeks, and erect nipples had me revved up, ready to take her up against a goddamn wall.

And it's been like that all week, which of course has only added to my frustration. She's so beautiful, so feisty, so . . . so mouthy that I'm turned on every fucking day with no way to take care of my building tension other than a stupid run.

When I was in the bathroom, ready to strip down while she was in her room, I would've done it. I would've let her see me naked. I wouldn't have cared. She was the one waiting for a show, and I had no problem giving her one. But out of respect for her, our professional relationship, and trying to keep her at a distance, I gave her a warning before I stripped down.

On my run with Brimar, he called me out on my attraction toward her. He said I wasn't even bothering to hide it. I don't think it was a choice if I could hide it or not, I can't. She pulls it out of me. She makes me lick my lips when she walks into a room. She makes me think of spanking her every time she mouths back. And when she purposely stares at me while eating a cookie, she's just begging me to take that filthy mouth of hers and fill it with my stiff cock.

Brimar being Brimar, he headed me off with a best friend warning, telling me to tread carefully with Lilly. I told him there would be no treading, that I wasn't going there with her.

Does she intrigue me? Of course.

Do I think she's absolutely breathtaking? Yes.

Do I fantasize about running her delicate fingers over my body? Nightly.

But when I say she's off limits, I mean it.

Because if she decides to say yes and become the goddamn queen of Torskethorpe, then I have absolutely zero right to her. *She can never be mine.* And even though I want her, I have to keep this boundary in place. There *is* no other option for me.

With all that being said, I thought about this last week—

and the hell I've put us both through—and believed a change of heart was necessary regarding how I teach her. She's right, not every day has to be spent in the room. I can make it more fun, and if I want her to make it through the training, I do need to attempt to create a pleasant learning experience. And, my ultimate goal is to make her love Torskethorpe. *So she'll stay.*

Which means, I need to fucking lighten up a bit.

"Okay, I'm dressed," Lilly says, disrupting my thoughts.

Decked out in a pair of navy-blue joggers and a gray hooded sweatshirt that's far too big for her body, she walks up to me, arms extended, a smile on her face. That smile, fuck, playful yet placid. It's the pinnacle of joy.

"Are you ready?" she asks, hopping around.

"Are you going to calm down?"

"No." She smiles even brighter.

Sighing, I turn her toward the stairs of the castle and lead her up to a small door on the left.

"Are we hanging out in a linen closet?"

I push the door open and step to the side, revealing a narrow staircase.

She pokes her head in. "Wait, this isn't a linen closet?" She looks over her shoulder. "Is this a secret passageway?"

"Secret would mean that it would be hidden, and this door is plain as day, out in the open."

"Disguising itself as a linen closet."

"Do you truly believe an eighteenth-century castle would have a linen closet?" I ask.

"I don't know what people did with their closets back then."

"If a royal needed a towel or linen, they wouldn't fetch it from the nearest closet. A servant would bring it to them from the servant quarters."

"Huh, I guess that makes sense. So, then, where does this lead to?"

"The roof," I answer as I move past her and turn my body to shimmy up the narrow, curved staircase.

"Oh my God, you're too big for the staircase. Are you going to get wedged in?"

"No, I was up here earlier. It's just tight." I reach out and take her hand in mine. "Mind the steps, they're slippery."

Her fingers curl around my hand, indenting into my skin as we make our way up toward the hatch. Still holding on to her tightly, I unlock the hatch and then push it open, lighting up the narrow hallway with the light from the never-setting sun.

When I reach the roof, I bend down and take both of her hands, helping her up until she reaches the top with me. She straightens up, and that damn smile of hers grows again as she takes in the view.

From the top of the castle, the grassy landscape and blue ocean feel endless. Fjords are cratered into the coastline, creating a jagged appearance to the black rocks, and wisps of foam stretch infinitely along the heavy sea waves. And despite it being summer, there's still a chill in the air, but fuck is it breathtaking.

"Oh my God, it's gorgeous up here. I feel like you can see for miles."

"You can," I say as I press my hand to her lower back and guide her to where I set up a blanket and some pillows.

She pauses when she sees the laid-out fur blanket and the plethora of oversized throw pillows Lara helped me collect. When she faces me, I'm met with a quizzical brow tugging above her glittering eye. "My, my, my . . . *Fitzy*, what is this? It looks awfully romantic if you ask me."

"It's not," I answer, wanting to make that abundantly clear. "The castle has nothing else that's comfortable to sit on that would fit up the staircase."

"Okay." She winks. "Sure."

Grumbling under my breath, I say, "It's fucking true," as we walk over to the blanket and pillows and take a seat.

I hand her a spare blanket as she gets comfortable. "In case you get cold."

"Thank you." She rests it over her lap. "So, what are we doing up here if this isn't a romantic interlude?"

It's not.

Remember, not going there.

"I wanted to show you the land, the best way I could without driving."

She offers me a genuine smile. "Now this is what I'm talking about." Hands clasped, she asks, "Where do we start?"

"Well, I believe we've spoken about this before, but eighty percent of the country is uninhabited."

"Because of the glaciers and volcanoes, right?"

"Right. So, the country is split into five regions." I point toward the coast. "We're on the southern peninsula, and if you look just past my finger, you'll see the red-and-white lighthouse that warns ships of the tip of our country."

She scoots in close, close enough for her lavender scent to circle around the both of us. Her soft hair tickles my cheek as she leans in, looking for the lighthouse.

"Do you mean that little dot?"

"Yes. But it's an important dot. Not only does it warn ships from the coast, but it was once used as a watchtower for invaders. Now it's run by a family. Their main responsibility is to help keep the coastline clear and call in anything that's out of the ordinary."

"I love that. Have you met the family?"

"Yes, King Theo had them visit the palace, and he gave them the King's Safeguard Medal, a noble honor of the highest degree. It means that they have spent a generous amount of their lives protecting our country."

"That *would* be an honor. Good for them. What else is on the southern peninsula?"

"Well, Harrogate, as you know, but what the southern peninsula is best known for are the hot springs."

"There are hot springs here?" she asks, excited, still right next to me, her leg bumping against mine.

"There are, but they're about thirty miles away."

"Which means we aren't allowed to go to them, right?"

"It would be a breach of security at this point, but I do believe there's an undisclosed location about ten minutes north by foot that has a smaller hot spring. Something I would be allowed to take you to."

She grabs my arm in pure joy. "That would be so much fun. I've never been in one before."

"I'll put it on the itinerary," I say. "Now, the capital is another region in the country. That's where the main population lives, as well as being the location of Strombly Palace."

"What is the total population of the country?"

"About twenty thousand."

"Gosh, Miami has a bigger population than that. I can see why traditions are so strong here."

"It's what we live by. Now, since the capital region is where most of the population is located, all the houses are lined up in rows, one right next to the other, only differing in height and bright colors. There aren't many yards, nor is there much space, but when you're trying to fit a population into fifteen percent of habitable land, things are going to be tight. But there's a lot of open space as well, which creates more of a community amongst neighbors."

"Fascinating. Are there tall buildings?"

I shake my head. "No, none, actually. The tallest building in the capital is the watchtower of Strombly. Every other building is either one-story or two-stories, even places of business. It's truly unlike any capital city you'll ever see. Nothing like Miami."

"I can't wait to see it," she says dreamily.

"Now, on the west side of the island, you'll find the biggest waterfall in the country, as well as the largest fishing port. The town is called Kirkfell. Surrounded by beautiful mountains, the town focuses on tourists, offering multiple tours up to the hot springs, bed-and-breakfast options, as well as the best place to get fermented cod cakes."

She places her hand on my shoulder and levels a stare. "Tell me, how do they really taste?"

"Not bad, actually. Paired with the right sauce, they're pretty good."

"I'm guessing I'm going to have to eat one at some point."

"You are, they're served everywhere, and it's insulting to the people if you don't accept their gift. Any gift, for that matter, including fermented cod cakes."

"Does Brimar make them?"

"He does. He makes the right sauce that has a hint of heat."

"I can handle heat. Maybe he needs to make them one night." She smirks. "So, if tourists come to Torskethorpe, they normally visit Kirkfell?"

"Yes. They float between Kirkfell and the capital. Since the capital is more inland, there aren't whale watching tours or the quaint seaside-town feel that tourists seem to enjoy, but the capital does offer quite a few driving tours that are very popular."

"Okay, you told me about the west, what about the east?"

"The prettiest part of the country, in my opinion. It's the only place on the island where the land is off limits. There are guards that protect that side of the country, round-the-clock security."

"Why's it so important?"

"It's where the birch forest exists, the only remaining indigenous trees on the island, as well as the sacred moss that takes over one thousand years to grow. The area is lush and green and free of any volcanic activity. It's pure in nature, one of the prettiest sights you'll ever see. Like . . . nirvana in the middle of a desolate, lava rock-filled land."

"Sounds dreamy. Do they do tours?"

"Yes, but only electric vehicles are allowed near the east side. They're trying to preserve nature the best they can."

"I love that. So, I'm assuming the east side is your favorite?"

I shake my head. "The prettiest, by far, but my favorite part of the country? We're in it right now."

"The southern peninsula? Why?"

"My parents took me here on their days off. We fished off the coast, camped down by the hot springs, and enjoyed the outdoors. I have a lot of memories down here."

"Where are your parents now?" she asks.

I look out to the ocean and quietly say, "They passed when I was twelve. A fire occurred in the servant quarters, and they couldn't get out."

"Oh my God." She grips my hand in hers. "Keller, I'm so sorry. That must have been horrific."

"It's in the past," I say, clearing my throat and sitting taller. "Not something I talk about."

"Well, if anyone understands what it means to lose their parents, I have experience, so if you ever need to talk—"

"I'm fine, Lilly," I say, sharper than I want while releasing my hand from hers. "Now, about the north."

"Keller," she says softly, while grabbing my hand again.

I let out a giant sigh and look her in the eyes, knowing she's not going to drop this. "Lilly, I'm fine, okay? I don't talk about it, because when I do, it dredges up old memories that haunt me. So, please, just drop it."

She nods, thankfully. "Okay." Then she says, "The north, what's there?"

"The volcanoes and glaciers," I say, realizing she's still holding my hand, and for some stupid reason, I let her.

At least I got her to change the subject so I don't have to relive that horrendous day.

━━

"IT'S CALLED KULNING."

"Kulning," she says, testing the word on her tongue. "And if you do it the right way, a herd of sheep will flock in from miles away?"

"Not quite. It's used only by farmers."

"Have you ever tried it to see if it will attract sheep?"

"No."

"Then you don't know." She sits up on her knees, takes a deep breath, and—

"What the hell are you about to do?"

She glances down at me where I'm lying on one of the pillows, looking up at the blue sky.

"I'm about to call the sheep. You know, make that *kunnn-nuuuu* sound. I have quite the vocal range."

"Great, but we don't need you making that sound while we're attempting to lay low."

"Who could really hear it? We've been up here for over an hour and we haven't seen one life form. The only company we have are your surly attitude and those white birds that keep eyeing us like we're a late-night snack."

"Surly attitude?"

"Yeah. Very unpredictable. Makes me think we should put Torskethorpe on hold and dive deeper into the man training me." She pokes my chest.

"That's not happening."

"Oh, come on. Give me a break for a second. I think I deserve it after you told me about the history of kulning. Not that it's a bad thing, it's just . . . you know, not my cup of tea, especially since you won't let me try it." When I don't answer her, she pokes my side again. "Please, Keller."

I heave a heavy sigh. "Fine, you get three questions."

"Oh, yay, that's more than I expected. But you need to ask me questions, too. Okay, this is a little get-to-know-you sesh."

"Fine," I say, exasperated.

"Calm down, dude, don't get too excited."

I crack a smile and glance away so she can't see it. Maybe she's right. Maybe a brief break will be good for us. Refresh the mind—plus, there's been something I've wanted to ask her for a bit.

"Okay, I'm going to go first since you're silent over there." She taps her chin. "Hmm, I'll start off easy, what's your favorite color?"

"You're going to waste one of your questions on that?"

"It's not a waste. Someone's favorite color tells a lot about them. So, what's yours?"

"Black," I answer.

"Ah, I presume like your soul."

"A percentage of my soul," I answer while sticking my hands behind my head. Lilly has yet to lie down, she's sitting cross-legged, turned so she's facing me. If she wanted to, she could rest her hand on my stomach, that's how close she is.

"Ooo, so mysterious, just like your favorite color." She winks. "Okay, ask me a question."

I want to ask her about her sexual behavior, what she liked the most at the sex club, and what turned her on. I want to dive deep into that conversation, but I know it's inappropriate. Probably not something I should ask the future queen of Torskethorpe. Plus, what am I going to do with that information when she answers? Just sit on it? Stew with it swirling around in my head over and over again, reminding me how much I want her but how much I can't have her?

Probably not smart.

"What's your most prized possession?"

"Ooo, okay, coming in with a solid first question." She rubs her hands together. "I guess it depends. I have a box of memories from my parents that I cherish, but it's hard to go through those memories because I end up missing them so much. The pain can be debilitating at times."

"I can understand that," I say quietly.

"So even though those memories mean the most to me, I put them in another category in my head. Therefore, my most prized possession? Hmmm, that would easily have to be my vibrator."

My eyes snap to hers, finding her smirking, completely pleased with herself. "That is not your most prized possession."

"Yes, it is." She wets her lips. "I'm a very sexual person. I love getting off, and I found a vibrator that's the perfect match for me. It's so valuable that I packed it and brought it with me, with extra batteries. But to my dismay, I can't use it because we're practically sleeping in the same room since the doors to the bathroom won't shut."

I would probably lose my goddamn mind if I heard her getting off in the next room. There's no way I'd be able to lie there in bed and not do something. Not storm through the bathroom, take the vibrator in my hand, and do the work for her.

"And trust me, I've thought about using it. I'm not making a move on you or anything, but the night of the broom, seeing you in a pair of briefs . . . I have to be honest, Fitzy, you have a great body. I could have easily masturbated to that image."

Fuck.

Me.

"We shouldn't be talking about this," I say, as I feel this overwhelming need to roll her to her back and let her feel how her words are affecting me. How I'm hardening at the thought of her masturbating to me.

"Don't be such a fuddy-duddy." She pushes at me play-fully. "I told you I wasn't trying to make a move, just speaking the truth, and the truth is always healthy. You're incredibly handsome. It's facts."

Not facts that I need in my head.

"Next question," I say.

"Ugh, fine. Let's see . . . oh, here's a good one—have you ever had a girlfriend?"

"Yes," I answer, leaving it at that.

"Uh, care to elaborate?"

"No, I don't."

"That's not what this game is about. You have to give me a little more detail. How many girlfriends? Were any of them serious? Wait . . . do you have a girlfriend now?"

"That's more than one question."

"Please, Keller." She shakes me. "Just share with me, you black-souled hottie."

Fuck, that makes me crack a smile, and this time she sees it.

"Oooo, I got you." She points at my face. "I got you to loosen up. Your jaw unclenched. Come on, tell me more."

Sighing, I push my hand through my hair and say, "One serious girlfriend—fiancée, to be exact."

"Fiancée?" she asks. "Wow, I didn't see that coming. So, you must have really loved her. What happened?"

"She got a job opportunity to work in London. We talked about what to do. I told her my life is with Torskethorpe, she didn't see it that way, and things were broken off."

"Oh, wow, that's hard. Do you ever miss her?"

"No," I answer. "She was my first girlfriend. I attached myself to her for all the wrong reasons. It was better off this way. I believe she's engaged again."

"You seem so cold about it. You really don't miss her?"

Not sure what kind of answers Lilly is fishing around for, I turn my head and look her in the eyes as I say, "I don't. We weren't a good match if you take into consideration her goals . . . and my desires."

"Oh." Lilly smiles awkwardly. "I can understand that. Not being sexually matched can be a real downfall." She pulls her legs in tight. "Okay, your turn to ask me a question. Make it a good one."

A good one?

Well, I have a good one, but I'm not sure I should ask it.

But, fuck, it's eating away at me. Every time I see her, I want to know the answer. I want to talk about it.

I chew on the inside of my cheek. Fuck it. "When you went to the sex club, what was your favorite thing about it?"

A slow smile spreads across her lips. "Mmm, good question." She places her hand on my stomach. It hollows out from her touch, but knowing enough about Lilly at this point, I know she's not touching me in a sexual way, it's just the way she communicates. "Well, there were quite a few things I liked about it. Mainly, I liked watching the kind of control the men had over the women. But it was never in a bad way, it was as if the women were the most important thing in their lives, and they were treating them like that. Cherishing them."

"As it should be," I say before I can stop myself.

Her fingers dance along my shirt, causing my heartbeat to pick up. "I liked watching how possessive the man was when he touched his woman, like every stroke was the first stroke. And there was something so sexy, so fascinating to me when the woman would give in and let the man lead her. The trust between them, it was beautiful." She moves her fingers over my shirt. "Is that what you like about that side of the sexual experience?"

"Is that your last question?"

"I guess so."

"Then, yes. I was born a protector; it's in my blood. When a woman puts her trust in my hands, I'll never break that trust, I'll hold it close to me and cherish it. That goes for inside the bedroom and outside of the bedroom."

"God, you're getting me all hot." She chuckles. "Urgh."

She lies down next to me. Shoulder to shoulder. "And once again, I can't use my vibrator."

"If you need privacy—"

"No, that would be weird. You going downstairs while I get off? No, thank you."

"The offer is there."

"Appreciated, but I won't be taking you up on it. Okay, ask your final question."

Her arm rubs against mine, causing the hairs on my forearm to rise, my mouth to dry, and my fingers to tingle. My body reacts to her in a way I don't think I've ever experienced before. Being near her like this, it's almost like this animal deep within me is clawing, begging, pleading to be let out of its cage, and every little touch she makes only drives that desire to more palpable levels.

When I don't answer right away, she turns on her side and props her head up on her hand. "Come on, you have to have one more question in there. Something that's been on your mind."

Yeah.

There is something.

Something that's been driving me nuts ever since she announced it during training.

"Your clit piercing. Why did you get it?"

From the corner of my eye, I watch her smile as she says, "After a few sexual experiences that fell completely flat, I wanted something that would help me climax better, something that was just for me. I didn't want to have to rely on a man to make me come. And with a clit piercing, the sensation is more intense."

"What was the man doing that he couldn't get you off?"

"All the wrong things." She stretches her hand out and traces my collarbone. "You know how the simplest touch in the right spot can get you high on that feeling of ecstasy?"

"Yes," I answer drunkenly as I allow her to drag her finger along my shirt.

"With the right person, that's all it takes, just a touch, here." She moves her finger over my pec. "Or here." Her finger caresses my abs. "Or . . . here . . ." She moves down to the waistband of my pants, and that's when I grip her wrist, stilling her.

"No, Lilly."

"No, what?" she asks innocently.

"We're not going there."

"Going where?"

Jaw hard as stone now, I turn to face her and say, "Sex. We're not fucking going there."

"You know it would be good."

"It would be fucking great," I respond. "But it's not happening. There are too many complications, too many unknowns." I swallow and then say, "And if I have one taste, I know I won't be able to stop."

Her eyes turn heady as she slowly lowers herself back down to the blanket, turns her face to her pillow, and lets out a muffled scream. Confused, I wait for her to lift up, and when she does, she says, "Well, I very well might need that private time now. Thanks a lot."

"OKAY, that wraps up the history of the cod in Torskethorpe," I say. "Any questions?"

Lilly blinks a few times and then starts slow clapping. "Wow, Keller, that has to be your most boring lecture yet. Didn't think you could top the history of patterned curtains in Strombly, but here we are, on the roof of a castle, the ocean beating into the rocks below us, and I'm bored out of my mind."

I was bored talking about it, but after the heated questions we asked each other, I had to douse us both in a tale of cod. It was the only way to ensure things didn't escalate.

Seems like it worked.

"It was an important topic—"

"Every topic to you is an important one. I'm going to tell you right now, that the cod story's importance is on the bottom of the totem pole, right next to 'unnecessary.' I'm truly shocked that I'm still awake after that. Best you told that story outside, where the sun doesn't set. Kept me more awake."

"Okay, I get it, it was boring."

She sits up and stares down at me. "It was more than boring—it was downright painful, the type of story that should be used as a form of torture."

"Well, be happy, that was the last lecture for tonight, and we can pack up now." I lift up, only for her hand to connect with my chest and hold me in place.

"No way. We're not ending the night on freaking cod and the image I have in my head of these demon fish swimming around in the ocean, eating other fish. I'm not going to bed with that floating around in my mind. No, thank you. You owe me."

Normally, I would tell her she's fine and to get her ass to bed, but in this instance, I think she might be right. The cod lecture was too much.

"What do you want?" I ask.

"Three more questions. But I'm the one asking this time. You know enough about me, but you're still a blank page."

I rest back on the blanket and prop my hands behind my head. "Fine, make them quick."

"Ha, okay." I catch the roll of her eyes. "First and foremost, I want it to be known that you have the right to veto my question, but I'd also like you to think about answering before vetoing."

What the hell did I get myself into?

"Understood?" she asks, using my tone of voice while

poking me. My brow lifts in question, which only makes her laugh. "Seriously, are you ready?"

"I'm not sure, but it doesn't look like I have a choice."

"Glad you see it that way, because you don't." She flips her hair over her shoulder. "Okay, first question—tell me one thing you miss about your parents." She presses her hand to my arm. "And before you veto, I'll share with you one thing I miss about mine." Her eyes plead with me.

Fuck. How does she already have that kind of control over me where I can't say no?

I heave a heavy sigh and say, "I miss their hugs. And not just the hugs they gave me, but the hugs they gave each other. I'd walk in on them at some point every day and find them embracing. They truly loved each other and leaned on each other for support. I miss that, walking into the kitchen to find my mom sitting on the counter and my dad leaning against the counter, my mom's arms wrapped around him tightly. I miss how they brought me into their embrace and held me there until I wiggled my way out. Just everything about it, I miss it."

Lilly is rubbing her thumb over my hand as I talk, and when I glance up at her, I catch the appreciation in her eyes. With a soft smile, she says, "That was going to be my answer."

"Really?" I ask. "You're not just saying that?"

She shakes her head. "No. You don't realize how much you miss a simple embrace until it's not there anymore. I truly miss the way my parents would squeeze my hand."

"Three times, right?"

She smiles softly. "Three times. Something I feel like I didn't know I was going to miss so much until it was gone. Now what I wouldn't give to have my mom and dad both hold my hand one more time and squeeze an *I love you*. Sometimes, when I'm dreaming, I swear I can feel them there, squeezing, but when I wake up, it all vanishes. Feels so . . . cruel. I hate dreaming about them."

"I do too," I answer, allowing myself to open up for a moment. As much as I love my role in Torskethorpe, it often requires many long days. Few days off. And if I'm honest, when I lost my parents, I lost my people too. They'd always been my friends. It's rare I open up to people, as there's rarely any time to do so, and no one of consequence to talk with. I, therefore, keep my life full and rarely consider the loneliness associated with my job. But there have been times when it's consumed me. "I'd rather not dream about them at all, because then I don't wake up feeling like I have to live through the loss all over again."

"Same," she says. "At first, I clung to those dreams. I'd sleep more often than I should have, hoping for a connection with them, but then my dreams started becoming more and more vivid, and . . . well, I couldn't take it anymore. Now I just hope to live with them through memories."

"I understand the feeling completely."

"I think you might be the only person who does . . . well, the only person I know." She slips her fingers into my hand and I allow it because I know, in this moment, that's what she needs. Hell, I need it too. I don't talk about my parents, ever, so I'm venturing into new territories for her. "Is it weird to say talking about that with you makes me feel closer to you?"

"No. I feel the same way," I answer.

"I'm glad." She releases her hand from mine and I almost reach out to slip my hand in hers again, but we've already crossed the line a bit too much tonight. Holding her hand is not something I should be doing. "Okay, sorry for the depressing question. Let me ask you something that will liven up this Q and A. What's the most embarrassing thing you've done in front of King Theo?"

"Ah, hell," I say, dragging my hand over my face.

"Come on." She chuckles. "You have to tell me; it will make you look more human in my eyes. Right about now, you seem far too perfect, and that's really annoying, so I need you to be self-deprecating. Thank you."

"Where do I even begin?"

"Ooo, there's more than one?"

"There's far too many to count," I answer. "Thankfully, Theo is a chill king and finds my blunders funnier than anything."

"Well, give me the story that you wish you could erase from your memory."

"It's so fucking bad." I shake my head.

"My mouth is watering. I need to know. Give me the juicy details."

I press my hand over my eyes and say, "I'll tell you, but I swear to God, Lilly, if you bring this up ever again, I will force-feed you fermented cod cakes for twenty-four hours straight."

She shivers next to me and holds up her hand. "Promise, what you're about to say will never be brought up again."

"Better not be." I prop myself up on my elbow and turn toward her so I can at least have a great view of her reaction to my utter misery. "I had this grand idea when I first became Theo's private secretary that I should learn the ins and outs of every position in the palace so if I ever needed to fill in, I would be skilled enough to do so."

"Is that why you sort of double as a bodyguard here?"

"Yes, I took extensive training with Brimar and Lara, but that's required of me when I'm with King Theo. He has his bodyguards, but if something happens to them, I need to be able to step up without thinking twice. If I wasn't Theo's private secretary, I know I'd be working with Brimar and Lara on security detail. It's in my blood to protect."

"So you've said." She winks. "So, you were training yourself . . ."

"Yes. I was doing quite well and learning a lot every week, going through different departments and learning their trade.

I've acquired much knowledge by living in other people's shoes, and I know it's enhanced my skills tremendously, but it was a fateful Friday evening that it all happened. That Saturday, King Theo was hosting a state dinner, so I thought it was the perfect opportunity to learn to serve dinner."

"Oh God, I feel like I can see where this is going."

"Not sure you do," I say before I push my hand through my hair. "Everything was going great. I was serving wine like a pro, the salad was easy to take care of, and it was all very smooth. That was . . . until we got to the soup."

"Oh, no." Lilly brings her legs up to her chest.

"One thing you need to know is that as a server, you need to hold one hand behind your back while you carry with the other. I practiced a lot and never had an issue, but that fucking soup bowl. It was fucking heavy. One of those massive plates, a foot in diameter, with a small scoop in the middle for a serving of soup. Well, I was carrying it with one hand from the kitchen to the dining room, which felt like a mile, and by the time I got to King Theo, my thumb was cramping. I tried to hurry, but before I could make it to the table, my thumb gave out, and the bowl fell from my hand and right into Theo's lap."

"Oh, God." Lilly covers her eyes. "You spilled soup all over him?"

"I wish that was the worst part."

She removes her hand. "That's not the worst part?"

I shake my head. "No, the worst part was that the soup was still scalding hot, because that's how Theo loved it. It scorched his lap to the point of blistering."

"Nooooo," Lilly says, her eyes nearly popping out.

"Yup. He was wobbling through the state dinner the next night, all because of me. I've never been more horrified."

She throws her head back and laughs. "Oh my God, that's so embarrassing."

"Tell me about it. I offered to bring him ice anytime he

needed it, which I did. He was cool about it, and glad I didn't burn anything off, if you know what I mean."

Lilly waves her hand in front of her face, catching her breath. "That's amazing. I'm sorry, but that's one hell of a story."

"That we don't talk about, right?"

"Right." She winks again and then blows out a low breath. "God, that's great. Not sure my next question can top that, but I'm going to ask anyway so we can finish out the night."

"Anything to move on from this story."

She smirks. "It's a quick one. Let's say you saw a girl that you thought was really pretty and you wanted to make a move on her, you know . . . get her attention, what would you do?"

"That's your question?"

"Yeah. I think you're a complex guy, but I've been able to break you down in different ways tonight besides the romantic side, and I'm just curious. I know you have that whole alpha side to you, but there has to be a softer side, right?"

"Not sure there's anything soft about me."

"That's obvious from one look at you, but just play along. If you were to try to win a girl over, what would you do? My guess is flex in front of her until she passes out into your arms."

My brow creases. "Do you really think that's what I'd do?"

She tosses her arms up. "I have no idea. Educate me on Keller's way of romancing."

I scratch the side of my jaw. "Haven't really had the time to do anything like that, so I don't have much experience, but I guess I'd go about it the same way my dad would, by introducing her to my poems and—"

"Hold up, you write poetry?"

I nod, which causes her to clutch her chest and fall back on the blanket.

"Ugh, that's so annoying."

"Why is that annoying?"

She pops up again, but this time she stands all the way up. "Where are you going?"

"This evening is over. I will not be forced to sit here and listen to you tell me about how you write poetry to woo women, not after spending the evening with you and learning about the love you have for your parents, your self-deprecating story, your love for cod, your sexual magnetism, or be subject to having to stare at your muscles anymore. It's enough."

"You're the one who asked me," I say.

"Yeah, and guess what, I thought you were going to say some cheesy pick-up line and be done with it. I wasn't expecting you to tell me you write poetry. That's a whole other level I don't think I can take, because I already think you're hot. I don't need a sensitive poet attached to that. No, fucking thank you." She moves past me, toward the hatch of the roof.

"But it's the truth."

"La, la, la, la, la," she says, plugging her ears. "I can't hear you."

I remove her hands and hold them at her sides. "Stop it."

"You stop it. Stop trying to make me yearn for you."

"Trust me, that's the last thing I want. I was just being truthful, that's all."

She grumbles and then says, "Fine, thank you for being honest. Your answer was appreciated, but I'll tell you this right now, if you find me humping your leg in the middle of the night, you know why. You can only blame it on yourself."

I chuckle. "I'll take the blame."

"Good." She smiles up at me. "Well, I'm serious, thank you for sharing tonight. I had fun, Keller. I think this little break is just what I needed."

"Yeah, I had fun too." I pull on the back of my neck as I stare down at her beautiful face.

"Ah, come here, you big lug." She loops her arms around me and gives me a big hug while pressing her face to my chest.

Stunned for a moment, I don't know what to do, but when

she wiggles against me, I realize she's looking for an embrace as well, so I drape my arms around her and offer her a hug. We stand there for a few moments, just holding each other. Two kids who lost their parents, who miss the simple act of an embrace. I can't help but think how this night just brought us a thousand times closer, and I'm not sure if that's a good thing or a bad thing.

⊂⊃

THE SMELL of smoke seeps into my nose.

The heat of a fire warms up my face.

The glow of flames stains my eyelids.

I try to open them, I try to get a better look, but I can't see anything. Just a glow. A deep orange glow, and then . . .

A scream.

A horrific, bloodcurdling scream that has my body breaking out into a sweat.

They're . . . they're in there.

I know they are.

But I can't get to them. I can't see them.

Fuck.

Just open your eyes. Open your eyes and you'll be able to—

"Keller."

My eyes shoot open so fast that I gasp and come face to face with another human. Unable to register what's happening, and who it is, I grab them by the shoulders, twist them to the bed, and pin them down so they can't move.

"Keller," a female voice calls out. "It's me, Lilly."

Her voice cuts through the fog.

I blink several times as the room around me comes into view.

And when I focus on her, on the worried look on her face, I realize what I'm doing.

149

"Fuck," I say as I jump off her. "Shit, Lilly, are you okay?" I ask, my heart beating wildly, the wake of my nightmare still haunting the back of my mind.

"Yes," she answers, sounding out of breath.

I take a seat next to her and move my hand over her arms, examining her. "Fuck, did I hurt you? I didn't—I didn't know." Frantically I push my hand through my hair.

She sits up on my bed and places her hand on my chest, right on top of my heart. "I'm okay, Keller. But are you? I heard you from the other room. You were having a night terror."

I nod, looking away, but she scoots closer, bumping right next to my side.

"Do you get them often?" she asks, her thumb making soothing strokes over my heart.

"Every now and again," I answer. "But I've never attacked anyone in my sleep." I turn toward her. "I'm sorry, Lilly. Are you sure I didn't hurt you?"

"You didn't." She takes my hand in hers and smooths it over her arm. "See." She brings it over to her other arm. "No lumps. No bumps. No cuts."

Still not convinced, I reach for the lamp on the night table and turn it on, illuminating the blacked-out space of my bedroom. When I turn back to her, I lift her right arm and examine it. On the upper part of her arm is a red spot from where I tightly gripped her. Pain zips through me as I go to her other arm, checking for the same mark. And there it is.

"Fuck, I hurt you." I back away on the bed as I attempt to process this. It goes against everything I believe in. I'm supposed to protect her, not hurt her.

"Keller, stop. It'll be red for a second. There won't even be any bruising. Seriously, I'm fine. I'm more concerned about you, though. Can you just settle down for a second and talk to me?"

I shake my head and rise from the bed. The nightmare,

the knowledge that I could cause her pain, that something even worse could have happened, twists and turns into an ugly reality. I grip my hair and pace the room, my pulse erratic as I try to catch my breath.

"Keller, you're going to have an anxiety attack." She hops off the bed and stops me, both her hands to my bare chest now. "Look at me. In the eyes. Look at me."

My gaze falls to hers, and in that moment, staring down at her iridescent eyes, I feel a warmth spread and crash into the frigid chill of my heart. Not sure I would've recognized that feeling before tonight, before our time on the roof, but I recognize it now.

Her palm cups my cheek and I find myself leaning in to her touch, leaning in to her strength. "I'm okay, Keller. Do you hear me?"

I swallow hard, as a hint of relief etches through me. "Yes," I choke out.

"Okay, good. Now"—she takes my hand in hers and brings me back to the bed, where we both take a seat—"we need to check on *you*. Are you okay?"

Exhaustion hits me all at once as the adrenaline fades away. "Yeah. I think so."

"Do you want to talk about it?"

I shake my head. "No."

Her hand smooths over my arm. "Was it about your parents?"

"Yeah," I answer quietly.

"Enough said." She scoots in even closer, leaving nothing between us. And I like it, I want her even closer, I want her in my arms. I want . . . I want another hug. "I get those dreams at times, and I realize the need to not talk about it. Do you want to talk about something else?"

I shake my head. "No, I'm good. I should get you back to bed." I rise from the mattress and hold my hand out to her. To my luck, she takes it, and I walk her through our shared bathroom to her room. I pull back the covers of her bed and help her onto the mattress. When she's seated, I move the covers over her legs and take a step back.

"I'm sorry for waking you."

"You don't have to apologize. I get it, Keller."

"Okay, well . . . get some sleep."

"Do you . . ." She bites her bottom lip and then asks, "Do you want to lie down with me?"

Yes.

I want you to continue to stroke my heart.

Stare into your eyes.

Feel your comforting warmth. Get lost in it.

I want to replicate that embrace, but in your bed, our limbs tangled together.

Because . . . because I think I fucking like you, and I have no idea how to deal with those emotions.

"That's not necessary," I answer. "I'll see you in the morning."

Before I do something really stupid, like climb into bed with her, I turn on my heel and go back to my bedroom, where I turn off the light, lie in bed, and stare up at the ceiling.

She's not supposed to see weakness in me.

She's not supposed to be scared of me.

She's not supposed to worry about me.

I'm fucking up. I have a job to do. Get Lilly Campbell to want to stay in our country and assume the throne. *And nothing about that means I have the right to touch her, let alone hold her.*

Get it the fuck together.

Chapter Eleven

LILLY

"Okay, where are we studying today?" I ask Keller, who's standing stoically in the living room.

He gestures to the dungeon—I mean lecture room. "Where we normally study."

"What?" I ask. "But . . . I thought after yesterday we were livening things up." I give my shoulders a slight shimmy.

"We'll be in the room, Lilly," he says, ignoring my shimmy and attempt to lighten the obvious morose mood he's in. "Let's get a move on."

Move on?

Okay, this morning when we were on our run and he was silent most of the time, I chalked it up to maybe a rough night of sleep and didn't bother him.

And at breakfast, when he didn't even look at me, I let him off easy, because maybe he was thinking about what we were going over today.

But now, no way, this is unacceptable.

I follow him into the room, and when he shuts the door, I spin on him, hands on my hips, and say, "What the hell is going on?"

"What do you mean?" he asks, still avoiding eye contact as he moves around the room.

"I mean, you're being weird and I want to know why."

"I'm not being weird, Lilly. Now take a seat, we have a lot to go over."

"Keller, will you just look at me?"

His shoulders drop and he lifts his head, his eyes meeting mine. "What?"

"Last night, we had fun, you even said you did. I thought we connected on a different level. And now, well . . . it feels like you're pulling away, and I don't know why. Did I do something wrong?"

"No. It's just time to get to work."

He's acting so cold, as if yesterday meant nothing. I don't get it. Was it because of his dream? Because he thought he hurt me?

"If you're worried about last night, your dream—"

"Lilly, I said let's get started."

"You didn't hurt me, Keller, see?" I show him my arms. "Totally fine."

"Sit down, Lilly."

"Or if you're embarrassed, don't be. I get night terrors too, it's totally—"

"I said, SIT DOWN," he shouts at me, his body now coiled with aggravation. "We're not talking about last night, we're not talking about my dream, and we're not talking about anything other than what I have planned. So, take a seat, shut your mouth, and just listen."

Oh.

No.

He.

Didn't.

154

⊏⊐

"HE'S AVOIDING ME, LARA," I say as we walk around the back of the castle.

"How's he avoiding you? He spent all morning in training with you."

"Yeah, in the stuffy room again, droning on like a boring lecturer. It's as if he locked up his personality. He's distant. I can feel it in his voice, in his body language. Not to mention he was a total asshole to me—I mean, cream of the crop, ripe for the picking, grade-A asshole." I lean in close to her and say, "He told me to shut my mouth five times. FIVE! It's a stark contrast from the man who told me about burning King Theo's penis with soup."

"He told you that?" Lara asks.

"Yes, and I swear to God, do not tell him I just told you that." I kick a loose rock on the ground. "Lara, he's pulling away, and I thought we'd made such great progress last night. Can one bad dream really change that?"

"Depends," Lara says. "If he felt you were getting too close, then, yes, that could change everything. Keller doesn't let a lot of people into his life. It's me, Brimar, and the king and queen. That's it. No one else. And even on that small list, there are things he doesn't tell us."

"So am I just supposed to sit back and let him retreat?"

"That also depends."

"Depends on what?" I ask.

"Your intentions with being here. If you're truly thinking about staying here, I believe there's some validity in you not letting him pull away, but if you're unsure, if there's a part of you that believes you'll be returning to Miami, then you need to let him pull away. You need to let him put distance there because he's doing it on purpose. He's guarding himself. So, if you're leaving at the end of this, let him guard himself."

"Ugh, Lara, you're a very smart woman, and that's annoying."

She chuckles. "I'm sorry."

I take a seat on the grass and bring my legs to my chest. "You know, when I said yes to all this training, I thought it was going to be different. Little less lecture-y and a little more fun. But it's just been one giant onslaught of information."

Ding.

"What was that?" Lara asks.

"My phone. It's a text message." I look at the screen and see that it's from Keller. Confused, I open the text thread.

Keller: *Forgot to send this to you this morning. Remember, this is confidential.*

Keller: *THE INFORMATIVE.*

I gasp out loud.

"What?" Lara asks. "Is everything okay?"

"Yes, it's from Keller. The Informative. I forgot about this. I'm sure you've read it already this morning."

"I have," Lara says.

"Well, excuse me while I delight myself in some gossip."

Keller: *THE INFORMATIVE. Known angler on the west was found philandering on another man's boat. Word on the street, he wasn't looking for extra bait, but rather the warmth of his opponent's wife. As for what will happen between the two, we're unsure at the moment, but fishing poles have been drawn and only time will tell whose bed the wife will choose. The harmony of the port rides on her decision.*

I set my phone down and look up at Lara. "Oh my God, an affair? Do you know who it is? Not that I would know the person if you told me their name, but still, do you know?"

She shakes her head. "No idea, but it's good to know if there's a supply shortage on cod this week, we'll know why."

"I guess so." I shake my head. "That's wild. From what Keller, you, and Brimar have told me about Torskethorpe, everyone seems to be so . . . perfect. But you're telling me there are people in this country jumping from boat to boat? Wow, just, wow."

"There's always gossip everywhere you go."

"I guess so."

Ding.

I glance down at my phone again and see another text from Keller.

Keller: *Lunch is ready.*

"Oh, lunch is ready." I stand from the grass, and together Lara and I head back toward the front door of the castle. Before we walk in, I turn toward Lara and say, "For what it's worth, I'm really trying to see if this is the right fit for me. I don't take this decision lightly, and getting to know Keller, I don't take that lightly either. I just thought you should know that."

Lara gives me a gentle smile. "I know your intentions are at their purest, you never have to worry about that with me. This is a big decision, and it'll take time. I get that. And I'm here to talk anything through, even those frustrations you have with Keller."

"Thank you." I spread my arms and pull her into a hug. "I'm really grateful for you, Lara."

She's stiff at first, but then she loops her arms around me and returns the hug. I don't hold on to her for too long, because it seems like hugs aren't her jam. Don't want to press my luck.

When we get inside, the boys greet us at the entryway. Keller's gargantuan frame blocks the doorway to the dining room, and when our eyes meet, I can sense he has something up his sleeve.

"Lilly, it's time you learn how to eat a simple meal, as a royal."

I groan. "Etiquette, again? You could have warned a girl." I turn to Lara. "Did you know about this?"

"Sort of." She cringes.

"And you didn't say anything to me?" I *tsk* at her. "Lara, us girls have to fucking stick together."

"No swearing," Keller's voice booms, startling me nearly out of my shoes.

"Jesus Christ," I say, clutching my chest. "Dude, we're right here, you don't need to shout."

"If you're going to step into this role, you need to start practicing now. No swearing, no *Jesus Christs*, and no inappropriate humor."

"Are you referencing my dick joke from earlier? That was to try to erase that scowl from your forehead."

"What was the joke?" Brimar asks, only for Keller to give him a scathing glare.

Ignoring Keller, I ask, "Why couldn't the lizard land a girlfriend?" When Brimar doesn't answer, I say, "Because he had reptile dysfunction."

Being the good man that he is, Brimar lets out a wallop of a laugh, while Lara chuckles next to me.

"See, they get it. This stone feature over here didn't even crack a smile," I say, referencing Keller.

"If you're done, I'd like to move on with lunch." Glad to see he's still the same asshole from this morning.

Keller moves to the side and gestures to a fully set dining table with multiple pieces of silverware, several drinking glasses, a folded napkin that resembles a fish, a plate on top of a plate, and candles.

"Um, what, uh . . . what is that decadence over there?" I point to the table. "That can't possibly be for lunch."

"You need to learn. Poor table manners reflect badly on the palace."

"Who says I have poor table manners?"

"You snorted out a cashew yesterday," Keller deadpans.

"Excuse me for enjoying a good chuckle while eating a meal."

"The cashew flew into my water."

"Oh my God, and I fished it out with my fork. No harm, no foul. Are you really still complaining about it? I told you I'd get you a new drink."

Calmly, Lara presses her hand to my shoulder and says, "I think Keller is just trying to help you out so when you do meet King Theo and Queen Katla, you feel prepared."

"Well, when you put it that way . . ." I move past Keller and into the dining room, where I choose the seat at the head of the table. Infuriating man. I thought we were friends last night. Well, he's definitely whipped away that thought.

Guess what? His loss, because I'm a freaking joy to be around.

Oh, and I'm really good in bed. Like phenomenal. And he threw away that chance as well—not that he was going to take it, because the man has will thicker than a freaking door to a bank vault.

Joining me in the dining room, Mr. Moody himself comes up behind my chair and helps me scoot it in, his hand briefly caressing my shoulder before he walks away.

What was that little touch? It causes me to look back at him. Rigid and prideful, he moves around the room with an air of arrogance, which is so annoyingly attractive to me that I feel the temperature in my body spike.

All from one single touch.

Damn him.

No, we're not heated and aroused. We're annoyed and angry.

"What are we having?" I ask, glancing around the table, trying to focus my mind on something else.

"A four-course meal," Keller answers as he comes up behind me once again. I try to look over my shoulder, to see what he's doing, but his hands connect with my head and he faces me forward. "Eyes ahead," he says in a commanding voice that speaks to my very soul. The kind of commanding tone that I find most effective in the bedroom. And, of course, my will is a blatant contrast to Keller's—it's a wisp of tissue paper—which is why I find myself listening, waiting for his next command. "Let's start with posture, shall we?" he says as he places something on my head.

"Hey, what's that?" I ask, trying to see.

"Don't. Move," he says, his voice like a crack of thunder.

It stills me.

It penetrates my soul.

It sends a flutter of chills over my arms.

Ooo, yes, say it again.

"I've set a plate holding a cup of water on your head. Anytime you slouch, lean too far forward, rest your arms on the table, or have any sort of improper posture, you *will* get wet."

Little does he know, I'm already wet.

When he releases the plate, letting me balance it on my own, his fingers glide over my shoulder, his touch like an aphrodisiac. I'm not sure why he keeps offering the small touches, especially after the way he shut down on me, but I'm going to shamelessly soak them all up.

"So, am I just supposed to eat like this?" I ask, feeling the weight of the challenge as I attempt to stay upright.

"Yes," Keller says while sitting next to me.

"But how am I supposed to lean forward to eat my food? I was always taught to eat while leaning over my plate to avoid messes."

"Are you an ape?" Keller asks me.

"Excuse me?"

"I asked, are you an ape?"

My eyes narrow as I keep my head still. "Do I look like a goddamn ape?"

Keller's fist slams on the table, rattling the glasses and startling me so much that I jump in my seat, jiggling the water and causing it to spill right into my lap. "No. Swearing," he says.

Drenched, water dripping down my face, the cup that once was on my head is now rolling along the floor. I glance up at Keller while brushing water out of my eyes. "Good golly, Miss Molly, you have some anger issues." I smile at him. "Is that better?"

"Yes. Now grab your cup so I can fill it up with water again."

I grab the cup, and Keller helps me place it back on my head while filling it up with water.

When he takes a seat, he asks again, "Are you an ape?"

Attempting the politest voice I can muster, I say, "Dear sir, does it look like I'm a hairy animal that picks ticks out of others' wiry hair?"

"You sure eat like one at times."

"Aren't you charming?"

Just then, Brimar brings in salads, beautifully arranged on plates that he sets in front of us. A spring mix is artfully arranged on the white plate, with a scattering of walnuts and an intricately cut pear fanned over the top.

"This looks great," I say. I go to reach for my fork, but I'm met with several options. "Uh, is this one of those things where you work your way in on the forks?"

"Fork closest to the plate is your salad fork. One in the middle is for dinner. The farthest fork is your fish fork."

"Oh shiii—uh, shoot." Keller stares me down. "I would've gotten that completely wrong. Good thing you're here." I pick up the fork closest to the plate and dive into my salad, only for Keller to slam his fist on the table again. I startle just enough for the water to fall on my lap. "What the hell was that for?" I ask, unable to control my swearing. The table slamming is uncalled for.

"You never eat until the king starts eating."

"What?" I brush water out of my eyes. "But the king isn't here."

"During this practice, I'm the king. Does it look like I'm eating?"

I remove my drenched napkin from my lap and dab at my face. "You know, that's information that could have been handed to me beforehand."

"You need to learn patience, and you need to learn to wait for your command." The way he says that almost feels as though he means it in a whole other way. And then it hits me like a ton of bricks. I know exactly what's going on with him right now.

This overbearing control freak that's sitting next to me, the same man who lay on the roof with me last night, isn't pulling away or being an asshole on purpose. No, he's trying to gain some semblance of control because he's spiraling.

I can see it in his eyes. The worry. The uneasiness. The need to stay focused on an immediate task in fear of the mind wandering. It's happened to me several times after a night-mare about my parents. This is his way of gaining control. He's grasping, reaching for anything to help him forget his thoughts from last night. It's why he's been short with me. It's why he's trying to control the situation now. He's in self-defense mode, and until his mind calms down, he's not going to get out of it.

This means one thing—I need to help.

"Uh, Keller," Lara says. "Maybe you're being a little tough on her. This is her first formal meal."

"No, Lara, that's okay," I say, holding up my hand and turning toward Keller. "If he wants me to wait for his command, I can be more than accommodating. I just wasn't aware that was what we were doing." I pick up my cup from the floor and place it on my head. "Fill me up, *sir.*" My eyes float to his, and I watch them turn dark as I sit tall, stretching my torso out, performing exactly the way he wants me to.

You want to forget, Keller? Well, sir, this is one way to do that.

"THANK YOU SO MUCH," I say to Brimar as he takes my dessert plate, which had held a decadent chocolate mousse. It took everything in me not to moan while I ate it.

Overall, eating with a steady hand and a stiff body takes a lot of energy, but it's doable. The hardest part of the meal was the soup. But the trick of it was, not to fill up the spoon and to ever so slightly lean at an angle, just in case you have a shaky hand.

After the initial two spills of water off my head, I held my composure the entire time, listening intently to Keller's instructions, waiting for him to show me what to do. And the more I obeyed him, the more his breath picked up. His chest filled out with pride, and the dangerous look in his eyes turned positively perilous.

The air grew thick.

Lara and Brimar ended up holding their own conversation on their side of the table. What I was doing was working.

While devouring my mousse, I put on a show for Keller, making sure to deliberately wrap my lips around my spoon and slowly pull it out while maintaining eye contact with him the whole time.

"So, does that conclude our meal for the day?" I ask, still holding up the water on my head.

"Yes," Keller says, his voice tight.

"Lovely." I remove the cup and set it on the table. "Now, if you'll excuse me, I'd like to go for another walk."

I stand from my chair and head toward the stairway so I can change, and over my shoulder, I ask, "Keller, will you be joining me?"

I hear Lara chuckle before she rises from the table and heads into the kitchen to help Brimar.

"If that's what you wish."

"Oh, it is."

And I can't wait to hear what he has to say to me when we're alone, without an audience watching our every interaction.

Hurrying up the stairs, I strip out of my clothes when I reach my bedroom, and I opt for a loose pair of sweatpants and a crop top. I search through my bras for something more comfortable when a thought pops up in my head. Maybe . . . we do no bra at all.

Cue evil grin

Oh yes, no bra is the perfect way to go with this long-sleeved crop top that's just loose enough that if I raise my hands, my underboob is exposed.

Yes, this is exactly what I need.

Keller will *rue* the day he tried to push me away after sharing a lovely evening. He has no idea who he's dealing with.

Once dressed, I brush my damp hair out and tie it into a bun on the top of my head, and then take a look at myself in the mirror. Perfect. Ready to go, I jog down the stairs to where Keller is standing, hands in his black jean pockets, watching my every move.

I pat him on the chest as I walk by and say, "All dry now, but I'm sure you'll have no qualms getting me wet again, right?" I wink at him, and he catches what I mean.

"Lilly," he says in a warning tone.

"Just slipping my shoes on." When I finish tying them, I reach for the door, but Keller beats me to it. Acting like the perfect gentleman, he opens the door widely for me, and as I walk past him, I feel his hand on my lower back as he follows closely behind, shutting the door after him. I try—*desperately*—not to react to his warm hand on my skin.

When outside, instead of going to the left like we always do, I go to the right.

"That's not where we normally walk," he says.

"I know. I want some new scenery. Plus, didn't you say there were hot springs up this way?"

"We're not going in the hot springs."

"Okay, Keller." Smiling up at him, I walk ahead and hold my arms out as I spin around. "Isn't it beautiful out?" I ask. When I fix my eyes back on him, he's not looking at my face, but rather my torso. I inwardly smile. "The perfect time for a walk." Walking backwards, I keep my eyes on his as I stretch my arms above my head and say, "Feels good to just stretch out, you know?"

He pauses mid-stride, no longer following me.

"Everything okay?" I blink innocently at him.

"Lilly, what the fuck are you doing?"

"Stretching, what does it look like?"

"It looks like after that display at the table, you're continuing your goal to provoke me."

"Is it working?" I smile at him.

"You know damn well it is."

Ooo, I did not expect him to be so honest about it.

Nor did I expect him to be so angry, but in a hot way, like he's about to devour me kind of way.

And as he closes the space between us, his strides eating up the distance, I realize that maybe I've provoked him a little too much.

I think we can all safely agree that my plan to get him to think about something other than his dream has worked, but it also might have backfired, from the looks of it.

When he reaches me, his hands fall to my hips as he holds me tight. His large body shadows me, enveloping me in his strength.

"That display back there was pathetic," he says.

Pathetic? Here I thought he was just about to ravish me, not insult me.

"Excuse me? I think I did a pretty good job."

"Not for the right reason. You were behaving because you were trying to get under my skin. You weren't trying because you want to do this for the country. And now, with this shirt?" His hands travel up my ribcage, and the feel of his large palms against my skin squeezes all the air out of my lungs. "You don't care about this country, this role, you just care about falling into my bed."

My eyes narrow. "That's not true. I care——"

His hands slide up even higher, his thumbs just below my breasts now.

"All you want is to get under my skin." He lowers his head so his lips are at my ear, as his thumbs stroke the underside of my breasts, causing me to nearly melt in his grasp. "Guess what, Lilly. You've been under my goddamn skin since the moment you showed up at the Moxy in that dress. You don't have to keep trying, you're there. You're buried in my goddamn veins, pumping my blood, causing me to go fucking crazy in my head because I've never wanted to fuck a woman as much as I want to fuck you."

His nose caresses my cheek as I attempt to not faint from his confession. Well, this has taken a delicious turn.

What I wouldn't give to be fucked by him—*controlled* by him. Possessed. Just like the way he's holding me now. I want more of it, I want him to tell me how he wants me, what he wants me to do, where he wants me.

I want to feel his lips on my body, his scruff on my skin, his hands feeling up my small breasts.

"Then fuck me," I say.

"That's exactly what I'm *not* going to do," he says, dropping his hands from my ribs. "Because you aren't here to be fucked by me, Lilly. I wouldn't be doing my job if I spent the amount of time I want to spend, spreading your legs and burying my cock inside your sweet pussy. And my job, to prepare you for a possible future role here, is paramount. I refuse to be sidetracked or seen as a joke."

He pushes me away as a gasp falls past my lips, a stark chill running up my spine. *A joke? Sidetracked?*

Turned on, irritated, and ready to maul the man, I ask, "Why can't it be both ways? Why can't we do both? We clearly want each other. Why are you denying it?"

"Because once you're in my bed, I won't be able to let you out. Because I have less than two fucking months to get you ready to be a queen. Because when it comes down to it, there's royalty in your blood, not in mine."

"Who cares about that?"

"Everyone," he shouts, holding his arms out. "You don't get it. You grew up in America, it's different there. There's an expectation of royalty here, and when it comes down to it, there's a definitive class difference between you and me. So, I'm not going to go there with you, Lilly. I'm not going to torture myself with a taste of you, knowing it'll go nowhere."

I fold my arms over my chest and look away. The wind picks up around us, rustling the tall grass. "So, what you're telling me is this. If I accept the line of succession, I won't be able to choose who I want to be with?"

He grips his hair. "You can, you always have a choice, but choosing someone like me is not a choice you should be making."

Fire fumes through me as I step up to him. "Why don't you let me worry about what choice I should and should not be making?" And then I turn on my heel and start walking away from the castle once again.

Insufferable man.

Chapter Twelve

KELLER

My phone buzzes next to me on the nightstand, stirring me awake. When I see the palace number on my screen, I quickly answer it despite the early morning hour and the lack of sleep from the night before.

"Hello?" I say into the phone, thankful the curtains of my bedroom have blocked the light from the sun.

"Keller," Theo says. "My boy, how are you?"

"Good," I say, whispering and getting out of bed. I throw on a pair of shorts and sneak out of my room and down the stairs. Not wanting to wake anyone up, I exit the front door and shut it behind me. "It's early for you."

"Yes, it is, but I didn't get much sleep last night. There's been another leak."

"What?" I hiss into the phone. "What was it?"

"They dropped her name. Lilly Campbell."

"Fuck," I mutter as I press my fingers to my forehead. "How did you find out?"

"Henrik has been doing a wonderful job, stepping into your role while you've been gone. He has sources outside the palace who informed him of the drop this morning."

"Wait, Henrik knows?"

"Yes, I had to tell him. What was I going to say you were doing for two months?"

"Theo, he could be the leak."

Theo lightly coughs into the phone and then says, "No, it's not him."

"How can you be certain?"

"Keller"—his deep voice rings through the phone—"if I tell you it's not him, it's not. Understood?"

"Yes, sorry," I say, still pinching my brow. "So, when everyone wakes up this morning, that's what the news will be?"

"Yes. Local news, at the moment. Outlets have asked for the palace to comment and we haven't said anything. We aren't confirming or denying."

"But it doesn't matter, they're going to figure it out, and once they do, there's no chance in hell Lilly will have a normal life after this."

"Well, it's not global, so it's not like people in Miami know," Theo says. "You act as if she's second-guessing her decision to step into this role."

"She hasn't committed, Theo," I say quietly. "She's still . . . fuck, she's still trying to comprehend the shock of it all. I'm trying, I really am, but I don't want to push her too hard."

"Keller, we don't have a choice. You either push her, or we give up our country."

"I know . . . I know, but . . . she's scared, Theo. I see her masking her fear, but it's there. She needs more comfort."

"Then offer her the comfort she needs."

"I—I can't," I say, the strain in my voice easily detectable.

"Why not?" he asks and then, "Wait . . ."

I squeeze my eyes shut.

Fuck, he knows.

How could he not? It's not as if I'm playing it cool on my end. But I'm tired. I'm so goddamn tired of trying to mask how I feel for her. Trying to act as though I don't want to touch her even though that's *all* I want. Like yesterday, even though I was reeling from my dream, I couldn't help but touch her any chance I could, even if it was a swipe of my finger over her shoulder. And that crop top, fuck me, I wanted to lift it up over her head and feast on her tits. My self-control is wearing thinner with every second I'm around her, and it's showing.

"Keller, is there something going on between you two?" Theo asks.

"No," I say quickly. "No, nothing is happening between us." That's true, nothing's actually happened . . . yet.

"Do you want something to happen?" he asks. I swallow, not responding right away, and that's all it takes. "You like her."

I heave a heavy sigh and say, "I don't want to."

"Why?"

"Theo, let's not get into this."

"No, let's." His cough erupts through the phone. "Tell me why she's not good enough for you."

"Not good enough for me?" I ask. "Theo, I'm not good enough for her."

"Where did you get that idea?"

I pace the front of the castle, the sharp sun beaming against my naked chest. "I'm here to serve Torskethorpe, to help protect the crown. That's my responsibility, that's what I was born to do. She's above that—"

"Do I not serve this country?" he asks. "That's what my entire life has been dedicated to doing, serving this country. Just because my blood is different from yours doesn't make you any less important. Let me ask you this, if you offered her comfort, would she take it?"

Yes.

With open arms.

I'm pretty sure she was following my every command yesterday just to turn me on.

It worked.

"That doesn't matter," I say. "I don't want to sway her decision in any way."

"I appreciate your noble attempt to be a good man. I've taught you well. But please do me a favor." Theo catches his breath. "If she needs comfort, if she needs a shoulder, please offer her what she needs. She's had a lot of loss in her life, the type of loss you can understand."

I push my hand through my hair. "Yeah, I know."

"I know you're doing a lot, but I need you to offer her everything she needs to make the right decision that will sway her to stay. Okay?"

"Okay."

But here's the rub—I doubt Theo understands that *offering her a shoulder to lean on* isn't the same as taking her from behind over the couch in her bedroom. *Offering her everything she needs* isn't making her kneel before me so she can take my cock down her throat. Contrary to what Lilly implied, giving in to our sexual urges wasn't as uncomplicated as she thought. And yet, I said okay to my king.

"Thank you. I know I'm asking a lot of you." *More than you imagine.*

"You're asking me to do my job," I answer. "But I need to know, what are we doing, moving forward? I know she wants to speak with you."

"And I desperately want to speak with her as well. I'm cautious, though, with the news spreading and not knowing who the leak is. I'm afraid if I speak with her, people will start to seek her out. We want to keep her safe. And safe right now is keeping her secluded in Harrogate as she tries to decide what she's going to do. If we bring her here, she'll be subjected to a life it seems she's not ready for."

"I believe you're right. As much as I would like to get out of Harrogate and move her into the palace, she's not ready. Not even close."

"Then in Harrogate she will stay. But I need you to keep me updated as to how she's feeling. Only then will we be able to move forward." He pauses for a second and then says, "Keller?"

"Yes?"

"What's she like?"

A stupid smile spreads across my face. "A spitfire, doesn't take any shit, and is a royal pain in the ass."

Theo lets out a boisterous laugh. "Then she very much has the Strom blood in her."

That she does.

We say our goodbyes, and when I hang up the phone and step into the castle, I'm greeted by Brimar, with a worried look on his face.

"Is everything okay?"

"No," I answer. "Lilly's name has been dropped, and it's going to be all over the news this morning."

Brimar winces while looking around. "Are they calling us to Strombly?"

I shake my head. "No, we're to stay put."

Brimar's brows draw together. "How can that be? Does King Theo truly believe we're safer here than behind palace walls?"

"He does because she hasn't committed to a decision yet. She's yet to decide if taking on the role of a monarch is something she wants to commit her life to. If we take her to Strombly, then she'll be subjected to a life she's not ready for," I whisper, not wanting my voice to carry.

"Well, we can't stay here forever," Brimar whispers back.

"Keeping her safe here in Harrogate is temporary. The public will find out."

"I know. But I don't want to push her. There's a fine line, Brimar. She doesn't deserve unnecessary pressure to make a decision."

"I think you need to set aside your feelings for her and think of this country."

"I *am* thinking of this country," I snap back at him. "That's why I'm not pushing her. She needs to love this country at her own pace, not because I'm pressuring her."

"What's going on?" Lilly asks as she steps out onto the balcony of the stairs, rubbing one of her eyes with her palm, looking fresh from her bed. "I heard whisper-shouting, and whisper-shouting can only mean one thing, that you're attempting to make sure I don't figure out what you're whisper-shouting about."

"We're just discussing safety protocols," I say.

Brimar gives me a look, and then with frustration, he pushes past me, saying, "I'm going to go work out."

When he's out of the entryway, Lilly asks, "What kind of safety protocols?"

I walk up the stairs, joining her. "Nothing you need to worry about." When I reach her, I ask, "Are you ready for our run?"

Her shoulders slump and she leans against the balcony rail. "Why do you need to torture me? Can we skip it today? Do something other than mindless running and stale lectures? Just have a fun day? Please?"

Offer her comfort.

This is what Theo's talking about. If I continue to push her too hard without meeting her needs, she's going to shut down and want to return to Miami. The pressure of having to convince her to stay and train her at the same time is overwhelming, but maybe letting up, giving her a break, would be best for both of us. Ultimately, we need Lilly to love this country, not just know its history. We need her to love who we are, where we are, and want to stay because what's in her blood is calling to her to stay. *Not just know the history until her ears bleed, Keller.*

"What did you have in mind?" I ask her.

She perks up. "Wait, really?" Her surprised expression is comical. Maybe I should lighten up more if she's this shocked.

"Depends. What do you want to do?"

"Uh . . . well, I wasn't thinking you were going to say yes, so I'm unprepared." She taps her chin. "Let's see, well, I definitely want to go to the hot springs."

"Lilly, I don't know—"

"Please." She comes up to me and tugs on my hand. "On the way you can quiz me about etiquette. I know how much you love to hammer knowledge into me." Smirking, she adds, "If only you were hammering something else into me."

"Easy," I say, causing her to laugh.

"And then maybe we can make bread or something."

"Bread?" My brows draw together.

"Yes, that kitchen just seems like it was made to bake bread. It doesn't have to be bread, though. It can be a specialty of Torskethorpe. Something people love eating."

"Vinatarte," I answer.

"Yes, that. We can make that. And then, after we bake, maybe we can just relax and play a game. Any games your country likes to play?"

"Crazy cods."

"Crazy cods?" She chuckles. "What's that?"

"Like crazy eights, but with a special deck of cards."

"Yes, count me in. That sounds like fun. And the whole time, if you want to teach me things, you can, but let's make it fun and not a lecture." She steps up to me and places her hands on my arms. "We need to loosen you up a bit. You're so tense and cranky with me all the time. Stop being cranky."

I'm cranky because I want you and don't think I can have you.

"I'm not cranky, just . . . alert."

"Well, after yesterday, this will be good for us. So, we can do it? Hot springs, baking, and then cards?"

"Yes," I answer.

With an excited cheer, she throws her arms around my torso and squeezes me tight, her head pressed against my chest. "Thank you."

Not sure what to do, I gently put one arm around her and pat her back.

"Ooo." She shivers. "Don't give me all your affection at once. I'm not sure I'll be able to take it." She pulls away and claps her hands together. "Okay, what should I change into for the hot springs?"

"Whatever you want," I say. "I'm going to let Lara and Brimar know the plan and then grab us some breakfast to go."

"Sounds perfect. And, Keller?"

"Yeah?" I ask as I start to head down the stairs.

"Thank you. I'm really excited."

———

"I DEFINITELY THINK these springs are farther than the ten minutes you claimed them to be," Lilly says as she walks next to me, her tits freely bouncing in the tight-fitted shirt she decided to put on.

When she met me at the front door, my tongue nearly fell out of my mouth when I caught sight of what she was wearing, or what she wasn't wearing.

Nipples hard, piercings on full display, no bra in sight, she jogged down the stairs in a pair of sweatpants that cinched around her waist and her shirt showing an inch of her midriff. Sure, the dress she wore at the Moxy was sexier, but this . . . this has me itching all over.

"Are you sure you've been to these springs before?"

"Yes," I answer. "They're just past that rock formation right up ahead."

"You better be right about that, Fitzy. Which, by the way, I meant to ask you . . . Fitzwilliam, that feels like a very English name, and I know Torskethorpe has a heavy British influence, hence all the British accents, but a lot of your names seem to have a more Scandinavian feel. Tell me how you have a well-known last name belonging to a British aristocrat."

"British aristocrat? Wait, are you speaking of Mr. Darcy?"

"Uh, yeah."

"You do realize his last name is Darcy, right? First name Fitzwilliam."

"Nu-uh." She pauses and then says, "Wait . . . is it?"

"Yes." I chuckle. "His last name is Darcy. That's why they call him *Mr.* Darcy."

"Huh, I guess you're right. For a second, I was thinking they called him Mr. Darcy out of respect. You know how parents will introduce you to an adult and be like, 'Now, Wally, this is Mommy's friend, Mr. Matt.' You know what I'm talking about?"

"Yes, but that's not the case in this situation. His actual name is Fitzwilliam."

"Either way, it still has that British feel to it. Was your dad British?"

"He was," I answer.

If I want her to feel comfortable, I need to open up to her, even though that's not something I generally do. With anyone. The only people I talk to are my core four: Brimar, Lara, Theo, and Katla. I hold anyone else at an arm's length—like I've attempted to do with Lilly—but it seems as though that's going to be impossible.

I should've known that from the moment I saw her spraying down people on the side of the street.

She's different.

She's the kind of person who will bury a piece of them in

your heart and leave it there, never wanting it back, never asking for more in return.

"He was? What was his name?"

"Roy," I answer.

"Did he look just like you?"

"No." I shake my head. "He had pitch-black hair and dark brown eyes. I have his build, but I look like my mum. She's from here. When I was five, they wanted to be closer to family, so they moved to Torskethorpe. My mum was the first to get a job in the palace as the curator for prints and drawings. Any picture you see in Strombly, my mum most likely touched. And then my dad followed shortly after her, getting a job as the royal pastry chef."

"Wow, do you have any of their talents? Can you draw? Can you bake?"

"I can sketch, yes," I answer. "I don't put the time into it to actually be good. It's more of a hobby. As for baking, I know how to make a few things."

"He bakes and he draws." She shakes her head. "A lethal combination. Toss that around with your impeccable body and mediocre looks and—"

"Mediocre? You better be fucking joking."

She laughs. "And he jokes around too. Ugh, a real catch." Lilly pauses just as we reach the rock formation and gasps as she catches sight of the steam rising from the ground. "Oh my God, is that it?"

"Yup," I answer.

She grabs my hand and tugs me toward the water, excitement radiating off her.

"Ahh, this is so cool." She squats down and touches the water with her hand, only to turn her shocked eyes on me. "It's so warm. We need to get in."

"Wait . . . what?"

Before I can ask her what she's doing, she kicks off her shoes and socks and pushes her pants down, revealing a black thong that clings tightly to her hips, and when she turns around, her back to me, my eyes are glued to her ass. Her pert, round, fucking perfect ass.

"Lilly," I groan.

"What?" she asks. "It's hot springs time. Strip down, Fitzy." And then she pulls her shirt over her head and drops it to the ground with the rest of her clothes. She wraps her arm over her breasts and then turns toward me, covering herself so I don't see anything, but I'm teased to the point of getting hard. "Uh, you still have clothes on." When I don't move, she rolls her eyes. "Am I going to have to strip you down myself?"

"No," I say quickly.

She snaps at me. "Then get with it. It's not like I haven't seen you in your underwear before. Stop being shy. Plus, I'm going to need your help navigating my entry into this thing."

Knowing I'm not getting out of this, I reach over my head, pull my shirt up and over my body, and drop it with her clothes.

"Oh, yeah, take it off," she hollers, causing me to give her a menacing stare. It does nothing but make her laugh.

I finish removing my clothes, leaving just my briefs on, and then move to the hot spring.

"You know, you have a really nice ass," she says. "This guy doesn't skip out on his squats."

I glance over my shoulder at her teasing grin, and because she's one of few who can loosen me up, I say, "I could say the same about you."

Her eyes soften before her smile grows even wider. "Oh my God, people, did you hear that? Keller Fitzwilliam likes my ass."

"Can you contain yourself, please?"

"Never." She winks.

I squat down to the water and then sink in, feeling the ground beneath me.

"Is it deep?" she asks. "I mean, I like it deep, but I just need to prepare myself."

"You realize that's not how a queen speaks."

"As far as you know." Her arm still wrapped around her breasts, she moves toward the edge of the springs and then sits on her butt, dipping her legs in the water. "Oh God, you're going to have to excuse me if I moan."

"Great," I say sarcastically.

"Give me your hand, help a lady out."

"From what flies out of your mouth, I wouldn't say you classify as a lady."

"What about a lady of the night?" She wiggles her brows.

"That feels more accurate." I take her hand in mine and then help her in, only for her to trip on God knows what and fall forward, straight into my arms.

Her tits press against my bare chest.

Her hard-as-shit nipples rub against my skin.

The cold steel of her piercings causes my entire body to break out into a sweat despite being in a pool of warm water.

"Oh, dear heavens," she says, gripping me by the shoulders. "We, uh . . . we're touching."

"We are," I say past a tight jaw.

"My boobs are against your manliness."

"Yup. Are you intending to remove them?"

"I am . . . I am, just trying to figure out how to do this in a classy way."

"There's no classy way of getting out of this. Just pull away."

"Okay. I'm going to count to three."

"There's no need to count. Just pull away."

"But counting feels right. A finality to these unforeseen circumstances."

"There could have been a finale several seconds ago," I huff out, praying to fucking God she doesn't feel how hard I am.

179

"Right, right. Okay, on three." She takes a deep breath. "We shall part."

"Just count."

Her eyes meet mine. "We part on three, not after. Right on three."

"Jesus, fuck," I say as I push her away, sending her to the other side of the spring.

"That wasn't on three."

"Yeah, well, you were taking too fucking long," I say, getting as far away as I can, my cock straining for her.

"Excuse me for attempting to be graceful." She reaches up to her ponytail, undoes her hair, and then dips her head back into the water. When she lifts, she looks like a goddamn wet dream—her skin wet, her tits just below the surface of the water, her expression completely relaxed.

It's too much to fucking bear, especially after the rubdown I just received from her nipple piercings.

With both hands, I cover my face and groan.

"What's wrong? Step on something wrong? An unexpected jagged rock, perhaps?"

"No." I lean my head back against the edge of the spring and close my eyes. If I close my eyes, then I won't be tortured.

"Then what was it?" I hear her still. "Oh God, is there an eel in here? Ready to snap my nips off?"

"For fuck's sake, no. Just . . . just relax."

"You promise there are no eels?"

"There are no eels."

"Okay." She shifts against the mud wall and rests her head. There, see, with my eyes closed and her far away, this will be completely fine. "Mmm," she moans. "This feels so good."

Or maybe not.

My eyes slide open and I catch her lift up . . . and my eyes fall to her naked breasts. It's the smallest glimpse, but that's all it takes. They're imprinted in my brain. Small, pink nipples with barbells horizontally through them, the tiniest of swells, just enough for a palmful.

I'm tempted.

I'm turned on.

My cock surges in my briefs, begging for more, begging for release from the pent-up tension I've been dealing with ever since I've met this woman. And given the lack of privacy, I've only been able to jack off once—in the shower—and it did nothing for the yearning I have.

I want to fuck her.

I want to see what it feels like to have her pussy wrapped around me.

I want to see her cheeks flush, her chest writhe as I pound into her, relentlessly.

"Uh . . . Keller, you kind of have this murderous look in your eyes. Now, as someone who finds that whole possessive murder look enticing, I'm okay with it, but you know, on the off chance that maybe you're actually considering murder, can I ask what's wrong beforehand?"

"You, that's what's wrong."

"Ah, I see. Let me guess—naked woman, possible boob show, hard penis? Am I right?"

Once again, she knows exactly what she's doing. I should've known.

"You think this is funny, don't you?"

"No. It's not funny. If I had it my way, you wouldn't be over there, growling under your breath, and I wouldn't be over here, accidentally showing you my boobs. If I had it my way, you'd be pinning me against this muddy wall, sucking on my tits, while your fingers drive deep inside of me, fucking me until I come."

I can practically taste her, the picture she painted like a 3D movie in my head.

"But you know . . . we're not going there," she says in a man's voice.

She's right, unfortunately.

"We *aren't* going there. So, please keep your tits under the water."

Smiling, she pops up out of the water and points to her breasts. "These tits?"

"Fucking hell, Lilly," I groan, covering my eyes again. "Jesus."

She just laughs. "Come on, they're just boobs. It's not like you haven't seen your fair share of them."

"They're not just tits, Lilly. They're *your* tits, there's a difference."

"I don't know, they seem normal to me." She floats toward me.

"What are you doing?"

"Showing you how normal they are," she says as she stands in front of me, lifting her chest up. She cups one of her breasts, letting her nipple piercing float by her fingers. My teeth pull on my bottom lip as I watch intently, my hand itching to touch my aching cock. "See? Normal."

"They're anything but normal," I say, plastering my hands behind my back so I don't touch her.

"Then what are they?"

"Let's not do this, Lilly. It's not going to lead to anything good."

"Or will it?" She takes another step closer. "Just play with me a bit. It's all innocent."

"The thoughts in my head are anything but innocent."

"Okay, how about this? For each thing I list off about proper etiquette at the table, you tell me what you like about my boobs. That way we're both learning and having fun." I look away and she pokes me. "Come on, we're in this beautiful hot spring, surrounded by rocks and the coastline, not a soul in sight. This is what fantasies are made of."

No, your tits are what fantasies are made of.

"Please." She pouts.

Fuck. I can't say no to her, not when she's looking at me like that, with those doe-eyes.

"Fine," I grumble.

"Oh, please, don't sound too excited." She chuckles. "Okay. I'm going to keep count on my hand of the things I list off. Ready?"

"Sure."

"First thing's first, we don't sit down until King Theo sits down. Once seated, my napkin is picked up from the left and draped over my lap. Spine straight, shoulders pulled back, chin parallel to the table. Never talk about myself, always talk about the people next to me. Research whom I'm sitting next to beforehand and have insightful questions to ask. When the food arrives, don't take a bite until King Theo takes a bite. When taking a drink, we silently sip and we always drink from the exact same spot to avoid lipstick getting all over the rim. When wiping my mouth with my napkin, I dab with one finger in the napkin and fold so no food shows on the cloth. Hmm, what else . . ." She smirks.

"I think that's enough."

"But I haven't gone into the proper usage of spoons, forks, cutting, what to do when you don't like something, how to sip soup—"

"I believe your knowledge of table etiquette is well-versed, and there's no need to dive any deeper."

"If you say so." Her evil grin spreads across her face. "Well, from what I counted, that's ten things you have to say about my boobs. Do you need to see them again so you can write sonnets about their beauty?" She lifts up one more time, and I watch as water drips down her chest, over her breasts, and back into the spring. They're the breasts that men of years ago painted. Wrote sonnets about. And it's why the poet within me has a plethora of words to describe them.

I wet my lips, and in a steady voice, I say, "They look luxuriously soft, like the finest cashmere. They're full but small, a great fit for my palm. Pale, with the most addictively attractive nipples I've ever seen. Nipples that make my mouth whimper with need." She heaves a heavy sigh as she comes forward some more, leaving very little space between us. And then she reaches out to my arm and tugs on it, loosening my hand from my back. When she brings my palm to her breast, I let her, because I can't fucking stop her. I don't want to. I want to feel her.

I cup her breast and groan as my thumb rubs across her nipple. "Tits made for a goddess, smooth, curved, responsive." I roll her nipple piercing between my fingers and she moans as her head falls back. "Tight, high, unmeasurable, incomparable . . . feminine." So goddamn hot.

"Keller," she whispers as I cup her breast harder. Shit, I need to stop. I don't think this is the comfort Theo was talking about but, hell, I've dreamed of what it would feel like to hold her tits in my hand, and now that it's happening, I'm having a hard time letting go. "When you play with my nipples like that," she hums, her chest lifting as her hands sift through her wet hair, "you make me want so much more."

One taste.

Just lean forward once and take her tit in your mouth.

You know you want to.

I wet my lips, my body barely leaning forward, my mind at war with itself.

"Yes," she says, encouraging me, her chest now rising and falling more rapidly.

Fuck, this is getting out of hand.

Before I can stop myself, I take a deep breath and reluctantly remove my hand and tuck it away behind my back.

Her eyes pop open in protest. "What are you doing?" she asks.

I swallow hard as I try to gain control of my tongue. "That was, uh, that was more than ten descriptions. I held up my end of the bargain."

Still breathing heavily, her eyes heady, she asks, "You're just going to end it like that?"

"Yes, that was the deal."

"But . . . you turned me on."

"Welcome to my hell, Lilly. I'm fucking turned on every goddamn time I'm around you."

"You know there's a way to fix that."

"Yes, I'm aware." I blow out a heavy breath. "But once again, we're not going there, so change the subject, and sit over there." I point to the other end of the spring.

"I don't want to sit over there. I'd rather sit on your lap."

"Lilly, I'm going to fucking lose it."

"Really? Does that mean you'll drop your incessant need to ignore the fact that we're both attracted to each other and finally take me the way you want?"

I pinch my brow and shake my head. "No. I'll storm away and put an end to this day. Go back to lectures."

"Urgh." She grumbles something under her breath and goes to the other side of the hot spring. "What now? Are we going to play another game?"

"No, we're going to sit in silence."

"Wow, you sure know how to carry on the fun." Her voice is drenched in sarcasm.

I can understand the frustration. I'm frustrated too.

She settles against the wall, but instead of keeping her chest under the water, she lifts her shoulders over the edge of the spring and sticks her chest in the air as she looks up to the sky.

Jesus Christ. Why did I think bringing her here was going to be a good idea?

I look away, but it takes all of two seconds before my eyes feast on her chest. And she knows it, because the smile that crosses her sexy lips is more than evil.

It's downright sinister.

"LAST TIME I WORE AN APRON, I didn't wear anything else under it," Lilly says as she ties an apron around her waist. "Should I do that now too?"

"No," I practically growl at her, causing her to chuckle.

"So grumpy. Are you still mad about having to walk back to the castle with a semi-hard-on?"

"I'm not sure you understand how painful that is."

"When you start having period cramps, then you can talk to me about pain. Your half-hard dick really gives me no concern."

She has a point.

After the heightened sexual awareness settled in the hot springs, we put our clothes back on over our wet bodies and made the trek back to the castle. Instead of trying to bombard her with more knowledge about Torskethorpe, I asked her to play twenty questions with me, but we shortened the game to ten questions and kept it to only celebrities. We both won two rounds, tying. The games mellowed her out and lightened me up. By the time we reached Harrogate, there wasn't much anger between us, but we were more at ease, which has carried into the kitchen, thankfully.

"Let's focus on baking." I place a bowl on the counter.

"I'd love to." She claps her hands together. "What should we do first?"

I hate admitting this, but I also think there's another reason we're both in a better mood. When we got back to Harrogate, we took turns showering. While Lilly was in the shower, I huddled in the corner of my room and rubbed one out, because despite being able to get back to the castle without my dick falling off, there was no way I'd be able to continue the day without relieving myself after the tit show in the hot spring.

And I'm almost positive from the smirk on her face and

the buzzing sound I heard while I was showering, she did the same.

Now, the air between us is light and breezy. Not tension-filled.

"We need to heat up the prunes," I say as I take out a saucepan and put it on the stove. I bring the pot filler from the wall and fill it up. "Grab the prunes for me."

Lilly grabs the box of prunes from the island and brings them over.

"You can dump the box in there."

"Okay." She opens the box and shakes the prunes into the water, letting some of the contents splash out. "Oops, sorry."

"It's okay. Now we're going to let that cook for about thirty minutes or until the water is evaporated."

"Lovely. Now what?"

"We make the dough."

Together, we add ingredients into two separate bowls, one dry, one wet, and I offer her direction that she takes easily, and we move seamlessly through the kitchen, almost like we've been doing this together for years.

"That's good, see how the dough has pulled off the side of the bowl clean?"

"Yeah," she says as I stand behind her.

"That means it's ready to be rolled and cut. Let's take the dough out." But she doesn't move. Instead, she turns around and leans against the countertop, her wary eyes meeting mine. "What's wrong?"

"You just said *rolled and cut.*"

"Yes . . . is that a problem?"

"No, I just . . ." She shakes her head. "Wow, I just had this memory flash through my mind, almost like déjà vu. When you said *it's ready to be rolled and cut*, that . . . that reminded me of a time when I was really young and baking with my mom. It was around Christmas. But we were making something called . . ." She presses her hand to her forehead. "God, she

187

called it cardamom cake. It was layers of cake and a mixture for between the layers." Her eyes turn to mine. "This feels so familiar."

Smiling softly, I say, "Because that's what we're making. Queen Katla always called it cardamom cake because she wanted to remind people that she loved more cardamom than cinnamon in the filling mixture."

"Wait, seriously?" Lilly asks.

"Yeah. So, you've made this before."

"Yeah." Her eyes well up. "My mom loved this cake. Every holiday, she would make it. Even Easter, which would make my dad mad because he loved lemon cake on Easter. Not my mom, though. She hung tight to her real love, cardamom." She smiles softly as a tear falls past her eyelid and down her cheek.

"Hey, come here," I say, pulling her against my chest and offering her a hug. Her arms wrap around my waist and her head presses against my chest. I smooth my hand over her hair and say, "This was my dad's favorite Christmas cake as well. He made several for the palace holiday party, and then when he got home, he'd make one for just our little family of three. He never got tired of making it."

"I had no idea, this is . . . this is special, Keller. This is what I was hoping for, this sort of connection with my mom. I wonder what else is a part of my childhood that comes from Torskethorpe that was just normal to me?" She glances around the kitchen. "She used to always make this carrot and beef stew."

"With celery and fennel?" I ask.

"Yes," she says, her eyes wide.

"Theo's favorite soup. It's not a tradition of Torskethorpe, but it's very much a Strom tradition."

"She always served it in brown crocks."

I smile at her, then move to a cabinet by the stove and pull down a brown crock bowl. "Like this?"

Her hands go to her mouth as she walks up to me to get a better look. "Holy shit," she says before taking it. "Keller, this is . . . this is exactly what she would use, and then she'd put those oyster—"

"Crackers over the top."

More tears stream down her face, and I gather her in my arms again, letting her have this moment. After what seems like a few minutes, I lift her chin to look her in the eyes. "There's so much more to come. Harrogate has rarely been used by Theo and Katla, but there will be so much more at Strombly, where your mother grew up. So many more memories, I'm sure."

"When do we get to go there?" She wipes at her eyes.

"When Theo thinks the time is right. Things are complicated right now. He's trying to protect you."

"I understand." She takes a deep breath. "Okay, sorry. I didn't mean to get emotional on you. I just, wow, I wasn't expecting to have a wave of memories hit me like that. I have very little from my childhood. After the estate sale to help pay off my parents' debts, I've sort of forgotten about the material things that were part of my childhood."

"No, it's fine. We lost everything in the fire, so I know how you feel." I give her another hug. "I'm here for you, Lilly."

She smiles. "Thank you." She takes a deep breath, claps her hands together, and says, "Now, let's roll this dough out." She turns back around and picks up the rolling pin. "I'd prefer if you lean over and help me."

"Like this?" I ask as I move my arms around her body and grip the rolling pin with her, my chest to her back, my head next to hers.

"Yes, like that." I can't see her smile, but I can feel it.

I've tasted this woman in my arms. This temptress. Vixen. This spitfire. She's pushed and prodded, determined to crack my self-control, and fuck did I want to make her come in the hot springs. And even though in this moment she has me exactly where she wants me, our confessions only moments ago have created a deeper, undeniable connection.

Despite Theo's words, though, my blood being different does make me different. *And I'd do well to not ignore that.* I'd do well to keep her at arm's length, but she's slowly pushing forward, taking up too much space in my head.

⸺

"THIS WAS DELICIOUS," Lara says from the kitchen. "I think the best I've ever had."

"Hey," Brimar shouts from where he's doing dishes, causing us to laugh.

"Yours is good too," she shouts and then quietly says, "The filling was so much smoother than his."

Chuckling, Lilly pulls her legs up to her chest as we sit next to the fireplace on a blanket she laid out for both of us. "What did you think of the cardamom cake?" I ask her.

"It was perfect." She stares off at the flames. Since her revelation in the kitchen, she's been very subdued. There's been no pestering, no teasing, no pressing her luck with me. She's been quiet, actually, with not much to say. Even through dinner, when she's normally joking around with all of us, she rather focused on her etiquette that she's mastered quite quickly and then retired to the fireplace after eating the cake.

I'm slightly concerned.

"Hey, are you okay?" I ask her.

She just nods as she stares into the flames.

"Are you sure? Because you seem . . . different."

"Just thinking," she says. And then a tear falls down her cheek that she quickly wipes away.

"Lilly . . ."

"It's okay," she says, wiping at her eye again. "I'm just . . . I'm sad, is all. I know we were supposed to play crazy cods, but I'm not in the mood, if that's okay."

"That's okay. Do you want to talk about it?"

Her eyes flash to the kitchen and then back to me. "Do you think . . . do you think we could go up to my room to talk?"

"Of course." I stand from the floor and lend my hand to her. She slips her hand into mine and I help her up. "You head up. I'm going to let Lara and Brimar know what we're doing."

"Okay." She wraps her arms around herself and disappears toward the stairs.

After I pick up the blanket from the floor and fold it, I walk into the kitchen, where Brimar and Lara are washing and drying dishes together. "Hey, Lilly is feeling off, so I'm going to talk to her up in her room. I'm assuming she'll go to bed from there."

"Sounds good. We'll lock up down here."

"Hey, heavy winds tonight," Lara says. "Make sure your windows are locked."

"Oh, good call," I say before grabbing two glasses of water just in case Lilly gets thirsty. When I reach her bedroom, the door is shut, so I give it a light knock and then let myself in. Lilly is standing in the middle of her room, wearing nothing but an oversized shirt now, what I've come to find is her favorite way to sleep. "I brought you water."

"Thank you," she says, walking over to her bed and taking a seat. She slips her legs under the covers and leans against the headboard. Once again, she brings her legs in close and rests her arms on the tops of her knees.

I set the glasses of water on the surface while taking a seat on the edge of her bed.

"What are you doing?" she asks as she flops down the covers. "Sit next to me."

Normally, I wouldn't do this, because it's getting too fucking close to her, but then again, I cupped her breasts in a hot spring today and also rolled out dough with her, as if we were in the movie *Ghost*, sculpting pottery together. So . . . sitting next to her in bed shouldn't be a problem.

"Scoot over," I say as I slide into her bed, but she doesn't scoot far. Once I'm settled, she presses up to my side and loops my arm around her back so I'm holding her tightly.

I give in . . . yet again, because I know she's in search of warmth.

Like Theo said, give her the comfort she needs.

I scoop my other arm around her and rest her head on my chest as she curls into my side. After a few moments of silence, she finally says, "I'm sad, but also . . . mad. Mad because I wish my mom had told me more about her life. There's so much she kept hidden, and now that I'm experiencing it without her, it makes me want to—to yell at her. To ask her why she needed to keep it all a secret." She sniffs, and I hold her tighter. "There's so much about this place that reminds me of her. And the more I think about it, the more it all comes into focus."

"Like what?" I ask as I stroke my thumb over her bare thigh.

"Well, in my parents' bedroom, there were three pictures over their bed, and they were all landscapes of this lush, green coastline. I never asked her much about it, I just assumed they were pictures she liked. But the more I think about it, the more I'm realizing they were photographs of Torskethorpe. And around Christmastime, there was always this one table runner she would use, it was very special to her. It had a *KS* stitched in the corner. I asked her once what the *KS* stood for and she said the initials of the person who made the beautiful runner. *KS* . . . that has to be Katla Strom."

"Katla did make quite a few runners for her kids."

"And there was a chest in our house, which Mom and Dad called their hope chest. It's where they kept all their cherished possessions. It looks just like the chest at the foot of this bed. And we also had very similar rugs to the braided rugs that are in the bathrooms and in the kitchen. Everything is so similar. The writing was there, growing up, the heritage, but I never bothered to ask because I was too young to understand. And now . . . now I feel so dumb."

"Lilly, you're not dumb."

"I am. It took baking a cake to see it all. To see the resemblance. Even though my mom left Torskethorpe, she still took so much of it with her."

"Apparently not the love for cod."

She chuckles and moves in tighter. "No, she left that here." After a sigh, she says, "I just wish she was here, you know? So I could ask her questions, so I could experience this with her."

"I wish you could too, Lilly."

"I just feel so alone. If it weren't for you, Keller, I'd be lost. This is so scary, all of this. I know I joke around a lot and tease you . . . tempt you. But it means so much to me that you're taking your time with me. That you're patient and, although sometimes you lose your temper, you continue to try to teach me and show me what my life could be."

"It's my job."

"I guess it is." She pauses and then quietly asks, "Is it your job to hold me like this?"

I shake my head. "No, but I promised you I'd protect you, and if that means protecting you from your own fears, then I'll do that."

Her legs curl against my side. "In an alternate reality, where my mom never moved, or better yet, she never passed away and, instead, she brought me and my dad to Torskethorpe, do you think we'd know each other?"

"We would," I answer.

"Would we be friends?"

"Probably not," I say honestly. "Not because I wouldn't want to be, though. My parents were very clear when it came to my role in the palace. I was not to speak within the palace walls. I was expected to stay quiet, to mind my manners, and to never bring attention to myself. If you were at Strombly, there's no doubt I'd be pining for you from a distance."

"Pining?" she asks, as she lifts her head. "You'd never make a move?"

"Never," I answer. "I know it might seem different or odd to you, but when you're a servant in the palace, you're there to comfort the sovereign, not mess with the equilibrium."

"But what if I demanded you talk to me?"

I smile. "Then I'd talk to you, but that's all it'd ever be."

"What if I kissed you? Would you kiss me back?"

"Out of desperation, I would've kissed you back, but then I'd have had to tell you it could never be."

"And if you saw me crying, in the palace, clearly distraught over your refusal, what would you have done?"

"I'd have pulled you into my arms, cradled you to my chest, and told you how I wish things were different. But I would've left it at that."

"That's so sad."

"Yes, but there are so many others who'd be able to give you more."

"You don't know that." She sits up now, looking me in the eyes. "What's *more* to you?"

"Does it matter?" I ask her. "This is all temporary."

"It might be, but you need to know, Keller, that you've given me so much more than any man in my life, and we're . . . we're friends. You always say you're here to protect me, and you have. You've made me feel safe ever since I arrived here. During this crazy, unpredictable, and out-of-this-world situation, you've somehow broken it down for me to understand. You've made it easy to slowly adapt, and maybe at times I've been bored out of my mind, but I see your efforts for me. I'm not sure anyone else in your position would've done the same."

"Because, like I've said from the beginning, Lilly, *you matter most.* That will never change."

Her eyes search mine as she presses her hand to my chest. "Do you realize how badly I want to kiss you right now?"

"Don't," I say, even though the feeling is mutual. "Because I'll have to turn you down, and I don't want to have to do that to you."

"I know." She lets out a heavy sigh and leans against my chest again. "I'll take this instead, the comfort of your arms."

I stroke her thigh and say, "You know I'll always be here for you, right? I can't be here for you like your mom could've been, or your dad, but I can tell you this. As long as you stay here in Torskethorpe, I'll never leave your side. I'll always be here for you."

"And if I choose to go back to Miami?"

"Then that's when we part ways, because you know my life is here. My duty is here."

"It's one of the reasons why I like you so much. Your loyalty is unlike any I've ever seen. It's very sexy, Keller."

"It's what's been engrained in my blood. There's no changing that."

"So, if I do decide to go back to Miami, would you at least write me back if I wrote you?"

"In my head, I want to say no, because a clean break would be best, but I know, deep in my soul, I'd never be able to fully walk away. I'd write you back."

"Good, because I wouldn't be able to fully walk away either."

Chapter Thirteen

LILLY

"Hey, Lilly?" Keller whispers into my ear.

"Hmm?" I mutter as I snuggle my cheek closer against his chest. My legs are tangled with his, and my arm's draped around his large torso.

"I should get to my bed."

"Why?" I ask, feeling far too sleepy and comfortable for anything to change.

"I can't sleep with you. This is crossing a line."

"Keller, the line is a blur at this point. Please just stay."

"Please respect my position here, Lilly." His voice sounds desperate because I know this isn't what he truly wants. If I were to look into his eyes at this moment, I know I'd see the man who touched my breasts earlier today, the man who wrapped himself around me when we baked, the man who held me tight, letting my sorrow become his. He wants this. But his dedication to "the job" wins out every time, and it's not fair for me to hold him back from what's important to him.

Sighing, I pull away from him and roll to the other side of the bed, curling into the cold pillow. "Okay. Sorry I asked," I say softly.

"Lilly," he whispers.

I turn my face to my pillow, gripping it tightly as I say, "Keller, it's fine. I'm not mad. You can go. I know I pushed you too far today."

He remains unmoving, staring at me. I can feel the blaze of his eyes. His indecision weighs heavy in the air, and even though I want to ask him to stay one more time, I know it's not fair to keep pushing his limits.

The mattress shifts and my heart sinks as I expect to hear him pad across the stone floor to the bathroom, but when I feel him close in behind me, I'm genuinely shocked. His arm loops around my stomach and he quietly says, "You know if it was my choice, I'd have it this way." His hand slips under my shirt and his warm palm presses against my stomach. "I'd spend the night, right here, holding you close to me, making sure nothing, not even a nightmare, hurts you."

God, when he says things like that . . .

I rotate to my back, and his large body hovers over me, his hand inches from my breast. "It is your choice, Keller."

"It's not," he answers with a shake of his head as his hand slides up to just under my breast, lighting up my entire body with tingles, with need, with the yearning to climb on top of this man and truly take what I want. "Fuck, but I want you, Lilly."

My heart beats so erratically that I can feel it in my throat as my cheeks flame with this burning desire I have for him.

"All you have to do is take what you want. Do you realize that? I'm all yours." I place my palm on his cheek. "Just take me, Keller."

The tension in the air grows so thick that it feels as if one slight movement could cause an unexpected explosion between us as he studies me, his eyes flitting back and forth. The desire in them mirrors mine, but uncertainty clouds that desire.

He wets his lips.

His hand grows tighter on my side, his fingers digging deliciously into my skin.

And he lowers his head to mine.

My breath catches. I prepare myself for his mouth, for his soft lips.

My hand floats behind his head, and just when I think he's about to finally kiss me, he rests his forehead on mine and squeezes his eyes shut.

"I . . . I can't, Lilly. I'm so fucking sorry."

The hope building in my mind vanishes in the blink of an eye, and the weird thing about it is that I'm not mad. How can I be? The man is anguished with his decision, so why would I make him feel even worse than he already does?

My hand slips from behind his head to his cheek, where I brush my thumb over his coarse scruff. "Don't apologize, I understand. I truly do."

His hand scoots up just another millimeter, his thumb now pressing against the underside of my breast, causing me to gasp. He offers me a stroke, so light I barely feel it, but it causes me to dig my fingers into his scalp.

"Keller," I whisper as our noses touch, his lips so close I can almost taste them.

His thumb moves carefully and then caresses my nipple. We both suck in a sharp breath, our mouths parted, our breath mixing. My skin prickles, wanting so much more. Wanting his mouth. Wanting his touch. Wanting his entire body.

Shifting, his cheek slides along mine, his mouth next to my ear as he cups my breast. God, yes, that feels so good. I spread my legs, welcoming him as I slide my other hand to his back, holding him close.

"Take me," I whisper, my lips dancing against his ear.

"Fuck," he says, squeezing my breast. His teeth pull down on my ear, causing me to moan quietly yet loud enough to snap him out of the haze we're both in. He pauses, and then in the blink of an eye, he releases my breast and pulls away, rolling toward the edge of the bed. He's clearly in agony, his hands digging into his hair while his back rolls with tension.

The wind outside whistles past the pointed edges of the stone wall, filling the silence that's fallen between us. My heart is beating wildly from being so close, but my mind is reeling with a mixture of anger and frustration.

Why get so close?

Why tease me?

Why make me believe that he's actually going to make a move and then pull away at the last moment? It's cruel.

"You should probably get to your room," I say, trying my hardest to hold back the edge in my voice.

"Lilly . . . I'm sorry."

"Stop apologizing," I say, that frustration coming out. "Just stop, Keller."

"Okay," he whispers.

"Just leave."

"Yeah," he breathes out. "Okay." He rises from the bed and starts to walk away, but because I'm so weak for this man, I call out to him.

"Keller?"

He looks over his shoulder. "Yes?"

"Can you at least do me one thing?"

"Anything," he answers.

My throat grows tight as I ask, "Your shirt, can you leave it here?"

Keeping his eyes on me, he reaches behind his head and

pulls off his shirt, revealing his sculpted chest, his muscles rippling with straining lust as he walks toward me.

Before he makes it all the way, I sit up and strip out of my shirt, leaving me bare-chested in front of him. His eyes scour my chest, brows turning down as he wets the corner of his mouth with his tongue. I hold my hand out to him for his shirt, but he doesn't hand it over.

He keeps it close to him as he sits next to me. He finds the neck hole of his shirt and offers it to me. I lean forward and once the shirt is over my head, gathered around my neck, he drags his fingers down my arm, over the side of my breast, and then picks up my hand. He brings my wrist to his mouth, where he presses the smallest of kisses. It's so light, a feather of a kiss, but it drives me wild, creating a force of sensual desire to billow in my stomach.

He helps that arm through the hole of his shirt, and then he moves his other hand up my stomach, runs his fingers along the side of my breast, and then down my arm. Just like my other arm, he brings that wrist to his mouth and lightly kisses it before threading it through his shirt. Once my arms are situated, he reaches for the hem and drags it down my body until I'm fully wrapped in him, his fingers dragging over my heated skin.

"Thank you," I whisper.

"You look . . . fuck, Lilly, seeing you in my shirt, it's messing with my head." He drags his thumb over my lip, tugging on it, and because I want him so bad, I pull his thumb into my mouth and suck on it. His eyes grow desperately hungry, right before he growls, pushing me back on the bed.

He pins my hands above my head and lowers his mouth to my ear. "If things were different, I'd have you do that all over again, sucking hard until I couldn't take it any longer and replaced my thumb with my cock."

God, yes. I would love that. "I want your cock in my mouth."

"You can't handle my cock in your mouth," he says, his nose dragging over my cheek. "You wouldn't be able to handle what I truly want to do to you."

"Trust me," I whisper. "I could handle anything you have coming my way. You've no fucking clue just how dirty I am."

"Fuck," he says before pulling my earlobe between his teeth. He tugs on it until I let out a sharp gasp. "How dirty?"

"My body is yours, so why don't you find out?"

He licks my earlobe. "I want to, badly."

"How bad?"

"So bad that all I can think about is shutting up that sassy mouth of yours with my dick. I want to force you to suck me off, to make me come so hard that I black out."

"You wouldn't have to force me, I'd take your cock freely, all the way to the back of my throat."

"Would you gag?"

"Yes, because I know you'd like it."

He caresses my cheek with his nose before he pulls away. It feels like a flame being doused in water. He pushes off the bed and leaves me breathless, staring at his retreating back. He pauses at the doorway to the bathroom. Gripping the frame tightly, he says, "Don't follow me. I can see it in your eyes that you want to. What just happened, it stays here."

"Nothing even happened," I say.

His eyes connect with mine. "More happened than you think."

KELLER: *THE INFORMATIVE: Still no decision has been made by the angler's wife as she continues to float between the two men, risking everything to find love. Some might say it's whore-ish behavior, but the true romantics believe she deserves happiness. A divide in the town of Kirkfell has been formed. The lovely tourist town is now facing the question on everyone's mind. Are you choosing love or duty?*

I set my phone down, a gasp on the tip of my tongue.

A town divided now?

That can't be good for the country's morale.

God, but it's so juicy.

But not as juicy as what's happening between me and Keller.

Or more like . . . what's not happening.

———

"LIKE THIS?" I ask Lara as I drag the thread all the way through the cloth.

"Yes, just like that," she says in a cheery voice. "You're a real natural, Lilly."

"You think so?" I look down at the square cloth napkin and the line of x's I've embroidered.

"There might be a few blunders on the back, but that's okay, as this is your first time. The top is truly beautiful, and I can see that you have patience for this that many might not have."

Keller is standing by the window, his eyes trained on me with his chin propped up in his hand. The wind has been whipping around so much outside that we've stayed inside the entire day. I can feel his gaze, interested in what I'm doing, so I lift up the napkin and show him.

"What do you think?"

He pushes off the wall and comes over to the sitting area, where he bends to look closely. "You're doing a beautiful job," he says, his voice soft, the rumble falling over me like a warm blanket, like the warmth his shirt provided me last night.

All morning, he's been attentive.

When I first came downstairs, he held his hand out on the last step, helping me down. It was unnecessary, but I took it anyway. When he served me breakfast—despite telling him I could get it myself—he set the plate in front of me and then dragged his hand over my back before taking a seat himself. When we were in the "learning room," he wasn't brash with his teaching. He opened his laptop and showed me pictures, discussing what we saw. At one point, his hand was on my thigh, his thumb slowly moving over my skin before he pulled away.

When it came to lunch, he offered to show me how to make one of King Theo's favorite sandwiches, which involved . . . cod. We joked around, he plugged my nose when I opened the canned cod, and he showed me how to toast the bread on the stove without setting it on fire. And then, when we sat down to eat, he tapped his sandwich to mine and we both took our first bites. It was delicious.

After, he told me Lara was going to show me how to embroider, a traditional hobby that every monarch, even King Theo, knows how to do. Apparently, it's custom during Torg for the royal family to trade different embroidered items they've created with the public. He hasn't left my side. His eyes haven't left me either. And even though he's only snuck in minor touches here and there, I swear it's been like he's held me all day, and I've loved every second of it.

I run my hand over the embroidery. "Are you just saying that or do you mean it?"

"Would I say something just to say it?"

"I guess not. Do you think it's trade-worthy?"

"I think it's close to it," Lara says. "I think if you practice a little bit more, you'll be just as great as your mother once was."

That puts a smile on my face. "I'm assuming when she was still here in Torskethorpe, she traded a lot of her pieces?"

Keller takes a seat next to me and drapes his arm over the back of the couch behind me. "King Theo once told me that Margret's pieces were most highly sought after and cherished by the public. There are pieces of hers in the homes of the public all over the country."

"I remember when the country found out of her passing," Lara says quietly. "It was as if the weather knew the loss we suffered because it rained for a week straight."

"Flowers lined the gates of the palace," Keller adds. "And when they held a memorial for her, those lucky enough to have one of her embroidered pieces, clutched them tightly in the rain."

A tear falls down my cheek from the thought of so many people loving my mother. I had no idea. Keller leans over and wipes away my tear. "I truly wish I would've known this, how strong her connection was to this country, how much she impacted the people. I can't believe she never came back, over all that time."

"Pride is a funny thing in this country," Lara says as she pokes her needle through her cloth. "We are a loyal bunch to our cores. We take care of our own, and we come together during dark times, but our downfall is our pride. If we have something stuck in our heads, we'll let it brew, unable to listen to the other side."

"I can see that pride, even with you, Keller, and Brimar," I say. "Stubborn pride."

From the corner of my eye, I watch Keller lower his head. *Yeah, you hear that, Keller? Stubborn pride.*

"So, you think pride got in the way of my mom coming back to Torskethorpe?"

Keller nods. "The fight with Katla was too damaging, and even though your mother loved this country, she desired more, at least at that moment. Katla trying to take that away didn't settle well with her."

"So, she fled," Lara says. "And she never came back. And because Katla carries her pride close to her heart, she never reached out."

"That's why Mom only wrote to King Theo," I say, remembering we spoke about this briefly.

"Correct."

"That's . . . that's so sad." I set my embroidery down and pull my knees to my chest. "I can't believe that they'd let a miscommunication destroy their relationship like that. Think of everything they lost, of everything I've lost. I didn't have any family outside of my parents, but coming here, there's so much more that I could have been blessed with when I was younger. I'm not talking about the royal aspect, but more about having grandparents, having an aunt and uncles, even though they've all disappeared in different ways. Maybe . . . maybe if my mom had mended that relationship with Katla, things could have been different."

"Possibly," Lara says. "But you can't focus on the *what if.*"

"Very true, I can only focus on the here and now." I look between Lara and Keller and say, "I'm so glad you guys are here with me. I know that my decision weighs heavily on you, but you haven't once pressured me or asked me what I'm going to do. You've shown me the history and the beauty of this country, but you've also shown me who I am and where I come from. My . . . heritage. And that's priceless. It means so much to me."

"If anything, we want you to just know your roots," Lara says. "Even if you leave, at least you'll be aware of the rich history of your ancestors and maybe pass down some of the traditions you've learned here to your future children."

Keller is silent as my phone beeps with a text. I usually keep my phone up in my room, because I'm not using it much, but today is Timmy's birthday, so I've been chatting with him. I also spent a good portion of time sending him deliveries through a meal delivery service so he knows that even though I'm not there, I'm still very much thinking of him.

I reach for my phone and unlock it to read the message from Timmy.

Timmy: *Uh, girl . . . you're famous.*

Brows drawn together, I whisper, "What?" just as another

text message comes in. It's a screenshot of an article. It says: "Miami Bikini Wagon Owner, a Real-Life Princess."

"Oh God," I say as I set my feet down on the ground and lean forward.

"What is it?" Keller asks, his protective instincts kicking in at once.

I flash him the screen. "Timmy just sent me this article."

Keller's eyes zero in on the title of the article. "Fuck." He stands from the couch and shouts, "Brimar, get out here."

Dishes clatter in the sink and then Brimar rushes in, a towel draped over his shoulder. "What's going on?"

"News broke out in the States." He flashes Brimar the screen. "Her name and everything."

"Shit." He presses his hand to his forehead. "That means all of her information is floating around not only Torskethorpe, but the world."

From his pocket, Keller digs his phone out and shoots off a text. As if he's robotic, he moves around the room and opens his laptop.

"Is this bad?" I ask, worry etching up my throat.

"Yes," Keller says, worrying me more. "Your privacy has just vanished." His phone dings and he checks the screen. He then goes back to the computer, types away on it, and in seconds, a screen pops up and it's King Theo.

I sit taller on the couch.

"Sorry to bother you," Keller says.

"No, it's quite all right," King Theo says as he clears his throat. "Is Lilija with you?"

"Yes." Keller brings the computer over to the couch and takes a seat next to me.

When I'm in view, I offer him a wave. "Hi."

"Lilija," he says, his voice growing soft. "I'm so sorry about this."

"I don't understand. What's happening?"

Calmly, but in a clipped voice, Keller says, "We've kept

you here, at Harrogate, to offer you privacy as we helped you navigate through training so you could understand what to expect if you decide to stay here and take on this role. But now that your actual identity has been revealed, we won't be able to give you the privacy of your decision. It's going to be very public."

"Especially here in Torskethorpe," King Theo adds. "Your name was released a week ago, but there were only rumors, and we were able to squash them. But now that you've been exposed in your hometown, the public will be expecting to see you. To meet you."

"This was what I was fucking worried about," Keller says. "That's not fair to her."

I place my hand on a fuming Keller and say, "Thank you for protecting me, but I don't believe there's any way around this, correct? If they're already publishing articles in Miami about this, it's going to be all over. There's no hiding, therefore, you should just introduce me."

King Theo's eyes light up. "Are you saying you're going to fall in line for the crown?"

"No," I say, causing everyone's shoulders to deflate. "I'm not committing to anything. I think there's a whole other side to this that I need to see before I can make that decision. And that means I have to leave Harrogate to do so."

King Theo smiles. "You're very smart, my girl. I believe you're right, there's a whole other part of this world you've yet to see." He covers his mouth with his arm and coughs a few times. "Excuse me."

"We need to control the narrative on this, though," Keller says. "We can't let the press control us. We control the situation."

"I agree," King Theo says.

"I say we spend a little more time here, in Harrogate," Keller says. "Let me finish prepping her, and in the meantime, we can have Henrik prepare statements and a welcoming to the palace that is well-thought-out, rather than rushed. If we're going to bring her to Strombly, we need to do it the right way."

"Yes, that's very wise," King Theo says. "I shall have Henrik reach out to you immediately."

"Don't you think it'd be better to get her to Strombly right away?" Brimar asks. "If we stay here, we're sitting ducks."

"No one suspects we're here, and if we continue to lie low, then we'll be fine. We need to do this the right way," Keller snaps back at Brimar, the tension in the room going from zero to one hundred in seconds.

"I agree with Keller," King Theo says. "Let's get our ducks in a row and then we'll have a welcoming. Lilija, are you okay with that?"

"Yes, whatever works for everyone."

King Theo focuses his attention on me and says, "I know this has been a whirlwind for you, and I truly wish I could've spent more time with you during your training, but I want you to know how much I truly appreciate you even considering your succession. At the end of this, even if your answer is no, I want you to know that I truly love you, my darling Lilija."

My eyes well up and my lips tremble. *"Darling . . ."* I whisper. "That's . . . that's what my mom used to call me."

King Theo's eyes grow soft as he presses his hand to his chest. "Ah, that's what I'd call my sweet Margret as well. I see the tradition carried on."

"It did." I smile. "Can I ask you something?"

"Anything, my darling," he says. I want to ask him about Queen Katla. I want to ask if she thinks of me and wants to meet me, or if the reticence between mother and daughter will continue between grandmother and granddaughter. But I'm fearful his answer will be yes. So, I push down those feelings of rejection and go with something safer.

"When I arrive at Strombly, will you please show me the different embroidered pieces my mother made?"

"I'll do something even greater than that. I shall show you her room, her treasured items, and the letters she sent me over the years."

"Really?" I ask.

He nods. "Really."

"Thank you."

Keller places his hand on my thigh and says, "I'll prepare Henrik."

"Thank you," King Theo says before we all say our goodbyes.

Once the laptop is shut, Brimar steps up, anger evident on his face. "You're being reckless." His boisterous voice snaps me out of the loving haze I was just in.

Keller rises from the couch. "Brimar, watch your tone."

"Don't tell me to watch my fucking tone. I'm the head of security. I'm the one who should be calling the shots here, and staying here in Harrogate is not smart."

"Brimar, I'm warning you," Keller says, his voice evilly controlled.

Brimar, on the other hand, curls his fists at his sides as he continues, "Do you truly think the public is dumb enough to assume we're not here?"

"I think as long as we keep quiet and maintain a level of peace here, no one will realize. Harrogate hasn't been occupied for years."

"You just want to keep her here because you know when you're at Strombly, you're not going to be able to fuck her."

"Brimar," Lara chastises, standing as well.

Oh shit. My eyes bounce back and forth between Brimar and Keller.

Keller's hands clutch at his sides and the muscles in his back flex as he very quietly says, "Your room, now."

Rolling his eyes, Brimar snaps the towel off his shoulder and takes off toward his room, Keller trailing behind him.

When they're out of the room, Lara takes a seat next to

me. "I'm so sorry he said that. That was completely out of line. What you and Keller do is your business."

"We've done nothing," I say, still stunned from Brimar's outburst. "Keller won't go there."

"Oh." Lara glances down at her hands. "That's surprising. I guess with the way he looks at you, the way he touches you on occasion, I assumed differently. I think Brimar assumes the same. Either way, it was uncalled for."

"Why are you apologizing for him?" I ask. "You didn't do anything wrong."

"I know, but . . . I just want you to know that I'm sorry he said that and that I don't condone what he said. He's just . . . he's very stressed lately. He wants to leave here."

"Do you think we're sitting ducks?" I ask her.

She shakes her head. "No, I trust Keller. He knows what's best, and if he thinks we're safe here, then we're safe."

"Okay."

A door slams, causing both me and Lara to flinch. Keller comes storming into the living room shortly after. Not saying a word, he grabs his computer and heads up to his room.

When he's gone, I turn to Lara and say, "Well, dinner should be fun."

THE WIND HOWLS against the stone of the castle, whipping so hard that the long blades of grass outside are running parallel to the ground. Dinner was a disaster. No one talked. We just ate our food and listened to the wind outside. When I took my plate to the kitchen, Brimar followed me and offered an apology for speaking out of turn. I thanked him for apologizing, and when I returned to the dining room, Keller was gone.

Lara and I sat in front of the fireplace again and worked on our napkins until my eyes felt blurry and I decided to retire for the night. My excuse for leaving was partially true, but I was also very concerned about Keller.

That's why I find myself now at Keller's door, my knuckles knocking on the hardwood.

"Yeah," he calls out.

My finger runs across the ancient wood as I say, "Keller, it's me. Can I come in?"

I'm met with silence, and right when I'm about to call out to him again, the door to his bedroom opens. He leans against it, wearing only a pair of sweatpants.

"Everything okay?" he asks me.

"Yeah, I just . . . I wanted to make sure you were okay. You haven't spoken to me since, you know, the blow-up, and I wanted to make sure you weren't mad at me."

His tense brow knits together. "Why would I be mad at you?"

"I don't know." I play with the hem of my shirt. "But you just seemed like you were."

"No, Lilly, I'm not mad at you. I'm just trying to figure out the logistics to your welcoming and what we have to go over in the next week or so. I'm busy."

"Oh, okay." I look up at him. "Just seems like you're pulling away after what Brimar said."

Keller's jaw grows tight. "What he said was completely out of line."

"I know, and he apologized. I just think tensions are high and I understand that. We all want to stay safe, but I don't want you pulling away," I say as I reach out for his hand, but he steps away. "Keller . . ."

"I have work I have to do, Lilly. It's late, why don't you get some sleep?"

"Are you really going to let what he said put distance between us?"

"What he said was correct. For a moment, I lost sight of that."

"When? Because last thing I remember, you've rejected me in every way you can."

"Not because I want to," he says quietly.

Frustrated with the man in front of me, I say, "Just forget it. Glad you're fine, just a moody asshole like usual."

I turn toward my door, but before I can retreat, he grabs my wrist. "Lilly, I'm trying to do what's best for you."

I shake free of his grasp. "How can you do what's best for me when you don't even know me?"

His eyes narrow. "I fucking know you."

"If you did, then you'd realize I don't care about your status. You act like in order for me to be happy, I need to be fulfilled by a man who has gold in his pockets and a prestigious title. That couldn't be further from the truth, but you don't seem to recognize that."

He doesn't seem to recognize the kindred spirit we share. He doesn't notice that when he's around, I feel protected, I feel seen. I feel as though I belong. He doesn't notice how I light up when he walks into the room, because he reminds me of happiness—of the days my parents swept me up in moments of pure joy. He puts me at ease, offers me support, and pushes me outside of my comfort zone.

When he doesn't say anything, I toss my hands in the air and go straight to my bedroom, where I lean against the door and take a few breaths. Absolutely infuriating. I hate that he thinks he knows what's best for me when he truly has no idea.

God, he makes me want to scream. Shaking my head, I move toward the bathroom, but through both our jammed doors, I spot him sitting on his bed, his fingers pulling on the strands of his hair.

Damn it.

Damn these non-working doors.

And damn this man.

This infuriating, insufferable man.

I will not feel bad for him. I will not give in to the slump of his shoulders or the way his muscles contract as he tugs on his hair. Nope. He's an idiot, therefore, he can be an idiot by himself.

CRASH.

I jack-knife on my bed, sitting up in a perched position, my heart hammering from the sound of broken glass echoing through the stone walls.

What the hell was that?

Eyes blurry, sleep still fogging my mind, I don't realize what's happening until I'm dragged out of bed and onto the floor.

I let out a scream, but then a large hand covers my mouth. When my eyes finally focus on the dark, menacing figure above me, I notice that it's Keller.

"Shh," he whispers. "Don't make a fucking sound."

My lips seal shut, my heart in my throat as fear pulses through my veins.

"What's happening?" I whisper.

"I don't know," he whispers back. "But we're not to move until we get an all-clear from Lara or Brimar."

Lying on top of me, Keller's large body eclipses mine, acting as a shield. Strangely, his weight isn't pushing me into the floor, because he's planking over me, protecting me.

"Keller . . . I'm scared."

"I know." His thumb caresses my cheek. "I got you, though. I promise, I won't let anything happen to you."

I clutch the hand that's cupping my cheek as my body shivers under him.

"Shhh," he says calmly as he strokes my cheek. "I'm here."

From below, I hear Lara and Brimar clear rooms, their

feet shuffling around. I stay stiff as a board under Keller, trying not to move despite my shaking legs.

"Clear," Brimar says in the distance.

"Clear," Lara says, their voices growing closer.

My teeth chatter, and adrenaline's pumping through me now.

"It's okay," Keller whispers.

"Clear."

"Clear."

And then, the creak of stairs. I grow even stiffer under Keller.

"It's probably Brimar," he whispers.

"Has Rogue secured Gisla?" Brimar calls out.

"Secured," Keller replies.

The door opens to my bedroom and Brimar says, "Clear. Safe to come out."

Keller moves off me and then helps me to my wobbly feet. He loops his arm around my waist and slowly helps me to the edge of my bed, where I take a deep breath. "What . . . what was it?"

Lara appears at the door and says, "An unlatched window blew open from the wind and broke when it hit the wall." She sticks her handgun in the back of her pants. "All rooms have been cleared. We're going to fasten wood to the window and secure it shut."

"Okay," Keller says. "I'll help." He takes one step but I'm clutching his hand before he can move any farther.

Call it the adrenaline, call it all the talk of wanting to keep me safe, but in a short minute, I went from sleeping like an angel to a freaking nervous wreck, and I need comfort. "Please stay with me." My lip still trembles.

He eyes me, and I notice the minute he sees that I need him to stay, because he softly nods. "Do you two have it covered?"

"Yes," Brimar says. "We'll take care of it. Sorry about the disturbance."

When they leave, I'm still shaking. "That was . . . that was terrifying."

In the corner of my room is an armchair, and Keller drags it closer to my bed and takes a seat. "Yes, but nothing to worry about, it was just the wind."

"Well, the wind needs to take a chill pill." I blow out a heavy breath. "Jeez." When my eyes meet Keller's, I tilt my head to the side and ask, "Did Brimar call you Rogue and call me Gisla?"

"Yes. Those are our code names."

"Why Gisla?"

"Princess Gisla, strong-willed and independent. Felt suitable for you." He grabs the blankets of my bed and tugs them down so I can slip in. "Go back to bed."

"My heart is still hammering. There's no way I'll be able to sleep now. And not to sound like I'm the biggest wuss in the world, but I'm also still slightly terrified with what happened."

"Do you need to talk about it?"

"Yes, that would be great." Not giving him a second to respond, I continue, "What would've happened if it was an intruder?"

"Well, Brimar and Lara would have done exactly what they did, gone room to room looking for any suspicious behavior, and I would've been here with you. Now, if someone entered our room, I would've shielded you. I told you, I would do everything within me to protect you."

"What if the person had a gun or a knife or something?"

"I would have fought them off. Just like Brimar and Lara, I've gone through extensive training."

"And what if you got hurt?" I ask, the thought of him taking a bullet making me feel physically ill.

"That's nothing you need to worry about."

I sit up. "But I *am* worried about it. I care about you, Keller."

"It's my job to put you first, so I would've done anything to protect you. If that means getting hurt in the process, then so be it."

"How can you be so casual about it?"

"Because your life matters more than mine," he answers.

"I don't like that answer."

"But it's the correct one." When I don't respond, he says, "Go on, get back under your covers."

"I don't want to." My hands shake. "I have too many thoughts running through my mind." My eyes connect with his. "You'd really protect me, even if that meant you getting hurt?"

"Yes," he answers with a pause.

My teeth clench together as I slip my legs off the edge of the bed.

"What are you doing?" he asks.

I stand, and as he watches my every step, I close the space between us until I'm right in front of him.

"Lilly," he rasps out.

I kneel on one side of his chair, and then the other, straddling his lap. Like he does every night, he's only wearing his briefs, so when I lower myself down, I feel him beneath me.

Breathing out a long, tortured breath, his hands fall to my waist. "Lilly, what are you doing?"

I place my hands on his chest, his thick pecs twitching under my touch.

"Lilly, you know I won't be able to stop you."

"I know," I whisper as I move my hands to his neck and lean forward. "But I can't stop myself either." I lower my head to his ear and drag my lips over his cheek. He sucks in a sharp breath while his fingers at my waist dig into my skin. "Never in my entire life, have I ever had someone treat me the way you do. You're the knight I never knew I needed. You offer me safety and solace. Just being in your arms makes me feel more comfortable than anywhere else on this planet. And I don't know what to do about it other than show you how it makes me feel."

"Lilly, please, I can't . . ."

I rock my hips, moving my pelvis over his growing bulge.

"Fuck," he whispers as his head falls back, giving me access to his throat. I take advantage of it and pepper kisses along his fiery skin.

"You make me whole, Keller." I kiss up his jaw. "You make me feel safe." I move closer to his mouth. "You make me feel cherished." I hover my lips just above his. "You make me feel like I matter." And then I lower my lips to his, giving him the faintest of kisses, and pause, waiting to see what he does.

He holds steady, still.

I don't move, waiting.

The silent night sweeps around us.

The tension grows thick.

And with every second that ticks by, I can feel myself losing control until . . . it snaps.

I release his face and reach for the hem of my shirt, pulling it up over my head and dropping it on the floor, leaving me in nothing other than a pair of cheeky underwear.

"Fuck . . . me," he whispers as his eyes fall to my chest. From the tempting lick of his lips and the slight thrust of his hips against mine, I take that as my green light.

I bring my breast to his mouth and run my nipple along his lip. His grip grows tighter, and his mouth slightly parts, just enough for my nipple to slip in.

And . . . he sucks on it.

I let out a low groan as he pulls on the tight nub. I place my hands around the back of his head, holding him close.

He pulls my breast deeper into his mouth, only for his tongue to lap at my piercing.

"Yes, Keller, please don't stop."

He doesn't.

Sliding his hands up my sides to my breasts, he cups both of them as he brings his mouth to my other breast. His coarse scruff marring my skin feels amazing, the scrape of it sending a chill up my spine. And the warmth of his mouth is everything I fantasized about, everything I need in this moment.

When his mouth releases my breast, I lower so we're face to face, our eyes meeting, and that's when I start rocking on him, grinding down on his length, watching intently as he wets his lips.

"Lilly, you don't know what you're getting yourself into."

"I have an idea." I bring my hands to his pecs and rock faster.

"You won't be able to handle me."

"Try me."

"I'm too rough." He slides his fingers under the fabric of my underwear and grips my flesh tight in his palms.

I let out a silent gasp as a wave of arousal falls through me.

"I like it rough," I answer.

"I'm demanding." He moves me faster over his lap. "I won't always give you what you want, and I take everything I need. I'll control you. I'll possess you. I'll make it so if you ever leave my bed, you'll never be satisfied by anyone else."

"I expect nothing less from you."

"You don't want this, Lilly."

I grip his jaw and force him to look at me. "I fucking want you. Give me what you can offer."

His gaze is wild, his grip grows tighter, and in the blink of an eye, he stands from the chair, carrying me with him, only to push me back on the bed. He grips my hands and places them above my head while lowering his mouth to my neck. His lips mark me, running up the column, and then down to my chest. His tongue drags across my skin, lapping at my breasts, right before he bites down on my nipple.

"God!" Pain pulses through me, followed by utter satisfaction as he sucks on my nipple, bringing the sensation to another level.

"Keep your hands above your head. Do not move them. Understood?" he asks.

"Yes," I answer.

He lifts up from me and stares down, his hand dragging over his mouth, down his powerful chest, over his rippled abs, and to the waistband of his underwear. He pulls the fabric down, revealing his extremely large cock. My eyes light up and my mouth goes dry from the sight of him. He strokes his length, pulling on the sensitive skin as he stares down at me, pumping fast, pumping hard. It's so sexy, I feel my underwear go wet.

When he releases himself, he lines his cock along my slit, and then he pulses over my underwear.

"Yesss," I nearly cry. I've wanted this for so long. All those days spent with him, all those little touches, those claiming glances, they've built up to this moment where I've wanted nothing more than him between my legs.

I hold on to his shoulders only for him to clamp down on my nipple with his fingers, pinching hard. I gasp out loud.

"I told you, hands above your head."

"S-sorry," I say as I raise them above me.

"Good girl," he says before taking my nipple into his mouth, soothing it with his tongue.

My teeth roll over my bottom lip.

His pace picks up.

My moans grow.

And as he dry humps me straight into this mattress, all I can think about is how much I wish there was nothing between us, how I wish he was actually fucking me, rather than taking the innocent way out. I want him to feel what it's like to be inside me. I want him to feel me while I come over his cock.

"This is all you'll get," he says, his hand sliding to my

collarbone, where he holds me tight, pushing me farther into the bed. "This is all it'll ever be."

"It can't be. Just feeling your cock between my legs, I want more. I want you bare, inside me."

He groans, squeezing his eyes shut as his hips pump faster, the friction now creating a pool of desire in the pit of my stomach. Burning, spreading through my muscles, through my veins, as he thrusts consistently over my pussy, hitting my clit at just the right spot.

"You'll never have me bare," he says.

"I will," I answer, both of us breathing heavily now.

He pumps faster, slides his hand up to my neck, and I smile as he loses control. I can feel him slipping further and further into his true self, and I love every second of it. His rough hold, the pounding of his hips . . . it adds to my building orgasm.

"What don't you understand about this being a one-time thing?" he asks. I look between us and watch as his abs bunch and lengthen with every pulse, his cock wet with pre-cum on the tip. My mouth waters.

"What don't you understand about your cock belonging in my mouth?"

"Fuck," he groans as he lifts me up at the hips, my pussy at his disposal as he runs his cock over it, but it doesn't seem to be enough, because he lets me fall to the bed right before he rips my underwear off. My left leg is dragged up and over his shoulder and he spreads my other leg wide. When I'm in the position he wants me in, he drags his bare cock over my clit again, but this time, he can feel my piercing.

"Fucking . . . hell," he groans, now pumping faster.

He never penetrates me.

He never kisses me.

He never lets me get too close, just close enough to drive both of us nuts.

The euphoric, light feeling of my orgasm climbs with

every thrust, with the feel of his balls slapping against me, with his cock sliding over my pubic bone, with the look of utter confusion, yet snapping desire, on his face.

"I need to know that I can come," I say, knowing he's the type of man who controls *everything* in the bedroom. When his eyes land on mine, I wet my lips and say, "I won't come until you say I can."

"That's not my choice," he says.

"I want it to be. I want you to own me."

His teeth push into his bottom lip as his head falls forward. "Fuck, Lilly. Don't do this to me . . ."

"Tell me, Keller, tell me when I can come."

He picks up his pace, my piercing sending waves of pleasure through me, my orgasm right there, on the edge, teetering. I can only hang on for so long until I combust. What he's doing is too delicious.

"Please, Keller, I want to come. Please let me come."

"Mother . . . fucker," he groans out, and then he digs his fingers so hard into my sides that my orgasm starts to ripple.

"Please, Keller, please give me permission."

"Fuck, Lilly. Come . . . Jesus Christ, come."

His command shakes me to my core as I let myself go, my orgasm clenching my body, pulling in tight to my center, only to shoot out through my limbs. I grip the comforter beneath me as my back arches and I moan out his name.

"Keller, yes, oh my God, your cock . . ."

"Fuck. FUCK!" he says even louder as he stills, shoots his cum all over my stomach, drop after drop, until he's completely spent.

So fucking good, but still my body is begging for more. And from the pulse of his muscles, I can tell he's feeling the same way.

His grip lightens up and his drowsy eyes focus on mine. "Shit, Lilly." He drops my leg from his shoulder and backs away as he stuffs his half-hard cock in his underwear. "What the fuck did I do?"

I sit up on my elbows. "Don't. Don't you dare fucking regret this."

He stares at me, his mind racing, the insecurity of his thoughts clearly pulsing through him. It takes him one freaking second to realize what he's done has crossed all his boundaries, has torn down his walls, has created a situation so grand in his head that the only response he can muster is . . . walking away.

To my dismay, he turns on his heel and exits my room.

Goddamn it!

I groan out a frustrated sigh and flop back on the bed, draping my arm over my eyes. What the hell is wrong with him? Why can't he get over this idea that he can't be with me? He clearly wants to be. He wants me just as much as I want him, so why can't he just let that happen?

Doesn't he see the absolute torment he's putting us both through?

Tears spring to the corners of my eyes, my frustration overflowing.

And then, the creak of a board. I open my eyes just in time to see him bend over me with a warm cloth that he drags over my stomach, cleaning up his mess.

When he's done, he takes my hand and lifts me to a seated position. From the ground, he picks up my shirt and helps me put it back on. Once I'm dressed, he pulls down the blankets of my bed and picks me up, only to place me under the covers. The way he handles me brings forth a whole new sense of *serve and protect*, but it also causes my throat to grow tight. Because I want this.

I want his gentle touch.

I want his aftercare.

I want him.

"Keller—"

He leans over my head, bringing his mouth close to mine, silencing me before I can even start saying what's on my mind. Quietly, he says, "I can't have you, Lilly."

His sentence slices through me like a sharp blade. I should've known that's what he was going to say, but I can't give up on him. We're so close.

I sift my hand through the hair on the back of his neck. "Don't pull away, Keller. Please don't."

"That's the fucked-up part, Lilly." He lowers his head, shaking it. I wait with bated breath as he gathers himself, and when our eyes lock again, he repeats, "I can't have you, but I also can't NOT have you." His voice is a growl, a proclamation, and before I can respond, his mouth descends upon mine.

And he kisses me.

Actually freaking kisses me.

Shocked, stunned, and relieved, I hold him in place as I part my lips, letting him slip his tongue into my mouth, where he tangles with mine. He rests some of his weight on the side of my bed as our kiss intensifies, as my hands dig into his scalp. *I never want him to leave.*

His kiss is demanding, controlled, filled with so much unrequited desire that I find myself melting into his touch, into the way he takes control. I've shared enough first kisses to know this is a once-in-a-lifetime kiss, the kind that marks you as a human, that brands your very soul, creating a memory so vivid that it will last more than a lifetime.

His lips move over mine, dragging out my tongue, creating such a bottomless sensation in my stomach. I'm careening, falling, tumbling into an unknown abyss, my only lifeline being his mouth and the way he makes me feel whole.

When he pulls away, I feel lost again. A part of me has detached and my body is drowning, looking for that life preserver that can only be translated as his touch.

"Stay with me," I whisper, not wanting him to go anywhere.

"No," he answers. "If I stay, I will fuck you."

"Then fuck me."

"No," he answers again. "This has gone too far tonight."

"But, Keller—"

"Lilly," he says in such a startling, deep, commanding tone that I close my lips and seal them shut. "I said, it's gone too far. Now rest your beautiful head, get some sleep, and I'll see you in the morning. Understood?"

God, yes.

I nod, and then to my delight, he lowers back down and gives me another toe-curling kiss before taking off into his room.

Chapter Fourteen

KELLER

"What do you do if someone asks for your political opinion?" I ask Lilly as we finish up our jog, Harrogate just in front of us.

"I don't give it. I have no political opinion at all. I'm a vessel of emptiness, only there to smile and wave. Kind of like I'm a vessel of emptiness right now."

She's been sassy this entire fucking run.

Ever since she tried to kiss me this morning and I didn't let her, she's been on a warpath.

I don't blame her, though. I feel the same fucking way.

Itchy all over.

Needy.

Like if I don't have her near me, I won't be able to breathe.

It happened so fast last night. She was on top of me, her nipple slipped into my mouth, and something unlocked within me, an unstoppable tidal wave of desire.

And I lost it. I took as much as I could from her, rubbing

my cock along her slick, wet clit. Fuck, it felt good—and that piercing, I can still feel it riding up and down my length. A cool metal, creating friction that has me addicted.

How I was able to kiss her good night and sleep in my own bed is beyond me.

And this morning, when she was wearing nothing but a shirt, knowing I'd had my lips on her only the night before, it took everything in me not to drag her to my bed.

It's been torture since.

Especially since she decided to run in just her leggings and sports bra, despite being cold. Her nipples are harder than the pebbles under our feet.

"And what if someone offers you a gift? Do you take it?" I ask.

We slow down as we reach Harrogate. Hands on her hips, she says, "No, I kick them in the face and run away." I give her a menacing look. "Come on, Keller, I know this shit. Yes, I take the gift. I thank them profusely. Are you done with the dumb questions now?" She blows past me and into the castle.

I follow her. "They aren't dumb questions. You need to know them."

She stomps up the stairs. "I know them, Keller."

I stomp up behind her and follow her into her bedroom.

"And for the record, you've told me that tiaras are for married women only at least five times on that run." She tears her sports bra off over her head, leaving her topless in front of me. I'd like to say I don't look, but breasts . . . I look. I look for far longer than I should.

But then I snap my eyes back up to her face as she strips off the rest of her clothes.

"I repeated it several times because you kept asking what kind of gems were in the tiaras. You emphasized that you look best with jade colors."

"That's a valid concern," she says, holding her arms out, and with the curtains now open, offering light to the room, I get to see her naked body with nothing blocking my view. And fuck is she so goddamn beautiful. She moves past me and into the bathroom, where she turns on the water to the tub shower. I follow her for some reason.

"It's my job to make sure you know the correct information."

"I know," she groans. "Christ, Keller. I think the moss on the walls knows the intricacies of your job at this point." She steps into the tub, picks up the nozzle of the shower, and starts rinsing her body. My eyes fixate on the way the water pebbles off her breasts.

It only takes seconds for me to grow hard.

"Is that what the rest of our time here is going to be like?" she asks as she sets the nozzle down and lathers some soap that she caresses over her body, her hands working around her breasts, over her stomach, and between her legs.

Fuck . . .

"Keller, I'm talking to you."

"Huh?" I ask, looking up at her irritated face.

"Oh, so you can stand there and watch me shower, but when I want a kiss, you won't give it up?"

I grip the back of my neck. "I'm trying to keep a professional distance."

"Oh yeah, you're really professional right now. More like a peeping Tom."

"You're right, sorry," I answer before I turn toward my bedroom and slip into the dark space, my curtains not yet pulled back.

What am I doing?

Last night, I lost control. I tasted her, and for the entire jog, I was asking dumb questions because my mind couldn't think of anything else as I watched her boobs bounce up and down next to me. All I could think about was how I'd had them in my mouth the night before. How they'd tasted, how she'd sounded when I sucked on them.

Or how it felt sliding along her clit.

Or her moans.

Or how her mouth tasted.

Fuck, I knew this was going to happen. One taste was all it took.

And then when I was saying good night, the slight sigh of relief when I kissed her one last time . . . I felt it all the way to the marrow of my bones.

So, what am I going to do now?

I clearly can't concentrate properly, not the way that I need to.

But I know if I take another taste, that will be the end of me, there will be no turning back.

Fuck.

I grip my hair, pacing my room as I try to decide.

And then, when I look up, she's standing in my doorway, a towel wrapped around her torso, looking so fuckable it's painful.

"What are your training plans for today? I need to decide if I should wear a dress to practice formal dinner wear, or something more comfortable." There's so much snark coming out of her mouth right now, it makes me want to silence it with my dick.

"Crisis management," I say.

"Oh, fun. That shouldn't be boring at all." She turns on her heel and heads into her bedroom.

"Wear something comfortable," I call after her.

She peeks into the doorway. "Do you really think I'm that dumb?"

Jesus Christ. The fucking mood on her.

Can't blame her, though. I didn't kiss her. So, yeah, she's going to be a wretched witch all day.

I tear my shirt over my head, strip down to nothing, and head into the bathroom. I turn on the shower, and since it's already warm, I get in and start hosing myself down, only for Lilly to walk in, wearing a thong . . . and that's it.

When she turns toward me, I watch her eyes travel down my body until they land on my hardening cock, caused by her inability to put on a shirt. Her tits will seriously be the death of me.

"Can you give me some privacy?" I ask.

"No," she says and then turns back around and starts brushing her wet hair, giving me a great view of her ass.

Fucking woman.

She's doing this on purpose.

She knows exactly what she's doing, trying to drive me crazy.

"You know, you have a really nice cock," she says. "Sad that it never gets used."

My nostrils flare. "It gets used."

"Oh yeah?" She turns around again. "By what? Your hand?"

Yes.

"Why are you provoking me?"

"I'm not, I'm just pointing out the obvious. You have a really nice cock, probably the best I've ever seen, and it's a shame it's not driving into a wet, soft pussy every night. You know, like mine."

My groin tightens.

"Or has a warm, tight mouth sucking on it . . . like mine."

My cock springs forward.

"Or, you know, a hand other than yours jacking you off until you come, like mine. Seems like a waste." She glances down at my cock again, which is stretched up to my stomach. "Also a shame that beautiful erection will deflate when you're done showering."

Leave her alone, or take what I want?

Risk the job, or give in to my feelings?

229

She turns around and grips her tits in both hands, massaging them right in front of me as she grows closer. "God, we would've been so good together too, Keller." She drags one finger up to her mouth, wets it, and then brings it all the way back down her body, slips it under the elastic of her thong and right to her clit, where I watch her fingers start to move back and forth. "Mmm, if only my fingers were your tongue. What I wouldn't give to come all . . . over . . . your . . . mouth."

My teeth grind together.

My mind turns black.

She snaps her hand out of her thong and walks up to me, then runs the tip of her finger over my lips. It takes about one second before I'm running my tongue along where she just touched, soaking up her essence. Smiling, she drags the tip of her fingernail down my body, to my cock, and sweeps it over the pre-cum that's gathered on the tip.

With a step back, she brings her finger to her mouth and sucks it in, her eyes closing as she devours my taste.

"Mmm, you taste delicious." Her eyes lock on mine. "Shame, Keller, such a shame."

And then she turns and heads into her bedroom.

I nearly snap the showerhead in half from the grip I have on it.

You know how when you enter into the reptile part of your brain, nothing else matters besides the feelings you're feeling at that moment?

Well . . . nothing fucking matters other than the one thing on my mind—getting between her legs.

I've snapped.

She's broken me.

There's only so much I can take, so much denial I can face before I crack.

Last night, I bent. Just now . . . I broke.

I rinse my body off, turn off the shower, wrap a towel around my waist, and storm into her bedroom, where she's rubbing lotion onto her skin. I charge toward her. She looks up just in time and gasps as I push her against the wall.

"You want to play with fucking fire, well, you just set off an inferno," I say, my forehead pressing against hers.

"K-Keller," she says breathlessly.

"Take my towel off, now." Her startled face means nothing to me as I repeat, "NOW."

Her hands fumble for a moment, but when she gains control of herself, she frees me of my towel and my cock springs forward.

She attempts to reach for it, but she hasn't earned that pleasure yet, so I pin her against the wall and say, "You will touch me when I say you can touch me."

Her eyes flash up to mine.

Not a hint of fear.

Not a hint of hostility.

But there is intrigue.

"Let's get one thing straight right fucking now," I say, breathing heavily. "You might be a future queen, but when it comes to the bedroom, I'm your goddamn king. Got it?"

She swallows hard. "G-got it."

"You will address me as 'my King.'"

"Okay."

"Okay, what?" I ask as I spread her legs with my hand.

"O-okay, my King."

"Good girl," I say, dragging my hand up her thigh to the triangle of fabric that covers her pussy. "You will no longer wear underwear. Ever."

"Yes, my King," she says, her voice smoother now.

"I'm waiting," I say.

"Oh." She scrambles out of her underwear and toes it to the side.

"And when I tell you to drop to your knees, you drop."

"Yes, my King."

I curl my hand into her hair and whisper, "Drop."

Keeping her hands to herself, she drops to her knees as I keep my hand twisted in her hair. Her eyes look up at mine, but I pull on the silky, wet strands, forcing her to drop her head. "I'll tell you when you can look at me."

The hand not holding her hair props me against the wall as I try to gather my breath, because, fuck, she's so responsive, so submissive. It makes me even harder.

I spread my legs and say, "Take my balls into your hand and make me come."

"May I touch your cock?"

"No. You teased my cock far too much, so you don't deserve it. You have two minutes to make me come. If you can't, then you'll be punished."

"And if I do make you come?"

"Then you did your job. Did you expect a reward?"

"No, my King," she says and, fuck me, the sound of her voice saying that makes me even harder.

"Good, now make me come."

Like the good girl she is, she rubs her hands together, warming them, and then she reaches between my legs, gently taking my balls into her palm. I sigh as she lightly pulls on them, just enough to not be ticklish, but not too much to cause pain. It's perfect, especially when she rubs her thumb down the seam of my testicles. She repeats the motion several times before she brings her mouth closer to them.

"My King, would you let go of my hair so I can get closer?"

"Yes," I answer, letting her wet tendrils fall over her shoulders. And then she slides between my legs and brings her mouth to my balls. She flicks her tongue out on the backside, and it feels so fucking good that I brace my other hand against the wall and curl my fists.

She flicks and flicks and flicks, making my cock swell between my legs.

"Fuck," I breathe out.

Keeping her tongue on my balls, she grips them in her hand and pulls them down slightly while she licks up. The difference in direction, the sensation of her movements, makes my stomach bottom out as I feel my balls pull together.

Still tugging, almost to the point of pain but not quite there yet, definitely turning me on, she brings them into her mouth and sucks as her thumb slides to the back of my balls, right to my perineum, where she taps.

Tap.

Suck.

Pull.

Tap.

Suck.

Pull.

"Good girl," I say. "Just like that. Fuck, you make me so hard." My balls tighten, the base of my cock swells. I'm right . . . there . . .

Tap.

Suck.

Pull.

Then her tongue drags up the seam, causing my whole body to quiver with euphoria. I'm seconds from exploding, my orgasm right on edge.

"Fuck, Lilly, I'm going to come. Take me in your mouth."

She lifts from my balls, slips her mouth over the head of my cock, and sucks. I come into her throat, my body freezing in place as my muscles ripple with pleasure.

"Shit," I mutter as I rest my head against my hands on the wall, feeling every spurt of my orgasm until there's nothing left. "Fucking hell." I glance down at Lilly as she removes her mouth from my cock. I place my fingers under her chin and encourage her to stand.

I help her up by offering my hand, and then I lightly pin her against the wall again. *She's a natural.* That was fucking incredible. I press a soft kiss across her mouth. She sighs and moves her hand up my chest. It's a sweet kiss, one we could both easily get lost in for hours. Actually, I could spend all day here, playing with her mouth, tangling our tongues, but I know we've things to do, so I pull away.

"Thank you," I tell her, looking her in the eyes.

"It was my pleasure, my King."

"Tonight, you'll get what you deserve."

Her eyes light up. "You're going to make me wait?"

"Yes, Lilly. You'll wait, but it'll be worth it." I drag my finger over her cheek. "If you need to take care of yourself, go ahead, but you won't get me until tonight."

She shakes her head. "I want to wait for you."

"Good answer." I kiss her lips again and then pull away, giving us distance. "Get dressed. We have work to do."

I attempt to push away, but she grips my waist and holds me in place. "Keller?" she asks, sounding insecure.

"Yes?"

"Can we just—can we just talk for a second? After last night and this morning, I want to make sure we're on the same page." Her eyes drift down as she says, "I know I put on an agitated front during our run, but when you wouldn't kiss me, it really hurt my feelings and made me feel incredibly insecure. I've made it clear that I want something with you. Before I get my hopes up, though, I just need to know what to expect."

If I'm honest, what I didn't expect was the many different facets of this woman's personality. When I first met her, I thought our country was doomed. Yet she's shown depth, integrity, intelligence, empathy, and now . . . passion. I don't know what we can have between us, but after her sexual submission to me, her natural reverence, I know I want to try.

I tilt her head up with my thumb to her chin. "Where do we stand?" Her eyes search mine as she lightly nods. "Tell me this, what do you want from me?"

"I want you," she whispers. "I want all of you. And I don't

want you to regret being with me. I don't want you to second-guess if what we're doing is the right thing. And when I lift up on my toes to kiss you, I want you to meet me halfway, not deny me your affection."

"It was out of self-preservation," I say. "You must know, at this point, the only reason I've been so controlled around you is because of the sensitive situation we're in. You would've been claimed as mine weeks ago if you were anyone else."

"What about now?" she asks, her fingers dancing up my bare chest. "Are you claiming me as yours?"

I pause, the weight of her question resting heavily on my shoulders. It goes against everything I've been taught, every-thing I've ever fucking known, but . . . fuck me, I like her. So goddamn much, and even though there's a little voice in the back of my head telling me what I'm about to say is against all my rules, I don't stop myself, because this full-body passion I have for this woman wins out.

She's the woman I want, and there's no way I can turn off that feeling.

And I doubt that it will ever go away.

So, I'm letting myself win.

"Yes," I whisper. "I'm claiming you as mine, Lilly."

Her smile stretches across her face as she loops her arm around my neck, pulling me in close so our foreheads connect. She reaches up so her lips are a whisper away. I know exactly what she's looking for. So, I meet her halfway and connect our mouths, stealing a searing kiss from her all over again.

So searing, that both of our mouths part at the same time as I press her against the wall, holding her ribcage so she can't move. I tilt my head to the side for a better angle and then drive my tongue into her mouth. Her moan vibrates through me, so I cup her breast and roll her nipple between my fingers.

She moans again and wraps her leg around mine, pressing her center against my once-again hardening cock. Christ.

I lift her up and she wraps both legs around my waist now as I hold her against the wall and rock my hips into hers.

"Yes," she gasps as her hand floats to the back of my head, where she tugs on my hair.

"Harder," I rasp as my mouth falls to her collarbone. I suck on her skin, marking her as mine, while she tugs on my hair even more. I continue to drive my hard cock against her thong-covered center. "Mine," I growl as I nip at her skin, sucking hard, knowing I'll leave a bruise, just what I want. "You're fucking mine."

"Yes, my King," she says with a gasp. "Oh God, you make me so hot."

I growl again, my hips moving so goddamn fast I don't have a moment to catch my breath. All I can think about is making sure she knows exactly who she belongs to in this moment. I piston my hips in and out, slamming her against the wall now.

"Come for me, Lilly." I drag my tongue up the column of her neck and when I reach her mouth, I kiss her, hard. There's no finesse about it. Our tongues slap together, her nails claw into my back to the point that I'm pretty sure she draws blood, but I say nothing because it's spurring me on.

I drive harder and harder and harder, the dresser next to us shaking from the force of my hips, and when I feel her tense around me, I don't stop.

"Fuck, I'm—I'm there," she says right before she lets out a low moan, her nails dangerously dug into my skin, and she comes. "Yes, oh God, Keller . . . yes."

It takes me two more pulses before I'm coming as well, my cum shooting between us.

Once my hips slow down and we're both sated, I lay her on the bed. I lean over and press a kiss to her lips and whisper, "Stay here."

When I lift up, I go to the bathroom, wash myself, and wet a washcloth for her.

Entering the room, I catch her smiling and watching me the whole time, a look of total satisfaction on her face. I situate myself between her legs, spread them, and then lean down and swipe my tongue all the way up her arousal, her gasp like a goddamn symphony to my ears.

"Fucking delicious," I say before taking the washcloth and cleaning her up.

She sighs into the mattress. "God, Keller, you're so hot."

"Glad you think that." I finish up, fold the washcloth over, and turn my back toward her.

"Oh God," she gasps and sits up. "I made you bleed."

I sit down next to her and hand her the washcloth. "Good, that means I'm yours now."

She dabs at the fingernail imprints. "Are you okay?"

"Perfect, Lilly." I grip her leg, the one that's wrapped around me, as she scoots closer to dab at my scratches. "You're going to have a serious hickey on your collarbone. Wear it with pride under your shirt. You hear me?"

"I wouldn't dream of wearing it any other way."

"No one else fucking touches you, from here on out. Got it? Even if you don't stay here, you're mine."

Her lips press a kiss to my heated back. "Yours, Keller. Only yours." And then she sets the washcloth down and wraps her arms around my waist in a hug.

I grip her arms from the front and say, "You were supposed to wait until tonight, but, fuck, you're irresistible."

"I can say the same about you."

"Today's going to be a tough day, Lilly. We have some intense things to go over. I want you to know, though, that I'm here. And no matter what, I will never—and I mean never— let anything happen to you. You're my responsibility. You're safe with me."

"I've never doubted it."

I turn and lay her back down on the bed, only to hover

over her. I press a kiss to her nose. "Get dressed, and don't forget, skip the goddamn underwear."

She smiles. "I will."

IN OUR LEARNING ROOM, I've drawn the curtains, eclipsing the space into complete darkness besides a single nightstand light. In the middle of the floor is one chair with Lilly strapped to it in zip ties.

Earlier, while we were eating breakfast, Lara and Brimar staged a kidnapping. They came in from behind, put a bag over her head, and secured her against her will. She screamed, being caught off guard, and they dragged her to the learning room.

It made me fucking sick to my stomach to watch. I wish this wasn't part of the training every royal has to go through, but it's the reality of the situation. Because of their status, there are enough threats—with a few successful kidnappings in the past throughout the world, where they've been held for ransom—to warrant the training.

After they secured her to the chair, keeping the bag over her head, Lara and Brimar came back out to the dining room, where we cleaned up and discussed the next plan of action. I would coach Lilly through the kidnapping while Brimar and Lara would act as the captors.

"Let me talk to her first, and then I'll have you come in," I say to Lara and Brimar.

They both nod. They hold a belt, and a few other things to threaten her with.

I step into the room and shut the door behind me, my eyes falling to Lilly, who's slouched forward, the zip ties pulling on her delicate skin. Walking up to her, I place my hands on her thighs and whisper, "How are you doing, Lilly?"

"Keller," she cries. "What's happening?"

"Crisis management. This won't be fun, but it's necessary, okay?"

She nods. "Are you going to stay here?"

"Yes. I'll be by your side the whole time, coaching you. Remember, this is an exercise, and we're trying to make it as realistic as possible. Lara and Brimar are going to come into the room in a second and act like they're your captors. Okay?"

She nods, and I continue to smooth my hands over her thighs. "Your goal is to become their friend, to gain their trust. You need to form a bond with them, because if you form a bond, it's less likely the captor will hurt you."

"Okay. I . . . I can do that."

"Good girl," I whisper as I move my hands up to her hips. "Are you hurting?"

"The zip ties are a little tight, but they're okay. I understand the need to take this seriously."

"Let me know if you need me to loosen the ties."

"I will."

I stand and press my palm to her cheek beneath the bag. She sinks into my touch, and that's where I stay for a few more beats, staring down at this beautiful girl. When I say I snapped earlier, I did. The willpower I was hanging on to, broke in the blink of an eye, and now that I've opened myself to what I've been feeling for this woman, I can't seem to stop myself from taking every morsel of what I want from her. Even a simple touch.

"I'm nervous," she says so, so softly.

Because I can't stand seeing her like this, I lean down and place a soft kiss to her shaking hand. "I'll be right here. I'd never let anything bad happen to you. Right?"

She nods. "Right."

"Good. I'm going to let them in now. Listen carefully, be a good girl, and focus."

"Okay," she says.

I crack the door open, letting Lara and Brimar know we're

ready.

Brimar kicks the door, shooting it into the wall, making a loud crashing noise. Lilly startles in her chair, and it takes everything in me not to reach over and soothe what I can only imagine is her terrified heart.

Lara walks up to Lilly and tears the bag off her head. Lilly blinks a few times, her tear-stained cheeks reddened from the heat of the bag. When she looks up at Brimar and Lara, they flash the light right at her face, causing her to wince and look away.

"Is that too bright for you?" Lara asks in an American accent.

"Yes," Lilly responds.

"Perfect, then we'll leave it as is." Lara walks around the chair and drags her fake gun over Lilly's cheek. "You're much smaller than I expected."

"She was an easy grab," Brimar says in an American accent as well as he snaps a belt against the wall, startling Lilly again. "You've made yourself a target for a while. Carelessly waltzing around in public, not following the protocol I'm assuming was taught to you."

Lara runs her gun along Lilly's neck. "It was almost as if she wanted us to capture her."

From where I'm leaning against the wall, arms crossed, I say, "Lilly, at this moment, you need to memorize everything you can, from the way they talk, their dialect, their clothes, how they look if you can see. What's in their hands, what they smell like, what the room looks like, if you hear anything like the ocean or traffic or anything that would indicate your surroundings. This is vital."

"Okay." She clears her throat and asks, "Why on earth would I want you to capture me?"

Lara twists her hand into Lilly's hair and pulls her head back. "Are you being sarcastic with us?"

Stepping in again, I say, "Lilly, I know this might be hard

for you, but don't provoke them. Don't joke. Keep calm, be patient, and listen to everything they have to say. Try to understand them. I know it's in your nature to defend yourself, but when you're kidnapped, you have to drop those defenses and concentrate on becoming agreeable."

"Okay, sorry."

"Don't apologize, you're learning."

"I asked you a question," Lara repeats, tugging on her hair.

"Sorry," Lilly says. "That was out of line."

"Ooo, she learns quick, doesn't she, sweetie?" Lara asks Brimar.

"She sure does. Now, let's see what else she can learn."

We spend the next hour role-playing, Lara and Brimar testing her, dropping hints here and there, and I watch as Lilly calmly asks them questions, listens to them intently, nods, and even gets Lara to talk about her childhood for a moment. I'm fucking impressed.

"Okay, I think that's enough," I say to Lara and Brimar, who quickly take the light out of Lilly's face. Lara cuts the zip ties and releases Lilly, who rubs her wrists, looking exhausted.

With concerned, unsure eyes, she looks up at me and asks, "How did I do?"

If we were alone, I'd take her into my lap and cradle her against my chest, making sure she was okay, but since we're with Lara and Brimar, I know we don't have that privilege.

"We need to see." Lara and Brimar bring in a table and extra chairs and we all take a seat. Lara passes Lilly a bottle of water, and I wince as she gulps it down. No doubt she was thirsty from nerves, adrenaline, and constant questions. Once I have the notepad and pen in hand, I ask, "Princess Lilly, can you please tell us everything you observed while kidnapped? The more we know, the more we can try to find the culprits."

"Oh." She nods and sits taller, crossing her legs at her ankles like she's been taught. Chin parallel to the ground, she speaks calmly as she says, "It was a couple. They called each other 'sweetie.' Both American with no particular regional accent. I couldn't quite see facial features thanks to the light in my eyes, but I was able to observe the woman had long, blonde hair in a ponytail and was about five-nine, would be my guess. The man had a large frame, bulky shoulders, and no hair. Boisterous voice. He was just taller than the woman. They mentioned Italy at one point, and I learned that the woman actually grew up just outside of Denver, Colorado."

"Great. And what about your location? Do you know where they took you?"

"It was cold, had stone walls, and the ocean was just outside the window. I could smell it and hear it, so I assumed it was close. They used clear-coated zip ties, and the man held a brown leather belt while the woman had a handgun that fits in the back of her pants. They argued at one point about a payment they had to make to a Salvador. They whispered it, but I was still able to hear them clearly."

"Salvador, that's a great lead," Lara says, acting as the detective now. "Anything distinctive about the male and female?"

Lilly thought for a moment. "I don't know if this would matter, but I was fairly sure the woman was lefthanded and the male was righthanded."

"Why do you think that?" Brimar asks.

"Well, when the woman grabbed my hair, I noticed that it was her right hand, which would leave her dominant hand available to hit me or whatever. And the male, I don't know. The way he pointed at me. He always gestured with his right hand."

"Good, Princess Lilly. Those things are helpful to note," I add. She's actually right, although I'm not sure if she picked that up during the simulation or from being around them for a week. At least she gave good reasoning, and that could be helpful.

"Anything else you can tell us?"

"Ah, yes, one more big thing, they both reeked of fish. Absolutely atrocious, I nearly passed out from the smell."

Lilly lifts her brow, and I laugh out loud as Brimar sniffs his shirt.

"We do not." Lara sniffs herself as well while Lilly chuckles.

"That's what you get for shining that light in my eyes for so damn long."

I lift from the table and say, "I think that concludes our kidnapping training. You did brilliantly, Lilly."

"You really did," Lara says.

Brimar breathes into his hand and smells. "I brushed my teeth."

Lara pokes his stomach. "She was joking."

"Well, just in case, I'm going to go take another shower." Brimar takes off, Lara following him.

"Yeah, maybe I'll change my clothes."

When they're gone, I help Lilly up from her chair and bring her wrists up to my mouth. "Are you okay?" I kiss her sensitive skin. "Are your wrists sore?"

"They're okay." She sighs against me and asks, "So I really did a good job?"

"You did. I'm really proud. You were composed, calm, and despite enduring a stressful situation, you remained poised. I was really impressed."

She smiles. "That means a lot to me." She drops her hands to my chest. "Now what?"

"Now, we take a break, and then after lunch, you're going to learn a new tradition."

"Ooo, I can't wait."

I tilt her chin up and move my mouth over hers, stealing a kiss before pulling away. It's going to be really fucking hard keeping my hands off her now that I've had a taste. I just need to make sure it's the right place, the right time.

Chapter Fifteen

LILLY

Keller: THE INFORMATIVE: A town is at the mercy of a love triangle. Fights have broken out on the streets, friendships have been lost, and family rifts have become so strong that businesses are now suffering. Shame has been thrown toward the angler's wife as she strolls the cobbled streets of Kirkfell. And now that the town is in shambles, she has decided to walk away from both men and is harboring with her sister to help heal the town.

"Holy shit," I whisper as I read the text a few more times. My phone chimes with another text message.

Timmy: Okay, I'm going to need an update. You're all over the news here. Is what they're saying true?

Lara, Brimar, and Keller are all preparing lunch, so I sink onto the couch next to the fireplace, one of my favorite places in the "castle", and text Timmy back.

Lilly: Long story short, I'm next in line for the crown here.

Timmy: WHAT? I mean, I knew you were royalty, but the next in line? So, if something happens to the king, you're the next monarch?

Lilly: *Correct, but they're giving me the option, and I haven't decided what I want to do yet.*

Timmy: *Which way are you leaning?*

I look up from my phone and stare out at the quaint living room. The rich history that these walls must have experienced. The people who've walked in and out of the front entryway. The wood-carved doors that replicate the landscape of the country. The wooden bowls carved by Torskethorpians from the past. The embroidered table runners and doilies. The oil paintings on the walls. There's so much about Torskethorpe that just feels right. That feels like home.

I turn back toward my phone.

Lilly: *I think I'm leaning toward saying yes. And that seems so crazy because my life is in Miami, but since being here, I've felt closer to my mom. There's so much of her here, I just . . . I feel like I don't have that in Miami.*

Timmy: *Because you lost everything, even the house you grew up in.*

Lilly: *And you know I love you and our wagon, we worked so hard creating the brand around it, but I just feel like I could make an impact here, you know?*

Timmy: *You make an impact every day on South Beach, showing off wet nipples with your wet T-shirt contests. But if you're speaking of more of a humanitarian impact, then, yes, you probably belong up there. LOL.*

Lilly: *I do kind of miss the wet nipples.*

Timmy: *They miss you, but you aren't needed here. And I mean that in a loving way.*

Lilly: *I know you do. God, Timmy, do you think I'm crazy?*

Timmy: *No, I think this is admirable. You're taking on a huge responsibility, putting others first over yourself. I'm proud of you.*

Lilly: *That means a lot to me.*

Timmy: *Now, tell me about Thor. How are things with him?*

I smile and bring my knees closer to my chest as I text him back.

Lilly: *Things are good . . .*

Timmy: *Umm, you're going to need to elaborate. Is that ellipsis alluding to something naughty?*

Lilly: *It is. After a lot of push and pull, Keller finally kissed me last night, and it was everything I hoped for. God, Timmy, he's so sexy, and not just in his looks, but in the way he grips me, how he talks to me, how he treats me like I'm the most precious thing to walk into his life. This might sound cliché, but he honestly treats me like a queen.*

Timmy: *I'm sweating. One look at him and he seemed like the kind of guy who holds his women up on a pedestal. Have you . . . done anything more than kissing?*

Lilly: *He dry-humped me last night.*

Timmy: *That's hot.*

Lilly: *Well, technically it went from dry-humping to wet humping.*

Timmy: *Even hotter.*

Lilly: *And this morning, I made him come by just playing with his balls. And then . . . he humped me against the wall.*

Timmy: *Uh, excuse me? Tell me more about this ball thing.*

Lilly: *LOL. He told me to. I've never done that before, but it's like he's so in tune with his body that when I started touching him, he was ready to go, focused on what I was doing and only that.*

Timmy: *I've never orgasmed from ball play, but I've heard of it happening. Now I want to try it. What did you do?*

Lilly: *Oh my God! I'm not telling you how to fondle yourself. Also, I'm pretty sure your mouth can't reach your junk.*

Timmy: *You fail to realize the many men I have at my disposal. I can be their teacher.*

Lilly: *Figure it out yourself! But I will say this, when he was about to come, he made me take his cock in his mouth and, Timmy, easily the biggest, nicest penis I've ever seen.*

Timmy: *Really?*

Lilly: *Yes. Just the sight of his penis gets me going. It's long and has the perfect girth, with a perfect head. It's just . . . it's picture-worthy.*

Timmy: *The only great penis I've seen in a while is mine. You're so lucky.*

Lilly: You're ridiculous.

Timmy: And he humped you against a wall, how was that?

Lilly: Carnal. Hot. Everything I needed.

Timmy: Goddamn you and your luck.

Lilly: Not sure I'd say my current line of succession is about luck.

Timmy: True. BUT, you're a princess, you have a beautiful penis in your life, and you're being treated like a queen. It seems as though things are going well. Aren't you glad I convinced you to go?

Lilly: I was waiting for that . . . but, yes, I am. Being here, it feels as if I've found that missing piece in my life.

Timmy: I'm glad, but I need you to remember that when you're waving to crowds and knighting people, I'm the one who convinced you to take a chance on something new.

Lilly: I'll never forget. And when things settle down, will you promise to visit me?

Timmy: I'm waiting for an invitation. You just tell me when. Also, on the business side of things, if you stay up there, we need to figure out what to do about the Wagon and me buying you out.

Lilly: Don't worry about it.

Timmy: That's not how business works. We'll work out an agreement. You put your time into our wagon.

Lilly: Okay, we'll figure it out.

"Lilly?" Keller asks, pulling my attention from my phone.

"Yeah?" I smile up at him.

"Lunch is ready."

I set my phone down and say, "Okay."

"Were you talking with Timmy?"

I nod as I get off the couch. "Catching him up on everything. Now that the news broke, I thought it would be okay."

Keller's jaw tightens. "You mean, you haven't told him anything about what we're doing up here?"

"No." I shake my head. "I've kept everything very confidential. I wasn't sure how much I could tell him. I actually haven't talked to him that much at all. We've talked more about you than anything."

I think he's going to ask more questions about that, but he doesn't. He scratches the side of his cheek. "Brimar was thinking that Timmy could be the leak."

"What? No way. Not Timmy. Drama might be his middle name, but his loyalty is as strong as yours. He'd never say anything. Plus, I haven't told him any details, so he wouldn't have much to talk about."

Keller doesn't respond, leading me to believe that he isn't satisfied with that answer.

Growing even more serious, I say, "Keller, he's not the leak."

"Okay," he says. "But I don't think it would hurt to just check it out."

"Are you serious? I'm telling you right now that he's not the leak. Why don't you believe me?"

Sighing, he fits his hand with mine and holds it tightly as he looks me in the eyes. "Lilly, one of the things you need to realize about this position is that anyone, and I mean anyone, for the right price, would be willing to sell information. We've seen our fair share of scandals, and a lot of the time, they come from people connected closely to the crown."

"Timmy is the only family I have left. I'm telling you, it's not him."

"Okay," Keller says. "I trust you."

"Thank you," I say as I release his hand and start to walk by him, but he stops me with a hand to my waist and tilts my jaw up with his thumb before placing his lips on mine. I sink into his kiss, and he washes away every last bit of irritation I was just feeling by this simple connection.

His affection is lethal, and I fear how he'll use it in the future.

"I'M MAD AT YOU GUYS," I say, causing all three heads in the room to pop up.

"You're mad at us?" Lara asks. "Why?"

Keller's eyebrows draw together, concern etching his features.

"Yeah, I'm really mad at you."

"Care to explain why?" Keller asks.

"Sure." I set down the scissors in my hand and carefully say, "We've spent how long in this freaking castle, and today is the day you decide to tell me about paper cutting? We could've been doing this nightly the whole time, but instead, you wait until a few days before we have to leave. That's truly doing me a disservice, because look at how good I am at this." I unfold my paper, revealing a row of connected penises cut into paper.

Lara snorts, covering her mouth.

Brimar chuckles.

And Keller gives me a look.

"I could have been cutting genitals this whole time."

"You're not supposed to be cutting genitals, Lilly," Keller says. "You're supposed to be working on mountain scenery."

"Yeah, well, the mountains didn't excite me like all the penises. I mean, look at how good this is." I stretch my paper out like an accordion. "It took some real imagination to accomplish this. Let me see what you guys have done."

Lara unfolds her paper, showing off an intricate, swirly design. It's pretty, but it's no penis lineup.

Brimar nearly rips his as he pulls it apart. He's been struggling the entire time, grumbling about how paper cutting isn't a tradition he's good at nor cares to be good at. His design is a simple line of hearts.

And then Keller . . . the overachiever, unfolds his, showing off an elaborate cut-out bird on a tree limb and leaves surrounding it.

"What the hell is that?" I point to his.

"Paper cutting done right," he says. "This is what's expected."

"That's unrealistic. Do you really think people expect me to be able to cut out something like that?"

"They do, that's why we're working on it."

After lunch, Keller sat us all down with paper and freshly sharpened scissors and went into the history of paper cutting —a *long* history of it—followed by a step-by-step tutorial. I compared it to cutting out snowflakes, and man oh man, the backlash I got for that. I was told "it's so much more than cutting out a snowflake." And, sure, Keller might've been right about that, but a whole bird scene on a tree? That's a bit much, don't you think?

"Well, if that's what's expected of me, then we should've started this a while ago. Sure, I have the obvious raw talent, but this seems as though it takes much practice. When am I to be expected to show off my paper-cutting skills?"

"At Torg," Keller answers.

"Explain what Torg is again." I smile sheepishly, but Keller just raises that perfectly posed eyebrow of his at me before sighing.

"Torg is our end-of-summer festival. It's a week-long—"

"Ah, right, sort of like the Highland games in Scotland, right? Everyone around the country joins together to show off their talents, baking, and enjoy the rich history of Torskethorpe."

"Correct," Keller says.

"And it's when the big trade happens too. That's actually what *Torg* stands for," Lara says. "It means *trade*."

"And that's when the royals trade their handcrafted items with the public, like the embroidery?"

"Right," Lara says. "It's the best time of the year."

"And the royal family is supposed to show off their talents within our traditions," Brimar says, chiming in as he attempts to cut another piece of paper. "You're not expected to be the best, but you're expected to be proficient."

"He's right," Keller says. "And I'm going to tell you right now, a row of penises for your paper cutting isn't going to go over well."

"Shame," I say, my prideful chest deflating. "I really know my way around a dick."

I glance up at Keller, who's now giving me a killer glare.

"Oh, wait, is that what a queen would call it? A dick? Or is that too crude? What about *crotch*?" I wince. "No, that just sounds gross. Hmm, *cock* is too vulgar. *Penis* seems normal, although funny, and I don't think I should be giggling when I say penis in front of other people. Maybe sword—"

"You won't be talking about penises in front of the general public or dignitaries, so no need to worry about it," Keller says.

I slip the scissors on my fingers and start circling them around. "What a shame."

"Can you not swing those around?" Keller asks. "They're very sharp."

"What, the scissors?" I ask just as they slip off my finger.

And then, as if the world has turned into slow motion, I watch them fly through the air, across the room, headed right for Brimar.

"Noooooooooo," I call out.

Unsuspecting and too busy working on another design, he doesn't see the death scissors approaching him—flying at him —freshly sharpened point first.

But the rest of the room sees the end target.

And together, we collectively gasp as they grow closer and closer.

And . . . closer.

My voice sounds like a stuck-in-the-mud robot as I say, "Briiiiii-marrrrrrrr."

He glances up at just the right moment, his eyes locking in

on the catapulted scissors, and quick like a cat, he lifts his beefy hand in front of his face, only for the scissors to impale right into the meat of his palm.

And like a dart stuck in the bullseye, the scissors stick where they penetrated.

"Oh, dear Jesus." Bile rises to the top of my throat.

"Fuck," Keller says, setting his stuff down and going over to Brimar, as Lara runs off for a first aid kit.

"I stabbed him," I yell as I hop off the couch and start running in place. "Oh God, I stabbed him."

Keller lowers Brimar's hand on his lap and calls out to Lara, "Grab some towels."

I shake my hands in front of me. "I'm a murderer. Bloodshed is on my name." I grip my forehead. "I'm so sorry. I didn't mean to. I wasn't aiming for . . . oh God." I dry-heave. "It's just, it's just sticking straight up."

I get down on my knees next to Brimar and grip his chair.

"What can I do?" When my eyes fall to the impaled part of his palm, I dry-heave again, and again. "It's just so disgusting. I'm sorry, but oh God, that's so vile."

"Lilly, maybe take a step back," Keller says as I dry-heave again. Lara arrives with the first aid kit and towels.

"Are you going to take it out?" I ask, hovering now. "I think you should take him to the hospital. Don't you think? I almost murdered him. There has to be some sort of penance for that. Is there? Does it go on my record? Do royals have records? Oh God, you're just going to pull it out? Wait, is his blood bubbling? Why is it bubbling?"

"Lilly, please step back," Keller says.

"I'm sorry, I'm just—I can't believe this happened. I mean, it was headed right for his face, and then *BAM*, his palm caught it. What if his palm didn't catch the scissors, what if . . ." My voice trails off as the worst-case scenario hits me straight in the chest. "What if—what if it impaled his eye?"

That does me in.

I can't hold it back.

My stomach revolts.

My body shakes.

And then, in seconds, I puke all over Keller's back just as he pulls the scissors out of Brimar's palm. The smell of the puke, the sound of Brimar's pain, and blood bubbling over his hand . . . it's more than I can take.

The world fades around me.

And my body crashes to the floor.

Chapter Sixteen

KELLER

"Jesus fucking Christ." Lilly's vomit seeps into my shirt, her body's lifeless on the floor, and I have a pair of bloody scissors in my hand.

"I'm fine," Brimar says. "Take care of her. I think she cracked her head on the side of the table."

"Shit," I say, unsure of what to fucking do with the puke on my back other than losing the shirt. I take the scissors and cut a slit at the collar of my shirt, and then, like the fucking Hulk, I rip the shirt open and say, "Lara, help me take this off."

She peels it off my back, gathering the puke, and then takes it to the kitchen, where she throws it out.

I turn toward Lilly, who's lying lifeless on the floor, and I gently examine her, rolling her to her side, where I find a gash on her forehead. The exact spot where she got hit in the head with the broom. The wound has reopened.

"Fuck," I mutter as I reach for the first aid kit. "Lara, take care of Brimar."

"Sure thing," she says as we both grab for gauze in the first aid kit.

I soak up her blood, dabbing gently while examining the rest of her body, making sure she didn't hurt anything else. I'm checking over her arms when her eyes flutter open.

"I . . . I can see your nipples," she says. Of course, that would be the first thing out of her mouth.

I glance down at my chest and then back up at her. "That's because you puked on my back."

"No, that doesn't sound like me," she says. "I don't do embarrassing things like that."

"Well, you did, then you passed out, hit your head, and reopened your wound."

"Are you sure?"

"Yes," I say, letting out a heavy sigh.

"You seem agitated," she says.

"I *am* agitated."

"Uh-oh," she whispers. "Was it something I did?"

Lara chuckles next to me, and I say from over my shoulder, "Don't humor her."

"Sorry," Lara says. "She's just so oblivious sometimes, it's funny."

"Ouch, be careful," Brimar says. "She might've stabbed me in the meat, but it still hurts."

"Wait . . . is that Brimar?" Lilly asks. "Oh God, that's right, I impaled him with scissors." She reaches out her hand . . . to nobody. "Brimar, I didn't mean it, I didn't mean to." She dry-heaves, and to fuck if I'm going to have her throw up again.

I grab the supplies I need, loop my arms under her, and then lift her up. "I'm taking her upstairs."

"Wait, no. Brimarrrrrrr," Lilly calls out as I leave the living

255

room and head up the stairs. "He's going to hate me forever. You need to take me back to him so I can apologize properly."

"You already said sorry, and I'm not about to watch you dry-heave some more."

I take her into her room, lay her down on her bed, and then spread out my supplies.

"You're all grumbly," she says as I unwrap a butterfly strip to close up her cut. "Am I in trouble?"

"No, Lilly."

"Then why are you acting like I'm in trouble?"

"I'm not acting like you're in trouble, I'm just trying to calm down. A lot happened in thirty seconds and I'm trying to process it all." She's right. Had Brimar not reacted as quickly as he did, the scissors would've impaled his eye. *Thank fuck he's as agile as he is.* I take a deep breath, clean her wound, stop the bleeding, and then place the butterfly bandage on her forehead. It's going to bruise. Hopefully, makeup will cover it. I check the back of her head and can feel a small lump forming. I'll need to watch that.

"I see . . . do you think I'm a criminal? Because if you do, I need to tell you, it's not in my nature to stab people. That's the first time I've ever punctured anyone. I mean, there was that one time in seventh grade when I accidentally poked Basil, a kid in my class, with a paperclip, and when I say accidentally, I mean on purpose, because he said his boobs were bigger than mine, and he was flat-chested. So, I opened up a paperclip, and as he walked by, I jabbed, but I didn't puncture his skin, only snagged his favorite sweater, which was more of a win, because it created an irreparable hole. But I swear I'm not a criminal."

"I know, Lilly."

"Truly an accident, so no need to be grumbly."

"I'm not," I say in a grumbly tone as I stand from the bed. "Now don't fucking move, do you hear me?"

"Where are you going? You say you're not grumbly but you still sound grumbly."

"I have to go take a shower. You threw up on my back, remember?"

"Like I said, that's not my brand. I don't throw up on backs. Toilets, yes. Trash cans, absolutely. Perhaps the gutter on the side of a street? A few times. And then there was one moment where I threw up on Carmichael's history book, but that's because I was going to throw up on his art project and he stuck his history book under me before I could. But backs . . . no."

I walk away. "Just stay put."

Once in the bathroom, I slip out of my clothes and step into the tub. Unable to scrub my own back, I dribble some body wash over my back and then turn on the water and do the best I can, washing the soap off and attempting to scrub myself. It's a quick shower, I'm in and out, drying off quickly and returning to my bedroom, where I throw on a simple black T-shirt and sweatpants.

When I return to Lilly's bedroom, she hasn't moved, and the only thing different from when I left is that she's humming while dancing her fingers across her stomach. When she spots me, she smiles sheepishly. "Now that I think about it, I believe I might've thrown up on your back."

Christ, this woman.

Shaking my head and trying not to smile from how ridiculous she is, I sit on the edge of her bed and cup her cheek softly.

"You're such a pain in my ass."

She chuckles. "Did I scare you?"

"What do you think?"

She taps her chin. "Hmm, well, given your grumpy disposition and the fact that you don't like to show your true feelings, I'm going to say yes."

"Yes, you scared me. Seeing you pass out like that . . . is not something I want to see again."

"Awww, Keller, you care about me." She pokes my stomach playfully.

"Yeah, I do, so don't fucking scare me like that." I connect my forehead with hers and press a small kiss to the tip of her nose.

She loops her hand around my neck, holding me in place. "It's cute when you're all grumbly and scared. I like you fussing over me."

"Yeah, well, no more passing out, and no more puking on my back. You're hot, Lilly . . . but not that hot to forgive a second round of that shit."

She laughs and then says, "Oh shit, I need to brush my teeth."

"I was going to mention that . . ."

"Are you saying my breath stinks?"

"Let's just say it's not minty fresh."

Her hand clamps over her mouth, her eyes wide. "Oh my GOD! Ew, don't look at me, I'm hideous."

I chuckle some more and help her up from the bed. With her arm looped through mine, I help her into the bathroom and assist her in brushing her teeth. Once she's "freshened up," I bring her back to the bed, where I gently lay her down.

"I'm going to go check on Brimar. You stay here, get some rest."

"I want to check on him too."

"Lilly, don't make me fight you over this. You hit your head again. You need to take a second to just relax."

"But I want to see if he's okay."

"You will in a bit, just relax for now."

"Fine, but only because the thought of walking down the stairs at the moment feels exhausting, not because you told me to stay here."

"At least you're honest." I start to walk away, but she clears her throat.

"Uh, excuse me?"

"What?" I ask her.

She taps her lips with her finger. "I'm going to need a kiss. That's unless you want me chasing behind you, looking for one."

I smirk and lower down as I say, "You're absurd." I kiss her lips sweetly and then lift off the bed. "Stay put. I'll be back to get you."

Pleased, I head down the stairs to where Brimar and Lara are sitting on the couch together, Lara holding a pack of ice on Brimar's palm.

"How are you?" I ask.

"Fine," Brimar answers in a clipped tone. "It's weird to think this is the first time I've had blood drawn since protecting the crown. And funny enough, it was from the person I'm trying to protect."

"Brimar, it was an accident," I say.

"I know, just frustrating is all. I think being in this castle, cooped up, unable to do our regular activities, it's starting to get to me."

"I think it's getting to all of us," Lara adds.

I pull on the back of my neck. "Yeah, me too. Only a few more days, though. How about this? Why don't you guys take off tomorrow to grab some last-minute supplies we might need for food, spend some time out, and maybe hit up the hot spring just down the road? I can handle Lilly."

"That's not a good idea," Brimar says. "We're here to serve and protect. I won't leave Lilly like that."

"Do you not trust me?" I ask him.

"I do, but my responsibility is to her."

"And you haven't had a day off in weeks. Take just the morning, the both of you, and come back refreshed."

"It might be a good idea," Lara says. "And we're running

low on supplies. We could try to make it until we leave, but we'd be pushing our luck. Plus, it might not hurt to have someone else look at your wound."

"There's nothing wrong with my hand. A butterfly stitch is all that's needed."

"Still, please take the morning," I say. "You need it. I promise, we won't go anywhere and we'll keep everything locked up. We'll be safe."

"Are you sure?" Brimar asks.

"Positive."

He nods his head. "Okay."

"And I'll be taking care of dinner tonight," I add. "Just sit back and relax, Brimar."

"Thank you, Keller."

"Hey, what are brothers for?" I ask as I walk away.

"ARE YOU SURE YOU'RE OKAY?" Lilly asks.

"Positive." Brimar offers her a curt smile. "I've had worse wounds growing up. This is nothing. Don't worry about me."

"Can I at least hug you? I won't feel right until I do."

Brimar nods and opens his arms to her. Lilly sinks into his large embrace and rests her head on his chest.

I made some simple sandwiches for dinner, nothing fancy, just used up some of the bread Brimar baked and leftover turkey we had in the fridge. Along with an arugula salad lightly dressed, it was a quick dinner.

We talked more about Torg, and by the time we all finished and cleaned up, it was time for bed. Long day, and we needed an early bedtime.

"Don't hate me," Lilly says.

"I don't. Now get some sleep. I heard you have a history quiz tomorrow."

Lilly's head picks up and swivels around to face me. "Really?"

"We shall discuss that tomorrow. Now say good night."

"Good night." Lilly gives him one more hug, waves to Lara, and then we walk up the stairs together. When we reach the top, she heads toward her room and I head toward mine. "Wait," she calls out. "Where are you going?"

"I'm going to my room."

"But . . ."

"Lilly, get ready for bed."

"Excuse me, but I don't expect to go to bed alone."

"Lilly," I say steadily. "Listen to me . . . get ready for bed."

"Urgh, you're frustrating." She storms into her bedroom. Can you tell she's feeling just fine?

When I reach my room, I take off my shirt and pants and stick them in my hamper before I head into the bathroom, where I brush my teeth. Shortly, Lilly joins me and does the same. I spit my toothpaste into the sink and rinse my mouth. When I'm done, I lean against the doorframe, watching her. She's in the shirt she borrowed from me, her hair tied into a loose bun.

When she's done brushing her teeth, she turns toward me and asks, "Are you going to make me say good night here, in this sterile bathroom?"

So fucking sassy when she doesn't get exactly what she wants.

I shake my head and walk up to her. I gently kiss her knuckles before pulling her to my bedroom. I make sure my bedroom door is shut and then pull back the covers of my bed. She lies down, and I remain standing.

"I had different plans for you tonight, plans that involved tying you up to this bed."

"Why are you saying that as if it's past tense?" she asks. "Because being tied up sounds yummy, especially if I'm naked."

"Because after today's events, that won't be happening." I slip into the bed with her and pull the covers over us.

"But I'm feeling fine."

"Yes, but your wrists are still red from the zip ties earlier, and I know if you were tied up in my bed, there's no way I'd be able to fuck you without fucking you too hard. And I don't want to hurt your head."

She turns toward me and rests her hand on my stomach. "You don't have to be so careful with me. I'm a big girl, I can handle a solid pounding, if that's what you desire."

It is what I desire, but I also don't want to give her a headache or cause any pain.

I tilt her chin up and look her in the eyes. "You're precious to me, therefore, I will be as careful as I fucking want. Do you understand?"

"Yes," she answers in an annoyed tone. Irritated, she rests her head on my shoulder, so I loop my arm around her and rest my hand on her thigh. Needing to feel her skin, I hike up her shirt and press my palm to her warm body.

"You're not wearing underwear," I say, feeling no fabric.

"You told me not to, so I didn't put any on. See, Keller, I can listen."

"I'm shocked," I say as I drag my fingers over her hip.

"I'm a very good listener," she says as her fingers move down my abs, one divot at a time, until her hand reaches the waistband of my briefs. It doesn't take much. Just her touch has me hard, ready to go.

"Are you? Because it seems as though you're about to slip your hand into my briefs without permission."

Her fingers pause. "Err, was I? Oops." She kisses my chest and quietly says, "I just want you, Keller." Her lips press against my jaw. "I want you bad. I want you inside of me. I want you to spread my legs and make me come. Being this close to you makes me feel desperate for your touch. Do you know how wet I've been all day, just thinking about what you might do to me tonight?"

"Tell me," I say.

She moves her fingers back to my chest. "Every time you touched me, innocently, it just reminded me of what was to come tonight. Every time you looked at me, our gazes catching in the middle of the room, I felt the need you have for me, and it only turned me on even more."

"And what about now?" I ask.

She rolls to her back and spreads her legs. Then she reaches down, swipes at herself, and lifts her fingers to my mouth, where I pull them in between my lips, sucking hard, tasting her.

"Dying for your mouth," she says. "Don't you want to make me come?"

"I do, but I also like making you wait."

"Keller," she groans.

"If you're turned on, then you may masturbate in front of me, but I'll need you naked."

"Are you going to touch me?"

"That will be for me to decide. Now, strip."

She sits up from the bed and pulls off her shirt. I push the covers down so her naked body is uncovered, and I watch as she spreads her legs and moves her hand between them. Her teeth roll over her bottom lip as she moves her fingers over her clit.

"God, I wish this was you instead," she sighs.

"Spread your legs more," I command, and she listens, letting them fall wider. "That's it. Now put your fingers on the outside of your labia and massage. I want you to tease yourself."

She listens and massages her labia, never giving herself what she actually needs, just turning herself on even more.

"That's right, Lilly." Moving my hand to her inner thigh, I drag my fingernails along her soft skin.

"Yes," she whispers.

My fingers dance over her stomach and down her other leg, never getting close enough to where she wants me.

"I need more, Keller."

I pinch her thigh, causing her to yelp. "Is that what you call me?"

"My King," she corrects herself. "I need more."

"Then stop."

"What?" she asks.

"Remove your hand, both of them, and place them behind your back."

She does as she's told and I let her lie like that. Nothing touching her, not giving her what she needs.

"You see, Lilly, when it comes to this bedroom, you don't tell me what you need, because I already know."

I reach over to my nightstand and pull out the vibrator I stole from her room. I switch it on and drag it over her breasts, letting the vibrations tingle through her top half. Then I roll it down her stomach and rest it on her pubic bone.

"You know, maybe I *will* tie you up tonight."

"I would like nothing more . . . my King."

My cock surges, and there's no stopping me. I know I should let her rest but, fuck, she wants this just as much as I do, so I rise from the bed, go to my closet where I keep my ties, and I grab four and toss them on the bed.

Gently, making sure not to hurt her already worn wrists and ankles, I tie her to all four posts of the bed, stretching her out.

I move my fingers over her arm and ask, "Does that hurt you?"

She shakes her head. "No, it feels amazing."

"Good."

Staring down at her, I take in the curves of her body, how the shadows of the room cross over her stomach and along her neck, her smooth skin ready to be marked by my eager mouth. And then those eyes . . . still a beautiful escape straight into her soul, and they've never been brighter than in this moment.

"You want me," I say as a statement, because I can see it in her body language.

"Badly, my King," she answers.

I kneel on the bed, my weight dipping the mattress as I straddle her shoulders with my hands, moving my mouth close to hers. Feeling the patter of her heartbeat against my chest, I press a soft kiss to her cheek, then to her eye, her other eye, and her other cheek. She sighs a heavenly sound as I bring my lips to her jaw, to the spot behind her ear, to her chin, and to the other side of her jaw.

Down the column of her neck, keeping my kisses soft, which causes a flood of goosebumps to break out over her skin. I drag my tongue along the rigid bone when I reach her collarbone. Her chest lifts as a light, almost undetectable moan falls past her lips.

Pleased with her response, I trail my lips farther south, right between her breasts. Her breathing picks up, and when I steal a glance at her, I catch her eyes squeeze shut in anticipation. Keeping my eyes on her, I flick her right nipple with my tongue. Her mouth parts and I take that moment to suck her breast into my mouth, making sure to pull on her nipple. Her arms tug on the ties as she lets out a deeper moan, this one more vocal.

I suck and play with her nipple piercing, moving it from side to side, knowing the sensation increases her arousal. When I switch to her other breast, I hear the vibrator fall to the mattress, so I pull back and reset it.

"Don't let that fall."

"It's teasing me."

"Good," I say then spend another five minutes just lapping at her breasts, sucking, nibbling, doing everything in my power to bring her close to her climax.

Her muscles tense beneath me, her breathing becomes more labored, and I know she's on the edge, so I pull away.

She groans out a protest, her eyes flashing open. I pull away from her, sitting up on the bed, leaving only her vibrator touching her, but not where she wants.

I grip the base of my hard cock, and I give it a few pumps, watching as her eyes take in every stroke. She wets her lips, and the utter satisfaction in her heady, hungry eyes spurs me on more. I bring my cock up to her mouth and without me having to say anything, she parts her lips and sucks the head of my cock into her warm, delicious mouth.

"Fuck, I could live here," I say.

Her tongue circles the tip, her mouth so fucking soft that I fear what will happen to my will when I finally get between her legs. If her mouth is this amazing, I can't imagine what her pussy will feel like.

While my cock is in her mouth, I grab the vibrator, turn it off, and move it to the side before moving my fingers to her slit. I gently slide them in to find her so goddamn wet that my cock surges in her mouth.

"Christ," I growl as I pull my cock from her mouth and move between her legs. I smooth my hands up her thighs and rest my thumbs on either side of her labia. I part her open and take in her glistening cunt. "Fucking beautiful," I say right before I flick out my tongue and take one long stroke. "Fuck me, you taste amazing," I say as she cries out in a long, drawn-out moan.

I grow closer, my cock pressing against the mattress, pained, begging for more of her mouth. But now that I've had this taste of her, there's no fucking way I'm leaving.

I prop my hands under her butt, angle her up, and I fucking feast.

I flatten my tongue and take long, drawn-out strokes against her piercing, lapping every last bit of her arousal. She writhes against the mattress, her hands clutching into fists, her breasts arching into the air, her nipples impossibly hard.

Turning my tongue into a point, I position it against her clit piercing making short, quick flicks, loving how responsive she is.

"Oh my God, my King. Please . . . please tell me I can come."

"You're free to come whenever you want," I say as I go back down on her, my scruff rubbing against her inner thighs as I suck her clit into my mouth, pulling just hard enough to cause her to cry out. When I glance up, tears caress the corners of her eyes.

I let her clit go and go back to flicking up and down.

Up.

And.

Down.

Until her legs clamp against me, her stomach hollows out, and a piercing moan falls past her lips.

"Oh, fuck me, oh my God, ohhhhhh . . . fuck," she cries, her orgasm ripping through her.

I let her ride my tongue until there doesn't seem to be anything left in her.

Her body sags into the mattress, her breathing settles, and the most satisfied look crosses her face when she opens her eyes.

I smooth my hands over her thighs and say, "So damn beautiful."

A lazy smile pulls at her lips as I sit up and stroke my cock again, offering myself some relief.

"I want you inside me," she says, tugging on her ties.

"Don't pull on those, as I don't want you hurting yourself. Relax."

"I want to hold you."

"Lilly, who's in charge?"

"You, my King," she whispers.

"Then stop telling me what you want and let me show you what you need."

I position myself between her legs and bring the tip of my erection to her pussy, still wet from her orgasm. I drag it up and down, causing her to release a hiss from her mouth.

"You don't need to hold me, Lilly. You need to feel how desperately I want you."

"Yes, my King," she whispers, urging her hips forward.

"Are you on birth control?"

She nods.

"Good, because I want this pussy bare. I want to feel every inch of your tight cunt, nothing between us."

"Please," she moans.

"Please, what?" I demand.

"Please," she moans again.

But I pull my dick away and straddle her body with my legs, bringing my cock to her mouth again. I'm addicted, I need to feel her tongue, her lips, one more time.

"Open for me."

She opens her mouth, and I slip my length inside, creating a different angle so I can pulse in deeper.

"Open wide, breathe through your nose." She does just that, and I slip in farther, hitting the back of her throat, and then pull out quickly. She gags but then opens her mouth again.

So, I do it again.

And again.

And again, until I feel my body start to tingle.

"Fuck," I say, pulling away and bracing my hands on the bed's headboard. "I could fuck your mouth all damn day, but I need that pussy."

I move back down her body, but pause and lower my mouth to hers, where I take her lips into a passionate kiss, mouths open, tongues tangling, moans mixing. Her enthusiasm to please me is such a huge turn-on and makes me feel like I've been missing something my whole life, and it's lying here, waiting for me.

"Your lips are so soft," I say, before giving her one more kiss and then trailing my lips across her breasts again, down her stomach, to her pubic bone, and then I part her once more and swipe my tongue along her slit.

"Yesss," she drags out.

And because I can't fucking stop, I lap at her clit a few more times before I pull away and line up my cock to her entrance.

"Deep breath, Lilly."

She takes a deep breath and then lets out the air as I enter her the first inch, causing her eyes to widen and her mouth to part in shock.

"I know, just take another deep breath."

She does, and I work myself in another inch, her pussy so tight that I know my life is changing with every goddamn inch I move inside her. This feeling ripping through me, this untouchable euphoria . . . I know I'll be chasing this high for the rest of my life with her.

I slowly work myself halfway in and then pause, giving her a second. "How are you doing, love?"

Her eyes flutter open at the sound of the pet name, a smile pulling at her lips. "Wonderful," she says, and I feel her entire body relax, opening her up even more. I take that moment to push inside the rest of the way.

She moans, biting down on her lower lip as I position my hands on the mattress for leverage. I take a few deep breaths as I take in how amazing this feels. So raw, so soft, so warm. There's nothing between us, nothing holding us back, and I'm connecting with her on a whole new level, a level I know that's scary to me but, fuck, there's no turning back now.

She might be the future queen.

I might be a loyal servant to this country, but at this

moment, there's no status. It's just me and her and our connection.

I move closer to her head, keeping my hips still, and I lift her chin, placing a kiss on her lips. She matches my kiss, my need. I reach up to one of her ties and loosen it, setting her hand free, which she immediately connects to my face, cupping my cheek.

"You make me feel so cherished, so wanted," she says in between kisses as I slowly rock my hips. She's so tight that I don't want to fucking hurt her.

"You okay?" I ask her.

"Perfect." Her thumb rubs over my cheek, her eyes watering again. "I'm so perfect."

I let her take charge of our kisses as I pulse in and out of her, picking up my pace with every stroke, the feeling of her clamping around me driving me to move quicker.

She slips her hand around the back of my head and sifts her fingers through my hair, holding on tight.

My hips hammer into her now, my will to keep it slow snapping, the feeling too delicious.

"Fuck, you feel too good, like goddamn heaven." I pulse harder, my pace relentless now.

"God," she cries out. "Yes, my King . . . right there. More."

Her lips return to mine, her fingers pulling on my hair, and something rips through me. I think it's the last thread of my self-control.

Everything around me fades to black, only the sound of her moans and our bodies connecting filling my ears. Every nerve ending is focused, zeroed in on one point, my muscles contracting inward, my pulse a steady beat.

"Fuck," I breathe out as sweat drips down my back, along my spine.

It's too good.

She's too fucking good.

I don't fucking deserve this, but I'm going to take it.

I pulse harder, faster.

My balls tighten.

My cock swells.

And a roar flies past my lips as the most euphoric orgasm of my life rips through me. Through the fogginess of my brain, I hear Lilly moan as well, her pussy squeezing me tight, drawing out my orgasm longer.

We ride the wave until there's nothing left to give, and then I collapse on top of her, my cock still hard, still inside of her.

"Fucking hell," I whisper before I remove myself. I untie her only for her to pull me against her, her arms and legs wrapping around me. I cup the back of her head, holding her close. "You okay?"

"Yes," she sniffles. "I'm so good, Keller." She pulls away, and I catch sight of a single tear cascading down her cheek.

I swipe it away. My strong, sassy, confident girl . . . crying. Maybe she isn't as tough as she seems. "Why are you crying?"

"I'm sorry, it's just . . . that was so intense."

"Intense is good."

"I know, I just wasn't expecting to feel like . . ." She looks away, but I gently force her to look me in the eyes by touching her jaw.

"You didn't expect it to feel like what?"

Her beautiful eyes shine up at me. "To feel like coming home."

And just like that, I feel my heart soften, and my thoughts, my ideas of what I can and cannot have, wash away into the past. This right here, this woman, she's mine.

I cup her cheek gently and kiss her. "Same, love. I feel the same exact way."

Chapter Seventeen

LILLY

Keller returns from the bathroom, after helping me clean up, and stands in the doorway, in all his naked glory. His strong set of shoulders relaxed, not tense. The solid stack of abs taut from the workout he just gave them. And even though his penis is no longer hard, straining between his legs, it still looks heavy. I have to tear my eyes away, or else I'm going to be begging for another round.

But with that all being said, I'm unsure what he wants now.

I know we said some passionate things while in the moment, but now that he's had me, what happens next? Do we sleep together? Do I go back to my room? I truly hate the "after sex" moment.

Cautiously, I sit up on his bed, the covers falling around my torso, and I ask, "So . . . do you, uh, do you want me to go back to my room?" I twist the sheets in my hand, hoping he says no.

Determination on his face, he struts toward me and leans on the bed as he grips my chin. Keeping our eyes connected, he says, "You're mine, which means you sleep in my bed. Understood?" A smile spreads across my face as I steal a kiss, only for him to flatten me to the bed, his large warm body covering mine. His hand smooths over my cheek as he stares down at me. "How's your head?"

"It hurts a little." I wince.

His face flashes with concern. "Fuck, I knew I shouldn't have—"

I cover his lips with my fingers before he can say anything else. "Don't. I just have a headache, that's all."

"I shouldn't have been so rough."

"You weren't," I reassure him. "I promise. You didn't hurt me. You were so perfect."

Still not pleased, he lifts from me and says, "I'm going to grab you some Ibuprofen and a drink."

There's no arguing with him as he slips on a pair of shorts and heads out of the room. There he goes again, needing to protect at all hours. So, I curl into his sheets and let out a heavy sigh.

I've had my fair share of sex before, the kinky kind that you only hear about, never experience, but they've never been as toe-curling, as satisfying, as what I just shared with Keller. There was an emotional level to our intimacy that I wasn't expecting. His need to protect, to provide, translates into the bedroom, and he made me feel so safe, so important.

He always says I matter most, and that's how he makes me feel. Like I truly matter.

I never realized how lost I was until I came here. I thought my life felt established. I had friends, some boyfriends here and there, still searching for the right one, and a thriving business. I thought that's what life was about to survive: friends, a job, and a place to live.

But that couldn't be further from the truth, especially for me.

For someone who lost the two most important people in her life, who lost her home, and her possessions, I need so much more than skimming the surface. I didn't need a routine, I need depth.

I need this country, where it feels as if my mother is surrounding me.

These people, who share the same traditions as I did growing up.

The culture, a culture I never knew was instilled in me until I came here.

And this man, someone who has my back, who fills an empty void I've been missing all these years.

I want to make him proud. I want to do the right thing, to show him that I'm more than the girl he first met, that this country means just as much to me as it does to him. Because it truly does, I've realized during the last few days, and it feels like home here.

I know it for sure.

Keller walks back into the room with a glass of water and medicine in his palm. Once I swallow the pills and take an extra sip of water, he retrieves the glass from me and sets it on the night table.

When he turns back to me on the bed, he cups my cheek as he speaks sincerely. "Let's get you some rest."

At the edge of the bed, he removes his shorts, and then he climbs under the covers, joining me. I curl into him, resting my head on his shoulder, as his arm that's around me rests along my back, keeping me close.

"Comfortable?" he asks.

"Very," I answer.

His thumb dances over my hip while he asks, "You'd tell me if I hurt you?"

"I would. And I promise, you didn't." I kiss his jaw. "I've never felt more cared for than when I'm in your arms."

"Good," he answers and then goes silent.

"Hey, Keller?"

"Hmm?"

"Can I talk to you about something?"

"You can talk to me about anything," he says.

I raise up and change my position so I'm leaning across his chest, looking down at him, face to face. "I want to say something to you but I don't want you to think it's spur of the moment, or because we just had sex or anything like that. I've been thinking about this for a while."

"Okay." His hand falls on my bare hip.

"I . . . I wanted to tell you that I've made my decision."

"Your decision?" he asks, looking confused.

"About whether I'm going to stay or go back to Miami."

His eyes widen. "Oh, that. But I thought you would wait until you got to Strombly to make that decision. Lilly, I know it's been rough here, but at least give us a chance to show you the other side."

I press my hand to his rapidly beating heart. "I'm not leaving, Keller. I'm going to stay."

"Wait . . . what?" He sits up now. "Really? You're going to stay?"

"Yes." I smile. "I'm not sure what'll happen when I reach Strombly or when I'm introduced to the public, but I keep feeling as if this is what I was supposed to do. I feel like I belong here, like that piece of me that's been missing all this time has been found."

"Jesus, you're serious?" he asks, his expression so adorably shocked that I lean forward and press my forehead against his.

"Yes, I'm serious."

"Holy . . . holy fuck, Lilly." He scoops me up and lays me flat against the mattress, where he cups my cheek gently and stares into my eyes. "You're really going to stay?"

"Yes, as long as that doesn't change anything between us."

"What do you mean?"

"I mean, I know you have some reservations about who you are and whom I'll become, but I don't want that to stop you from being with me. I don't want you to pull away."

His eyes search mine, his mind processing what I'm saying. If I stay and become queen, then he'd be dating the queen, and I need to make sure that's okay with him.

He swallows hard.

The pause in his answer, the shiftiness in his eyes . . . it sends a fearful chill down my back. You can see the backpedaling on the tip of his tongue.

"Keller, I know you've always put up that wall, but I can't do this without you—"

"You won't have to," he says finally. He brings my knuckles to his lips, where he places a gentle kiss. "I'm yours for as long as you'll have me."

"Really?" I ask. "Because I know how you feel about—"

"The only thing you should worry about is your training, nothing else. I'm yours and I'm not going anywhere."

"Keller." I lift into his arms and hold him tightly. "Truly, you mean that?"

His arms encase me against his chest and his hand grips the back of my head. "Yes, love, I do."

I pull away to look him in the eyes, just to make sure. "Because I'll need you, Keller. This is terrifying and a large responsibility. I don't know if I can handle it alone. I need you by my side."

"I know, and I promise, I'll be there for you."

I place my hand on his dark scruff and bring him in close, resting a soft kiss on his lips. "Thank you."

"No, love, thank you for making a selfless decision."

I shake my head. "No, it's not selfless. There's nothing selfless about my decision. It's based purely on being selfish. I was going through the motions while living in Miami. I had a successful business and friends, but I never felt fulfilled. Here, there's so much filling my life with joy, even on the days you're droning on about the history of codfish."

He chuckles. "It's important information."

"But seriously, I feel as if I'm a part of something here, I feel as though I can feel my mom here. I feel the love. I want to hold on to that. I want to mend things with Queen Katla, mend a relationship my mom never could. And I want to learn from my grandparents." I kiss him once again. "And I want to do that with you next to me."

"Well, I'm all yours."

"And I'm yours."

I kiss him again as he lays me back down on the bed, where he curls me up to his chest and doesn't let me go the entire night.

⌥

A LARGE YAWN escapes me as I sit up in bed, wincing as I feel the heaviness of pain in my head. I peep my eye open but can't see Keller. Unsure of the time, I drag myself out of bed, needing more Ibuprofen, and head to my room, where I throw on a pair of pajama shorts and a T-shirt.

If it were Keller and me, I would've just slipped into his shirt and called it a day, but I'm not sure what his plan is when it comes to telling people about us, so I'll let him take control over that, and I'll dress in my own clothes.

The sun is bright, feeling like laser beams straight to my eyes, so I hold on to the stair rail as I head down the stairs. The cold wood under my feet wakes me up as I make my way to the kitchen, expecting to hear Brimar and Lara talking over a pot of coffee, but instead, I find Keller leaning against the counter, wearing nothing but a pair of shorts, his hair rumpled in all the best ways, while holding a single mug of coffee.

When he looks in my direction, his eyes light up. "Morning, love."

The rumble of his morning voice.

The pet name for me.

The smile in his eyes.

It all brands my soul, marking me as his.

"Good morning," I say shyly as I approach, unsure if I should keep my distance or not. "Where are Brimar and Lara?"

He sets his mug on the counter and closes the distance between us. His hands rest on my hips as he presses a sweet kiss to the top of my head. "They took the morning off and drove into town for some supplies."

"Really?" I ask. "So, we have the castle to ourselves?"

"We do," Keller says with a heart-melting smile. "But that doesn't mean we can take the day off. We have a quiz planned for today and some wood-carving lessons."

"A quiz? Is that necessary?"

"You'll like my quiz." He winks, takes my hand in his, and leads me to the counter, where he lifts me up and scoots between my legs. His hand reaches up to my cut. "How are you feeling? Does it hurt?"

"A little."

He frowns.

"But nothing a little Ibuprofen can't fix, and maybe some coffee . . . and some of that fresh bread Brimar made. And perhaps an egg or two?" I wince.

Keller chuckles. "I think I can manage that for my girl." He kisses the tip of my nose and then gets to work, pulling out the ingredients and pans he needs.

"Can I help?" I ask.

"No, love, you just sit right there and keep me company."

Warmth spreads through me. This is new to me, someone taking care of me like this. I've been on my own for so long that it feels good to just sit back and let someone else do the heavy lifting for a moment.

While he slices up the bread, he asks, "How did you sleep?"

"Amazing," I say with a wistful sigh.

Head down, he glances to the side at me, a wicked gaze in his eyes. "Yeah?"

I smile, unable to play it cool. "Yes. I honestly think it was the best night's sleep I've had since we've been here."

"You flatter me," he says as he cracks four eggs into the heated pan. "Are you sore?"

"A little." I twist the hem of my shirt in my hand. "But in a good way, like those muscles haven't been used in a while, not in a way that you hurt me."

"Promise?"

"Promise," I answer.

"Good. Oh, by the way, I got the update from the Informative."

"Really?" I ask. "Can I see it?"

He picks up his phone from the counter and hands it to me. In a text that he sent me, I read it to myself.

Keller: *THE INFORMATIVE: A duel in the town square. Two Anglers, two fishing poles, one decision. While the angler's wife has been hiding away, attempting to leave the town to find its peace, the men have been battling it out on the ocean, trying to catch the most cod this week, pride the only thing to lose. The town has rallied behind the two fishermen, wearing the colors of the boats as a representation of who they support: the green and the yellow. Word on the street is that there's an equal divide, and despite the fight over the fish, the men are now trying to win back the love of the angler's wife.*

I set the phone down, my heart full in my chest.

"Oh my God, I swear, Keller, this is some sort of juicy soap opera I didn't know I needed in my life. And I feel bad saying that because these are real people, but, oh my God. The angler's wife walks away, only for the men to come back to fight for her. I mean, what kind of spell has she cast over these men? And . . . how could they still want her after the cheating, especially when she cheated on the husband with his competitor? I'm all about finding love, but I'm also for respect and loyalty, you know?"

"It's good to hear that," Keller says as he flips the eggs in the pan. When he turns toward me, he says, "Loyalty always comes first."

"Does that mean you'll remain loyal to me?"

He walks up to me and slips his large body between my legs as he cups my cheek. "Lilly, if you don't already know that, then you haven't been paying attention." He brings my mouth to his where he nips at my bottom lip with his teeth, then pulls away.

A distant sigh releases from me as I reach for him but come up short. "You can't just do that and leave me here, unsatisfied."

"I can do whatever I want when you question my loyalty to you."

"I wasn't questioning it, just, you know . . . confirming."

"Ah, is that so?" He lifts a brow in my direction.

"Yeah, so no need to get your nuts all in a jam."

"So eloquent." He turns off the stove just as the toast pops in the toaster. He butters the bread and fills our plates before taking them to the table, where he sets them right next to each other.

I hop off the counter and fill a mug with coffee for myself, adding my milk and sugar, and then grab his mug as well.

When he sees me approach, he says, "I could've gotten that."

"I know, but I could too. You don't have to do everything."

He tips my chin up with his index finger. "But I want to do everything." He lightly brushes his lips against mine and then pulls away, only to sit in a chair at the table. I go to pull out my chair when he says, "What are you doing?"

"Sitting down," I answer.

"Lilly, your seat is right here." He pats his lap.

"Please, you expect me to sit on your lap during breakfast?"

"I don't expect it, Lilly. I require it." He tugs on my hand and forces me onto his lap. His arm loops around my waist, holding me in place.

"I thought you were only the king in the bedroom?" I say with a smile.

"I am, but you'll respect my rules and requests outside of the bedroom as well, which reminds me . . ." He slips his hand past the waistband of my pants and cups my ass. "Mmm, good girl. No underwear."

"Don't need underwear at breakfast," I say.

But he doesn't answer. Instead, he stares at his plate, unmoving.

Confused, I ask, "What's wrong?"

When he looks up at me, the devil plays in his eyes. "I can't decide if I want eggs for breakfast or your cunt."

My mouth goes dry and I try to remain calm as I say, "Maybe both?"

"Great idea. The moment I finish these eggs, your pussy is mine." He then picks up his fork, stabs one whole egg, and places it in his mouth, leaving only one left on the plate.

Oh God.

—————

TO SAY Keller likes to perform oral is an understatement.

The man lives for it.

After scarfing down his second egg, he pushed our plates away, laid me across the table, and pulled down my pants. He then lapped at my clit for about a minute before I was screaming out his name.

From there, I sat back down on his lap, his very hard lap,

and I finished my breakfast while he slid his hands under my shirt and played with my nipples. By the time I finished, I was so turned on that I begged him to finish me off, which he did by pushing me back on the table again and making me get off on his tongue. *Again.*

While I lay spent on the table, he cleaned up, the whole time his cock straining in his sweatpants. When he was finished, he scooped me up and took me up the stairs to the bathroom, where he set me in the shower and took my shirt off.

He joined me, his erection pressing against my back while he wet us with the showerhead, my back to his front. His hands caressed every inch of my body, playing mainly with my breasts, and then between my legs, which he told me to spread for him. And that's when he put the showerhead on the pulse setting and pressed it against my clit. As my orgasm ripped through me, he held me up at the waist.

When we got dressed, he slipped me into one of his T-shirts and that was it, nothing else, claiming he wanted access to me whenever he desired. And while I sat on his bed, watching him dry off, his cock so impossibly hard I couldn't understand how he could move around, he did nothing to ease his discomfort. He simply slipped on a pair of shorts, and that was it.

When I reached for his erection, he told me I was not to touch him.

I argued with him, telling him I wanted to make him come, which only spurred him on to pick me up, pin me against the wall, and finger me until I was on edge. He tossed me to the bed, spread my legs once more, and made me come on his tongue.

Now that I was utterly spent and unable to walk, he scooped me up, brought me back down to the living room and sat me on the couch to show me his woodworking skills, but I couldn't pay attention, not with his erection in full frame.

Wanting to entice him, I sat back on the couch and spread my legs.

I thought that would do the job, but it didn't, not until I brought my hand between my legs and started pleasuring myself. That's what made him snap. Across from me, he pulled his cock out and stroked himself, his eyes on my hand the entire time. I slid my finger along my clit, really drawing out the sensation of my piercing, and within minutes, Keller was groaning and falling back on the couch as he came all over his stomach.

I took it upon myself to clean him up.

And now that his erection is gone, I can concentrate.

Thank God. What a morning.

Keller comes back into the room, his muscles still tense from the buildup he endured this morning, and sits next to me on the couch.

Pulling my chin toward him, he lays a desperate kiss on my lips but releases me almost right away.

I groan as a plea. "What was that for?" I ask.

"No more enticing me."

"Enticing you?" I ask. "Uh, I have done nothing. You're the one who's getting all handsy. I'm trying to be a good student."

"Widening your legs so I can see your addicting pussy isn't enticing?"

"Well, you see, I couldn't stop staring at your dick, therefore, I had to do something about it. It's all your fault. If you'd just taken care of your erection, then we wouldn't have had a misstep during wood carving."

"You're turning this around on me?"

"Uh, yeah, Mr. Walks Around With An Erection. Who does that? Just jack off, or better yet, fuck me, and then we both win."

"Have you ever heard of delayed gratification?"

"Yes, but, Keller, you were so hard."

"I'm aware, Lilly. But I'll come when I want to come, understood?"

"Yes . . . my King."

"Good." He scoots back on the couch and spreads his legs. "Now sit between my legs and bring your wood so I can help you."

"*Bring your wood.*" I chuckle. "Shouldn't I be saying that to you?"

His brow raises. "Don't test me, Lilly."

"But it's so fun."

"I told you, no fooling around today, we have things to get done."

A loud guffaw pops out of my mouth. "Me, goofing around? Uh, excuse me, sir, but you're the one who hasn't let me shut my legs since I woke up."

"Are you complaining?" he asks in such a rich, threatening tone that I feel a chill run up my back.

"No, just pointing out the obvious."

"Not needed. Now get over here so I can teach you a lesson in woodworking."

"Oh yes, teach me, big man."

"Lilly . . ."

"Ooo, a warning tone." I settle between his legs and hold my piece of wood out in front of me. "I like it when you use that tone. It makes my nipples hard."

"Are you trying to make me angry?"

"We haven't had angry sex yet, so we could go for the trifecta today. Sweet morning sex, shower sex, and angry sex. Talk about being accomplished."

His arms come around me and his lips fall close to my ear. "Focus, Lilly, or else you're not going to get what I've planned for later."

"Oh, the quiz? I'm sure that'll be fun."

His hand slides under the hem of my shirt and up my side

until it reaches my breast. He pulls my nipple between his fingers and gives it a good squeeze.

Fuck . . .

Mouth right on my ear, he says, "Trust me, Lilly, it's more than a quiz."

Then he releases me and takes the piece of wood from between my hands.

And he thinks I'm the one teasing him?

"Basswood is the best wood to carve, especially as a beginner," he says, as if everything is fine and him pinching my nipple didn't just spur me on once more. "And you want to make sure it's fully dry. If you feel it's wet in any area, the wood will be of no use to you because when it dries, it'll crack leaving your carving broken."

Okay, I'll admit it, it's kind of sexy hearing him talk about this carving stuff.

"And you see the way the grain in the wood is flowing?" He runs his large hand over the wood. "That's the way you want to carve, with the grain." He picks up a carving knife, a thin, curved piece of sharp metal on a wooden handle. "See the curve in this knife? This is so you can use both hands to push the blade through the wood. One to guide, one to push. It will offer you better control."

He adjusts his hands on the piece of wood, presses his thumb to the curve of the blade and, as if he's carving through butter, he pushes the blade through the wood, taking off a chunk.

"Think you can handle that?"

"I think so," I say as he hands me the wood and the knife. Looking over my shoulder, arms around me, he helps me get my hands into position, and then with his own, he overlaps mine and helps me make my first cut. Together, we shave a long strip off the end and onto the floor.

"Perfect, Lilly," he says, his praise settling in my stomach, like a warm drink. "This time, do it on your own."

He lifts his hands and rests them on my thighs while I take my time, pushing down on the blade and shaving off a piece of wood.

"I did it," I say, excited.

"Yes, you did. Now, remember that when removing the wood, you have to do it in thin layers. If you go in too deep, you risk taking out a bigger chunk than intended."

"Okay. Should I keep shaving?"

"Yes, for practice. When I think you have the technique down, we can attempt your first carving."

I continue to shave layer after layer off the block of wood, collecting a pile of curled wood shavings on the floor while Keller watches, offering instruction and helping me with angles.

"I can see why people enjoy this so much. It's very soothing. I like the feel of it."

"My father and I spent nights together carving fish when I was younger."

"Why fish?" I ask. "Well, besides the fact that you're all obsessed with cod."

He leans his chest against my back, his cheek nearly pressing against mine. "We traded them at Torg."

"Oh, right. Were you and your dad good?"

"Dad was. At the time, I was still learning, so my fish weren't nearly as smooth as his, but Dad always made sure our trade was a packaged deal. Whoever got his, got mine too."

"That's so sweet." I dig my knife in a little too far and notice that it's tough to push through. Keller helps me adjust, his warm hands on top of mine. "Do you have any of your fish still?"

"I have one. King Theo gave it to me after the fire. We lost everything in that fire, but King Theo had a fish from my dad, and instead of keeping it for himself, he gave it to me."

I pause and lean to the side to look him in the eyes.

"You've never really spoken about the fire, only mentioned it. I didn't know you lost everything."

"I keep that pretty close to my chest," he says and then leans forward, trailing his lips along my cheek. "But you've snuck inside my bones, and it doesn't seem as though I can shake you."

"Does that mean you trust me?"

He nods. "I do."

"Would you mind telling me more about your parents, then? I know you don't like talking about them because it hurts, but it helps me to know that I'm not the only one who has felt alone in this life—at least, that's what I assume you must have felt losing them at such a young age."

"I did." He turns his attention back to the wood. "I had a family in the palace that adopted me," he says offhandedly, "but it was never the same. Recovering from losing your parents in a fire is horrible as the nightmares are so vivid. Sometimes, I'll have dreams and they'll be in them, but they've aged. We sit on the back porch of the quaint house we had in the servants' quarters, staring up at the northern lights as they dance above us, just like we used to. But in my dreams, my parents never say anything, they just hold my hand and remind me with their touch that they love me."

A tear falls down my cheek, and I set the wood down so I can turn and face him. He leans back on the couch as I straddle his lap and place my hands gently on his chest. "I have the same dreams, but my parents haven't aged. They're as I remember them, and we're out on the beach, lounging in chairs, watching the waves roll in. But there's no sound. It's almost as if the dream is in slow motion and I get to feel the comfort of them around me all over again."

"How do you feel in the morning?" he asks.

"Comforted, but also sad, empty."

"Same," he says, while he takes my hands in his. "Almost

287

feels worse after, because I got them back for a short moment."

"And then they're taken away all over again."

"But for those few minutes you do have with them, it's like . . ."

"Nothing can take that away from you."

"Exactly." His hands glide up my ribs. "Fuck, Lilly. What are you doing to me?"

"What do you mean?"

"I haven't felt this connected to a person . . . ever. And now that you're here, in my life, it terrifies me that you'll be taken away as well."

"I understand that feeling," I say as I rest against his chest, my head to his shoulder. "Being here, it's made me feel like everything I've been missing in my life has actually been hiding away in another country, and that terrifies me too. I didn't think I could feel this way again."

"What way is that?" Keller asks, his hand stroking the back of my head now.

"Safe," I whisper.

His grip grows tighter on me. "You'll always be safe with me."

"I know. I can always count on you."

"Always."

Chapter Eighteen

KELLER

Lara: How is everything over there?

    Keller: Peaceful and quiet.

    Lara: Okay, well, I don't think we'll be back for another two hours. Is that okay?

    Keller: Fine, no rush. Take your time.

    Lara: Uh-huh . . . any reason why you want us to take our time? *wiggles eyebrows*

    Keller: No, I just want you to have a nice time out.

    Lara: Right, so this has nothing to do with the moans we heard last night?

    Keller: No idea what you're talking about.

    Lara: Keller, we're not stupid. How long has it been going on?

    Keller: That was the second night.

    Lara: Do you realize how risky this is?

    Keller: Yes, but I can't stay away. I can't avoid her anymore, Lara. She makes me feel whole.

    Lara: As long as you know what you're doing. There are consequences. Who knows if King Theo will approve, and then what if she decides to walk away?

Keller: *She won't.*

Lara: *Brimar thinks differently.*

Keller: *Brimar doesn't know her the way I do.*

Lara: *He's worried about you.*

Keller: *I can tell, but trust me when I say, she's not going anywhere. And neither am I.*

Lara: *Are you falling for her?*

Keller: *Yes.*

Lara: *Wow, that's unexpected. You know I like her a lot, and I genuinely think she'd be a great match for you. She balances you out. But I'm not sure she's ready for what's to come. I don't want you getting hurt.*

Keller: *I appreciate that, Lara, but I think you and I both know, I tried staying away. I fucking did, but the connection is too strong, and the need is far too electric. This is so much bigger than thinking she's beautiful. I know her on a basic level, and she sees me to my core.*

Lara: *Okay, just be safe. We care about you.*

Keller: *I know, but don't worry about me. Take care of yourselves. And, hey, I got a text from Henrik earlier. They think they found the leak.*

Lara: *Really? Who?*

Keller: *Someone within the executive staff. They're going to speak of some false stories and see which one is outed. They'll know soon.*

Lara: *Thank goodness. If we can clear that out by the time we get there, that would benefit Lilly's welcoming.*

Keller: *Agreed. Okay, have fun. I'll see you tonight.*

"Who are you texting?" Lilly asks from the couch, where she's still carving the first side of her fish. "You have this weird, pinched look on your face."

"Lara," I answer. "They'll be returning later than planned."

"Oh." Lilly holds up her fish and shows it to me. "What do you think?"

Fuck, she's so beautiful. That smile on her face, the pride

beaming in her steely eyes, she's breathtaking. And that fish . . . it's actually halfway decent.

"I think you're going to be better than me soon."

"You sure know how to flatter a woman." She sets the piece of wood and knife down and shakes out her hands. "I need a break."

"I have the perfect idea for that," I say as I stand from my chair and hold out my hand to her.

She willingly takes it. I link our fingers together and guide her out of the living room and up the stairs to my bedroom, where I have everything set up that I need.

"Ooo, I like this already," she says when we reach my room. "Should I be naked?"

"Yes," I answer as I let go of her hand and pull up the hem of her shirt until she's completely naked. I drag my fingers over her side, loving how soft her skin is. "Get on all fours, on the edge of my bed."

She smirks and turns toward the bed, where she gets into position.

"Are you comfortable?"

"Yes, my King," she says.

"Good." Since she's closer to the left side, I move next to her and smooth my hand over her back. "Now listen carefully, as I'm going to ask you a series of questions. Every time you get one right, you get a reward, but every time you get one wrong, you get punished." I press a kiss to her shoulder blade, then to her neck, and then her cheek. "You're not allowed to come until I grant you permission. Understood?"

"Yes, my King," she answers.

"Good girl." I gently caress her ass and ask, "What is the name of the palace?"

"Strombly," she answers with confidence.

"Good." I lift my hand and smack her ass, leaving a red mark.

"Oh, fuck," she says, her back bowing and her head dropping. "Oh God, I wasn't expecting that."

To ensure that's what she wants, I finger her pussy, and to my surprise, she's already very aroused.

"Did you like that, Lilly?"

"Y-yes, my King," she answers.

"Then we shall move on. Next question, what is the name of the festival at the end of summer?"

"Torg."

"And what do we do there?"

"It's where people from around the country get to trade their handcrafted items, as well as show off their talents that have been passed on from generation to generation. It's also where you'll find the best cooked cod cakes in the country. A celebration before the winter months."

Smack. Smack.

I deliver two spankings to her, causing her to grip the comforter tightly in her grasp.

As she moans, I say, "Good answer."

"Thank you, my King," she replies, her voice strained.

"Doing okay, love?" I ask. She offers me an enthusiastic nod, so I continue. "What is King Theo's full name?"

"Uh . . . oh shit. It's, uh, Theodore, uh . . . ramakin . . ."

"Lilly, you disappoint me," I say as I pick up a clothespin from my nightstand. I show it to her, opening and shutting it, and then place it on her nipple, pinching it tightly. A hefty hiss escapes her lips.

"I'm s-sorry, my King," she answers. "Please correct me and tell me his full name?"

"Theodore Holti Strom, the Third."

"Thank you for correcting me."

"Yes, of course." I smooth my hand over her back, which has broken out in a light sweat. "Next question—what is mead?"

"Fermented honey water, usually drank at Torg after King

Theo offers a toast to the country."

"Very good," I say to her as I deliver three more slaps to her ass.

"Ah, God," she yells, her body contorting. The sight of her is so sexy that I adjust my hard-on in my pants.

"Tell me, Lilly, when you get to Strombly, will you be wearing a tiara?"

"No, my King," she answers. "Tiaras are only for married royals."

"Good girl," I say as I reach under her and take the clothespin from her nipple. I roll her sensitive nipple between my fingers and she cries out in pleasure. Moving close, I whisper, "Remember, you don't come until I tell you."

"Yes, my King."

As her body heaves, I bring my hand back to her ass and ask, "What is kulning?"

"The art of herding by using your voice."

"Very good," I say as I reach for her vibrator and turn it on. I slowly move it inside of her wet pussy and watch as her body adjusts to the new sensation.

"Fuck . . . me," she whispers while shifting on the bed.

"When in public and asked for your opinion on the current affairs, what do you say?"

"Nothing," she answers. "I don't have an opinion on politics or current affairs."

"Excellent," I say right before I spank her ass four times now.

"Uhhhhh," she moans, her butt lifting, looking for more.

"Where is Strombly located?"

"In the capital, population thirty-two hundred."

"Now you're just showing off," I say as I remove the vibrator and tease her other hole with it.

"Yes, my King," she says, her body urging me on. "Please, yes."

Smiling, I reach for the lube I found in her nightstand, and

I dribble it along her crack. I gather it with the vibrator and slowly push it into her tight hole. Her head lowers to the mattress as a feral sound falls from her lips.

"Tell me how you feel."

"Unbelievable, like my body is aware of every pulse, every slap, every pinch. I never want you to stop."

"Then make sure you keep answering correctly." Keeping my hand on the vibrator, I ask, "What is my job title?"

She pauses, her head slouching. "Oh God, I . . . I don't know. Protector?"

"Nice try." I switch the vibrator off, and she moans in protest. "Private Secretary to the King."

Instead of saying anything, she groans, her body subtly lowering to the mattress.

"Sit up, Lilly."

"Sorry," she says, her legs shaking now.

"What's wrong?" I run my hand along her backside.

"I . . . I'm just feeling so much right now."

"You tell me if it's too much."

She nods.

"No, Lilly, you have to use words."

"Yes, my King."

"Better." I ask her question after question, and she answers them correctly one at a time. I turn the vibrator back on, I spank her beautiful ass, I spread her legs, and then start licking her sweet clit into my mouth.

She's rolling with pleasure, crying out my name, begging to come, but not yet.

"Lilly, how much of the country is uninhabited?"

"Eighty . . . percent," she breathes out heavily.

"Good girl."

"Please keep sucking on my clit," she begs, her voice hoarse now.

"No, love, you don't tell me what to do. Did you forget that?" I lift from the bed, push down my shorts, and release my aching cock. I position myself at her entrance, keep the vibrator going in her other hole, and then slowly enter her.

"Oh fuck, Keller." Her upper half falls to the bed, and I grip her hips to hold her bottom half up. "You okay?" I ask.

"So . . . so good," she replies, her entire body slippery with sweat now.

Continuing to move inside, I say, "Last question. Get it right and I'll finish fucking you. Get it wrong, and I'll stop everything now, leaving you unsatisfied." I move my cock inside of her and give her a few pulses. Her legs quiver, her body shakes, and her breathing is so erratic that I'm not sure I will hear her answer. "If you don't take the crown, who is the constituent country that takes over Torskethorpe?"

"Oh God," she whispers, her eyes squeezing shut. "Keller . . . I don't . . . I don't know."

"Ah, love," I say, pulsing into her a few more times before I remove myself and the vibrator and let her limp body fall to the mattress. "It's Arkham."

"No," she cries out, her hands tangled in the sheets. "Please . . . please don't leave me like this."

I step away, my heart hammering in my chest as I watch her flip over, a tear falling down her cheek as she drapes her hand over her eyes.

"It shouldn't matter," she says, her frustration peaking.

"What shouldn't matter?"

"Whatever country takes over. Because it's not going to happen. I'm taking the crown. It doesn't end with King Theo. And I'll be sure to provide enough heirs to continue the legacy and show them how amazing this country is. Teach them to learn to love it, as you've taught me."

My heart swells in my chest, and fuck if I can stop myself. I move to the bed, lie next to her, and flip her onto my lap. I place my hands behind my head and say, "Fuck me, Lilly. Use my cock, and fuck me."

Her eyes widen in surprise. "But . . . but I got it wrong."

"But you just gave me the most beautiful answer yet. Now, fuck me."

Still breathing heavily, she positions my cock at her entrance and slowly slides down on it until she's completely full.

"Keller," she whispers, her eyes pleading with me.

"What, Lilly?"

"It's—it's too much."

"No, it's not, love. Just relax."

She nods and takes a few calming breaths. Slowly she relaxes and then starts to move over my cock, her teeth biting into her lip.

"Not going to last," she says while shaking her head. "Not at all. Fuck, Keller, I'm going to come so fast. Please tell me I can."

"You have my permission."

Her hips rock faster, and usually I'd like to say it takes longer to get me off, but seeing my girl above me like this, pumping her hips over my cock, has my orgasm spiking early, building at the base of my spine, and starting to spiral out of control.

"Oh God, Keller . . . I . . . I . . ."

Her eyes squeeze shut and her orgasm rips through her, her pussy clenching around my cock so tight that I crest in seconds.

"Motherfucker," I yell as I push my hips up into hers, an insane amount of pleasure pulsing through my every vein, making me groan so loudly, I'm pretty sure people from miles away can hear me.

And it doesn't stop, it keeps going as Lilly continues to come all over my cock, rocking her hips until there's nothing left inside of her.

When she collapses, she falls to my chest, her slight body curling against me. Her arms grip me tightly as her head fits into the crook of my neck.

I gently rub her back, my fingers trailing along her spine as I ask, "Are you okay?"

She lets out a heavy breath. "Barely," she whispers and then places a kiss on my jaw. "No one has made me feel the way you do."

"Same," I say. "And that answer at the end, you meant it?"

"I meant every single word of it," she says. "This is what I'm supposed to do, this is where I belong. If I must keep reminding you of that, then so be it, but I'm not going anywhere."

I lift her chin, turning her toward me, still in awe of her words.

"I'm taking the crown. It doesn't end with King Theo. And I'll provide enough heirs to continue the legacy and show them how amazing this country is. Teach them to learn to love it, as you've taught me."

I kiss her lips and roll her to her back, then cradle her head softly and spend the foreseeable future kissing her all over her body, because it's the only response I have.

She's staying.

She's mine.

———

"TOMORROW IS our last full day here," I say to everyone at the dinner table. Brimar made another soup, this one full of potatoes and beef, and of course fresh-baked bread, which Lilly has had three pieces of so far. "Which means I need you, Lilly, to finish your fish."

"Can't I finish it when we arrive at Strombly?"

"No." I shake my head. "It's going to be hectic when you get there. You'll be pulled in every direction. And you need the fish for Torg. You'll be trading it."

"Oh, okay. I just have to smooth it out a bit and paint it. So, not much left to do."

"Brimar and Lara, are you able to pack up the castle and

make sure all is left in its proper place?"

Lara nods while Brimar grumbles about him taking care of the kitchen.

"I have some phone calls with Henrik tomorrow and some prepping to do, so I won't be able to do much to help."

"We can handle it," Lara says. "Plus, I have some protocol to go over with Lilly."

"What sort of protocol?" Lilly asks, surprisingly still using the table manners we've taught her. She's been working hard, and it shows. When we first arrived, she would have been hunched over her bowl, spoon in one hand, bread in the other, slurping up her soup. Now she's poised. Regal.

"Since we've been here, we've been relaxed when it comes to following the protocol of what you need to remember when out in public. As your bodyguard, I need to go over some things with you, like how you need permission and clearance before entering a building or going outside, how you don't open a door, and logistics that need to be remembered. It's simple, but I do feel like it's something we need to touch upon before we leave."

"Oh, yeah, anything you guys can think of, I'd love to know, because I don't want to make a fool of myself when I arrive."

"You won't," I say. "You're prepared."

"I feel like I am, but I'm also nervous, and when I'm nervous, I forget things."

"Well, we'll all be there for you," Lara says. "And I can whisper in your ear if you need help or reminders."

"That would be so great. Thank you so much," Lilly says as she sets her spoon down, turned over on her plate, indicating that she's done. She then places her hands in her lap and smiles at us all. "I know you're going to say it's your duty to serve and protect, but I want to tell you how thankful I am for everything you've done for me since we've been here. I'm not sure you're aware how terrifying this has all been, but you've made it a thousand times easier by being there for me, walking me through everything I need to know, and even poking fun at me when needed."

I reach out to Lilly and take her hand in mine. I feel the heat of Brimar's and Lara's eyes on the connection, but I hold her hand anyway. "You've done an exquisite job of handling everything we've thrown your way."

"I couldn't have done it without you guys. Seriously." She takes a deep breath. "I truly feel as though you're family, the family I've been missing since my parents passed away. And you've shown me the history I've been missing my whole life, the history I've craved. This has been a scary, but also fulfilling, few weeks, and I'm so thankful for all three of you."

"Wow," Lara says, dabbing at her eyes with her napkin. "Does she have the regal thing down or what?"

We all chuckle, and I squeeze Lilly's hand and say, "She does."

Shortly after, I carry the plates to the kitchen while Lara and Lilly work on some self-defense moves that Lilly has wanted to learn. I decide to stay in the kitchen and help Brimar.

"What can I do?" I ask him.

He whips a towel in my direction. "You can dry."

"Easy enough." I saddle up next to him by the sink, and as he rinses the dishes, he hands them to me. "Want to talk about whatever's on your mind?" I ask him.

"Nothing's on my mind."

"Brimar, I've known you since we were kids. Trust me, I can tell when something is on your mind."

He scrubs a dish extra hard as he asks, "Do you actually like her?"

Not a fan of his tone, I ask, "What do you mean?"

Glancing at me, he says, "It all feels too convenient. So, is this something you worked up with King Theo?"

"What?" I ask him. "What the fuck are you talking

about?"

He turns toward me now, hands sudsy. "I know Theo wishes you were king, that you could take his place, but we all know that can't happen. Unless . . ."

"What the fuck are you alluding to?" I growl at him.

"She's already lost a lot, and she's a flight risk. She might think this is all fun and games now, but until she steps foot in that palace and goes day to day with the schedule thrust upon her, she has no fucking clue what this is going to be like. If you jump in, make her fall for you for ulterior motives—"

I have my hand wrapped around his collar and him pinned against the sink before he can finish that sentence. "If you ever accuse me of such treachery again, I'll have your fucking head, do you understand me?" I seethe. "My love for this country and for Lilly are two separate things. I'll do anything for Torskethorpe and its traditions. I'm a servant, not a noble. I'm well aware of the difference and that I have no place belonging in the latter. As for Lilly, my feelings for her have nothing to do with her title and everything to do with the person she is. Trust me when I say, the last thing I ever wanted was to get involved with her, given who she is. I've battled nightly over that decision, so don't presume I thought with my dick because that's never been the case." I push him away from me and toss the towel on the counter.

He can do the goddamn dishes on his own.

When I start to walk away, I pause and turn back around. When our eyes meet, I ask him, "When did you start questioning my loyalty to this country?"

"Your loyalty to Torskethorpe has never been in question," Brimar says. "Your intentions have been."

"You should know me better than that, Brimar."

"You're right, I should." And without another word, he turns to the sink, washing the same dish he was washing moments ago, as if he didn't just question our entire friendship.

Chapter Nineteen

LILLY

"What are you carving?" Lara asks from across the living room, where she's finishing up embroidering a table runner that I begged her to give me when she's done.

"Something special for Keller," I answer.

"Not to be rude, but it looks like a boob."

I hold up my carving and smile. "It is. With a very hard nipple."

Lara laughs. "Why are you carving him a boob?"

"Well, for one, it's pocket-sized, so in case he ever needs to cop a feel, he can just reach into his pocket."

Lara laughs some more.

"And secondly, he's been in a weird mood today, and I thought that making this would cheer him up. A pocket boob."

"I know it would cheer Brimar up," Lara says, and then she moves closer to me, taking a seat on the couch. "Brimar said they got in a fight last night. He wouldn't tell me what about, though."

"Keller wouldn't talk to me either." Although, we didn't do much talking last night, if you know what I mean.

"I don't think I've ever seen this much tension between them."

"Do you know why they might be at each other?" I ask as I press my thumb against the blade to carve around the very prominent nipple I've created. I plan on making a hole through it and putting one of my spare nipple rings through the hole. I know when I reach Strombly, I probably won't be able to do something like this, given how I need to be composed, which is why I want to do it now.

"I'm not sure. I know the stress is high for both of them. They never want to let King Theo down, so that might be a part of it."

"Do they think I'm going to fail?" I ask, insecurity crawling up the back of my neck.

"No." She shakes her head. "I don't think that's the case at all." She looks to the side and says, "I don't want you to feel bad about what I'm going to say, okay? But I think it has something to do with Keller's involvement with you."

"As in . . . us coupling?"

"Yes," she answers. "I think Brimar is worried that Keller might scare you away, you know, if something ever happens between the two of you."

"That's not going to happen," I say. "I know it's easy for me to say because I'm the one feeling it, but what I have with Keller is so far removed from the crown, it's more on a primitive level. Just me and him, nothing else."

"I can understand that. When Brimar and I first started dating, I knew Keller had reservations about it, especially since we're on the same security team. We never want anything interfering with the job."

"Ah, I see what you mean," I say. "Because the job always comes first."

"Unfortunately, it does, for everyone involved." She grows even more serious when she says, "Something you need to remember when you step foot in Strombly—it has a rich history of sovereigns who've always put the crown ahead of everything else. I know King Theo has reservations about doing so. He blames his responsibilities and his tunnel vision when it comes to the country on his inability to have raised his children to appreciate the roles they were born into, to have the same loyalty that someone like Keller has, who would do anything in his power to serve the country. So, even though you need to go into this knowing, no matter what, the crown always comes first, I think you need to remember there's life outside of the crown, and if you don't nurture it, everything can tumble to the ground."

I place my hand on Lara's and say, "That's probably some of the best advice I've gotten. Thank you."

"You're welcome." She takes my hand and squeezes it. "I want to see you succeed. There'll be people in the public who want nothing more than the girl from Miami to fail, and they'll be vocal about it. But just know, the core people who are surrounding you, they aren't waiting for you to fail, they're excited to watch you succeed."

My emotions get the better of me as I say, "Thank you, Lara. That truly means a lot to me."

"Well, you mean a lot to us."

———

"ARE YOU READY?" I ask Keller, who still seems to be in a weird mood.

"Ready for what?" he asks as he stops in the middle of the living room. He's been up in his bedroom all day working on the welcoming and preparing the staff, so much so that I haven't seen him. And the way his hair is all rumpled from his hands running through it, and the stiff set to his shoulders . . . it makes me want to loosen him up in all the right ways.

"Two things." I hold up my fingers. "Thing one, I have some tricks to show you that I've learned. And thing two, I made something for you."

His eyes narrow skeptically. "Did you finish your fish?"

"I did." I gesture toward the windowsill. "Right over there, in all its glory, my Torg fish. Compliments will be accepted."

He walks to the windowsill, picks up the fish, and examines it. I spent a great deal of time carving out the scales, which he told me I didn't have to do since I was a beginner, but I wanted to. And then I painted only the head and the tail in a pale blue. I put a clear coat over the whole thing and—voilà—a fish!

"You carved the scales."

"I did." I rock on my heels. "Impressed, aren't you?"

"I am. Very impressed. You did great, Lilly," he says softly. "I only wish I could keep it for myself."

"Funny that you bring that up," I say as Lara chuckles behind me.

Keller turns to face us, confusion on his brow. "What's going on?"

"Well, I told you I made you something. And this . . . this is all for you. Hold out your hands and close your eyes."

Still eyeing me skeptically, he does as told, and that's when I take the mini boob, no bigger than a golf ball, out of my pocket and set it on his palms. Hands clasped together in glee, I say, "Okay, open your eyes."

His eyes flutter open and zero in on the mini boob in his hands with its . . . adornment. Then they flash up to mine as he clutches his long fingers around it.

"Lilly . . ." he says in that bedroom tone of his.

"Yes?" I ask innocently.

His eyes flash to Lara, who's still chuckling behind me, and then back to me.

"Do you like it? Can you tell it's a mini replica? I made the nipple extra hard for your liking."

Lara laughs out loud now, and I can see Keller waver between loving it and wanting to reprimand me.

"Can I speak to you privately?" he asks.

"Uh-oh," I say to Lara. "Looks like I might be in trouble."

"Lilly," Keller snaps as he motions to the entryway. Still smiling, I fall in line behind him, and when I reach the circular room, he moves in on me, trapping me against the wall.

He holds the boob in front of me and asks, "What's the meaning of this?"

"Well, Keller, dear, you see, it's a boob. And that boob is supposed to be placed in your pocket, so whenever you think of me, you can caress it, you know, since we won't be able to be all ooey-gooey, lovey-dovey at Strombly and in public."

"You shouldn't be carving boobs. You're the future queen. Where's your decorum?"

"Waiting for me at Strombly." I smile at him and then move my hands under his shirt, feeling his rippling abs beneath my fingers. "Tell me you love it, because I know you do."

He lets out a heavy sigh and then says, "I fucking love it."

"Ooo, I knew you would." Now calling out so Lara can hear me, I say, "He loves it, Lara, he's just trying to act all tough."

He pinches his brow with one hand and asks, "Why are you like this?"

"You love that I'm like this, admit it." I bring my hands to his pecs, and they twitch under my touch.

"I do." His eyes meet mine. "I really fucking do."

"God," I breathe heavily. "I'm going to suck your cock so hard tonight."

His eyes turn dark as he lowers his head so it's closer to mine. "Watch it. You can't be saying those things, not anymore."

"I can and I will, but I'll whisper them to you instead. Despite my role moving forward, I want you to know that I'll always and forever want your cock in my mouth." I smile brightly, causing him to shake his head and laugh.

"You've got to be the dirtiest future queen ever."

"I'll wear the title proudly."

He leans in closer and cups my cheek. "How are you doing? I'm sorry I've been busy all day." His thumb drags just under my eye.

"I'm doing great. Made my man a boob, finished my fish, and I have some other things that I've worked hard on to show you."

"You're such a good girl," he says, quietly enough for me to realize the praise speaks from the sacred place we share. Then he leans forward and moves his mouth over mine in a desperate kiss. I match his desperation and slip my tongue past his lips, causing him to groan and pull away. "Tonight," he whispers. "Okay?"

I nod and then release him, only to take his hand in mine. "Come on, I want to show you my moves."

One eyebrow quirks in question, and then he asks, "What kind of moves?"

"Some special ones. Come on."

I lead him back into the living room, and out of the corner of my eye, I catch him pocketing the boob, just where I wanted it.

"Lara, we're ready."

"Oh, great. Help me move this table."

I go to move the coffee table with Lara, but Keller steps in quickly and takes care of it.

"I can lift things, you know?" I say to him.

"Not when I'm around," he answers back.

Speaking to Lara, I say, "You know, I could be quite annoyed with that answer, but unfortunately for all feminists, I find it incredibly hot."

"Nothing wrong with a man picking up a table for you." She winks. "Brimar would have done the same."

"Where is Brimar?" I ask.

"Packing up, working on some security details with the palace. He'll be making dinner shortly."

"Oh, cool." I move to the center of the room and say, "Keller, come attack me."

"Excuse me?" he asks.

"You heard me." I motion with my arm. "Come try to get me."

"Why?" he asks.

"I told you, I have moves. I have a few to show you here and one to show you in the car."

"The car?" he asks and then looks at Lara. "What the hell did you teach her?"

"The fun stuff," I answer for Lara. "Now, come try to kidnap me. I'll pretend to be talking to a little girl about her flower crown." Getting into character, I squat down and say, "Oh, hello, sweetie, what a lovely crown. Did you make that yourself?" When Keller doesn't do anything, I look over my shoulder and say, "Uh, hello, that's your cue. Come try to take me."

Sighing, he walks up to me as I turn back around, slips his hand over my eyes, and then one arm around my waist, picking me up as if I'm a simple sack of flour.

I wiggle in his grasp, attempting to do that thing Lara taught me with my legs, but fail miserably against the stone god behind me.

"Are you supposed to be doing something to me?" Keller asks.

"Yes," I grunt, trying hard to loop my leg around his to trip him up. "But, Jesus, you're so big."

"Never complained about it before," he whispers in my ear, causing my cheeks to flame.

I wiggle some more.

I kick around.

I even attempt a karate hand on his arm, but nothing breaks him.

"Am I supposed to be impressed?" he asks as he sets me down, my worn-out body needing a break.

"Well, it worked on Lara."

"Yes, and Lara is three-quarters my size."

"Not something we considered," Lara says, tapping her chin. "But what about the full-frontal attack? Try that one."

"Ah, yes." I lift my finger to the air. "The full frontal. I'm going to really get you now." I position myself and set the scene. "Now, I'll be greeting a world leader when out of nowhere, you try to attack me head-on."

"That would never happen. Your security detail would be extensive in a meet-and-greet with a world leader that you'd never have to worry about a frontal attack."

"Ugh, fine, I'm meeting with someone in town, and they decide they don't like my dress and attack me."

"Also, if Lara does her job, none of this happens."

"What if Lara gets a charley horse on the job? Huh? Ever think about that?" I ask him. "Those death cramps come out of nowhere and can take a grown man down. We must be fully prepared for all scenarios, so stop being difficult, stand over there, and attack me from the front."

"Sure, in case of a charley horse." He rolls his eyes, and I ignore it.

"Okay, come at me. I'm just going to pretend I'm greeting a dignitary. Oh, hello, Mr. President, how kind you are to compliment my yellow dress. I made it from hay."

Keller pauses in his approach. "Hay?"

"Just attack me, for fuck's sake." His brow raises at me. "Errr, I mean, for crying out loud."

He moves in on me, and I pop my arm out, aiming for his nose as I let out a "hi-yah."

Keller grabs my hand, twists it around my body, and in seconds, has my back pinned to his chest.

"Ha, got you," I say. "That *hi-yah* hand was just a decoy. This is where the fun begins." I move to stomp on his foot. "Take tha-aaaahhh."

He spreads my legs, causing me to almost tumble forward, only for him to scoop me up and toss me over his shoulder.

"Uh-huh, sure, good move, but what about this?" I say as I smack his ass. "Look out, the saw-hand is coming. *Brrrrrrr-ummmmm.*" I start chopping at his back repeatedly, gaining some ground with every pound.

"Little to the left," he says. "Yes, right there."

I pause. "This isn't a massage. These are my deadly weapons." I chop at him again.

"Feels like a massage," he says when he sets me back down.

"Oh yeah? But what about this?" I spin in place and try to chop him at the waist, but he stops my hand, so I go in for a right hook. He stops that as well and ties me up in a pretzel. "Uh-huh, I see you, but what about this?" I go for the good stuff, plowing a fist right to his crotch, but he lifts his knee, deflecting my hand. I spin again and attempt to body slam him into the wall, but instead, I bounce off his large body and land on my butt on the floor.

When I stand, I brush off my backside and nod.

"Quite the competitor. I tip my hat to you but—oh no, look out, a codfish." I point to the side, and to my luck, he glances over as I roundhouse kick him, aiming for the stomach.

But the man has catlike reflexes, and before I can enjoy the feeling of my foot connecting with his abs, he grips my ankle in his large hand and then somehow drags me close and lifts me in the air so I'm hanging upside down in front of him, breathing heavily.

"This . . . uh, this is unexpected," I say.

"Wow, Lilly, you sure learned a lot," Keller says sarcastically. "I don't think you're going to need Lara." He sets me down on the floor, and I quickly stand, adjusting my shirt. "You can clearly handle this all on your own."

"You know . . ." I place my hands on my hips. "You're incredibly sexy, but you can be a real wet blanket sometimes."

Lara is in the corner, cackling, her hand over her mouth, probably entertained for a lifetime at this point.

"Glad to be of service, my queen." He bows his head.

"You're annoying." I move past him and, in a sneak-attack move, try to punch him in the arm, but he grips my fist and spins my back into his chest. He wraps his arms around my waist and presses a kiss to my neck.

"You looked hot doing all of that."

And like butter on a hot day, I melt. Damn him and his sensual voice.

"I have one more thing to show you."

"Can't wait." He kisses my neck one more time and then releases me. "If it was anything like I just experienced, I know it'll be great."

"Oh, it will be. Lara, shall we?"

She's wiping under her eyes where her tears of laughter are streaming, and she nods. "We shall."

Together, we walk to the entryway and out the door, Keller following closely behind.

"Where are we going?" he asks.

"Keys." I hold my hand out to Lara.

"Keys?" he asks, confused.

Lara places the keys to our ride in my hand, and I go over to the car and take a seat on the driver's side.

"What do you think you're doing?" Keller asks.

I turn the car on, roll down the window, and then, in my

best Bruce Willis voice, I say, "Get the fuck in the car, we're booking it out of here."

"What the actual fuck?" Keller says as I roar the engine.

"Hurry up, they're coming, and I'm leaving you behind if you don't get in this car immediately."

Lara gives him a push and I watch as Keller jogs over, his pecs bouncing under his shirt as he makes it to the passenger side and gets in.

"I suggest you buckle up."

"Lilly, what are you doing?"

"And hang on, you're about to get the ride of your life."

He buckles up quickly as I put the car in reverse and press hard on the pedal, sending us backward.

"Jesus, fuck!" Keller yells as he holds on to—what I like to call—the *oh my God* handle of the car.

"Yippee," I scream as I shift the steering wheel to the right, causing the car to do a complete one-eighty.

"Motherfucker, Lilly, what the hell are you doing?"

I put the car in drive and pound on the gas, shooting us forward again.

"Those bastards aren't going to get us, not with me at the wheel."

"No, you're only going to kill us," he says, gripping every handle he can as we bump along in the field. "Fuck, Lilly, slow down."

"That's exactly what they want us to do. Not on my watch." I make a hard turn, forcing Keller to slam into his side of the car, his hands slapping the window, and then I gun it again, flinging him backward.

"Lilly, fucking stop."

And then I scream at the top of my lungs, "Ahhhhhhhhhh-hhhhhhhh!" startling what I can only imagine is some pee right out of Keller. He clutches his chest as I yell, "They have guns. They're shooting at us. Quick, grab your Glock. Take a shot."

I toss him the fake gun and roll down his window. "Quick, give them the old *pew-pew*." When he doesn't do anything, I say, "Keller, they're gaining on us. Shoot or be shot."

"Fucking hell." He sticks his hand out the window and pretends to shoot.

"Oh, fuck, they're surrounding us. There's only one thing to do," I say as we come closer to the coastline.

"Uh, Lilly, if you say drive off the cliff, I'm going to fucking put my foot down."

"It's the only way," I say, picking up speed.

"Lilly . . . what the fuck." He grips the dashboard as we get closer and closer. "Lilly, stop." Closer . . . "Lilly!" And closer . . . "Fuck, Lilly, stop!" he screams just as I put the car in reverse, spinning the wheel, turning us in a one-eighty at the edge of the coast, and then put it back in drive and speed back to the castle.

"Fucking Jesus Christ!" Keller yells.

"Yahoo," I scream, braking right in front of the castle, and put the car in park. "We did it." I clap for myself. "We lost those punks."

Not speaking a word, Keller steals the keys from me and then flings his door open, only to melt out onto the ground.

I get out of the car as well, while Lara claps for me. "I think he's impressed," I call out and round the car, where I find Keller breathing heavily and gripping the ground. "Aren't you glad you shot those people trying to get us? A valiant effort on your end." I smile and then prance back to the castle, knowing I'll pay for what I just did later.

And I'll welcome his payback with open arms.

⸻

"KELLER, stop . . . please . . . please just make me come."

"You think you can tell me what to do, especially after that stunt you played this afternoon?"

312

He has me tied up. My arms are behind my back, and my legs are spread and elevated, attached to the rails at the top of the bed. He tied multiple ties together to make them reach, and there's absolutely nothing I can do as he "teaches" me with his mouth, his hands, his cock, and my vibrator.

I've been like this for what feels like an hour.

Him taunting.

Tasting.

Edging me to the point of an orgasm, only to take it away.

He has dipped his cock in my mouth, in my pussy, and then back in my mouth. I've sucked on his balls, he's rubbed his cock over my breasts and along my clit piercing, and I watched him masturbate, stroking his long, hard cock until he came all over my stomach.

But he hasn't allowed me my pleasure, and I'm starting to worry that he won't tonight, because, man oh man, was he angry about the driving.

Fuming.

I don't think I've ever seen him that mad.

And when he took me to his room, he gave me a lecture about being safe as he spanked me repeatedly until I was dripping and needy.

"I learned my lesson. I promise it'll never happen again, my King."

"Of course it won't because I won't allow it."

"Is that how it's going to be? You dictating?" I ask, unsure why I need to poke the bear.

He walks over to the side of the bed and leans down so his hands straddle my face and he's inches away. "When it comes to your safety, I'll always dictate how it will be. You're my top priority, and if you're ever in danger, that's because I wasn't doing my job, do you understand me?"

"Yes, but—"

"But nothing," he chokes out, his voice growing gravelly. I realize that maybe he isn't just playing the demanding role of my boyfriend, of my lover, of *my King*, but he's truly worried. His hand cups my cheek softly. "I can't . . . I can't have anything happen to you, Lilly. It'll fucking destroy me. Tomorrow, everything changes. Everything. And I need you to know that you'll be safe, that you'll make safe choices because when you step foot in Strombly, I won't be able to protect you from everything, and that terrifies me."

"Keller," I whisper. "I—I wasn't trying to make you feel this way. I had everything under control."

"That was obvious," he says. "But moving forward, Lilly, please, please promise me you'll make smart choices. Promise me you'll protect yourself because you're protecting what matters most to me." He wets his lips. "I already lost my parents. I can't lose you as well."

My heart hammers as I try to free my arms. "Untie me, Keller. Now."

He does as I say, and when I'm free, I push him back on the headboard so he's leaning against it. I straddle his lap, placing my hands on his shoulders.

"You're not going to lose me," I say, pressing my thumb under his chin so he has to look at me. "I'm yours. I'm here to stay. Nothing is going to happen to me."

"You never know for certain." He wets his lips as his hands fall to my waist. They shake ever so slightly, and I can feel just how terrified he is. "We don't know how people will accept you. They might be so angry that you're not from Torskethorpe that they try something stupid, and if I'm not there to protect you and something happens . . ."

"Stop. You can't think that way. I have Brimar and Lara and whoever else joins the team, people you trust and know will protect me when you're not around."

He nods but still looks terrified. So, I do the only thing I know to do. I lift up and move his once-again hard cock to my entrance and slowly lower myself. We both suck in a sharp breath once I'm fully seated.

"You feel that?" I ask him. "You feel that connection?"

He nods, his hands helping me rock over him.

"That connection is unbreakable, Keller. Nothing is going to get between us, and nothing is going to hurt us. It's you and me, together in this world." I connect our foreheads as my rocking starts to pick up, my orgasm building.

"Lilly." His voice is distraught. When I look him in the eyes, he says, "I . . . fuck, I shouldn't say this, not like this, but I need you to know . . . I need you to understand how much I care for you."

My heart hammers, pounding so hard my pulse feels like fire in my veins.

"Say it."

He wets his lips again and looks me in the eyes. "I . . . I love you, Lilly."

His cock hits me in all the right places, and even though the words are on the tip of my tongue, I can't voice them as my orgasm tears through me, shooting through my limbs and causing me to feel weightless as I come all over his cock.

To my surprise, he flips me to my back and pounds into me a few more times before he stills and groans as he comes as well.

When our eyes connect, we both attempt to catch our breath. He tries to maneuver out of me, but I clamp my legs around him, holding him in place. With my hand on the back of his head, I bring him close to my mouth and say, "I love you, Keller, so much."

"You do?" he asks, insecurity clear in his expression.

"Yes, I do. You make me feel truly whole."

"Love . . ." he says softly. "Fuck." He presses his forehead to mine and then kisses me softly.

We spend the next few minutes cleaning up and getting ready for bed. Once we're done, we fall back into his bed, my back to his chest as he spoons me from behind, his large, warm body offering me all the comfort I need in this world.

MEGHAN QUINN

He gave me his heart.

"I need you to understand how much I care for you. I . . . I love you, Lilly."

It's been years since anyone's said that to me. Years since I heard my parents' voices telling me they loved me. *Years since I felt this safe. This loved.*

———

TIMMY: *Is today the big day?*

Lilly: *Driving to the palace now.*

Timmy: *How do you feel?*

Lilly: *Like I'm going to puke.*

Timmy: *Fair reaction. Is Keller with you?*

Lilly: *His hand is on my thigh as I text you.*

Timmy: *Good. As long as someone is there to metaphorically hold your hand.*

Lilly: *He's here. He's barely left my side all day. He keeps telling me I'm going to do great, but all I can think about is, for the love of God, don't puke on the king.*

Timmy: *I think that's something solid to repeat in your head. But also . . . don't forget the filter. You're not spraying down wet tits anymore. You're dignified now.*

I snort, and Keller leans in, whispering, "What's so funny?"

"Timmy," I answer. I flash him the text, and Keller chuckles as well.

"Yeah, no more wet tits." He keeps his voice so quiet, so close to my ear, that I know only I can hear him. "Unless it's your wet tits in the shower, with me."

"Like this morning?" I ask him.

His hand slides farther up my leg, the dress I'm wearing riding up with his hand. "Yes," he whispers again, and I'm not sure if he's doing it on purpose, but his touch, his voice?

316

They're washing away the nerves and making me focus on one thing alone—the desire I have for this man.

"Don't start something you can't finish," I tell him quietly.

"I don't mind finishing you, as long as you're quiet," he whispers back.

My eyes flash to his, and I shake my head while smiling. "No way can I be quiet with you."

"Missed opportunity."

I lean into his touch and rest my head against his shoulder. "Keller?"

"Yeah, love?"

"I'm scared."

"I know." He wraps his arm around me and holds me tight. "You have all the right to be scared."

"What if . . . what if King Theo doesn't like me?"

"I would be hard-pressed to see that happening. He's going to love you. Just like I do." He kisses the top of my head. "Now stop worrying and think about all the good things that are going to happen. You're going to meet your grandfather for the first time. Now that's something to be excited about."

"You're right," I say. "That is exciting. But also . . . puke worthy."

He chuckles. "If you need to puke, you tell me. I'll get you everything you need."

Chapter Twenty

KELLER

"Wow," Lilly breathes as she looks out the window at the fast-approaching Strombly Palace. Ever since we reached the capital, she's been glued to the window, taking in all the buildings, saying how they look like something you'd see at EPCOT, which made me laugh. "It's breathtaking. I wasn't expecting it to look so . . . medieval. I had more Buckingham Palace vibes in mind, you know? But this is . . . this is breathtaking."

Strombly Palace sits on the top of a secluded hill, surrounded by an expansive stone wall that circles the entire perimeter. Only accessible by the famous Strombly Bridge, with its imposing heights over the Torske River, the palace's structure is made up of tall towers, bastions, a myriad of stone carvings perched high, gracefully large windows, and burnt-orange roofs. Outfitted with a plush green courtyard at the center of the majestic building, a marble ballroom, and an endless number of bedrooms.

"It is, isn't it?" I say, marveling at the building I've known as my home.

Brimar pulls the car into the castle and around to the grand entrance, where staff is lined up, waiting for us.

I lean close to Lilly before this all begins and say, "Remember, they're here for you, to support you. You'll be amazing, Lilly. Chin parallel, full of grace."

The car parks and a footman opens the car door. I step out first and offer him a nod before holding my hand out to Lilly. She takes it from inside the car and carefully steps onto the concrete of the grand entrance.

Wearing a canary-yellow dress that reaches her calves, she looks regal. I release her hand when she's standing and gently put my hands behind my back. When my eyes fall on the staff surrounding her, I see the appreciation in their eyes and the relief. We all know what's at stake, *and* the sacrifice she's making.

"Miss Campbell," I say, gesturing toward the door. "Right this way."

I spoke to her about my use of her title when we arrived at the palace, how I needed to remain professional in front of the staff, and she understood. But trust me when I say I'd want nothing more than to take her hand at this moment and hold her tight while she steps into this new role in her life.

We walk through the doors, where more staff is lined up. To my shock, King Theo and Queen Katla are standing at the base of the split staircase. Lilly pauses. The entryway is silent as their eyes connect.

King Theo, out of bed and looking healthier, takes a step forward, Queen Katla at his side.

Out of the corner of my eye, I catch Lilly curtsying, just like we taught her, and I don't think I could be prouder. I bow as well.

And when we both rise, King Theo's eyes are filled with

tears as he uses the help of his cane to close the distance between us.

"My darling Lilija," he says in awe. "Come here." He holds his arm out, and hesitantly, Lilly leans into his embrace, before he fully grips her in a bear hug. I stand idly by, watching as Lilly loops her arms around him and returns the hug.

Trying to remain stoic, I hold it together even though a bout of emotions rises at the base of my throat. I can't imagine what she's feeling right now, but if I know my girl like I think I do, she must be swarmed with emotions.

When they finally pull apart, Theo wipes at her eyes, clearing her tears, before looking up at me, appreciation and gratefulness in his eyes.

"Keller, thank you."

I nod. "You're welcome, Your Majesty."

And then Queen Katla steps up, tears clouding her eyes as she takes Lilly's hands in hers and quietly says, "You're a beautiful replica of Margret." A tear slips down Katla's cheek. "Thank you, Lilija, for coming here, for giving us a chance."

For the first time since I was brought to the palace, Queen Katla's characteristic cool façade is absent. She looks . . . *warm. Welcoming.* It's a sight to behold, and I'm sure I'm not the only staff member shocked.

"It is my pleasure," Lilly says.

"Please, come sit with us in the red room. Keller, please join us."

I nod and follow behind, keeping at least one step behind Lilly as we walk slowly toward the red room, the king and queen's private drawing room. Lara and Brimar follow closely behind as well.

When we reach the red room, Lara and Brimar man the doors, shutting them behind us, as Theo and Katla take a seat on an upholstered settee and gesture to the one opposite Lilly.

She rests her hands in her lap and, from the shake in them, I can tell she's still nervous. I remain standing next to the settee.

Theo looks up at me and says, "Keller, take a seat."

I sit down on the same settee as Lilly, but I put at least two feet between us. Theo looks between us, and I know he knows when the corner of his lip twitches. Nothing gets by him.

But, being the classy man he is, he doesn't start the conversation with the knowledge that Lilly and I are an item. Instead, he says, "Lilija, tell me, how do you like it in Torskethorpe?"

"Honestly, I love it." She smiles. "Granted, it took me a moment, but after I got used to the perpetual sun and the summer weather, which doesn't even come close to the heat of Miami, I started to immerse myself. I found little pieces of the house I grew up in all around Harrogate. I know there was a falling out between my mom and you, but I want you to know that there was so much of this country that she kept close to her heart and instilled in me without me even knowing about it. And with every day that went by with training, the hidden secrets my mom planted started to unfold."

"Really?" Katla asks.

"Truly," Lilly says. "And the more Keller taught me, the more I realized that this country I knew nothing about has been my home all along."

Theo's eyes widen as he grips the cane between his legs now. "Wait, Lilija, are you saying . . . are you saying you're going to stay?"

Lilly glances at me and then back at Theo. "I am. I've thought long and hard about it, and even though I loved my life in Miami, I felt a piece of me was missing. When I came here, I found that piece. This feels right. This feels like home."

King Theo clutches his chest as he leans back on the settee, his eyes misting with tears. "My darling, you have no idea the joy you've brought us, brought this country."

"It was more of a selfish decision on my end. Being here, it feels like I'm close to my mom again."

"Well, your decision feels heroic to us," Theo says. "I'm just—I'm beyond words. I don't know what to say."

"I do," Katla says, placing her hand on Theo's leg. Queen Katla has never treated Theo with anything but utter adoration, their PDA never concealed. She's not a cold woman, but a slightly broken one. Proud, yet sad. I know that deep within there is a warm-hearted woman who longed for restoration with her estranged daughter. *And now she has a chance in some ways.* "It takes a courageous woman to fly to a foreign country, find out she's a princess, and being the remarkable adult that she is, accept the responsibility that's been handed down to her. I know I've done some heinous acts in the past regarding communication with my children, but, Lilija, I need you to know that I'll spend the rest of my time making up for it. I'm a stubborn woman, but I also know where I've wronged this country, and pushing my children away is my fault. Having you here, it feels almost like I don't deserve it."

"Katla," Theo says softly. "We've spoken about this."

"I know, but I need Lilija to know where I stand." She levels herself with Lilly. "And I stand with you, Lilija. I shall be your backbone, your support, your concierge. I'll be everything you need."

"How about a grandma?" Lilly asks softly. "Never really had one of those, and it was what I was excited about most when coming to Strombly."

Katla's eyes now well up as she nods. "Yes, yes, I can do that for you."

"There's a lot I don't know about you guys, and I would love to spend some time getting to know you. And maybe you can show me some of the things my mom made. Maybe some pictures of when she was younger?"

"We would be most pleased to do so," Katla says. "Is there anything else you request?"

"Um, well, not sure you need to know this, but . . ." She twists her hands together and looks at me, and the hairs on the back of my neck rise. Fuck, she's going to tell them. "Keller, well, he's . . . uh, we're sort of an item."

Theo smirks.

Katla shifts her attention to me.

And a light sweat breaks out on my upper lip.

"Is that so?" Theo asks. "Keller, care to explain?"

"Yes, sir," I say. "Although I know it's not in my position to let my personal business mingle with my professional, and I apologize for that, I attempted to avoid getting involved with Lilly, but as time went on, that was harder and harder to do."

"I didn't make it easy on him, either," Lilly says. "And I didn't tell him I was going to admit this, so he's caught off guard, but I want to be open with you both. Keller means a lot to me. He's been my lifeline during this whole process. If I could request anything, it would be that we're allowed to continue to date, because I would be devastated if that wasn't allowed."

"Lilly," I say quietly. "Maybe we should talk about this—"

"I see no problem in them dating, do you, Katla?" Theo says, still grinning.

"No, I don't see why it would be an issue. Keller is an excellent young man. You have good taste, Lilija."

My gaze falls to theirs as the insides of my body start to itch, my insecurities roaring to life. It's true that I've had a lot to do with Queen Katla over the years. She loved my mum dearly and was devastated when she died. But I've never felt the same connection with her that I feel with Theo. She's always kept herself more aloof than warm with me. *Is she honestly pleased or saying what she believes Lilly wants to hear?* I pull on the back of my neck and whisper, "We can talk about this later."

"Oh, sure, okay," Lilly says, looking incredibly unsure.

"Lilija, why don't I show you some of the table runners

your mother embroidered over the years?" Katla stands from her seat and holds out her hand.

Lilly lights up as she says, "I'd love that." She stands as well, Katla takes her hand, and together, they walk over to a dresser on the other side of the room, leaving me with Theo.

He grips the armrest of the settee and then lifts himself up. "Keller, join me in my office."

I can only imagine what this will be about.

I open the hidden door that leads to his office and watch him slowly walk through. I'm so glad that he's actually out of bed and not coughing. That relieves me, but it also feels as if he's aged ten years since I last saw him.

I shut the door behind us, knowing he's going to want the privacy to lecture me, and we both take a seat in his seating area, each opting for a fabric captain's chair in a navy blue. They match the curtains that run floor to ceiling in his circular office.

Theo sets his cane down and says, "So, you and Lilly."

"Yes." I shift uncomfortably.

"Did that happen after our conversation when I told you to comfort her?"

I shift again. "Yes."

"Uh-huh, comforted her a little much there?" he teases, but I don't find it funny.

Looking him in the eyes, I say, "I wasn't planning on giving in to my feelings, I truly wasn't. I was trying to keep her at a distance, but . . ." I rub my forehead. "Hell, I just couldn't stay away. She's . . . she's special, Theo. It feels as if she's always belonged to me."

"Okay, so then what was that all about back there?" He points to the drawing room.

"We didn't discuss how we would go about telling you."

"I think how she did it was perfectly fine." When I don't say anything, he continues, "Why are you so uncomfortable?"

"Because—she's going to be queen one day, Theo."

"I'm aware and quite happy about that."

"Yeah, well, she deserves to be with someone who can provide for her, someone with a higher ranking."

Theo's brows tilt down in a frown. "When has that ever been an issue with this family?" he asks. "That's never been a requirement, nor will it ever be."

"But that's not what I grew up with." I punch my hand through my hair. "I grew up knowing my place. My parents instilled it in me. Reminded me every day where I belonged. I'm here to serve, not to pretend I'm someone else."

"I see, and what exactly do you think that someone else is? Because no one is asking you to pretend. No one is asking you to be anyone but yourself, and from what I can tell, that girl likes you . . . for who you are, nothing else."

"She does," I say softly.

"Do you believe you're not good enough?"

"Yes," I answer without even having to think about it. I know I'm not good enough.

Theo blows out a breath and then says, "Let me ask you this. Do you love her?"

My gaze meets his and I nod slowly. "Yes, sir. I do."

"And have you told her this?"

"Yes."

"Are you worried about what the staff might think? Is that the issue? Because you know I have no problem with the love you share for each other."

"I'm afraid people will think I'm posing as something I'm not."

"How about instead of looking at her as a part of the crown, you look at her as someone you just met. Would you think twice about being with her?"

"No, but I'm not afforded that luxury," I say. "Because that's not the case here. She's going to be queen, and if we stay together, if we . . . if we marry one day, that affords me a title, a hefty title."

"A title you are more than able to handle," Theo says. "A title I'd be proud to see you wear. But how about this, instead of worrying about the future and what might come, focus on the now. She needs you, and I need you. Please don't hurt her heart because you're scared. She's been hurt far too much."

I nod. "I'd never want to hurt her. I love her, Theo, I truly do. But, sometimes, don't you think love isn't enough?"

"Never," Theo says, straightening now. "Love is always enough. If love weren't enough, then I wouldn't be in a position where Katla is at my side. We've had our ups and downs, the history has written itself, and without love, I'm not sure we would've made it through all the tragedy we've faced. The first thing you need in a relationship is to like each other, and that's then followed by love. You have both, so don't be a fool and scare yourself away from that. Now, you go back into that drawing room and reassure that girl that her coming forward with the truth is not to be punished, but commended."

"Yes, sir," I say, standing from my chair.

"And, Keller?" When I turn to face him, he continues, "Thank you . . . thank you for showing her the true beauty of this country when I wasn't able to. Your hard work has not gone unnoticed."

"It was my pleasure," I answer.

"And from now until the foreseeable future, Henrik will be staying on board as my secretary."

My heart trips out of my chest. "Theo," I say softly. "You . . . you're just going to give away my job?"

He shakes his head. "No, you'll be at Lilija's side now. I don't matter as much as Lilija does. I need you to stay close to her to continue to help her through this transition. Henrik is wonderful, but he's not you. If you resume your position with me, you'd be wasted. Your responsibility now is to guide Lilija." When I look down, he adds, "This is not a demotion; it's a promotion. She's our future, and I'm the past. You need to keep moving forward."

"I understand," I say, connecting my eyes with his. And although I understand his words and his sentiment, I'm shocked. I haven't believed I could have Lilly, and now . . . *now that seems possible.* Not only that, I'll have even more capacity to serve this country I love. This man, who has treated me like a son, has given me a blessing beyond what I ever thought possible. *Fuck.* "I'll do you proud, Theo."

"I know you will. And you'll also make your parents proud, Keller."

I nod humbly. What can I say to that?

I excuse myself and go back into the drawing room, where Katla and Lilly are huddled over quite a few table runners. Lilly is speaking quietly, running her hand over the embroidery work, her expression in complete awe.

Being here in the palace makes our situation profoundly different. It puts things into perspective. We don't have our safety bubble anymore. There are eyes and ears everywhere. And I can't be as candid as I want to be with her. Now that we're here, now that she said she'd take the throne, everything has changed.

She glances in my direction, and when she sees me, she gives me a wary smile, and it nearly splits me in half. *She's unsure.* She's questioning herself when she did nothing wrong. And as Theo said, she needs to know what she said is not to be punished, but commended.

I close the distance between us, making sure to approach cautiously in case they're talking about anything sensitive, but when Katla invites me to the conversation, I know it's safe.

"I was just showing Lilija Margret's beautiful stitches."

I walk up right next to Lilly, put my arm around her waist, and bring her in close to press a kiss to the top of her head. It's my way of letting Lilly know everything is okay. Katla smiles warmly as I reach down and pick up one of the napkins. "She did exquisite work. With more practice, I believe Lilly will be just as good, if not better."

Lovingly, Lilly looks up at me. "You think so?"

"I do."

━━━

"OKAY," Lilly whispers at the dinner table. "The cod cakes were actually really good."

I chuckle softly. "See, nothing to be scared of."

"I will always be scared of fermented cod."

"What are you two whispering about?" Theo asks as he brings a goblet of water to his lips.

"The cod cakes," I answer as Lilly grips my thigh under the table, giving me a warning squeeze.

"Delicious, right, Lilija?"

"Very." Lilly dabs her mouth with the corner of her napkin, just as I taught her. Before we walked into the dining room for dinner, she pulled me aside and asked me to review meal etiquette one more time. I told her she had nothing to worry about, but she wanted to impress King Theo. So, we had a quick crash course before entering the dining room. "The entire meal was great. Although, Brimar is quite the chef. He would bake fresh bread every day, and I couldn't get enough of it."

"Ah, yes, Brimar has made quite a few loaves for us," Katla says. "Brilliant with his sourdough starter."

"I think a part of this gut is from Brimar's bread," Theo says, patting his stomach. He's unlike any king I know. Pretty sure the Queen of England wouldn't be patting her belly at the dinner table. Theo yawns and says, "Excuse me. How rude of me. It's been a long day. Didn't get much sleep last night. I was nervous about meeting you, my darling."

Lilly smiles shyly. "I barely got any sleep either, but I think I can confidently say the nerves are mostly gone. They'll probably shake away with every day that goes by."

"They will," Theo says.

"Has Keller walked you through the itinerary?" Katla asks.

"I'm not sure Lilly even knows Keller's new role," Theo says.

"What new role?" Lilly asks, looking concerned.

"Keller will continue to be at your side. Even though he's been my private secretary for years now, I know his work will be more valuable to you. I want you to be comfortable, and with Keller leading the way, I know you'll be taken care of."

"I will," Lilly says, slipping her hand into mine under the table. "It's surprised me how comfortable I've felt around Keller. Yes, I've depended on him to prepare me for this role. But personally, I feel so connected too."

Katla smiles. "That's so wonderful to hear. It'll be a perfect match, then. So, that means tomorrow will go swimmingly. Keller will be giving you a tour of the palace and our everyday routine while Theo and I prepare for Friday."

"What's Friday?" Lilly asks.

"Your first public appearance," Theo says. "We've held off the public as much as we could, but they are anxious to meet you, and I believe if we wait much longer, they'll become antsy and think something is wrong."

"Oh, wow, okay," Lilly says, taking a deep breath.

"Don't worry, we'll be there, and so will Keller, who's been working on the welcoming with Henrik."

"You'll be fine," I reassure her.

"You will," Theo says as he pushes his chair away from the table. "Now, I must get to bed for fear of passing out at the dinner table. Face first into the dinner plate isn't very kingly." He stands, and so does everyone else at the table. Theo walks over to Lilly and me, one hand on each of our shoulders. "Go to bed, get some sleep. I'll see you two tomorrow."

Before Theo takes Katla's hand, she leans in to stroke Lilly's cheek. "I'm so thankful you're here with us, Lilija. Sweet dreams, darling," she says, causing Lilly's eyes to well.

"Thank you. I am, too," Lilly replies.

Then Theo and Katla walk out of the dining room, leaving me with Lilly. "Want me to show you to your room?"

"Yes, please," she whispers. "I must get out of these heels, or I might die."

I chuckle. "You'll get used to them."

"Says the man in the comfortable shoes."

"Who says these are comfortable?"

"How about this, we trade shoes and then make a decision?"

"Nice try," I say as I press my hand to the small of her back and guide her toward the stairwell. "So, how has your first half day been?" I ask.

"Overwhelming," she answers as we head up the sweeping staircase. We pass by quite a few staff who bow or curtsy, and I can feel Lilly's discomfort with the gesture. She smiles gracefully, and when we finally reach her room, I open the door for her and let her step in first.

"Oh, wow," she says as I shut the door behind us. "This is . . . this is opulent."

That's an easy way to put it. The walls are covered in a cream damask wallpaper, the windows are shrouded in yards and yards of green velvet fabric, and the four-poster, gilded bed, which takes up a good portion of the space, is decorated in purple and green velvet bedding. The creaky wood floors are covered in Persian-style rugs, and the ceilings are adorned with intricate carvings. A decadent chandelier hangs from the center of it all, casting a dim light throughout the space.

"You have the option to change things if you want, if it's too much for you," I say, watching her examine the intricacies of the décor.

"It's not that, it's just . . . sort of unbelievable." She chuckles. "Like this is the stuff you see in movies, not in real life. Like . . . Keller, there's a chandelier in my room, a legit chandelier."

"Yes, well, all the rooms are like this."

"Even yours?"

That makes me laugh. "My room is in the servant quarters, remember? My room isn't even half this size, nor is there velvet material anywhere."

"What's it like, then?"

"Well, it has a double bed, thankfully. A braided rug on the floor that my mum and I made together, one of the few things that weren't destroyed in the fire, and pictures of everything important to me. A desk where I journal, a dresser for my clothes, and that's pretty much it. I don't require a lot."

"It sounds nice."

"It does the job." I sigh and then gesture toward a door on the left. "That's your en suite bathroom. Everything you need is in there. And the dressers and closet are full of your clothes as well as shoes. Your lady's maid will come by tomorrow morning to wake you up and help you with anything you need. Her name is Runa. She was prepping your suite today but had a family emergency, so that's why she's not here right now."

"Oh no, is everything okay?"

"Yes, she just needed to leave to help her mum. She's excited to meet you, however. And if you need anything before Runa returns, there's a phone on your night table. You just need to pick it up and someone will answer. Okay?"

She nods.

"Well, I'll let you get settled." I take a step back, but she quickly clutches my hand.

"Where are you going?"

"To my room," I answer.

"You're going to leave me by myself?" she asks, her eyes wide. "Keller, you can't leave."

"Love, I can't be here with you."

"Why not?" she asks, her eyes panicking now.

"Because my room is in the servants' quarters."

"Yes, and I'm used to sleeping next to you, your warm body wrapped around me, so unless you want me to follow you to the servants' quarters, I need you to stay here, with me."

"Lilly—"

"Please, Keller," she begs. "Please, don't leave me in this room all by myself. Not after the day I had. Please, just stay with me."

Hell, when she looks at me like that, with those pleading eyes, there's no way I can deny her what she wants.

"Okay," I answer.

"Thank you." She stands on her toes and pulls my mouth to hers, giving me a soul-searing kiss as she holds me tightly. When she releases me, she slips out of her heels and then turns her back toward me so I can undo her dress.

She moves her hair to the side, and I carefully pull the zipper down until the dress is loose enough to fall to the ground. Wearing a matching bra and thong, she turns toward me and takes my hand. Together we walk into the bathroom, where we brush our teeth, her eyes on me the entire time. I know that fucking look. I know exactly what she wants from me, and even though I think I should leave right now, I know my heart, *and my body*, won't let me.

Once we're done, I set her down on the edge of the bed's mattress. "You need some pajamas."

She unclasps the front of her bra, exposing her breasts, and shimmies out of her thong. "Why? I like sleeping naked, especially with you."

"Yes, but Runa will be in here in the morning. Do you want her to see you naked?"

"Better get it out of the way. Give her an eyeful first thing in the morning." She tugs on my pants. "Seriously, I'm not worried about that right now."

"What are you worried about?"

"Getting close to you, finding my happy place in this crazy

new day, and settling into the comfort of your arms. That's what I need most right now." Her fingers dance under my shirt. "Please, Keller."

As I said, I can't deny her.

I reach behind me and pull my shirt over my head. Instead of dropping it on the floor like I usually would, I fold it and put it on her dresser before taking off my shoes, socks, and pants. When I turn around, I watch her eyes roam over my body, mainly fixating on my chest and abs. I turn the chandelier light off, then shut the curtains, leaving only a sliver open to add light to the room, because I know that's the way Lilly likes it. When I reach the bed, she's already climbed inside, so I join her.

I've always wondered what these beds feel like, whether they were comfortable or simply luxurious looking.

I can make an accurate assessment right now and say that they feel incredible. Or as Lilly said, *opulent.*

Once I'm settled on my pillow, Lilly curls against my chest, her breasts pressing against my bare skin. Her legs tangle with mine, her head rests on my chest, and her arm loops around my waist.

Chuckling, I ask, "Think you can get any closer?"

"I'm trying." She grips me tighter as I move my arm to her back and hold her close.

When she finally settles in, I ask her, "Comfortable?"

"Very. Thank you for staying, Keller. I wouldn't want to sleep in this giant room by myself. I'd be far too scared, questioning every sound I hear. But with you here, I know I'll sleep well."

I gently move my thumb over her back, soothing her. "How are you feeling? Still think you made the right decision?"

"Yes," she answers right away. "Granted, it's been an out-of-body experience today, and I'm not sure I'll ever get over the fact that people bow and curtsy to me, but I know I made the right decision. The relationship between my grandparents and me is still new, but just from their welcoming arms, I know they're the missing piece in my life I've been searching for."

"Good." I kiss the top of her head.

Her fingers dance across my chest. "Can I ask you something?"

"Anything."

"Today, when I told Katla and Theo about our relationship, and you acted like I did something wrong . . . did I? Did I do something wrong?"

"No," I say softly. "That was more about my insecurities than anything."

"What insecurities?" she asks.

"Nothing you need to worry about," I say, but that doesn't settle her.

She lifts up and moves so she's lying more on my chest, looking me in the eyes. "If it's about you, I want to know about it. Why were you feeling insecure?"

She won't drop this, I know she won't, and if I want her to get some good sleep tonight, then I need to tell her the truth.

"Growing up, I was told that my place in this world is to serve the royal family. Being with you, dating a future queen, puts me in a different position. In my parents' eyes, you would've been completely off limits, no questions asked. But I went there because I couldn't stay away. When we were at Harrogate, we were in a bubble, yet it still felt normal, but now that we're here, it's different. The vibe is different, and the people are different. I can feel my parents and what they might've said. I can see the looks in the eyes of the staff and—"

She presses her fingers to my lips, silencing me. "Keller, when have you ever cared about what people think?"

"It's not that simple, Lilly. I was programmed differently. I was raised to know my place, and crossing over that line is what's causing me to struggle mentally."

"I was programmed differently too, Keller. I grew up in America, where royal families don't exist. I was raised to have a mind of my own, to live freely, and here I am, lying in bed, in a foreign country, reflecting on my day as the future queen of Torskethorpe. Life changes constantly, and if you live in the past, you're going to miss it." She grips my jaw and forces me to look at her like I've done so many times to her in the past. "I choose you, Keller. I choose the man I fell in love with, the protector, the man who knows everything I need before I even know it. Your status, your job, your wealth, whatever it is that's holding you back, that doesn't register in my mind. All I care about is you. Just you, Keller." She cups my cheek, her fingers traveling to the back of my head, where she sifts them through my hair. "I love you, that's all that matters. And you love me, right?"

I nod. "I do. I love you, Lilly."

"Good answer." She smirks and, hell, I love that smile so much.

"I'm sorry," I say as I shift her off my chest and back onto the mattress, where I hover over her. "I didn't mean to worry you. I just need to work some things out in my head."

"I get that. But while you work those things out, don't push me away."

"I won't," I say. "I'm sorry." I brush her hair out of her face.

Her hands slide down my back to my briefs, and she slips her fingers past the elastic waistband. She grips my ass and pulls my pelvis closer.

"Lilly."

"Hmm?" she asks as her fingers dig into my skin.

"We're not doing that."

"Why not?" she asks, moving her hand to the front of my briefs. She dips her fingers past the waistband.

"Because you need some sleep."

"Yes, but I also need you. So, give me all of you, and then let me pass out from there. But I need that connection, don't you?"

I do.

I need it badly.

It's why I push down my briefs and kick them to the side of the bed before I pin both of her arms against the mattress and move on top of her body.

Her eyes become heavy with lust as she looks up at me and spreads her legs, accommodating my body.

"Show me how much you love me, my King," she says just before I match our lips together, greeting her with an open-mouthed kiss that leaves both of us breathless. She is mine. And in this bed, we are one. I am *her king*.

And for the rest of the night, I slowly and deliberately make love to my girl.

I forget about my fears.

My insecurities.

And everything else that's bothering me.

Instead, I focus on the comfort I find when I'm with her.

Chapter Twenty-One

LILLY

Light beams into my closed eyes as the curtains are drawn in my room.

"Good morning," a female voice says as I scrunch my eyes, trying not to let my retinas burn from the onslaught of light.

I turn toward the large man next to me, seeking his warmth, when I realize there is no large body next to me. Instead, I'm met with a cold side of the bed. I part my eye open and look for my man.

Nothing.

But a female appears at the side of the bed, wearing a black dress with a white collar, the same uniform I've seen the other staff around the palace wear. She also has an apron around her waist and a flower broach attached to the right side of her dress.

"Good morning, ma'am," she says. "May I introduce myself? I'm Runa."

Oh shit.

I smile and cover up my breasts. "Sorry about that. Old habits die hard, you know? I, uh, I'll at least wear a shirt in the future." One of Keller's shirts. I need to remember to ask him for some.

Speaking of—where is he? Did he really sneak out in the middle of the night? Or did Runa shoo him away without me knowing?

"Whatever you prefer." She clasps her hands in front of her. "But dare I say, I admire your piercings."

Oh hell, I forgot about those. That must have been eye-widening for her.

"Uh, thank you."

"I've always wanted to do such a thing but have been too scared. This might be bold, but may I ask, did it hurt?"

I let out a giant yawn and stretch one arm above my head while the other keeps the blanket close to my chest. "Only for a second, but the pleasure outweighs the pain, if you know what I mean."

She smiles. "That I do. Well, Miss Campbell, it's a pleasure to finally meet you. I'll be your lady's maid, and I'm here to make your life easier. Anything you might need, you just ask, and I'll be happy to oblige. I work closely with your team to ensure you're prepped and ready for what's to come each day. Since today you're just touring the palace and getting acquainted with the staff, I have laid out a simple outfit for you that is both comfortable and professional. You'll find it in the bathroom and everything else you might need to prepare. As for a morning drink, I wasn't informed of what you might wish to wake up to, but if you tell me, I'll be able to make sure I have a drink ready each morning."

"Oh, wow, that doesn't seem necessary. I don't want to put you out."

"It's not putting me out. It's my job."

"I know, but I'd feel bad asking that of you."

Runa takes a step forward and holds her hands in front of

her as she says, "May I be bold for a moment, ma'am?" That *ma'am* stuff must stop, but I don't bother saying anything immediately.

"Of course," I say. "If we're going to have a good relationship, I always want you to be bold."

"Well then, I know this lifestyle might be new to you and quite different from what you're used to, and I'm quite aware that is not of your doing. But please attempt to understand our ways. The people here serving you do it because it's their life. It's not because we're forced to or to simply pay the bills. We take great pride in the excellent service we provide our sovereigns. We undertake thorough training to get to this point, and to make it to the palace is the dream. This is how we know to serve our country. This is our life. Staff may be insulted if you deem us unnecessary. It's an honor to serve you, ma'am. So, please, tell me how I may serve you best."

"Oh God, Runa, I'm so sorry," I say, clutching my chest. "I didn't mean to insult you."

"It's quite all right. I know there will be some cultural differences at first, and as long as you have an open mind"—she glances at my chest again with a smirk—"then so will I."

"Deal," I say. "And I do love a coffee in the morning, with milk and sugar."

"Very well." She bows her head. "Now, if you'd like to get ready, Mr. Fitzwilliam is waiting to start your day outside your door."

"Fitzwilliam?" I say, confused, and then it hits me. "Oh, Keller? He's outside?"

"Yes, ma'am."

I'm seconds from asking her to call me *Lilly*, but then realize maybe that might insult her, so I hold back.

"Can you send him in?"

"But, ma'am, you're hardly decent."

"It's fine," I say, offering her a wink.

"Ah, I see. Well, shall I retrieve your coffee?"

"I think I'll just have some with breakfast. But thank you, Runa. Maybe later in the day, we can sit down and get to know each other better?"

"Ah, while we prepare you for dinner, we can speak then."

"Okay, sounds great. Thank you."

Runa nods and leaves the room, only for the door to open again and for Keller to slip in. He's wearing a black suit, white button-up shirt, and black tie. His hair is styled, his face freshly shaven, and I can smell his delicious cologne from where I sit on my bed. There's a binder in his hand, and his eyes go dark when he looks up at me and sees me in my bed.

"Good morning," I say as I stretch my arms above my head, allowing the blanket to slip down to my waist. His eyes roam my chest. I move the blankets from me and hop out of bed. Walking up to him, I wrap his tie around my hand and say, "You left me this morning." I peck him on the jaw.

"I didn't want to startle Runa." His hand lands on my side. "But it seems you might've given her a show?" His mouth lowers to my neck, where he trails kisses.

"Mmm, I did." I grip him tightly. "But I wish you were the one who found me in bed, naked, instead of her."

His palm lowers to my ass, which he gives a good squeeze. "Fuck, you're so warm."

"And you look incredibly hot in this suit," I whisper as I kiss his throat. "But I must shower. Care to join me?"

"I'm already dressed for the day."

"That's the great thing about clothes," I say as I pull him toward the bathroom by his tie. "You can take them off and put them back on."

"Lilly," he groans. "I shouldn't even be in here. I thought you were dressed when Runa told me to come in."

"Runa blasted my retinas by flipping open the curtains like a mad woman. I was still dreaming about you."

"Dreaming about me?" he asks as I move to the shower and turn it on. "What kind of dream?"

"Oh, you know, the sexual kind," I say as I go to the sink and brush my teeth. Keller leans against the wall, his eyes never straying from me.

"Yeah? What was I doing to you?"

I spit into the sink and rinse my mouth before heading to the shower. "You were fucking me in the shower."

"Liar," he says. "You're just saying that to entice me."

"Is it working?"

"No," he answers, even though I know he's lying. He's already set down his folder and removed his suit jacket while loosening his tie.

The shower is almost like the one in Harrogate, round, tub-like, but built entirely of tile with no door or curtain. The showerhead is above me, acting as a rain shower and a detachable shower, but there's zero privacy, which is what I want right now.

I step under the water and turn toward him so he can watch the water drip down the front of my body.

I don't bother looking at him. I focus on washing myself because I know that's all it will take. I start with my hair, puffing out my chest the whole time. When I rinse out the shampoo, I make sure to moan quietly while parting my lips. And I do the same thing with my conditioner. When it comes to soaping up my body, I take the bar of soap provided and slowly move it all over my skin, making sure to spend extra time on my breasts.

By the time I turn off the water and glance at Keller, he's at the sink now, gripping the counter's edge tightly, the veins in his neck firing off.

A towel awaits me on the heated towel rack, and I wrap it around my body, secure it under my arm, and then walk over to him, placing my hand on his obvious, bulging erection.

His eyes fall to mine, and before he can say anything, I drop down to my knees and undo his pants. He hisses when I take his cock out of his briefs, and when I wrap my mouth around the tip, his chest expands, and his head falls back.

"Fuck, Lilly. We shouldn't be doing this."

"I do believe work hasn't started yet, therefore, if I want to suck your cock, I will."

He grips my jaw and says, "But I dictate when and where."

"Are you going to deny me your cock?" I blink up at him and see the indecision waver in his eyes.

Just when I think he's going to tell me to stand, he wraps his hand around my wet hair and says, "Suck me. But when I say stop, you listen."

"Yes, my King," I say. And as usually happens when I call him that, he takes a deep breath.

Pleased, I take him into my mouth again, and my hands fall to the base of his length, where I tug, drawing pleasure up his shaft.

I watch as he sags against the counter, guiding me with his hold, relaxing when he's usually very rigid, very uptight. But he must know I need this connection as much as he does. To start the day, I need to know that I'm his. I need to feel his touch. I need to feel him inside of me.

I roll my tongue over his head, sucking hard and then drawing him into the back of my throat.

"Fuck, Lilly, you're so good." He moves my head over his dick, dragging himself in deeper and deeper until he hits the back of my throat. He pulls me away and gives me a moment to breathe. His thumb passes over my cheek. Then he brings me back to the tip and I suck him even harder, pulling a groan from his throat.

So sexy.

Such a turn-on.

I can bring this man to his knees with just my mouth. I feel so empowered.

While my mouth and one hand pump over his length, I

cup his balls with my other hand and carefully palm them, rolling them around in a deliberate rhythm.

His muscular thighs quiver.

His hand grows tighter in my hair.

And when I release him, only to flick the underside of his cock with my tongue—something I know he loves—he groans, which echoes in the bathroom.

"Enough," he says, tugging on my hair.

Even though I don't want to stop, even though I desperately want to finish him off with my mouth, I listen.

"Stand up," he commands. "Touch yourself. Are you wet?"

I am, I don't need to touch myself to know, but I do it anyway and slip my fingers between my legs before pulling them away. Keller wraps his long fingers around my wrist and brings my hand to his mouth. He sucks my fingers between his lips and then makes a satisfied noise.

"Put one leg up on the counter."

I prop one leg on the counter, bringing my pussy to his aching erection. He grips his length at the base and then rubs the tip along my clit.

"God, yes, Keller."

He then slips inside of me, and with his hand on my ass, keeping me from falling back, he digs his fingers into my skin and pulls me closer, hitting a spot I didn't even know existed.

"Oh, God." My head falls back as Keller's other hand caresses my breasts, his fingers toying with my nipple piercings.

"Heaven," Keller whispers. "Being inside of you, it's goddamn heaven." He pulses his hips, and I know with one wave of friction between us, I will not last long.

"You're so deep," I say, my breath escaping me with every thrust. I can barely hold any air. It's being snatched by the immense pleasure pulsing through me. "I . . . I won't last," I say. "I'm sorry."

"Same," he grunts, pounding harder now, using his hand on my ass to keep me steady as he slams into me. "Fuck, this will never get old. Ever. So good."

His voice.

His touch.

His relentless efforts to make us both orgasm, it frees something within me, unlocks a vessel. Before I know what's happening, a low, guttural moan falls past my lips as my body seizes around him.

"Yes, Keller, fuck . . . yes." I grind on him, my orgasm ripping through me in one fell swoop, knocking me so hard in the chest that I lose my balance and nearly slip. But my man is there to catch me. He holds me up by the ass with both hands while he pounds into me, right before the sexiest noise comes out of him.

"Shit," he whispers. "Oh . . . fuck, Lilly." His hips still, and I feel his cock pulse inside of me as he comes, both of us using each other until every last ounce of pleasure has been claimed.

I wrap my legs around his waist, as always amazed at his strength. I grip his shoulders and hug him while peppering tiny kisses along his collarbone.

"Thank you," I whisper.

"You don't need to thank me, Lilly," he says softly, now rubbing my back with his hand.

"I know that wasn't on your schedule this morning, but I needed it. I needed that connection." I lean away to look him in the eyes. "Waking up without you was sad. Today will be overwhelming, and I needed that quiet moment with you first."

"I'm yours, love. Whenever you want me."

"Promise?"

He nods. "I promise." And then he leans in and offers me a kiss, which I greedily take.

"I love you," I whisper when our foreheads connect.

"I love you, Lilly," he says softly, and even though there is so much unknown coming my way, I know one thing is for sure—this man is mine, and I can do anything with him at my side.

⸻

"HI." I wave to the kitchen staff. "It's so great to meet you. And can I just say, it smells fantastic in here. I don't know what you're cooking, but my stomach is growling." They chuckle.

It's been a day full of hellos and introductions. We first took a more extensive tour of the palace. I even got to go into the crown room, which was immaculate. So much history, so many jewels, a total robber's dream. I was assured that the security in the crown room was next level, and not even a Hollywood screenwriter could devise a way to steal anything from the room.

And in every part of the palace we toured, staff lined up to say hello. I was educated on their jobs, which, wow, there are so many specific things that need to be done around the palace that I had no clue about. One person, in particular, is in charge of vacuuming the west wing carpets daily.

Every.

Freaking.

Day.

"Lunch is almost ready," Keller says and then presses his hand to my lower back, ushering me toward the exit.

"It was so nice seeing all of you." I wave again. "Thank you all for everything you do."

They also wave, a bunch of very friendly people, and once we're in the hallway, I turn to Keller and ask, "Do you think they liked me?"

"You've asked me that every time after you've met some-one. When are you going to realize you're a likeable person?"

345

"Not for a while. I'm an outsider coming in, so I can't be their favorite."

"You're also saving this country from falling under the reign of another country, so I don't think they care where you're from, as long as you have Strom blood."

"I guess that makes sense."

"Ah, Lilija, there you are," Queen Katla says from the other side of the hall. "I'm sure you've had a busy day so far, but would you mind joining me for some tea sandwiches and fresh fruit in my stateroom? I'd love to have a chance to speak with you on a more personal level."

"Of course," I say as I look up at Keller. "That would be fine, right?"

He smiles. "Of course. We're finished with this portion of our tour. Does the kitchen staff know of your dining arrangements, or shall I inform them for you?"

"They're aware. Thank you, Keller." Queen Katla comes up to me and loops her arm through mine. "Right this way, my dear."

Weathered but beautiful, Queen Katla is not the typical grandma I would've envisioned. You know, white hair with a short perm, possibly some Alfred Dunner clothes decorated with birdhouses and styled in a dusty blue. That's not Katla at all. She's dignified. Refined, with her thick, salt-and-pepper locks that are styled in a blowout and pinned back with a jewel clip. Her makeup is light and very subtle, but her bright eyes are highlighted with mascara, her cheeks are pinched with blush, and her lipstick is pristinely painted across her lips. Her style reflects what Emily Gilmore would wear on a random Tuesday—comfortable, but rich.

And she smells divine.

"Thank you for allowing me to steal you away for lunch. I know Keller has you on a tight schedule, but I wanted to speak with you."

"Of course. I'm here for whoever needs me."

We walk up a flight of stairs to the right, where large, stately doors part as we approach. Queen Katla walks me right through the doors, and then the footmen close them behind us, the sound of birds chirping outside the window the only noise filtering through the vast room.

Decorated in a beautiful light blue, her stateroom is like all the others in the palace. Sweeping, curtained windows offer soft contrast to the high ceilings, which are decorated with intricate, gold design work. Cream carpet runs the length of the room, with soft, cream-colored furniture dotted throughout. A fireplace sits to the left, and the mantlepiece is adorned with picture frames of who I can only assume are her children. *My aunt and uncles.*

"This room is gorgeous," I say.

"Thank you." She gestures for me to take a seat in one of her chairs lined up with a round side table, which is decked out with tea sandwiches, fresh fruit, and finger desserts.

Well, don't mind if I do.

But being the civilized, classy person that I've become, I wait for her to offer me food before I start poking my finger into the pink petit fours. I hope they're strawberry flavored.

"Would you like some iced tea?" she asks as she lifts a pitcher.

"That would be lovely," I say, feeling as though I'm in some out-of-body experience where I've turned into a posh elitist who says things like *that would be lovely.*

Normal response before would've possibly been something like . . . *I'm dying of fucking thirst, so yes, please.*

I've evolved.

Once the drinks are poured, Katla hands me a small plate and says, "Help yourself."

Now, these finger sandwiches look amazing. And they have my name written all over them, but I need to take my time, place two on my plate, add some fruit, and then back away.

"I know you must be wondering why I brought you here."

Not really, kind of glad, because, WOW, this pumper-nickel thing with cucumber is amazing.

"I'm aware Keller gave you some history of what happened between your mum, Margret, and myself."

I swallow and say, "Yes, he did. Was that okay?"

"Yes," she answers. "Keller has always been honest, and I know that's something that he probably needed to tell you in the moment, and I honor that. I just . . . well, I wanted to see how you felt about it, how you felt about me. And I know that sounds self-indulgent, but I want you to know that letting Margret drift away is the biggest regret of my life."

So, this is a heavy lunch . . . okay.

I set my plate on the table and wipe my fingers on my napkin.

"That's not self-indulgent. I think I'd wonder the same thing if I were in your shoes. Can I ask you something?"

"Of course, anything," she says.

"Were you close with my mom before she left?"

She nods. "I was. We'd spend many summers in the court-yard garden, embroidering together over a fare like this one."

"Did you know she wanted to leave?"

"I did, and although it worried me, I knew that it was truly what her heart desired. However, after Pala left to be with Clinton, I was destroyed. I spent all this time grooming Pala, teaching her the ways of a queen, having a gentle heart and a lifting soul, and then she fell in love." She shakes her head. "I know what it means to fall in love, and from the looks of it, so do you." I give her a brief smile and she continues. "And I'm not mad at her for falling in love. She has a beautiful life with her husband and three children, but I was scared because I barely saw her, and I didn't want to lose Margret as well." She lets out a pained sigh. "I handled everything so poorly. I took what I was feeling toward Pala and tried to trap Margret. I think we all know if you attempt to tame a mustang, they'll run."

"Why didn't you ever reach out like King Theo?"

"Pride. Embarrassment. Hurt. I thought that if I ignored the situation that maybe she'd come back, maybe come to her senses and find home again. But the more I waited, the more she created her own home." Katla lifts a napkin to her eye. "I feel such shame over it all, and when Theo said he sent Keller to find you, well, it felt like this sprig of hope blossomed in my stomach. But I didn't want to let that hope turn into something more. That's why I wasn't on the calls with you and Keller. I knew if I saw you, I would break down and beg you to see us. Theo was very adamant about you making your own decision."

"So was Keller, and I respect that about all of you, that you let me process the role—*my history*—on my own terms. I was able to make an unbiased decision on what to do."

"That was Theo's hope, because this is a different life from what you're used to. He wanted to make sure your heart was in the right place."

"And it is," I answer.

"I know, Lilija, you don't have to prove anything to me. I can see it in your eyes. Being here makes you happy."

"It does." Now it's my turn to fidget with my napkin.

Over the last week or so, I've had to comprehend that my mom and dad basically lied to me. And that's a tough one to digest, because they were my world. Knowing they withheld the truth about my heritage, family, and homeland has made me angry. I think part of my lashing out at Keller, pushing him to want me, possibly stems from that. But they're not here to work through this . . . grief. Anger. And I refuse to hold on to that either. If I can forgive my parents for that, I need to forgive my grandmother for any part she played as well. I've missed out on twenty-seven years of having her in my life, and I don't want to miss out on any more.

"I want you to know that I hold nothing against you. What happened between you and my mom? That's in the past. I want to build a foundation from here. I want to spend time with you and Theo. I want to hear your memories. I want to see more from her life here. And I want to continue learning about Torskethorpe and this country's amazing people. I want to make my mom proud."

"She'd be so proud of you," Katla says, reaching out and taking my hand in hers.

"You think so?"

"Yes, I know so."

My eyes get misty, and I quickly pull away to blot at them. "Ugh, I don't think I've ever cried as much until I came here. Something is happening to me."

She chuckles. "Well, why don't we talk about something that won't make you cry?" She sips from her glass of iced tea. "Tell me more about you and Keller."

I can't help the smile that pulls across my lips. "It started as enemies to lovers, and slowly over time, I wore him down."

Katla laughs. "I like the start of this story."

―――――

"ARE all days going to be like this?" I ask Keller as I lie on my bed and spread out my arms. "I'm exhausted, and my feet hurt so bad."

"Some days might be worse," he says softly as he sits on the end of my bed. He takes one of my feet in his hands, removes my sock, and massages the bottom with his strong thumbs.

"Oh God," I moan. "That feels amazing."

"Moan like that again, and you'll find out what else is amazing."

"Is that supposed to be a threat?" I ask while I rest my head back on the bed.

"It can be," he says in a dark voice that sends a shiver up

my spine. No use in testing him, he's proven himself sufficiently.

"Aren't you tired?" I ask him.

"No, I'm used to long days with little sleep."

"Did you get little sleep last night?" I ask him. "What time did you leave me anyway?"

"Three. I didn't sleep after I vacated your room."

"Why not?" I ask.

"Just my thoughts keeping me up."

"Care to share what those thoughts are?"

He moves his hands to my heel, and I nearly kick him in the stomach from how good it feels.

"You know the thoughts already. They just seem to be haunting me."

"Is there anything I can do to help?"

"I don't believe so," he answers, and that doesn't sit well with me. I didn't expect him to ask me for a three-step process of getting over his fears, but I thought that he'd maybe say something like . . . *being here helps. Holding you helps. Feeling you helps.*

But as he rubs my foot and stares off into the room, I notice something more and more as the hours get closer to my welcoming. He's distancing himself.

Sure, he might be in my room, at night, rubbing my foot, and that seems like he's close, but his heart and his head are not. They're elsewhere.

It's been slowly happening all day, and I'm starting to see why.

I lift up on my elbows to look him in the eyes. "Keller, I feel like you're pulling away from me." Might as well get it all out in the open.

"I'm not." He shakes his head. "Just trying to find my footing again. Being at Strombly with you means I need to make some adjustments, not to mention the new role I have. I'm dealing with much change and navigating it."

"Are you second-guessing being with me?"

His eyes glaze over, and my pulse picks up when he doesn't answer.

"Keller, are you?"

"What?" he asks, his eyes focusing on me again. "No, Lilly, I'm not."

"Okay, because it kind of feels like you are."

"I'm not. Like I said, just a lot to unpack." I shake free of his grasp and move to straddle his lap.

"Unpack it with me. Let me help you. You don't always have to be so strong; you can be vulnerable too."

"You have enough to worry about and don't need my baggage."

"Keller," I whisper while placing my hand over his heart. "What don't you understand about you and me being in this together? This isn't always about me."

"You matter most, Lilly."

"Enough with that," I say. "You matter just as much as I do."

His eyes lift to mine, and they seem almost sad as he says, "Lilly, I love you, but that will never be the case."

"Forget the crown, forget the country, forget all of that. What we have is between you and me, Keller and Lilly, and no one is equally more important than the other. So, tell me what was troubling you. Tell me how I can help."

"You can't," he says with frustration. "So just fucking drop it."

Caught off guard by his sharp tone, I back off his lap and sit on the edge of the bed, unsure of what to do, how to get through to him. Doesn't he see this as an equal partnership? That I need him just as much as he needs me?

When he doesn't say anything but remains quiet, I decide to get ready for bed. I slip into the bathroom, my heart heavy as I change into a pair of pajamas that Runa laid out for me. It seems like she's alluding to something, and even though I wish it were Keller's shirt I was climbing into, I settle for the pink silk shorts set. Once I brush my teeth and put my hair into a loose ponytail with a scrunchie, I head back to my room, where Keller sits on the edge of the bed, his hands clutching the mattress.

When his eyes meet mine, I see how tortured they are, and my heart breaks all over for him.

"I think I'm going to head back to my room," he says softly.

Once again, my heart crumbles for what feels like the tenth time since we got back to my bedroom. "Why?" I ask.

"I don't think it's good that I stay here tonight."

"Keller," I say, my panic starting to climb up my throat and choke me. "You're pulling away, and I don't know why or how to stop you from doing it. What changed from this morning until now?"

"Nothing," he says.

"But in the bathroom, you told me . . ." My voice catches. "You told me you love me."

"I do," he says as he stands. "That's the problem, Lilly. I fucking love you when I shouldn't."

Growing frustrated now, I say, "Are you that loyal to something your parents taught you many years ago that you can't look past the fact that you've grown since then? Even Theo and Katla approve of us. Wouldn't their opinion matter the most? Katla told me today how happy she is to know that I'm in your life in a romantic capacity. Why doesn't that weigh in?"

"It's not that easy, Lilly."

"It seems easy to me."

"You don't get it," he says, pushing past me.

"What don't I get? Losing two parents? Because I'm pretty sure if you look my parents up right now, you won't find them." A tear slips down my cheek that I wasn't expecting. "I know what you're going through, Keller. But the difference between you and me is that I'm willing to change."

At that moment, our phones ding with text messages, but neither of us bothers to look.

"This wasn't supposed to be my life," I say. "I should be in a bikini truck in South Beach, Miami, but I've been able to adapt, so why can't you?"

He presses his hand to his forehead. "I don't know, love . . ." His voice trails off when he looks up at me. "I don't fucking know."

He looks so tortured that even though I'm angry with him and want to knock some sense into him, I can't help the pull he has over me. I place my hand on his chest as his grip falls to my waist. We both lean in as our foreheads connect.

"I'm so fucking sorry," he says quietly.

And I can feel his apology, all the way to the tips of my toes.

"I know," I say softly as I run my hands up to his cheeks, holding him tight.

"I'm dealing with some unexpected demons and struggling with it."

"That's okay, Keller. But if you don't push me away, we'll make it through this."

He nods.

"I need you. This is so scary and crazy, and you're my rock. We have to stick together."

His hands slide up my shirt to my ribs, where his thumbs dig in. "Just be patient with me."

"I will, as long as you don't leave me."

"I won't leave you, love," he says quietly before backing me up to the bed. When I sit on the edge, he kneels in front of me and rests his head on my lap. My hands instinctively sift through his hair and hold him close as he grips me. "I'm sorry, Lilly."

"I know, Keller. I know."

He lifts up, and our eyes meet. His hand goes to my cheek right before he pulls me close and brings his lips to mine.

I cling to him, kissing him deeper, more thoroughly, reminding him that he's not here alone, that he has me, that he can rely on me. Our tongues tangle, our hands grow tight, and our passion for one another heightens as he lays me back on the bed and unbuttons my top, exposing my breasts. His mouth leaves mine and descends to kiss my chest, where he deliciously sucks on my nipples, peppers kisses along my skin, and even nibbles my breasts. I arch into his mouth, loving the way he knows what turns me—

Ding.

Ding.

Ding.

Ding.

Keller pauses and glances over at my phone.

Ding.

"Is everything okay?" he asks.

"I think so," I say, my breath short. "Timmy is the only one who texts me."

Ding.

I look over at the nightstand.

"But never this much unless it's important."

He pulls away from me, reaches for my phone, and hands it to me. "I know you'll worry."

He's right, I will.

I sit up in bed and close the sides of my shirt, so my boobs aren't just hanging out. Once covered, I open my text messages and see that Timmy has sent me a few, and then I see one from an unknown phone number. From the preview, it says The Informative.

"What's going on?" Keller asks.

"That's weird. Did you give my phone number to The Informative?"

"What?" he asks, confused.

I open the text message and read it out loud. "'The Informative: breaking news alert. With a new princess in town, all eligible bachelors are lining up at the palace gates. But be warned, she isn't available. Our very own private secretary to the king has finally gotten what he's wanted all these years, a straight shot to the throne.'"

"What," Keller roars. "What the actual fuck?"

My pulse quickens. Although, it almost doesn't feel like it's pumping blood through my body anymore. As my limbs turn numb, I continue to read. "'Little known fact, he was adopted by the king and . . . queen . . .'" I trail off and look up at Keller, his eyes searching back and forth as he digs around in his pocket for his phone. "'Unable to take the throne because he doesn't hold the Strom blood, he's taken the only route he knows that will get him there, through the future queen. Let's just hope she sees this before she falls too hard for his fake charm.'"

The phone drops out of my hand and falls to the ground.

Adopted?

Keller must have gotten the exact text because he's reading it on his phone, his hand driving through his hair aggressively. When he's done reading, he shoots up to his feet and turns toward my door to leave.

"Hey," I call out to him. "Are you going to fucking explain any of this?"

Realizing I'm still in the room, he says, "Fuck . . . it's not true."

"What's not true? The adoption?"

"No . . . that's, uh, that's true, but the part where I'm trying to take the throne, that's not true."

"Keller, how could you not have told me?"

He's pounding through his phone, not paying attention to me.

"Keller," I shout, drawing his eyes up to mine. "Focus on me."

"I'm having a hard time doing that when I'm trying to figure out how this random number texted you, how they knew about The Informative."

"What are you talking about?" I ask.

"It's not real."

"What's not real?"

"The Informative. It's just something I came up with to fuck with you since you were trying to fuck with me. No one knew about it. No one but——" His eyes darken. "No fucking way."

"What?" I ask, but he takes off toward my door. "Keller, wait, talk to me."

But he's gone before I can stop him, my door clicking shut.

I stare toward his retreat, waiting for him to come back, for him to charge through the door, but he doesn't.

He doesn't return all night.

And in the morning, when he's supposed to greet me once I'm ready and lead me to the grand entrance, where I'm supposed to parade around the capital in a car . . . he's not there either.

Chapter Twenty-Two

KELLER

My feet pound against the stone floors through the servants' quarters. People ask me if I'm okay as I make my way through the halls, but I ignore them. There's one thing on my mind, one person, and nothing will get in my way until I have answers.

When I reach room 270, I raise my fist and pound on the door. "Lara, open up," I yell. I pound some more until the door unlocks and Lara's startled face comes into view.

Looking her dead in the eyes, I ask, "Where is he?"

"Who?" she asks.

"Who the fuck else would I be talking about?" I ask as I toss her door open, slamming it against the wall.

"Brimar?" she asks. "He's not here. What's going on?"

"Don't act as if you have no fucking clue what's happening."

Hand to her chest, she backs away, her eyes wide with

concern. "I don't, Keller. I have no idea what's happening. Is everything okay with Lilly?"

"You're telling me you don't know about this?" I flash her my phone's screen and she takes it in her hand, reading the text.

I watch carefully as her eyes scan the message, scrolling back and forth, her mouth falling open in shock. When she's done, she asks, "You think Brimar did this?"

I hold up two fingers and say, "There are two people I told about The Informative and the trick I was playing on Lilly, and there are two people who know about my adoption. You . . . and Brimar. From the look on your face, I'm guessing it wasn't you."

"It wasn't," she says. "I'd never do that to you, and you know that. You know where my loyalty lies." When I don't say anything, she shakes my shoulder. "Keller, you know I didn't do this."

"I know." I believe her. But then I add in a seething tone, "Where is he?"

"I don't know. Do you want me to text him?"

"Yes. Don't tell him I'm looking for him."

"I won't." She picks up her phone from her table and quickly types away. While we wait for a response, she asks, "Does Lilly know?"

"Yes, he texted it to her."

"How did she react?"

With my hand on my forehead, I pace Lara's small room as I say, "I don't know, not great. I left before we could talk about it."

"That wasn't smart."

I pause and say, "Tomorrow is her welcoming parade through the capital, Lara. I need to figure this shit out and see if he's told anyone else. The last thing we need is people booing her as she's making her way through the streets of Torskethorpe. Brimar is out to ruin this, and I need to see what he's done so I can fix it." I also need to know why the fuck he did this.

"Are you sure that's what you're doing?"

"What do you mean?" I ask.

"I know you, Keller, and I know what that kind of text does to your head."

Yeah, it does all sorts of fucked-up things. The gnawing brunt of that text message, the words behind it, the history behind it . . . it's a knife to the chest.

"It's not fucking true," I shout. "I never wanted the throne, ever. It's why I've struggled with being with Lilly. Because I know my goddamn place in this world, and it's not with a goddamn crown on my head."

"I know," Lara says, placing her hand on my shoulder. "I know that's not who you are."

"Then why would he write that?" My shoulders sag as this overwhelming sense of pain circulates through me. "I thought we were friends . . . brothers."

"You are," Lara says as I start shaking my head.

"No, a friend wouldn't do this. A friend wouldn't purposefully use the insecurities I'm feeling and punch me in the face with them. This was intentional, and there was a reason behind it, but I just don't understand why."

Lara's phone dings and she looks at the screen.

When her eyes meet mine, she doesn't say anything.

"What? Where is he?"

"This isn't a good idea, Keller. Wait until tomorrow."

"Where the fuck is he, Lara?" I seethe.

Her face droops in defeat as she says, "The Crowned Cod."

The pub.

I turn on my heel and head for the door, but Lara stops me. "Keller, you're angry and hurt. Going there to confront him isn't going to do any good. You're only going to damage an already fragile situation."

"This needs to be dealt with."

"Just wait until the morning. Please, Keller, I'm begging you."

I yank my arm from her grasp, and without another word, I head out her door and down the hall.

⊏▭⊐

LILLY

ARMS CLUTCHED AROUND MY LEGS, bringing them tight to my chest, I lightly rock back and forth on my bed, the sun peeking through the curtains, barely shining light on the enormously empty room.

Thanks to the ever-present sun, I have no idea what time it is.

I have no idea how long I've been sitting here, hoping and praying Keller comes back.

And I have no idea how many times I've read that text message, trying to find every little piece of information I can. Seeking out any clue or play on words, anything to help me better understand.

Theo and Katla adopted Keller? Why didn't he say anything? He's spoken so highly of them, but in a king and queen capacity, never as parental units. I just assumed he liked them as people, not as someone who has been there for him as a mother, as a father. Why did he hide that from me?

And the whole wanting to be king thing . . . Well, from the demons he's been battling since we got together, even before we got together, I know that's not what he wants. He's told me many times—he knows his place, and it's not with a crown on his head. But he's made exceptions for me, so why has he kept it a secret?

There's a knock at the door, and my head turns just as the door eases open, my heart hammering in my chest, willing it to be Keller.

But instead, it's Lara.

"May I come in?" she asks.

"Of course," I answer, grateful I'm wearing the pajama set Runa laid out for me. Maybe in some cosmic way, she knew tonight was going to happen, and I'd require clothes.

Lara slips into the room and shuts the door behind her before walking up to my bed and taking a seat. "How are you doing?"

"Not great," I answer. "I'm assuming since you're here, Keller told you what's going on. Unless you got the text as well."

"I didn't get the text. But Keller did come to my room."

I pause, the night rolling through my head. "Wait . . . did you send that text?"

Her eyes widen. "What? No. I'd never betray Keller and you like that."

"You're right; I'm sorry." I shake my head. "When he left here, he made it seem like he knew who it was, and when you said he went to your room, I just assumed. I'm sorry."

"No, that makes sense, and he does know who it is."

"Who?" I ask. "Who would do that?"

"Brimar," Lara says, her voice sad and full of shame simultaneously.

"Brimar?" I ask, shocked. Stunned. "That can't be true."

"Keller is right. Only two people in this world know the information in that text message. One of them is me, and the other is Brimar."

"But . . . why? Why would he do something like that? Provoke Keller?"

"I wish I could tell you. He hasn't said anything to me, but I feel so sick about it and embarrassed."

"Why are you embarrassed? You didn't do anything."

"I know, but he's my boyfriend and we're attached, you know? That's why I came here, because I wanted you to know I had nothing to do with the text, and I wanted to make sure you were okay. Keller said he didn't really talk to you about anything."

"He didn't. He just left, and now I have no idea what's going on."

"Are you upset about the information? Do you believe it?"

I shake my head. "I don't believe the part about Keller wanting the throne. From all the conversations we've had, I know that's not the case with him. Am I upset about the adoption? No. I mean, do I wish he had told me something like that? Something so important? Of course I do, but I'm not upset about it. The text was mean-spirited and clearly meant to hurt Keller and play on all his insecurities, which in turn hurts me. But the information in that text, I'm not mad about that. I just wish he was here to talk to me. To hold me."

"I understand that." Lara reaches out her hand to me and I take it.

"Where is he now?"

Wincing, Lara tears her eyes away and says, "I think he's going to confront Brimar. I begged him to do it in the morning, to not go, but he left my room without a word."

"Where's he headed?" I ask, worry etching up my spine.

"Where Brimar is, the Crowned Cod, a pub just outside of the palace walls, mainly patronized by Strombly staff."

I flip the blankets off me and stand from the bed.

"What are you doing?" Lara asks.

"I'm going to go to the cod place."

"Uh, no, you're not," Lara says.

Turning toward her, I say, "Lara, I need to speak to Keller. I need to stop him before he does something stupid. I don't want him getting in a fight or . . . I don't know . . . I just need to get to him."

"That's a terrible idea, and I truly care about you, Lilly, but I refuse to take you there."

"Then I'll go myself."

"You won't," Lara says, standing as well. "Not only do you not belong in a place like the Crowned Cod, but it'll ruin your welcoming tomorrow, which has been thoughtfully planned to make the best impression. If you show up at a pub the night before, rumors will spread, and it won't be a good look. So many people are counting on tomorrow, so don't ruin it out of a gut reaction."

I hate that she's right. My head is nodding, knowing precisely what she's talking about, but my heart is bleeding, the need to stop Keller, to speak with him, driving me to do stupid things like step out into the capital in a pair of pajamas, looking for a man. Out of all the training I've been through, I know that gut reactions are not permitted. I need to be thoughtful about what I do and what I say.

Sad and worried, I climb back on the bed and pull my legs in again. "I hate this," I say. "I texted him, I called him, left him voicemails begging him to come back to me, and he's not listening. I just assumed that it could help if I saw him in person."

"There's no use now. In his head, he needs to fix this."

"So, what am I supposed to do? Just wait?" I ask.

"Yes, wait and hope he doesn't get into trouble."

―――

KELLER

SILENCE HAS BEEN ECHOING in my ears since I sat down in this dark abyss of a room. Not even a distant cough or laugh, just complete and total silence, which has caused me to live in my thoughts.

My insecurities are roaring to life.

My need to distance myself leaving me feeling cold.

And that text message, burning a hole in my pocket, as I fucking wait.

And wait.

And wait.

Until it's four in the morning and I hear the distant sound of feet clomping down the hallway. A familiar gait that I've come to know well. The slightest of limps from when he was training to become a guard and was cracked in the knee by an oncoming car. He rolled over the windshield and landed on his feet, but the damage was done.

And now, as I hear that limp come closer and closer, I dig my fingers into the arms of the chair I'm sitting in, trying to steady my breathing and my temper.

Lara was right, I couldn't go to the pub, not with the risk of all eyes on us. So, instead, I went to his room, where I've been waiting ever since. And this is where I've been, in this chair, fucking waiting.

The doorknob jingles, and then the door pushes open. Brimar flicks on the overhead light, and when he looks up to find me in the middle of his room, staring at him, he startles backward into the wall.

"Jesus Christ," he says as I stand and slam the door shut behind him. He pinches his brow and asks, "What the fuck are you doing here?"

"Why do you think I'm here?" I ask, gauging how drunk he is. From the clarity in his eyes and the steadiness in his legs, I'm going to say not drunk at all. But there's a lipstick stain on his neck and a noteworthy perfume that's unfamiliar swirling around him.

Outrage and anger take over as I press my hand to his

chest and back him up against the wall. "Are you fucking cheating on Lara?"

His eyes lift as he stares directly at me. "Is that why you're here?" he asks.

"You know why I'm fucking here, but answer the question."

"Yes," he says. "For months now."

The absolute fucking audacity of the man. Before I can stop, I bring my fist back and slam it into his jaw.

He doesn't fight back. He slinks down to the floor, spitting out a gob of blood and smiling while holding his jaw.

"You used to punch harder than that. Lost some of your steam now that you're fucking some American?"

"Watch it," I say.

He stands and moves around his room, setting his things down and taking off his suit jacket. "So, figured out the text was from me, huh? I'm surprised it took you this long."

"I've been waiting for you, not wanting to make a scene in public."

"Ah, but the boys down at the pub would've enjoyed that." He wipes his white sleeve across his mouth, blood staining the fabric. "They were all talking about the new princess, wondering if she was single and looking for someone to help continue the strong Strom name. Lots of guys are lining up to get a piece of your girl. You could have defended her honor, let them know your dick claims her . . . and the throne."

My jaw tenses.

My fists clench at my sides.

I know he's provoking me, trying to get me to fight him, and even though I'd like nothing more than to beat the ever-loving shit out of him, I didn't come here for that right now. I came for answers, and that's what I'm going to get.

"Who have you told?"

He unbuttons his shirt. "Who have I told what? You're going to have to be more specific."

"About my relationship with Lilly. About the adoption."

"Ah, I see. You're worried about your reputation."

"No, I'm worried about Lilly," I say. "You know how hard it's been for her to make a decision—"

"Oh, boo-fucking-hoo," Brimar bemoans. "She's plucked from a life in America and brought to a beautiful foreign country where everything will be handed to her. What a rough life."

"What the fuck is your problem?" I ask, my frustration reaching new levels. "You're supposed to be my brother."

"That's where you're wrong," Brimar says. "Because a brother wouldn't treat someone the way you treat me."

"What are you talking about?"

"You think you're better than me."

"How do I act like I'm better than you?" I ask.

"For one, you're so far up Theo's ass, I don't know how you breathe. He's the king, but he doesn't have the power to make you one."

"Why do you keep saying that? When have I ever wanted to be king? Never. Not once."

"Or how about the fact that you think you're better than me because Theo adopted you?"

"As a formality," I yell.

"What?" Brimar asks.

"The papers never went through because of the complications with Theo and Katla being royalty. So, they said I'd always be their son, despite the paperwork not going through. It was never real."

"So why the fuck did you lead us to believe that was the case?"

"I don't know," I yell again. "Because I was desperate to feel like I had something, someone to take care of me. I had someone to fall back on. You, out of all people, should know that."

"And you, out of all people, should know what it feels like to have someone brag about having parents when you don't."

"I wasn't bragging. Plus, that was over fifteen fucking years ago, Brimar. Have you been holding on to it for that long? Why are you dredging this up now?"

"Because you've been on a power trip, and I assumed that was why. Since Theo asked us to go find Lilly, you've taken it upon yourself to lead the way."

"Because Theo asked me specifically."

"Yes, but I'm the head of fucking security, meaning I'm the one who should be calling the shots." He points to his chest. "I'm the one who should be figuring out where we're going and who's allowed near us and who isn't. But you've treated me like your goddamn assistant this entire time, and I'm sick of it. We come from the same cloth, from the same upbringing, and it's about time you realize that."

"I do," I scream at him. "I fucking realize it every day. Every time I look at Lilly, I realize it. I know I don't belong in the same room as her, but she wants me there for some reason. Do you realize the mental anguish I've had to filter through to love the woman I want to love?"

"Love?" Brimar asks, his thick brows kissing his hairline. "You barely know each other."

"We know way more about each other than what I apparently know about you." I push my hand through my hair. "I can't—I can't fucking believe you, man. You broke my trust. And for what? Pride? Pretty fucking stupid. I need to know who else you told. Did you leak it . . ." My voice trails off as a thought hits me square in the chest. My eyes flash up to his again, and I ask, "Are you the fucking leak we've been looking for?"

"Took you enough time to figure that out too," he says, his voice full of arrogance.

And with that, I can't stop myself, I charge at him, plowing him into the wall and creating a dent in the plaster with his body. He hits me in the stomach with an uppercut, causing me to back off him for a moment, but it's enough time for him to cock back and drive his fist into my eye. I stumble backward, my vision blurry as I see his fist come at me again, but this time I duck and blow my fist into his stomach.

He buckles over, and I take my chance at hitting him with an uppercut to the jaw so he falls backward.

When he's on the ground, his head lolling to the side, I say, "That was a fucking security risk, and you know it."

"And not once did you ask me for my advice. Thought you'd be able to step off your high horse and notice—"

"Notice what? That you've been slacking on your job? Because that's what's been happening. That's why I haven't asked you. Because before we went to Miami to find Lilly, you were slipping up. You were making mistakes. You were putting the people we're supposed to protect at risk and I wasn't about to let you do that with Lilly. She's all we have left." I grip my head. "Jesus, fuck, Brimar. She's it. That's all. Without her, we have nothing left of this country. And because of your pride, you'd let that get in the goddamn way?" I get close to him, inches from his face. "Now tell me, who else did you fucking send that text message to?"

His jaw works to the side, and then he says, "The Tribune."

My nostrils flare with anger, but before I can beat him into the floor, I tear out of his room and head straight for the palace.

LILLY

LILLY: *Keller, can you please text me back? It's five in the morning and I want to know if you're okay.*

Lilly: *Keller, please. I'm scared. I need to talk to you about all this, and I don't want to do it through text message. Please, just see me. I'm awake.*

I stare down at my unanswered texts as the clock in the top left corner of my phone switches to half past five. Lara left about forty-five minutes ago after I promised her I wouldn't do anything stupid, like attempt to find Keller. And I'm holding myself to that promise, because even though I'm desperate to see Keller, to work things out, I know the value and importance of my actions.

So, I've stayed up, still waiting for Keller, texting him often, hoping he'll respond or visit me in my room.

But . . . nothing.

Absolutely nothing.

And the more the silence goes on, the more my heart breaks.

KELLER

"I NEED to speak to the king," I say to the footman at his bedroom door. "Now."

Thankfully, I still have the authority to override the guards at his door, and they knock on it before opening. When the door parts, I push through into a dark room, the curtains completely blocking off all the light from outside.

"Your Majesty," I say, using formal terms. "I need to speak with you. It's urgent."

"What's going on?" he grumbles as Katla switches on a

light, casting the room in a yellow glow. Theo sits up and spots me. He rubs his eye and asks, "What time is it?"

"Almost six," I say. "And I'm sorry for barging in like this, but I need to speak with you about the protection for the welcoming parade."

"What's going on?" Katla asks, keeping the comforter close to her chest. "Has there been a threat?"

"No, but I found the leak we've been looking for. It's Brimar."

"Brimar?" Theo asks with a surprised cough. He pats his chest. "Our Brimar?"

"Yes," I answer, still pained from the thought of my best friend turning on me. "I've noticed he's been slipping on his responsibilities, not making the right calls, so I stepped up with Lilly to make sure she was protected. Not enough, apparently, because he was leaking information right under my nose." I hang my head. "I'm so sorry."

"Do not apologize to me," Theo says sternly. "This is not on you. Tell me, what's happening to ensure Lilly's safety?"

"I've gathered with Henrik, and we've been working on a plan. We detained Brimar, since he's broken the code of trust with the crown. We've also taken his phone and searched it for any leads he might not have told us about."

"Is there a security risk for the parade?"

"No, we've spoken with the rest of the security detail, and they're all on the same plan we originally had. They haven't been tipped off about any threats, and from the rounds they've made on the parade route, everything seems to be in order."

"So, everything is okay?" Katla asks.

I take a step forward, and I must come into the light just enough for them to see the gash and bruising under my eye.

"Dear God," Theo says. "What happened to you?"

"Nothing you need to concern yourself with. I'm fine."

"No, I'm concerned. I asked you what happened, and you will tell me."

I let out a deep sigh. "I lost my temper with Brimar," I answer, my head hanging in shame as I pull on the back of my neck. This entire twelve-hour period feels like a goddamn week at this point.

Theo stands from the bed and wraps his robe around him before moving to the seating area, Katla joining him. "Take a seat and start from the beginning."

Knowing this will be a painful conversation, I sit across from them as they put on their glasses. "We got a text last night, Lilly and I. We were, uh . . . together."

"It's no secret that you're staying in her room," Theo says.

"Just the first night," I say, as if I'm in trouble.

"I don't care," Theo says. "If you're in a relationship with her, it doesn't matter to me."

"Right . . ."

I explain to them about the prank I was pulling on Lilly with the Lady Whistledown gossip, which makes them chuckle. "And when I was with Lilly, we both got a text from The Informative, and I was fucking confused since I'm the one who sends those texts."

"What did the text say?" Katla asks.

"To paraphrase, that men were lined up to date Lilly, and the only reason I was with her was because I've wanted to take the thrown since I was adopted by you guys, but since I'm not blood . . . I can't take it."

"What?" Theo rages. "That's preposterous."

Katla rests her arm on his. "We all know that's not how you are, Keller."

"I know, but only two people in this world know about The Informative and the adoption."

"Lara and Brimar," Theo says.

"Yes, and it wasn't Lara. She had no idea it was happening. Needless to say, she was distraught. But it took me a moment to bring this to your attention because Brimar said he sold the story to the Tribune. I was working with Henrik on getting the story squashed."

"And did you?" Katla asks with hope.

"Yes. Thankfully, Henrik, since he once worked for them, had friends who terminated the story and forced people to sign an NDA, so the story won't be out there."

"So, then, everything is good?" Theo asks.

"Yes, I believe so," I say, taking a breath for a moment.

"Then why doesn't it seem as though you're good?" Katla asks.

Because Brimar stoked my insecurities into a roaring flame.

Because I'm fucking worried that in the heat of the moment, I didn't check everything.

Because I'm so terrified that something will happen to Lilly that I can't breathe.

"Just processing," I say. "It's been a lot."

"I can see that," Theo says. "Brimar was your best friend. I can understand you might be shaken right now."

"Yeah, just a bit."

"Well, take a moment to gather yourself," Theo says. "Because today is a celebration and should be treated as one."

"You're right," I say, standing from the chair and offering them a forced smile.

"Why don't you stop by the medical staff?" Katla suggests. "Make sure your eye is okay, and then spend the day with your girl. I know she's been looking forward to this moment with you by her side."

I swallow hard and nod before I head out the door.

Chapter Twenty-Three

LILLY

I wipe my mouth with a piece of toilet paper and then stand from the bathroom floor, where I just lost all contents of the breakfast I barely ate.

"Miss Campbell," Runa calls out and then steps into the bathroom, where she finds me. "Oh dear, are you okay?" She rushes over to me.

"Yes," I say as she helps me to my feet. "Just nerves."

She gently rubs my back. "Are you sure?"

"Yes," I answer as I place my hand on my stomach. "I'm not sure there's anything left inside of me, so I think we're okay to proceed. I just need to brush my teeth first."

"Of course." Runa rushes to the sink and prepares my toothbrush before handing it to me.

"Have you, uh, have you heard anything from Keller?" I ask, for the tenth time, I'm sure.

Runa's face turns down in a frown. "I'm afraid not, Miss

Campbell. I'm so sorry, but when I hear from him, I'll be sure to have someone inform you."

"Thank you," I say before I start brushing my teeth.

Looking at me in the mirror, Runa says, "You know, Miss Campbell, you'll have a wonderful day today. I've spoken to a few staff members who have friends around the capital, and they're thrilled you're here." She rests her hand on my shoulder. "Not to put pressure on you, but they consider you their angel. Given the history of the Strom family, we truly thought the crown ended with King Theodore, but you've come in and saved this country. We're indebted to you."

I spit the toothpaste out of my mouth and rinse before dabbing my lips with a towel. When I'm done, I say, "I'm indebted to this country as well. Before I came here, I was lost and didn't realize it. Being here feels like coming home. It's a mutual appreciation."

"I'm sure the people of Torskethorpe will love to hear that." She smiles at me. "You'll be wonderful today, Miss Campbell. I just know it."

"Thank you, Runa." I take a deep breath. "Okay, I'm ready."

Runa holds up a perfume bottle and smirks. "Just in case there's any lingering scent clinging to that beautiful dress."

I wink at her and hold my arms out wide. "Smart. Spray me."

She offers me a few spritzes, and I spin around in the floral mist before heading to the bedroom, where Lara is standing in a black suit, hands behind her back, looking tired but ready. When she sees me, she smiles genuinely.

"Miss Campbell, you look beautiful," she says, and I know even though she's hurting right now, she's being the support that I'm missing.

Runa picked out a beautiful lavender dress for me to wear today. An asymmetric design that hits just above my shins, with a ruffle top and sleeves. It's very flattering but covers up everything that needs to be covered up.

Katla appears at the door, and her eyes well up when she takes me in. "My dear girl," she says, walking in and holding her hands out to me. "You're the spitting image of your mother." She swipes at her tears.

"Are we decent?" Theo asks.

"Yes," Katla answers, and he walks in with his cane.

When his eyes land on mine, he lets out a small exhale before clutching his chest. "My darling, look at you. You're stunning."

"Thank you," I say as I take in his white suit with a yellow tie and Katla's yellow dress. "You both look wonderful yourself."

"Not as wonderful as you," Katla says. "Runa, do you have the flower crown?"

"Right here, Your Majesty," Runa says, pulling a fresh flower crown from a box I didn't notice on the bed. Violets are secured in a circle with greens intertwining, with a lavender ribbon that breaks off at the back and flows a few feet. She takes it from Runa and lifts it over my head. I bend at the knee before her and let her adjust it over my hair. When she's done, she lifts my chin and looks me in the eyes. "Violets, your mother's favorite."

My lip quivers as I gently touch the flowers. "This is . . . this is so special."

"She is here with you, at this moment. Remember that," Theo says, coming up to me and offering his arm.

"Th-thank you." I turn to both of them. "Thank you so much for everything."

Henrik appears at the door and says, "The carriage is ready."

"Do you mind if I walk with Lara?" I ask Theo and Katla.

"Not at all," Theo says as he grabs Katla's hand, and together they lead the way.

Runa gives me a wink before I leave with Lara at my side. Keeping my voice quiet, I ask, "Have you heard from Keller?"

"Yes," she says, her voice the same volume as mine.

I whip my head toward her. "You did? Is he coming?"

"He was just checking on security measures. He hasn't said anything beyond that."

"Really?" I ask, my heart falling. "He's supposed to be here. I don't understand."

Lara walks closer and says, "I'm sure he'll show up at the grand entrance. He's probably just doing some last-minute checks."

"Okay," I say as we make our way down to the first floor, taking our time because Theo needs the slower pace. The whole time, even though I can feel my heart cracking with every step, I smile at the staff lined up along the walls, bowing and curtsying as we pass.

I remember what Runa told me, that they work hard for moments like this when they can be a contribution to history. And I want to make sure I make them feel just as special as they're trying to make me feel, so I push my feelings to the back of my mind and try to focus on my steps. One foot in front of the other. And I try to focus on my breathing. In and out. And I control my lips that want to quiver with nausea. Steady and smiling.

When we reach the first floor, the kitchen staff are all waiting, watching, hands in front of them. I offer them a smile and a wave, and then we head to the grand entrance, where I steel myself, looking toward the door for Keller.

But when I don't see him, my stomach flips as my nerves skyrocket.

He's not here.

"Where is he?" I say to Lara as Theo and Katla walk to their carriage.

"I don't know, Lilly, I'm so sorry."

"Can you text him?"

"We don't have time. You have to get into the carriage."

Panicking now, I turn toward her and say, "I . . . I can't do this. Not without him." And I know I can't. Keller taught me everything required for today, but I don't think I'll remember everything. What if I completely fuck this up? "I need him. What if I mess stuff up?"

"Miss Campbell, are you ready?" Henrik asks, clipboard in his arms, ready to move me along.

I turn back to Lara, pleading with her. "I can't, Lara."

Looking me in the eyes, Lara grips my shoulder and says, "You can and you will. Do you hear me? You've trained for this, and the people out there want to shower you with love. This is nothing to be scared of, and I'll be right there with you, walking alongside your carriage, close enough that if you need anything—and I mean anything—I'll get it for you. But you won't need anything, because you're ready for this. You're capable, and you're going to forget about Keller for this moment and relish in this new journey. Do you hear me?"

I nod, my lip quivering, my eyes watering.

"Someone hand me a tissue," Lara calls out, and out of nowhere, one appears. She reaches up and dots the corners of my eyes. "I'm so proud of you, Lilly, and everything you've done to get to this point. Don't let your worry over Keller ruin it. Okay?"

I nod. "O-okay."

"Now, deep breaths."

I take a few and then she smiles at me.

"Are you ready?"

"I think so."

"Good."

When I turn to Henrik, he offers me a soft smile. "Good to go?"

"Yes," I answer.

"Then, right this way." He gestures toward the gold carriage with two white horses leading the way. It feels like a fairy tale you see at the end of a movie, riding off into the sunset, only with this fairy tale, the prince is nowhere to be found.

———

"YOU GOOD?" Lara asks over the bustling, screaming crowd that is taking any chance they can get to wave, say hi, or capture pictures of me as we parade around town.

"Good," I answer even though my arm is tired, my face hurts from smiling, and my heart feels weak, like a piece of it broke off this morning.

This should be a joyful moment for me, with all the people of Torskethorpe so happy to see me, so proud, but it's not. Keller's absence overshadows it.

And he promised . . .

He promised he wouldn't leave me. Guess I was completely wrong about that.

———

"YOU MUST BE EXHAUSTED," Theo says as he sets his fork down on his plate.

After a long parade of riding down the streets of the capital, I was given a tour of the statehouse and introduced to all the significant dignitaries in Torskethorpe, of which there were five since the country is so tiny. And then we went on a tour of some local businesses where I met quite a few people who offered me several gifts. Homemade flower crowns, jams, scarves, carved cods, and some doilies for my bedroom. I graciously accepted every single gift, talked about the process of making the gifts, even threw in some technical terms I learned during my training, and shook many hands while pictures were snapped of me left and right.

Not a single negative comment.

Not a single boo.

Just warm love, welcoming me to the island.

But the warm welcoming didn't negate the fact that I was a nervous wreck, that I tripped over my words a lot of the time, and when I looked for assistance on a term, Keller wasn't there to help me.

Despite feeling abandoned in a moment of need, once we returned to the palace for dinner, I knew I had made the right decision by coming here because I found a family. I found people who embrace me. I feel like I've found a purpose. A place where I can hopefully make a difference. Be more. But hell was the day exhausting.

"I am," I say with a yawn. "But good exhaustion. Today was unlike anything I've ever experienced."

"You were wonderful," Katla says. "Truly, I don't think I could be prouder."

"Same," Theo says. "You were so eloquent and regal. You made a few blunders here and there, but that was to be expected, and overall, you made a positive first impression."

"I hope so." I fold my hands on my lap, a question burning inside me that I can't hold back anymore. "Do you know where Keller was today?"

Theo glances at his plate while he grips the table's edge. "I'm not sure," he says, his voice full of disappointment.

"Oh . . . wasn't sure if he had a task or not?"

"He did," Theo says, now looking me in the eyes. "His task was to be at your side, to help you navigate the day."

A bout of ice spreads through my veins.

So he was supposed to be here.

He was supposed to stick by me.

With everything that happened last night, I convinced myself during the parade that he wasn't there because he was cleaning up the mess Brimar left behind, but that wasn't the case. He was just neglecting me.

"Oh, I see," I say as I rest my napkin on the table, indicating I'm finished with my meal. "Well, I'm quite tired. Do you mind if I excuse myself and go to bed?"

Katla and Theo exchange looks, and then gently, Katla says, "Maybe you should talk about what's on your mind."

God, don't you hate when people say that? Because I'm on an emotional ledge right now and one little comment about feelings could tip me over the edge, just like this has.

Tears begin to blind my eyes and choke my throat. A sickening feeling takes over.

He doesn't want you.

He's done his job of grooming me—fucking me—but doesn't want to be by my side. *My King* is only in the bedroom.

I was born a protector; it's in my blood. When a woman puts her trust in my hands, I'll never break that trust. I'll hold it close to me and cherish it.

He lied.

His love, if I can believe it was love, was fleeting. A show. Something I could hang on to while I navigated through this new turn in my life. He fooled me about The Informative, so it makes sense he could fool me about loving me too.

Droplets of sorrow find their way down my cheeks, and I pick up my napkin to dab at them.

"I'm sorry," I say. "I'm still learning how to control my emotions."

"No need to apologize," Katla says, coming to my side and pulling me into a hug. "It's been a busy, overwhelming day, and you had expectations of who would be there."

I nod. "I know it sounds stupid, but I wanted to make him proud, you know? We worked so hard to get me ready for this, and his absence hurts."

Katla rubs my back gently. "I understand completely, Lilija."

Theo clears his throat, and when I glance in his direction,

I see the tension in his neck, the grip of his fist, and the anger in his eyes. And I want to tell Theo not to get mad at Keller, that it's no big deal, but why would I? Why am I going to protect him?

What he did today was not okay.

And I'm not going to make excuses for him.

After another hug from Katla, I stand and take a deep breath. "I'm going to lie down. I hope that's okay."

"Completely fine, dear," Katla says. "We have a ladies' luncheon tomorrow in the courtyard, but that's the only thing I believe. We wanted to keep the schedule light for the first few weeks, leading up to Torg. Getting your feet wet seemed better than making a splash."

"I truly appreciate that," I say.

"And you . . . you like it here, right?" Katla asks, insecurity in her eyes. I can see how scared she is to lose another one of her children, so I press my hand to hers.

"I do. It truly feels right here, and I have no plans to go anywhere, despite what might be happening in my personal life." I offer them a small smile and a goodnight and then take off toward my room.

⊏⊐

"MISS CAMPBELL, do you have everything you need?" Runa asks when she enters the bathroom.

I'm already in a pair of navy blue silk pajamas, my hair's braided, and my teeth brushed. I couldn't get out of my dress and heels quick enough. Or wipe the makeup from my face. I realize this is something I will have to get used to—makeup, dresses, and heels. It's a far cry from my bikini and sandals.

I place my toothbrush in its holder and turn toward her. "I need your help."

"Yes, of course, how can I be of assistance?"

"I need you to take me to Keller's room in the servants' quarters."

She frowns. "Oh, that's something I can't do."

"Runa, please," I say, pleading with her. "He's not answering my texts or my calls, and if I don't at least speak to him tonight, then I won't be able to get any sleep. Please help me."

"Miss Campbell, the servants' quarters are not a place where the princess of Torskethorpe goes. It would be against all our rules of privacy."

Saddened, I turn back to the mirror, staring at my reflection, another tear cascading down my cheek. They've been intermittent at this point. Not sure they're going to stop. "I understand. I'm sorry I asked."

I wipe at my face and then move past her and into the bedroom, where I slip under the turned-down sheets of my plush bed.

Runa stands by my bed, staring at me, her hands in front of her, not showing an ounce of emotion.

"I think I'm good, Runa, if you want to retire for the night."

But she doesn't move. Instead, she takes a step closer to my bed and whispers, "There's a secret passageway to the servants' quarters that lead straight to Keller's room, which is the first one on the right."

I perk up. "Really? Where is it?"

"Just outside your room behind the picture frame of Strombly Castle. Follow the tunnel down through a series of doors, and keep going straight until you reach the last one, which will bring you to the quarters. First door on the right. I shall pick some clothes for you, so you aren't recognized immediately."

She goes to my closet and pulls out a pair of sweatpants and a hoodie. "Here." She passes them to me. "The guards change in about five minutes, and if you hurry, you'll be able to sneak past them. I shall wait by the picture frame for you to knock on it when you return, and I'll distract the guards so you can sneak in. I shall do this once and only once."

"Thank you, Runa," I say as I quickly put on the sweatpants and hoodie. Runa fashions the hood over my head and pulls on the drawstrings. She offers me some shoes and heads to the door. She looks at her watch and my pulse picks up as we wait.

"And . . . now," she says quietly as she opens the door.

Together, we move down the hall to where there's a giant picture frame. She opens it, the picture hinging like a door, and I climb into the barely lit tunnel.

"Hurry now," she says before shutting the picture.

The tunnel darkens even more, which is frightening given I don't know where I'm going, but determined, I walk forward and reach the first door. I open it and walk through, the tunnel lighting up with sporadic sconces on the wall. I quicken my pace, going through doorway after doorway until I reach the last one, which brings me into a cream hallway with carpeting, resembling a dormitory.

First door on the right.

I turn toward it—thankfully no one is around—and I knock on it, hoping he's home.

I wait impatiently for him to answer, but when I hear rustling, my hopes leap. The door opens, and standing in nothing but a pair of shorts is Keller. His hair is a mess, his eye's bruised, and there's a gash on his cheekbone. When he notices it's me, his eyes widen, and he quickly drags me into his room and slams the door.

"What the fuck are you doing here? You shouldn't be down here, Lilly."

"Well, I had to do something since you weren't answering my texts or calls." I spot his phone on his night table and walk over to it. I press the screen and it lights up. "Oh, would you look at that? It works."

He tugs on the back of his neck, and that's when I notice bruising near his ribs. What happened to him? "I got your messages," he says quietly.

"Okay, well, starting on an honest foot, that's good to know. Anything else you care to tell me? I don't know, like . . . why you weren't there today?" I fold my arms over my chest, taking a defensive position.

"I was there," he says.

"Oh, did you borrow Harry Potter's invisibility cloak?" Sarcasm is my best friend right now, because the hurt I was feeling moments ago has turned into anger after finding him hanging casually in his room. He shouldn't be here. He should be in my room, telling me what's going on. But instead, *I had to go after him.* "How much did it cost? Must have been a pretty penny."

"Lilly," he says softly. "I was in the crowd, making sure everything was smooth."

"Ah, I see. Funny, because I was told that you were supposed to be at my side, making sure I was comfortable and knew what the HELL I WAS DOING!" I yell the last part.

His brow creases, forming a ball of tension between his eyes. "You did know what you were doing. I heard from Henrik that everything went great."

"You heard from Henrik." I sarcastically laugh. "You shouldn't have had to hear from anyone. You should have been there."

"I wasn't in a position to be there."

"What are you talking about?" I ask. "Because of what Brimar said? Is that what's holding you back?"

He lets out a large breath and rests his hands on his sides.

"Because I don't believe any of what he said. Let's skip over the fact that you didn't tell me about the adoption, but the sheer idiocy that you'd want to be anywhere near the line of succession is comical. You don't even want to be with me. That's how desperate you are to stay away."

"I want to be with you," he says, his eyes pleading now. "Don't fucking say that. I want to be with you, Lilly."

"Well, you sure have a weird way of showing it. Maybe it's different here, but in America, we don't ignore the person we're in love with. We answer their text messages and phone calls." I take a step closer, my throat growing tight as the emotion of the day and the moment rock through me. "Do you have any idea how scared I was today? Any freaking clue, Keller?"

"Lilly, I can explain—"

"Terrified," I shout at him. "Not only because I didn't want to do that alone, but because I had no idea what was happening to you. The only reason I knew you were okay was that I was that desperate girl, asking anyone who would listen where you were and if you were okay. It was pathetic. I was freaking pathetic. You put me in a position where I couldn't do anything else but look like the forlorn female in search of her knight in shining armor. How is that fair to me? All you had to do was text, and that was it. But you couldn't do that."

I try to bite back my tears, to hold on to them, but there's no use. They tumble down my cheeks as a sob escapes my lips. Keller attempts to console me, but I step away.

"No, don't touch me. I want to know what made you act like I didn't matter today."

"You do matter, you matter—"

"Don't fucking say it." I point at him. "If I mattered most, I wouldn't be here, yelling at you, my heart breaking with every breath I take. We would be in my room, cuddled under the covers, reflecting on the day."

He rubs his hand over his forehead and says, "It's not that easy, Lilly."

"Really? Seems easy to me. You read a text, and you respond. You have an assignment, you show up. I can't fathom how that's not easy."

"It was the text," he says, growing impatient with me. "It

touched upon everything I'm insecure about, everything I don't want people thinking about me. Coming here to Strombly, you know I had some adjustments. There've already been whispers about us, about my intentions. This isn't normal, Lilly, for someone of my status to date someone like you."

"Oh my GOD! Who cares! Jesus Christ, Keller. It's not like we're living in a time where women's rights are suppressed and men rule with an iron fist. We're living in this modern day, with a king and queen who approve. So, your whole excuse of class differences doesn't check out."

"But that's how I grew up," he shouts. "And I'm working on coming to terms with it, but it's not that easy. I'm still trying to impress. I'm still trying to feel like I earned this job, that I'm doing it right. There's much pressure on me."

"So that means you just ignore me?"

"I didn't handle today correctly, okay? I was fucking terrified that I left a stone unturned after having to take Brimar off security. I wanted to make sure you were safe, that everything would go okay today, and nothing would ruin the welcoming."

"You ruined it," I say with a snap in my voice. "You might've thought you were taking care of me, but you weren't. I was worried and self-conscious the whole time, wondering why you weren't there. You did nothing but hurt the day for me, for us." Another sob escapes me. "This was supposed to be our day, Keller. A day we worked so hard to get to, and you weren't there." I wipe a tear off my cheek and then quietly say, "You abandoned me, left me alone, the one thing I begged you not to do. The one thing you promised you'd never do." Tears are now coming in droves.

"Fuck, I'm sorry," he says, trying to take me into his arms, but I duck away and move toward the door. "Lilly, please, just let me make this better. I fucked up and thought I was doing what was right for you, for us, but——"

"But you weren't." With my sleeve, I wipe away my tears.

"You left me . . . alone, and that, including lying to me, Keller, that's something I don't think I can forgive. If you loved me, you would've been there, instead of letting your insecurities control your actions."

With one more wipe, I reach for his door, but he quickly comes up to me and holds the door shut. "Please, Lilly. Please don't leave yet. Let me . . . fuck, just let me work through this with you."

I tilt my head to the side as I ask, "Work it out? Like actually talk to me, what you should have been doing all day? Why should I let that happen now? You didn't even tell me you were adopted."

"Because it wasn't . . . it wasn't fully true."

"What do you mean?"

"The paperwork never went through because of complications with the crown. It was more of a formality. I never mentioned it because . . . because it was never true."

"But it was true in your heart," I say.

His eyes flash to the side as he says, "Yes . . . yes, it was."

"Which means it was something you should have told me," I say through clenched teeth. "What has this relationship been to you?" I ask. "Has it just been about sex?"

"No," he says quickly. "Lilly, you should fucking know it's not just about sex."

"Well, that's what it seems like to me."

He steps back, looking insulted. "It hasn't been about sex. It's way deeper than that for me. I fucking told you I love you, and I haven't said that to anyone."

"Then maybe you don't know the meaning of love."

"I do," he growls back at me. "Because I haven't said those words to anyone else, means I know how impactful they are, how important they are. I saved them for the right person, for you, because I know, deep in my fucking soul, that you're the person my heart was supposed to fall for."

I place my hand on his doorknob and twist it. "If you

loved me, then you wouldn't have left me to fend for myself today. You would've realized that today trumped your insecurities, and you would've done everything in your power to be there for me. But you weren't, and as I said, Keller, that's unforgivable."

I move past him, open the door, and leave, heading right back the way I came, my eyes puffy and still tearing up as I make my way through the tunnel. When I reach the picture frame, I knock.

Runa opens the door and says, "Coast is clear." She helps me back into my room, where I sit on my bed, my body feeling empty.

"Here, let's get you out of this," Runa says as she carefully takes off my hoodie and sweatpants. The whole time, I stare at the wall. Even as she helps me lie down, I don't say anything. After I'm tucked in, she sits on the side of my bed and says, "You know, Miss Campbell, it's within my job responsibilities to take care of you, to make sure you have everything you need, and to be a guide when need be. It's not a requirement to act as a friend or a confidante. It's frowned upon to grow too close to the one you're serving." She brushes a stray piece of hair out of my face. "But I can't help but feel drawn toward you. You remind me very much of my sister who I lost just five years ago."

I look up at her now. "I'm so sorry, Runa. I didn't know you lost a sister."

"I did. And she was vibrant and beautiful, just like you. She had the world at her feet, and the possibilities were endless. But with one wrong decision, one dark night, we lost her. I'm trying to tell you that you have the world at your feet with so much to offer to this country. I'm not sure what might be going through with Keller, who by all means is a wonderful man inside and out, but don't let the devil swoop in when you have so much promise moving forward. You're strong, Miss Campbell. You might think you need him, but you never did. A man doesn't define your ability to stand on your own two feet. Your brain and your heart do. Perhaps continue to use them in the right way."

I nod, my lips curled in together as I hold back my tears. "Thank you, Runa."

Chapter Twenty-Four

KELLER

On a deep breath, I walk into Theo's office chambers and shut the door behind me.

This morning, I received a text from Henrik stating that Theo wanted to see me in his office at seven in the morning, no later. I didn't have to read into the text to know what it was about.

I was in fucking trouble, because not only did I let down Lilly, but I also let him down yesterday.

I'm still struggling with the conversation we had last night. It was . . . it was eye-opening. Everything she said was right, but she forgot to mention that I was a coward. Sure, I was taking care of security and ensuring everything was in check, but I also avoided Lilly. I knew it was going to hurt her, that she was going to be devastated that I wasn't there, but I stayed away, for my selfish reasons, and the entire night, that's all I thought about—how I fucked up—and I'm not sure there's any way I can make it up to her.

But I plan on doing that.

First thing's first, apologizing to Theo.

"Take a seat," Theo says as he points to a chair across from him.

The room is deathly silent as I move across the dark blue Persian rug and take a seat in an upholstered chair that I've sat in many times before, but never under these tense circumstances.

"Care to explain where you were yesterday?"

I shift in my chair and grip the armrests. "I was ahead of the parade, ensuring all security was in place."

"Isn't that why we have Ottar? He's the second-in-command to security, is he not?"

"He is," I answer.

"Was he not doing his job?"

"No, he was."

"I see, and what were you supposed to be doing?"

Fuck. My mouth goes dry as I attempt to answer his fast, hard-hitting questions.

"I was supposed to be with Lilly, assisting her through the parade."

"I see." He nods. "And you didn't perform that duty."

"I did not," I answer.

"Any reason behind that other than your own selfish decision and disobedience?"

I wet my lips and shake my head. "No, sir."

"I appreciate your honesty, but unfortunately, we'll have to suspend you from your duties."

My stomach crashes to the ground as I sit taller. "Suspend me?" I ask. "Wh-what do you mean?"

"I mean, we'll be reviewing your decision and assessing whether or not it's grounds for termination. Until then, you are not to step foot inside the palace. You're only allowed in the servants' quarters and will not be privy to any private intel."

"But, Theo, sir, what about Lilly?"

"She seemed to carry on perfectly fine yesterday without you, despite the obvious heartbreak she was suffering through that only Katla, Lara, and I were aware of."

That stings more than you know.

I'm proud of her for being able to fulfill her duties without help, but it doesn't feel good not to be needed, especially given the line of work I'm in.

"But . . . I was trying to help with Brimar and—"

"I'm grateful for the work you did in the early morning, taking care of Brimar and cutting the story before it could ruin the day for us, but that was all that was needed at that moment. Ottar had security under control. You should have been with Lilija, which was most important at the time. You lost sight of your duties."

"I was trying to help," I say, hanging my head.

"You were trying to avoid her. Your personal life encroached on your responsibilities and that's the last thing I expected from you."

He's right.

"I'm sorry, Theo. I let you down."

"You let Lilija down."

And that is probably the most painful realization out of all of this.

I don't know what to say, so I just nod.

"Ottar will escort you back to your room and take away your security passes until further notice."

"I understand," I say as I go to stand.

"Have you been dismissed?" Theo asks in his commanding voice that I've only heard a few times in my life. Theo's usually a jolly man with a smile that stretches to his ears, so you don't see this side of him very often.

"No, sir." I sit back down.

"Now, on a personal note . . ." He pauses and leans

slightly forward in his chair. "What the fuck were you thinking?"

Color me shocked because I'm not sure I've ever heard Theo speak like that before.

"You told me you loved Lilija. Was that a lie?"

"No." I swallow hard, sweat forming on my lower back. "That wasn't a lie; that was God's honest truth."

"I see, and what does love mean to you, Keller? Is it something to be toyed with? Something to be tossed around without a care?"

"No, sir."

"Or is it to be cherished, protected, and nurtured with the utmost care?"

"Protected."

"So, why the hell have you been freaking out since you arrived at Strombly with her? I see how she looks at you, *and* how you can make her happy or break her heart. She's infatuated with you, and yet, you're acting like a fool. Tell me, where did you learn this type of behavior? It surely wasn't from your parents, who had a beautiful, loving relationship, and it wasn't from Katla or me, who pride ourselves on the devoted bond we have with each other. So, where is this coming from?"

I rest my hands on my lap and quietly say, "Fear."

"Fear of losing?" he asks, his voice softer.

I nod and lift my eyes to his as they brim with tears. "I love her so fucking much," I say. "And since I've gotten here, I just . . . I fear what people might have said about me being with her. I fear that their opinions might encroach on her thoughts of me. I fear that she could get hurt and see that I'm not the man she deserves. I fear that I'm just not good enough, and all those fears lead to one thing. Losing her. And . . . I can't fucking lose her."

"But don't you understand you've lost her by pushing her away? By not being honest? By letting outside factors hinder the bond you two share?"

Royally Not Ready

"I do now," I say.

"I thought we'd taught you better than that, Keller. Fear doesn't determine your future. Fear is what holds you back. I hate to say it, my son, but you've taken the coward's way out by ducking away, by not facing those fears, and that's incredibly disappointing."

A tear falls down my cheek as I nod. "I'm sorry. I . . . thought I was doing the right thing."

"You thought you were protecting your heart from further damage." He leans even more forward, his hand connecting with my knee. "But instead, you've created a gap in your soul by relinquishing the most important aspect that holds us all together—the ability to persevere and to love. And that's a decision you'll have to live with."

I wet my lips and wipe at my cheeks. "I realize that."

Theo leans back in his chair and says, "And the crazy thing about it all, when I spoke to her last night, I saw in her eyes that she still loved you. That's what you don't get. Her love for you is not conditional, my boy. You've been blessed with her unconditional love, and instead of protecting that gift, you've mishandled it. I just hope for your sake that she'll give you another chance because, Keller, that girl, that woman, she's going to change this country for the better with one smile, one kind gesture, and one speech of hope. And if you want to be on the right side of history, you better do everything you can to win her heart back." He lifts the glass of water on his side table and takes a sip before saying, "You're excused." He presses a button, and the doors open, Ottar standing, waiting for me.

One hand on my shoulder, he guides me out of Theo's office chambers and straight to the servants' quarters, where I spend the rest of the day trying to figure out what the hell I'm going to do.

395

AS I'M bent over my desk, I hear a knock at my door. Not bothering to turn around, I answer, "Come in."

The door opens and then shuts, followed by the soft voice of Lara. "I heard what happened."

Everyone's heard what happened. News about my suspension quickly spread throughout Strombly, and it's probably the most embarrassing moment of my life. I can't even think about it, it makes me so sick.

Keeping my head down, I say, "Yeah, it was the right move for King Theo to make. I fucked up, didn't show up for the job, and now I'm paying the consequences."

"Those are the facts, but how are you feeling?" She sits on my bed, which is next to my desk.

I flick my pen onto my journal and lean back in my chair. "Like absolute piss," I answer.

"Well, you don't look any better."

I bring my hand to my cheek, feeling my bruise. "Yeah, I'm sure." I blow out a heavy breath. "Fuck, Lara, what was I thinking?"

"That's the problem, Keller. You've been doing too much thinking. You've been trying to overanalyze everything when you should've just been living your life without worrying about what others would think or what your parents said. I know you love them dearly, and you would do anything to honor them, but you need to realize their way of thinking was old school."

"I know." I pinch my brow. "I fucked everything up, Lara." I pause and then ask, "Wait, how are you doing? Have you spoken to Brimar?" I hate that I will have to tell her what else he's been doing. Breaking her trust as a security officer is one thing. But his betrayal of their relationship is dreadful. *Unexpected.*

She shakes her head. "No, and I have no plans of speaking with him. He's been fucking cheating on me, Keller. I was talking to Runa, and she told me that he's been seeing her cousin's friend on the side."

"I just found out yesterday morning when I confronted him. I'm so sorry he did this to you, Lara."

She sighs heavily. "I just feel so wronged. I loved him. Gave him my all. I thought . . . I thought we were in this life together, and he double-crosses both of us."

"It's fucked up."

"I wonder if he did what he did to you because he knew you would probably find out about the cheating and wanted to hurt you before you hurt him?"

I pause and give it some thought. "You know, it's a good possibility. Especially since everything was reported to me. Either way, he's not the man we thought he was, and I want to ensure you're okay."

"He's been distancing himself lately. When we were at Harrogate, we got into a few fights, and I even slept on the couch a few nights. I never said anything because I didn't want our relationship woes to be a distraction from the training, but that was one of the reasons he was so adamant about leaving."

"Shit, that makes sense," I say. "You should've said something to me. I would've switched out security."

She shakes her head. "No, being at Harrogate, getting the opportunity to protect and train with Lilly, was a great honor, and I didn't want to miss the opportunity because of a lovers' quarrel. I thought if I could just hang on with Brimar, and get back to Strombly, then maybe we could work things out, but that wasn't the case. And even though I'm heartbroken over it, I feel like a weight has been lifted off my shoulders. I know how much of a burden our relationship has been lately."

"I wish you would've talked to me about it. I could've done more to involve you, so you weren't spending so much time with him."

"But then you wouldn't have been able to spend that much time with Lilly, and you needed that. You needed her. She brought something out of you that I hadn't seen in many years, a genuine smile. She truly makes you happy."

"She does," I answer. "And now . . . hell, now I'm not even allowed in the palace or even near her, for that matter, to make it up to her. To tell her what a fool I was, to show her that I love her, more than anything, and that I would do anything to earn her trust again."

"How would you even go about earning her trust back if you were allowed in Strombly?"

"Probably show her by small acts."

"Well, that could still be accomplished," Lara says.

"How?"

"You have Runa and me. Although Runa is not entirely happy with you. She mentioned how upset Lilly was over your foolish mistakes, and she hates seeing Lilly upset. I think with the proper coaxing, we could get her involved."

"You think so?" I ask.

"With a big apology, I think so. But the question is, what would your small acts be?"

"Court her from a distance."

"I like the sound of that. So, does that mean you'll try to win her back?"

"Until my dying day, I will fucking try because I won't be whole without her."

Lara smirks. "Seems as if we have some planning to do, then."

Chapter Twenty-Five

LILLY

"Are you feeling better?" Runa asks as she hands me a cup of water.

"Sort of," I answer, my head still pounding, my eyes still puffy, my heart very heavy. "I think . . . I think I can start getting ready for the luncheon."

Runa adjusts my blankets, so they sit better on my lap. "No need, Miss Campbell. Queen Katla has called in your absence and said you came down with a cold."

"What? She didn't have to do that. I can get it together." I take a deep breath, my eyes watering up again. "I just . . . need a second." Another tear cascades down my cheek, and I curse myself for being unable to control my emotions. "God, I'm sorry. I really can do this."

Runa gently rests her hand on my shoulder as she says, "Please don't try to stifle your feelings in front of me; it will only make it worse. You might not be comfortable talking to me, but it might help. Holding it all inside isn't healthy for the body or the mind."

"I know you're right," I say as I lean back on my pillows.

Since I woke up this morning, I've been crying. Poor Runa has had to bring me a box of tissues and tend to me while I attempt to get it together. Spoiler alert, I haven't gotten it together.

I let out a pent-up breath and ask, "Have you ever been in love, Runa?"

"Yes, Miss Campbell. While going through training, I fell in love with a boy named Ergo. He was, well, he was my everything. He was training to be a footman. It was easy to fall for his charm and his looks, but what mattered most was that we bonded at the heart."

"What happened?"

"When we graduated, he was offered a position in another country, while I was hired to work here, at Strombly. Even though our love for each other was quite strong, our dedication to serving was stronger."

"Have you heard from him?"

"I have. He's married now with a boy on the way." She takes a deep breath. "It was devastating to hear he found someone else."

"Oh my God, Runa, I'm so sorry."

"No need to apologize. That's love, right? It's life's greatest challenge. Sometimes you get to live and love, and sometimes you must love and forget." She looks me in the eyes. "Are you telling me you're in love with Keller?"

I nod slowly. "Yes, and I've never truly been in love like this before. Like I depend on him to bring joy to my life. I never depended on anyone before, as I've always been so independent, but we connected on a deeper level at Harrogate. A level so deep I think only a few people would understand. In a time where I was so lost, he was a lifeline, my safety net . . . my hero. And I know that sounds corny, but it's true. I feel like he opened my eyes to a whole new world. He showed me that I didn't have to walk through this life alone, and then . . . and then he just left me out to dry. He abandoned me when I needed him the most. I—" My tears fall once again. "I don't know how to handle that."

"Ah, I see. I understand the feeling of loss. It's painful. It feels like you can't breathe at times."

"Yes. Especially after all the promises we made to each other." I take the tissue she hands me and dab at my eyes. "I hate that he's affecting me this much, but this whole experience has been with him. I feel . . . empty."

"That's very understandable. I'm not sure I'd be as strong as you."

"What are you talking about? I'm missing a luncheon because of a broken heart. That's not being strong."

"Ah, but you're talking about your feelings. You're wading through them, trying to make sense of it all. If I were in your shoes, I'm not sure I'd be sticking around in this new country, where my biggest advocate just broke my heart. I'd probably flee to my comfort home."

I shake my head. "I'd never do that. I made a promise to King Theo and Queen Katla and to this country. This is where I belong."

Runa smiles softly as she takes my hand in hers. "You know, Miss Campbell, we have a lot in common. There might be different DNA running through our veins, but our desire to serve others is a bond I take very seriously." She pats my hand. "Now, rest up, cry, be sad, have a moment. I'll bring eye patches to clear the puffiness. Make sure you have plenty of water, and if there's anything I can get you, please, feel free to ask for it."

"I'm not very hungry, but whenever I was sad, my mom always brought me a donut."

"Consider it done." Runa stands from the bed and then hands me my phone from her pocket. "This was buzzing while you were napping. I took it away so it wouldn't disturb you."

"Oh. Thanks." I take the phone from her, and when she walks out the bedroom door, I glance down at the screen, hoping to see a message from Keller. But when I see a text from Timmy, my heart sinks all over again.

Timmy: *How are things? I read some articles about the welcoming parade. Baby girl, you looked breathtaking. I can't believe this is your real life. When can I come and visit?*

Even though I feel like my heart has been ripped out of my chest, I text my friend back.

Lilly: *Please visit whenever you can. I could use a friend.*

Lucky for me, he texts back right away.

Timmy: *That sounds ominous. What's going on?*

Lilly: *I think Keller and I broke up. Well . . . more like I know we broke up.*

Timmy: *WHAT? WHY?*

Lilly: *It's such a long story, but something spooked him, and instead of working it through with me, he ghosted me.*

Timmy: *What? That doesn't seem like the man you talked to me about. I thought he was attached to your hip.*

Lilly: *So did I, but things turned awkward once we got to the capital. It was like the bubble we were in burst, and he didn't know how to handle it. He felt weird about staff knowing about us being together, even though Theo and Katla didn't care. It still doesn't make sense to me. I'm just . . . sad.*

Timmy: *Ugh, I wish I was there to hold your hand. Maybe he just needs a second to get his head on straight. From what you told me, the man was infatuated with you, and an infatuation like that doesn't just wash away. Plus, he still has to work with you, right? That means he'll see you every day.*

Lilly: *Which will make things incredibly awkward.*

Timmy: *Or it'll make him realize what an idiot he's being. Let me ask you this, would you take him back?*

Lilly: *I don't know, honestly. I love him still. I'm not sure that* *feeling will ever go away, but the trust we built vanished in the blink of an eye. He truly hurt me, Timmy.*

Timmy: *Then you have to think about whether or not the pain he caused you is greater than not spending your life with him. And that's something only you can figure out.*

"I FEEL WEIRD," I whisper to Lara in the car.

"Why?"

I tug on the hem of my floral dress. "Because I'm all dressed up, looking like a garden in this fabric, and I'm about to meet a bunch of anglers. Doesn't that seem weird?"

"No, that seems normal, but I understand that this is still new to you. At least it's the only thing you have scheduled today. It's nice that they've stretched out your schedule, so you aren't bombarded."

"Yes, I agree. But I still feel weird."

"You'll get used to it. These people are excited to meet you."

"I'm excited to meet them as well, to be honest. They're the top anglers over the last few years?"

"Winners of biggest fish caught over the last five years," Lara says. "Quite an accomplishment. Every year, they record the fishes caught and their size for that year, and around Christmastime, they're crowned."

"Wait, is that where the name the Crowned Cod comes from?"

"Yes. The owner who opened it was crowned back in the nineties. There's prize money associated with the crown, and the woman who won took that money and opened the Crowned Cod. Since she passed about seven years ago, management hasn't been great, and it's more of a risky place to go if you're not a regular."

"Well, that's sad."

MEGHAN QUINN

The car pulls up next to a bright yellow boathouse, the color a beautiful contrast to the green mountains behind it and the blue water just at the edge of the rocky foundation.

"This is so cute," I say.

"Kirkfell is one of our biggest tourist attractions, besides the capital, because of all the brightly colored buildings, trails to hike, and small-town feel. Great food here as well."

Kirkfell, that's where Keller planned his fake story about the angler's wife, and being a romantic at heart, I want to know what would've happened to the angler's wife and who she chose. I know, it was made up, but it's like your favorite author writing two books in a series, ending it on a cliffhanger, and never writing that third one for you to find out what happened to those characters. Oh, they make promises, they tell you one day, but it never . . . ever . . . happens.

"Are you ready?" Lara asks.

"As ready as I'll ever be," I answer.

Lara steps out of the car first and holds the door open for me as we practiced at Harrogate. I swing my legs out, keeping them shut, because . . . you know, Britney showed us what not to do, and then I stand, the sun beaming down on this warmish day. Either the weather has given me a break, or I'm starting to get used to it. Either way, I'm not a shivering icicle.

Henrik appears from the front of the car. He has come with me today since Keller's been suspended. I understand why Theo did it. Keller didn't report to his job as he should have, but I'm still in shock.

And saddened.

I know I walked out on him when I went to his room, but call me a glutton for punishment, I still thought I'd be able to see him. But that's not the case, and this feels very . . . final. Like our relationship status is over. Done.

So, I've been mentally trying to deal with that as well.

"Miss Campbell, right this way," Henrik says as we move toward the yellow building.

404

Henrik is friendly, a little stuffy, and doesn't seem to have a sense of humor like Keller. I attempted to joke around with him earlier, you know, cut the tension since I'm feeling all sorts of emotions, but he didn't laugh. He didn't even crack a smile. It made me miss Keller even more, and I hate that because he hurt me.

Gripping my clutch, which has nothing in it besides my lipstick and a mirror, I follow Henrik into the boathouse. It takes my eyes a few moments to adjust from the light outside to the darker interior, but when they do, I'm met with I'd say at least thirty people, all lined up, waiting for my greeting. I thought it would only be five, but then again, it seems they brought their families.

"Princess Lilija," a man with a gray mustache and bald head says as he walks up to me and bows. "It is my pleasure to meet you."

"This is Magnus Hearborn," Henrik says. "The chief angler of Torskethorpe. He oversees the competition throughout the year."

I hold my hand out to him. "Mr. Hearborn, it's a pleasure to meet you."

He gently takes my hand in his and bows again. "The pleasure is all mine." When my eyes connect with his weathered ones, he adds, "It means a lot to us, to our country, that you're here. We've felt lost without an heir, and you've truly saved us."

Maybe a month ago, something like that would've made me scoff, but after being in Strombly and talking to many, I realize just how significant my decision is.

"I'm so honored to be here and to be welcomed with open arms."

"And I hope I'm not speaking out of turn when I say you look just like your mother. We loved her dearly."

"Thank you, that means a lot to me," I say kindly.

"We appreciate you coming by. I believe I shall introduce

you to our anglers now. They've had pins and needles waiting to meet you."

Magnus moves me through the line of anglers and their families. I listen to their stories of how they caught their crown-winning cod, and some of the stories were quite entertaining. I laughed, I shook hands, and I accepted a few wood carvings of fish, one of which was a life-sized replica that came up to my hip. And when we get to the final man, my eyes deceive me, because for a moment, I think he's Keller from the broadness of his shoulders and the style of his hair.

But that can't be.

Can it?

My breath is stolen from my lungs when he lifts his head, and his deep blue eyes connect with mine.

Why is he here?

Lara didn't mention he was going to be here, or did she and I was daydreaming? Either way, he's here, and he looks . . . God, he's so handsome. The bruise under his eye has faded, but his expression looks weathered, as though he's been through the gauntlet and barely was able to crawl out.

But still, the most handsome man I've ever seen.

And even though I feel the broken pieces of my heart barely holding together, it still leaps from the sight of him. My body still craves his warm, strong arms. My mouth still desires his. And I desperately want to crawl against his body and let him take care of me, tell me everything's going to be okay.

"And I believe you know Mr. Keller Fitzwilliam," Magnus says. "His story is entertaining because he caught the biggest fish by accident."

As if someone has programmed me to do so, I lift my hand to Keller, who takes it in his long fingers as he bows. But there's something paper-like between our fingers, and when I have a second to figure it out, I see that he's slipping me a note.

Before he releases my fingers, he gives them a gentle

squeeze . . . three times.

My breath stills in my chest as my pulse roars through my veins.

Three squeezes.

It's what my parents used to do to tell me they loved me.

Is that what he's doing? When his eyes connect with mine, from the forlorn expression in them, I know that's exactly what he's doing.

Three squeezes . . . he loves me.

When our fingers release, I grip the note tightly. And with a steady voice, I say, "Mr. Fitzwilliam, what a surprise to see you. I was unaware of your fishing abilities."

He brings his hands together in front of him and says, "It was a mistake, unfortunately. I was fishing with King Theo off the bank of Kirkfell. He had a few lines hanging off the back of the boat and had to go to the bathroom, so he asked me to watch his lines. The minute he left, a fish was hooked and I reeled it in. But during the reeling, I fell into the water."

"Really?" I ask, a smile peeking from my lips as I think about Keller falling off a boat. Not because he could have drowned, but because such a strong man like himself, I couldn't imagine him not being able to hold his own against a fish.

"I have a bad case of sea legs unfortunately and, yes, I fell into the water. While being fished out, I hung onto the pole and reeled the fish in, only to be pulled out of the water with my fish."

I chuckle. "What a spectacle, I'm sure."

Magnus holds up a picture of a wet Keller clinging to a fish. I chuckle even more. "Our favorite crowned cod story."

"I can see why. A mishap gone right."

"Indeed," he answers before taking another bow, ending our conversation.

And just like that, our interaction is over, but I cling to the note. As Magnus shows all the pictures from previously crowned cods, Lara comes up to me and I slip her the note for safekeeping until I can read it later.

I want to say I paid attention to the rest of the visit and dove into the grand tales of fishing, but my mind was on one thing alone—whatever that note said, and the three pulses Keller gave my fingers before our hands parted.

After what felt like half a day, Lara and Henrik walk me back to the car, where I stand in front of the door and offer everyone a wave. I spot Keller's towering height by the entrance of the boathouse, his eyes intent on me, his hands in his pockets.

Why did he show up today? Given his current suspension, I'd think he wouldn't want to be seen in public. He's so worried about what people think about him that this public appearance with a mark on his name seems very uncharacteristic.

I have so much to ask him, but the biggest question of them all? *Why weren't you strong enough for me?* Why wasn't I important enough for him to push through the insecurities?

With another wave, I duck into the car and wait for Lara to sit next to me. With Henrik in the front, out of earshot thanks to the glass between the front and the back, I keep my eyes ahead and ask, "Do you have the note?"

"I do." She slides it over to me on my leg, and I take it in my hands. I give the people one last wave, and then we're off, driving down the road, a motorcade in front of and behind us.

I let out a deep breath and rest my head back, clutching the note. "Did you know he was going to be there?"

"I had an inkling. I wasn't sure if he'd show up or not."

"Why didn't you warn me?"

"I didn't want to add to the nerves that you already have with these public outings. This was your first without Queen Katla or King Theo and I wanted to make sure you were going into it with a clear head and not worried about the possibility of seeing Keller."

"That makes sense." I rub my lips together. "He looked so . . . sad, but also determined, in a way."

"He did."

"Have you talked to him at all?"

Lara rubs her hand over her thigh as she says, "I have. Every night."

"What?" I ask, turning toward her now. "Why didn't you tell me?"

"I'm treading a hard line here, Lilly," she says. "You're not only my responsibility to protect, but you've also become a friend. And I've known Keller since we were kids. He might've acted poorly and made foolish decisions, but he's also my best friend. I know you've been hurting, so I've wanted to keep things close to me so as not to hurt you more."

"Well, I appreciate that, but you don't have to tread carefully around me."

She gives me a look. "Lilly, I appreciate you trying to be strong, but I know it'd hurt you if I spoke about him. I'd rather talk to you about other things that make you happy."

"He used to make me happy," I say quietly, clutching the note. "Do you know what this is about?"

"I don't know what's in the note."

"But you knew he would give this to me?"

She looks away and says, "How about you don't ask me questions about Keller, that way I don't feel the need to break anyone's trust?"

"Okay, yeah, I'm sorry. I didn't mean to put you in the middle."

"It's quite all right. I'd be the same if it were Brimar and me. That is, if Brimar didn't commit treason or cheat on me." She smiles. "At least Keller didn't do that."

"Very true," I say softly. "I'm so sorry that you're going through this. It's never okay to cheat."

"No, it's not. It hurts, but I'm more angry than heartbroken, if I'm honest."

"I can understand that." And then, because I can't help myself, I ask, "Do you think I'm being ridiculous?"

"Not in the slightest. He hurt you and probably in one of the worst ways. Your feelings are completely justified. Now, read that note."

"Okay." I unfold it and focus on his familiar handwriting. I scroll over it briefly and say, "I think it's a poem."

Lara smiles. "Ah, that seems right."

"What do you mean?"

"Well, there's some Viking in that man, if you haven't noticed."

"I have," I say, my mind going to his large frame and blond hair, his protective instincts.

"One of the ways a Viking would express their love to someone was through simple poetry. There's no structure, no format, just a declaration of their feelings. This makes sense to me."

"Oh." And then I remember something he said to me at Harrogate. If he ever tried to woo me, he'd write poetry. Is that what he's trying to do? Only one way to find out. I focus on the poem and read it quietly to myself.

There is no way to explain,
This burning, merciless feeling,
Biting through my bones.
It eclipses my thoughts,
It burrows into my veins,
A cataclysmic force so strong,
I can't breathe.
I need you.
I broke us.
It's broken me.

My teeth run over my bottom lip as I read the poem a few more times, his words hitting me like a tornado, swirling around, confusing yet comforting.

I look up and stare at the road ahead.

Quietly, Lara asks, "Was it good?"

I nod, my tongue peeking out to wet my lips. "It was good."

"Not surprised," she says.

And the rest of the drive, we're both silent, Keller on my mind the whole time.

⌐══⌐

"RIGHT THIS WAY, MISS CAMPBELL," Henrik says as he moves me past a swarm of people and into an art gallery.

I can feel Lara right behind me as we make our way into an open, wood-planked room with vaulted ceilings, white walls, and beautiful art hung all around the perimeter, ranging from landscapes to abstracts to portraits.

"Oh, wow," I say as I take in all the walls. "This is stunning."

"We have some truly brilliant artists in Torskethorpe," says Olga, the art curator. "I'm going to take you around the room and have the artists speak of their work."

"That would be wonderful," I say as we walk up to a beautiful landscape depicting the ocean. Familiar hot springs are nestled in the corner, and as I get closer, it hits me. I know exactly where this is located. My eyes drift to the name of the picture. *My First and Only Love.* And then underneath the title is the name. Keller Fitzwilliam.

What on earth?

There's no way.

"Ah, and here is the artist now," Olga says as a large presence steps into my line of vision.

Keller stands before me in a navy blue suit and black button-up shirt, the top two buttons undone. His hair is slicked to the side, and his face is freshly shaved. Just the slightest hint of the bruise under his eye remains. If I didn't know it was there, I wouldn't have noticed.

"Mr. Keller Fitzwilliam."

As I've been taught, I hold out my hand, and Keller takes it, slipping another piece of paper into my fingers as he bows.

"Princess Lilly, it's a pleasure," he says, his fingers lingering on mine for a brief moment before he squeezes them three times and pulls away.

I love you.

It's subtle. I'm the only one who knows what he's saying and doing, but it feels like the entire world is watching my reaction.

"H-hello," I say, stumbling over my words thanks to my racing heart. I'm holding on tightly to the piece of paper in my hand. "Please, tell me about your beautiful painting."

"This is called *My First and Only Love*, inspired by the place where I fell in love off the coast of the southern peninsula. I've never felt a love as fierce, as powerful, as for the woman who captured my heart. I wanted to express the devotion I have for her through art."

My heart is hammering so hard I can barely hear Keller over the roar. "It's . . . it's breathtaking," I say.

He nods. "Just like the love of my life."

Dear.

God.

I clear my throat and offer him a small smile before Olga directs me to the next artist. I gently place the note in Lara's hand, knowing she'll keep it safe for me.

We walk through the gallery, and I hear story after story for every piece of art. The whole time, I can feel Keller's eyes burning for me, following me, and when it's time for me to leave, he's still standing next to his painting, his hands in front of him. There's a proud set to his shoulders. He looks less defeated, more empowered—as he should. I can't remember a single thing about any of the other paintings in this room, besides his.

"I've never felt a love as fierce or powerful as for the woman who

captured my heart. I wanted to express the devotion I have for her through art."

I don't even know if I acted the way I was supposed to, because my mind has been molded into only thinking about Keller.

As we make our way to the car, I'm tempted to reach out to Lara, to lean on her for support, but I know it wouldn't look right, so I wait until we get into the car to let out a large exhale.

"Oh my God," I whisper as we all buckle up. The car begins to move, and I turn toward Lara. "Please tell me it felt like there was a lack of oxygen in that room."

"The minute your eyes connected with his, yes . . . the air seemed to shrink."

I press my hand to my chest. "I was not . . . expecting that. I knew his mom was an artist, but he made it seem like he wasn't that good."

"He didn't represent himself well when talking about his talents, then. His pieces are magnificent."

"Does he focus on landscapes?"

"Everything. Lately, late at night, while we talk, he draws portraits."

"Oh? Of who?"

"Of you," she answers. "Wherever you've been photographed for the day, he'll spend the evening sketching you in his notebook while he tells me how beautiful you are."

Okay . . .

Act normal.

That's no big deal.

It's just, you know . . . art.

It's not like a romantic thing or anything like that. I have a sketchable face. That's it.

Lara slides the piece of paper over to me. "It's a shame when we realize the moment we lost the most important thing in our lives, isn't it?"

I give her a side-eye. "I thought you were staying out of it."

She holds her hands up. "I am, I'm just, you know . . . talking."

"Uh-huh." I unfold the piece of paper and read the poem to myself.

So desperate for love,
Beating, screaming,
Begging for one glimpse.
My heart is yours,
A servant to your being,
Forever yours but hopefully,
Never, never.

It takes me a few moments to reread it, to understand what he's saying, and when I do, I mentally hear myself say, *forever . . . never, never.*

"LISTEN, Lara, if I walk through that door into the wood-whittling place, I need you to tell me, will I see him there?"

She grimaces and quietly says, "There's a high probability he's in there."

"How high? Give me a percentage."

"One hundred," she says just as Henrik opens the door, and I come face to face with three men. One of them is pretty old, wrinkles etching his face, a hump in his back. One is quite charming, with rich dark hair and a crooked nose. And the third is Keller, wearing jeans and a button-up shirt, with a heavy cloth apron tied around his neck and torso.

His hair has grown longer on the top so he can fix it into a ponytail, and the bruise under his eye is completely gone. I don't know how it's possible, but he looks bigger, stronger than a week ago.

"Princess Lilija," Henrik says. "Allow me to introduce you to some of our best whittlers in the capital. This is Eriek."

Henrik gestures to the old man. "And this is Jon, and you're already acquainted with Keller."

"Hello," I say while trying to speak to all of them, not just Keller. "It's nice to meet you."

Eriek steps up and says, "We're very pleased to have you here. With Torg just around the corner, we're excited to show you how we put together a fish for trading, using some of the oldest utensils on the island."

I smile and act as though I'm interested, but the entire time, I feel him so close. His energy is so palpable, that I almost cut myself at one point while trying to shape the fish. I nick myself, nothing a small bandage won't fix. Eriek and Jon are both lovely men, very involved in the history of whittling, while Keller watches over us, waiting his turn.

And when his time comes, he bows and, hoping for a note, I hold out my hand, which once again, he squeezes three times. To my satisfaction, he slips me a note. That piece of paper? It feels as though it lights up my entire body. It may be only parchment with scribbling on it, but it's so much more than that to me. It feels like glue, repairing the damage that's been done to my heart.

"Princess Lilija," he says. "Thank you for joining us. I'll be going over the painting portion of the fish. Would you mind stepping up to the table?"

I do as I'm told. The command in his voice is soft, so no one else would notice it, no one but me. He stands next to me, the heat of his body so powerful that I feel it in the depths of my soul. As he speaks, his shoulder brushes against mine, sending chills up my spine, one wave after another, until I feel almost breathless. He shows me how to paint the fish, just like he did in Harrogate, taking me back to when we couldn't be apart from each other.

Memories flood me.

Emotions tickle my brain.

The need for him now is so strong that I can't quite remember exactly why we aren't together.

And when he looks me in the eyes, the desperation causes my heart to bleed because, despite it all, I feel the same way. I want him badly. *I've missed him terribly.*

When we're back in the car, Lara slips me the note, but I don't look at it right away. Instead, I stare out the window at the retreating Keller, who doesn't tear his gaze away until I can't see him anymore.

Still looking out the window, I whisper, "I love him, Lara."

"I know."

"And I don't think I can go on without him. He hurt me, but . . . the hurt I feel when he's not around, that's stronger."

"I can see it in your eyes."

I lean back in my seat and turn toward her. "How's that possible? How's it possible to love someone who hurt you?"

"Unconditional love, Lilly. You can't control it. It just sits there, buried in your heart, forever. I don't think I've ever seen the type of love you two share. It almost seems as though you both breathe deeper when around each other. That's something to hold on to."

I don't respond to her. I look at the paper and read his words.

When our eyes meet,
It feels like the ink
In my pen won't seize.
My words are tangled,
Contorted in my mind.
I desperately want to say,
How the world spins,
Only when you are near.
But the best I can write,
Is always mine, eternally yours.

Chapter Twenty-Six

KELLER

"Come in," I say over my shoulder.

I don't turn to face Lara. I know it's her, as she's come at the same time every night since I lost everything.

I've gotten into a routine since I've been put on suspension. I still wake up every morning at the same time, but instead of getting ready for the day, I go on a five-mile run and then work out in the gym provided by the palace. After that, I shower and help around the quarters by cleaning, offering to help with meals, and even doing repairs. When I have downtime, I sit in front of my journal and focus on my poems, focus on my feelings, and why I had such a hard time coming back to Strombly. Why I felt the need to jeopardize the best thing that ever happened to me.

And after much reflection and speaking with Lara, it comes down to one thing—to prove to my parents that even though they're not here anymore, I'm still the man they always wanted me to be. But above all else, above the rules, above their societal expectations, they would've wanted me to be happy. And I'm not fucking happy. Not even in the slightest.

So, I came up with a plan. I worked with Runa and Lara and found out Lilly's schedule, and I made sure I was there at the events I knew I'd be able to attend. And then I worked on my poems; I went over them repeatedly until I felt they were the epitome of what I was feeling.

On the days when I knew I'd see her, I didn't sleep. I kept thinking over and over what that interaction would be, what I'd say to her, and how I'd look at her. And after, I'd reflect on how goddamn beautiful she was. How perfect she was, handling the people of Torskethorpe. How she was an absolute natural. And how her hand fit into mine when I passed her the note.

I tried asking Lara for reactions to the notes, but she said she was already walking a thin line between us, that she wanted to keep Lilly's reactions to herself, and I respected that.

So, I've been waiting by my phone for a call, a text, anything that tells me she wants to talk. But she hasn't contacted me. I don't blame her. She was right—*my desertion was unforgivable.* Brimar may have pressed on my insecurities. But I stomped on Lilly's fears.

"Are you just going to sit there, or are you going to greet me?" a booming voice says from the door.

I fly out of my seat and turn around quickly to find King Theo standing in my room. The door is shut, but that doesn't mean the people around me didn't hear his deep voice.

"Theo," I say, stunned. "I'm sorry, I thought you were Lara."

"Is that how you greet a friend?"

"No, sir. Sorry." I push my hand through my hair, knowing it's a mess. I'm not wearing a shirt, and I haven't shaved in a day or two, so I probably look like an absolute mess.

His eyes scan me as he takes a seat on my bed. "You look like hell."

"I know," I say, staying standing.

"Take a seat, Keller."

I sit back down in my desk chair, but I turn it to face him. "If I knew you were coming, I would've made myself more presentable."

"I prefer to see you like this—no smoke and mirrors about how you're truly doing. And from the looks of it, not great."

I shake my head. "Am I able to speak freely?"

"I'd hope that you do."

"Being suspended from my job felt like everything I've worked toward in my life was ripped from my grasp. I thought my pride, my fulfillment in life, relied on what I did for you, for the crown." I shake my head. "But the guttural pain that I feel daily, the reason I find myself grasping for a life preserver in this sea of uncertainty, is not from losing my job. It's from losing Lilly. And that's when I realized it doesn't fucking matter what I do. Granted, I love my job, but I love Lilly so much more, and I'm worried that I won't get her back."

Theo rests his hands together as he leans forward. "And what exactly are you doing other than passing her notes at public events?"

Shit, how does he know?

"You, uh . . . you know about that?"

"Yes, Henrik is just like you. He doesn't miss a thing. He's kept me informed of all the places you've shown up and your interactions with Lilija."

I knew Henrik was too good.

"I, uh . . . I've been trying to express to her how I feel, how I love her, through poems."

Theo cracks the smallest of smiles. "Ah, I see, taking a cue from some of our ancestors?"

"Something like that," I say. "Since I wouldn't see her every day, going to public events I knew she'd be attending would give me a small chance to show her how much I love her. How much I want her in my life."

"I see. And has it worked?"

I shake my head, hanging it in front of me. "No, I don't believe so. She hasn't contacted me."

Theo slowly nods. "And this is more important to you than your job?"

I swallow hard and look Theo in the eyes. "If I give up one thing, it would be the job. I can't give up on her."

His grin stretches wider. "Good answer." He shifts on my bed. "Now, it's to my understanding that she misses you. Between reports from Lara, Henrik, and Runa, they all believe she'd take you back in a heartbeat."

"They told you that?" I ask, hope springing in my chest. "Lara hasn't said anything to me and I see her every night."

"The power of being king," Theo says with that grin I know and love. "And I've heard from the head of staff that while you've been suspended, you've been helping out wherever it's needed. Instead of sulking in your room, you've still contributed to the monarchy in the best way you know how. That, to me, speaks volumes about your character and the exceptional man you are, Keller."

"Thank you. Strombly, and the people inside of it, mean everything to me."

Theo nods. "Does it mean enough to you to set aside what your parents once told you?"

"Yes," I say. "I realized I was trying to uphold their ideals despite being outdated, and I realize how foolish that's been."

"Ah, so during this time of suspension, you've finally found some much-needed clarity?"

"Yes," I answer.

"Then, I shall reinstate you as Lilija's private secretary, beginning tomorrow morning."

I grip the arms of my chair, my fingers digging into the wood. "Really?" I ask.

"Yes, but we shall be looking for your replacement and training them as soon as possible."

My brow creases. "But—"

Theo holds his hand up. "My boy, if you say you love Lilija as you do, and I can see her love for you, there will be wedding bells in the future, which means you'll be placed into a different role."

Understanding crosses my mind. "Oh."

Theo straightens up. "You realize the responsibility that will ensue, correct? She'll be queen, and you'll be her prince, her advisor, her advocate, her protector, her shield, and her rock. Will you be able to handle that without running away?"

My skin breaks out in a sweat. The answer to his question is monumental, and without a second thought, I know what to say, because I feel it deep in my soul.

"It would be my absolute honor."

Theo's eyes soften as they sparkle back at me. He holds his hand out to me and I take it. He gives me a squeeze.

"I'm not sure you realize the impact of that statement, but it truly gives me hope for the future of Torskethorpe." Theo rises from the bed and grips his cane as he says, "Report first thing in the morning."

"I will." I stand as well, and when we both pause, looking each other in the eyes, Theo opens his arms, and I take what he's offering. I wrap my arms around him and hug him tightly.

He pats my back and quietly says, "I love you, my boy."

Tears fill my eyes as I clutch him tightly. "I love you, too."

When Theo releases me, he cups my cheek. "Don't mess this up. Lilija is a once-in-a-lifetime love."

"I promise you, I'll spend the rest of my life honoring her and the love she has for me. You have my word."

He pats my cheek. "I know I do." And then he takes off, leaving me stunned.

I sit back in my chair just as Lara walks through the door, a wary look on her face. "Please tell me that conversation was a good one."

I smile up at her. "Lara, it was a fucking amazing one."

Chapter Twenty-Seven

LILLY

"This dress is beautiful," I say to Runa as I look at myself in the standing mirror in my bathroom. A baby-blue wrap dress with lace details, lace sleeves, and a ruffle hem. It's stunning, and I still can't believe I get to wear clothes like this. Plus . . . it's so soft. I keep touching the fabric, which I need to stop doing because if I do that in public, it'll look like I'm feeling myself up.

"I believe it's my favorite so far," Runa says as she adjusts the tie in the back. "Have you seen the style blogs that've been popping up about you?"

"No. Are you serious? Ha, if they only knew what I really like to wear. Although, this dress is comfortable and flattering. Would it be horrible to see what other dresses this designer has?"

"Not at all. She's local, actually."

"Really?" I ask. "I like that a lot. She does great work." I adjust my hair, which we curled into soft waves and pinned back on the sides. "Okay, I think I'm ready."

"Very well. I set your shoes on the settee for you to put on. Your clutch is ready and I added the notes you like to keep in there as well."

I feel my cheeks blush at the mention of Keller's poems. I've carried them with me, wherever I go. Runa knows that when we change clutches, those change out as well.

"Thank you," I say softly.

"I shall let Henrik in to go over your schedule while you put on your shoes."

"Thank you." We walk back into my bedroom together, but while Runa leaves, I walk over to the settee, where my light-blue heels are waiting for me.

I sit and reach for a shoe as the door opens again. Expecting to see Henrik, I smile and look up, only for my breath to be stolen from my lungs as Keller walks in. His imposing stature fills the room as he shuts the door behind him.

Wearing a black suit with a black shirt and black tie, he looks devastatingly handsome.

"K-Keller," I say, sitting tall now. "What are you doing here?"

Not saying a word, he walks across the room and to the settee, where he sits next to me. The first thing I notice is the clarity in his eyes. The next thing I notice is how much bigger he seems, like his arms are about to burst out of his suit jacket. And the final thing is that delicious scent of his, a masculine cologne that clung to me when we were in Harrogate. It's wrapping around me, gripping my heart like a vise.

"I'm here to talk to you about your day," he says.

"Wh-what? Like you, uh, you got your job back?"

"Yes, I was reinstated last night."

I gulp.

"So does that mean you'll be——"

"By your side, every day, guiding you through your events? That would be correct."

"Oh." I swallow again. "Okay, well, that's, uh, that's a new development."

"Would you prefer Henrik?"

"No, I mean . . . I don't know," I say, my mind a total mess. I let out a deep breath. "I don't know what to think."

"Am I free to speak outside of professional norms right now?"

"Of course," I answer, feeling weird about the formality with him.

"Lilly, I need to apologize to you. What I did to you on the day of your welcoming parade *was* unforgivable. I was trying to solve a problem, trying to keep you safe, and trying to avoid these damaging thoughts in my head. I quickly realized my behavior, my way of handling everything, did nothing but steal you from me. And I lost the best thing that's ever happened in my life. It's unforgivable, I realize that, but what I'm hoping is that you can allow me to make it up to you, to show you."

"Is that what you've been doing with those poems? With the squeezes to my hand?"

"Love poetry dates back to our ancestors, a form to show a woman what they meant to the poet. I lost my ability to speak with you and I had to earn that back, therefore I wrote to you. I wrote every night. I thought of your bewitching eyes, your courageous heart, and your gracious soul. And I dreamed of what I'd say to you if I ever got the chance."

"And what would you say to me?" I ask, my skin prickling, my heart pounding, my need for him so strong that I'm surprised I've been able to keep myself together.

"That if you give me another chance, if you allow me back in your life, I promise you, till my dying day, I'll spend it keeping your heart close to mine and showing you how much you're meant to be mine." He reaches out and takes my hand in his. "I'm not asking for forgiveness. I'm asking for the chance to prove to you my undying love." And then he squeezes my hand three times, causing a tear to cascade down my cheek.

I look at him and say, "I don't want to do this without you, Keller." Hope springs in his eyes. "The last couple of weeks have been dreadful. The best part of them was when I saw you. You hurt me, but it hurts worse not being with you." I move off the settee and straddle his lap. His hands fall to my waist, and as I run my hands up his chest, I can feel the rapid beat of his heart. "I need you to promise me you're mine and that you won't ever abandon me again. Don't lie to me. I need you, Keller, by my side."

"I promise you, love," he says softly, his hands smoothing up my sides. "Nothing is more important than you and me, than us."

That puts a smile on my face, and as I lean closer to him, I cup his cheeks and look him in the eyes. "I've missed you so much."

"Fuck, Lilly. I've been a wreck without you. And watching you from a distance, reading about you in the paper, seeing the reactions from everyone in Torskethorpe made me so goddamn proud. I hated myself for not being there with you and sharing your accomplishments."

"But you're here now."

"And I'm not going anywhere."

I lower my mouth to his and one of his hands moves to the back of my head, his fingers tangling through my wavy locks.

"I love you," I say.

"I love you, Lilly," he replies right before our lips collide.

Desperate, our kiss sears through me, reminding me how much this man owns me, every inch of me. As if I haven't been able to breathe the last couple of weeks, he fills my lungs with life, reclaiming what's his.

I melt into his embrace as he wraps me up tightly. His slow, drugging kisses are just what I need in this moment, and when I swipe my tongue over his lips, he parts them, letting me in. Our tongues tangle, our breath mixes, and before I know what's happening, his hand is up my dress and my hand is trying to unbutton his shirt.

"Fuck, Lilly," he says as his mouth falls to my neck. "I missed you so damn much."

"I missed you," I say just as the door opens and a throat is cleared behind us.

We still, and on a gulp, I look over my shoulder, where I find Runa.

"Oh . . . uh, hi, Runa."

"Miss Campbell, you're to report to the grand entrance in ten minutes, and they're not expecting you with disheveled clothes and smeared lipstick."

I awkwardly laugh. "Uh, sorry, I got carried away."

When I slide off Keller's lap, Runa gives him the evil eye. "I'm pleased you two have found reconciliation, but, Keller, you know better than this. Not before an event."

"Sorry." He clears his throat as his hand clasps mine. "Won't happen again."

And then, with three squeezes, he stands from the settee and helps me rise. "Runa, can I have five minutes? I promise she'll be ready."

"She better be," Runa says with a smirk before leaving.

Turning toward me, he lifts my chin and looks me in the eyes. "Forever mine?"

"Forever yours . . . my King."

He smirks and presses another kiss to my lips, filling me with so much love and life that I know, from the depths of my heart, that even though I was so not ready for my royal adventure, I'm more than happy I took it.

I found family.
I found friends.
I found purpose.
And I found the love of my life.

Epilogue

KELLER

"Don't move."

"But . . . but I need to."

I pause and lift from where I rest between her legs. "Who makes the rules in this bedroom?"

"You, my King," Lilly whispers.

"And I said don't move. So don't fucking move."

Her chest rises and falls, arching her back off the mattress, while my silk ties hold her arms and legs tightly in place.

I move between her legs and continue to lightly lap at her clit, barely touching her. Enough to drive her crazy but not to bring her the climax she's chasing.

With her legs spread wide by the silk ties, I don't have to do much other than flick my tongue and play with her entrance with my cock. I've been switching between penetrating her and then licking her.

I barely enter her, pump a few times, and then return to her clit.

It's a goddamn tease to my own release, but more of a tease to her as she's now writhing beneath me, needing more.

"You like that, love?"

"No," she says breathlessly. "You're teasing me. I want to come, but I can't get there."

"Mmm, shame," I say as I rise up and bring my cock to her pussy. I slide it along her slit and watch her eyes roll back from the sensation.

"Yesss," she breathes out as I take my cock away. "No . . . goddamn you."

I chuckle and go back to flicking my tongue against her clit. But this time, I apply more pressure and feel her arousal grow, her pussy getting wetter with every flick.

"Fuck, yes, Keller . . . please, please keep going."

But I pull away and grab the vibrator I was playing with earlier. I press it to my balls and turn it on, letting it vibrate the very base of my erection. I hiss out in pleasure as I start pumping my cock, giving myself what I need.

"Ah, fuck, this feels good."

Her eyes grow heady as they focus on how my hand pulls over my length.

"You want a taste, love?"

"Yes," she says, and I move up the bed and place my tip in her mouth. She sucks me in, and it's so fucking good that I push farther into her mouth.

"Heaven," I mutter as I pull out and then push back in. It feels so good that it's only a few pumps until I pull away. "I'm tempted to fuck your mouth until I come, but I need that greedy cunt."

I move back down to her body, rub the head of my cock over her slit a few more times, and then slip inside, all the way, bottoming out.

"God . . . yes." She gulps as her chest lifts. I capture her breast in my mouth and suck on her nipple. I play with her piercing, rolling it between my teeth and nibbling as I pulse in and out of her. I feel her clench around me, and I know it will be soon. I lift from her chest, grip her hips, where I dig my fingers into her skin, and I pump into her rapidly.

Her moans meet my groans.

Her attempted thrusts match mine.

And the tension in her body pulls tight on the ties.

I pause and release all her limbs and then fall on my back, where I let her take control.

Riding me, she thrusts her hips over mine, repeatedly, her pelvis moving so fast, I can't control the expedited climb of my orgasm as I watch her tits jiggle above me, her head thrown back in ecstasy.

And then her pussy clenches around my cock and a long, drawn-out moan falls past her lips as she comes.

With that, I flip her to her back, press down on her stomach, and I fuck her so hard, I can barely breathe as white-hot pleasure tears through me, my orgasm taking over and stilling my body until there's nothing left to take.

I pull out of her and roll to the side, bringing my arm over my eyes as I catch my breath.

"Christ," I mumble as I feel her curl her bare body around mine. I lift my arm and see her beautiful eyes peering up at me. I smile at her. "Fuck, I love you."

She chuckles. "You better, since you proposed to me today."

I bring her left hand to my lips and press a kiss to the impressive aquamarine stone that's the center of her engagement ring. A vine motif curls around the stone and is dotted with leaf-shaped diamonds. It's worth more than I could imagine. Katla gave it to me to propose with, and I couldn't have thought of a more appropriate ring—a ring that once belonged to her mother.

I took her to Harrogate, where I told her there would be a small gathering of artists to paint the castle, but in reality, it was just her and me. I took her up to the roof, which had been decorated in violets and candles, and under the northern lights, I proposed to her. It was a sweeping yes, followed by much crying.

We called Theo and Katla to tell them the good news. They cried too and told us to have a good night at Harrogate. Lara and Ottar stayed with us and have been downstairs the whole time.

Lara will deny it every time I ask, but I know something is going on between her and Ottar. He's the silent type, quite serious, but I see him soften when he's near Lara. They'd be perfect together because Ottar is a loyal man to his core, and I know he'd never hurt Lara as Brimar did.

Brimar . . . well, he was put through a trial, found guilty, and is serving time in a neighboring country. I still have mixed feelings about my former best friend committing treason, but I know that's something I'll have to reconcile slowly.

After Lilly gave me a second chance, I haven't left her side. I asked Theo for permission to stay with her in her bedroom, and he said it wasn't his decision. It was Lilly's. Lilly, of course, wavered over her decision jokingly, and that first night together, we barely got any sleep as I made love to her repeatedly.

A few short days later, it was Torg. And I believe it was the most fun I've ever had at Torg. Lilly traded her embroidered tablecloths and the fish she worked so hard on. Naturally, *not* the boob she gave me in Harrogate. The public was overwhelmingly loving toward her. She wore a flower crown every day, danced with the people, sang, and we all toasted with mead.

By the end, we were exhausted but so full of joy. Lilly told me she found where she was supposed to be on the last night of Torg.

"I still can't believe we're engaged," she says, kissing my chest.

"Why not? I told you, you were mine forever." I drag my fingers over her back.

"I know, but . . . it feels so crazy. Like . . . you're going to be my husband."

"As it should be."

"When are they announcing it to the public?"

"They're giving us a few days, but when we return to the capital, we'll have to speak with the press, and there'll be an official statement released, and that's also when I'll turn over my position to Henrik."

"So, you're no longer a private secretary?"

I shake my head. "My job now is to be there for you, for anything you need, and of course to fuck you until you're pregnant." I wiggle my brows.

She smiles. "How many kids do you want?"

"As many as you'd like."

"I'm thinking three. What are your thoughts on three kids?"

"I think we get married first, and then we work on as many kids as you want."

Her hand smooths up my chest. "Is the wedding going to be big?"

"You know it is, love. When the country finds out we're engaged, there'll be celebrating for days. It'll be a big ordeal. Does that scare you?"

She shakes her head and then rests her chin on my chest. "No, because the people of this country feel like family, so why wouldn't I celebrate it with them?"

I stare longingly into her eyes. "You're going to be such a good fucking queen."

"With you by my side, I will."

She rests her head, and I grip her tightly.

It feels like just yesterday when I went to Miami to find the future of Torskethorpe and found her spraying down people for a wet T-shirt contest. At the time, her eyes and smile took my breath away, but I had no idea she'd bury herself in my soul.

Now, I can't imagine life without her. I can't imagine this country without her. And one day, when Theo passes and it's time for Lilly to reign, I know she'll be the embodiment of Theo, her mom, and this country.

She saved us and me, and I'll forever be indebted to this beautiful woman. My love, my future wife, our future queen.